Natural

Child

Books by

CALDER WILLINGHAM

Natural Child

by Calder Willingham

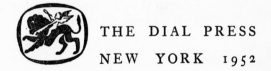

THE DIAL PRESS
NEW YORK 1952

DESIGNED BY WILLIAM R. MEINHARDT
PRINTED IN THE UNITED STATES OF AMERICA
BY THE HADDON CRAFTSMEN, SCRANTON, PENNA.

For my mother
Eleanor Willcox Willingham

"Do not let yourselves be tainted by a deprecating and barren skepticism, do not let yourselves be discouraged by the sadness of certain hours which pass over nations."

—LOUIS PASTEUR

Natural
Child

Part 1

The Blues Jumped a Rabbit

Chapter I

DUE TO THE apartment shortage, I am now sharing with someone a place known as a cold-water flat. Such apartments usually are in poor, run-down neighborhoods if not slums, and
they generally have hot water despite being called "cold"-
water flats. That is an oddity of the city—the name really
means they have no central heating. This particular flat has hot
water and is in a fairly good neighborhood, though of course
the building itself is very old. I share the apartment with
someone, a boy or young man or whatever you would call
him. He sleeps on a cot in the kitchen. It's nothing but an
army cot and only cost three dollars, and he complains and
curses continually about it. Of course he wants to sleep in the
double bed, but I am in the double bed, and perish the
thought forever. I have enough trouble as it is, and he can
continue to curse and groan on the cot. For various reasons,
I'll identify him only as Mr. X—no other identification is necessary, he has no connection with this story and just happens to
be here at the moment, so he can be nameless.

He (Mr. X) has just gone out to get the Sunday *Times*,
which he reads every Sunday, though of course he considers
it stupid, the way he does everything else. He regards everything in the world as stupid. This is stupid, that is stupid, to
listen to him, everything in life is stupid and the conclusion is
to sit and look into space with your mouth full of golf balls.
But he reads the *Times*. If you ask him why he reads it, he
gives a nonsensical answer, such as, "It's raining outside," or

he doesn't believe in going to movies on Sunday. Like this—
I'll say:

"Why do you *read* it, if it's so *stupid*?"

He'll answer, "It's raining."

I'll say, "It *isn't* raining, and what's that got to do with it, anyhow? It isn't raining."

"Well, it might rain," he'll say.

"Hmm," I say. "I don't see what the rain's got to do with it."

"You might not like rain," he'll say. "But the farmers like it. It makes the flowers grow."

This is the type of argument you get in with him. That is, sometimes. At other times, there's no describing the arguments, he's so utterly mean, vile, cruel and hateful, though of course *later* he's sorry, however that's bad, too, because if you don't forgive him he'll do such things as refuse to eat or even crawl around the apartment on his hands and knees endlessly pretending he's a dog. But then if you do forgive him, he'll turn around and act hateful all over again.

In any case, now that he has gone out, I'll be able to start this. I made up my mind to write this book some time ago, and should have begun yesterday. It would have been all right, that was a Saturday, and though he's usually home Saturdays, yesterday he was at the library—or so he said, who knows where he really was. It's no concern of mine and doesn't interest me, but probably he was off with some girl, I wouldn't put it past him and he's certainly been going to that library constantly during the past few weeks, not that he would do anything but grin at the girl and talk to her foolishly, if he did see any girl in the first place. Anyhow, I could have started this book yesterday as I intended, since he was gone all day, but I put it off and went instead to a movie that didn't have any point, except that sex makes you happy. That's no point.

For that matter, as far as *he's* concerned, it probably wouldn't make any difference if I did type while he's here. He has long since stopped looking at any of the things I write. He says, "Lamb, your insanity is enhanced by that machine. Please don't play with it, dear." In the last week, though I

4

couldn't bring myself to start this book, because of its depressing aspects, I did manage to write a few stories, but he paid no attention. These days when he sees me at the typewriter he just makes some remark such as, "At it again." Thank God —in the past he would read what I'd written and analyze what was wrong with it. But even if he paid no attention, I would feel peculiar writing *this* with him in the room. It would be very bad if he saw it, because he himself is more or less one of the characters and he will be presented in his true colors, and he would hardly like that.

He always says, "Leave me out of your opuses." Once he said, "Don't ever put *me* in one of those epics, lamb. Who knows, some idiot might publish it. Look at what they do publish. And it would be just the epic I'm in. I don't deserve that, pet. (Oh, yes you do, Mr. X, that's EXACTLY what you deserve!) That would be a fate wors'n Gawd knows what, to be enshrined in one of those opuses of yours, and considering what these lewd publishers publish, why they might take something of yours, especially if you lynch forty-five niggers or something. Those *South*ron books and everything—stranger things have happened, but leave me out of it, I'm not Rhett Butler or Jeeter Lester either one, or any of those *in*sane *South*roners." He chuckled. "But if you ever *do* plunge the poised dagger in my back, lamb, at least make me an old darky that hobbles around with rheumatism so bad he scarcely can catch those little six-year-old white gals—*disguise* me anyhow." Disguise him?— oh no, I couldn't disguise *you*, Mr. X, you'll be down in this book *just* the way you are, which is EXACTLY what you deserve. This will be neither an opus nor an epic, it will not be about imaginary characters, but about real people. *Everything* in this book has actually happened, and I mean to tell it all from beginning to end, leaving out nothing, if only for my own satisfaction, though personally I would rather leave out 90% of it.

But I'll leave out nothing. It's all right to write realistically today, though why they write that way puzzles me. And since this *really* needs to be written realistically to some extent,

5

there's no point in omitting anything, that is, very little. Besides, though extreme realism is depressing, why should I mind admitting that during the period covered by the events of this story I was nineteen, and during that time, a difficult period, I was in several different difficult situations. I was nearly twenty, or nineteen, which isn't really young, but neither is it so old, sort of "in between," an interesting period of life, for a girl, and probably for a man, too.

But I must say that anyone coming to New York from a small town and running into people like George and Phil necessarily —what can I say? I don't know exactly how to express it. Those boys argue so much it would make anyone dizzy, and they are wild. Wild in the way they talk, but more than that they *act* wild. One time George dared Phil—no, it was Phil that dared George—he dared him to have a fit on the street. All sorts of people do it, he said. Everything happened on the street. "*Go* on," he urged, "*have* a fit, George, show Sue and Bobbie what a fit you can throw. He can throw a fit that's out of this world. You'd swear he was an epileptic idiot. For that matter, he probably is." George said he wasn't in the mood, however then he stared across the street for a moment, then suddenly right there on 58th Street, he half-collapsed against a car fender, shaking and making horrible noises. It was certainly convincing. Phil was so amused he wept with laughter. It looked very ridiculous and it was funny the way the people around there (including one old lady with a dog) looked at George—no doubt they thought he was crazy, especially when all at once he suddenly cut off "the fit" right in the middle and calmly lighted a cigarette, his usual look on his face. The lady glared at him, but he didn't pay her any attention. How many people in their right mind would do a thing like this? Is it modern? Artistic? Intellectual? No, it's just silly, but they talked about it being an art form, about how it "expressed" something, and so forth—they talked on that way all the way to the Automat. "In an insane world," said Phil, "insanity is *naturally* the very *greatest* of the arts."

6

"I share your sentiments on that," said George. "I don't know how but you've spoke a great truth."

"Well, you're the living proof of it," said Phil. "Have another fit when we get to the Automat, have one on the floor there by the change booth, it'll be a sensation, the Automat'll be like a madhouse."

"Oh, no," said Sue. "That's enough fits. Just relax, both of you."

"That's what *I* say," said Bobbie. "Don't do that any more."

"You gals ca'am daown," said George. (Mocking what he thinks is a Southern accent.) "Just res' yo'selves real peaceful, nohow, heah?" There never was such a Southern accent, but it amuses him beyond words to talk what he calls "Southron style, wif humminy grits in mah mouf no how." He thinks his own humor is hilarious. When he says something like that, it amuses him so much he practically collapses, and few things in this world amuse him as much as a Southern accent.

In any case, they are both wild, these boys, and though I wasn't actually extremely young when I met them, Southern girls (accent or no accent) are different in some ways from Northern girls. I don't mean that to sound critical of the North, but in the South people seldom act like that, at least not the people I know in the South. Down there people are either entirely crazy, or normal. They don't act insane one minute, then like a normal person the next, which is the way George and Phil do. I was having a perfectly normal conversation with one of them at the Automat the other night while eating dinner, then I said something he didn't like, so he let one of those sugar containers run in his coffee without stopping till he had about a third of a cup of sugar in the cup, all the time acting cool as if he wasn't really furious, just sitting there holding that thing while the sugar poured out and staring at me, then he tried to drink the coffee. A woman at the next table looked at him as if he was crazy, but did that bother him? He looked back at her as if he would cut her throat, and that was nothing in comparison to the way he looked at me, and all

7

because I'd said something or other he didn't like, some little thing another person wouldn't even pay any attention to.

But to get on with the story.

It all begins in July, one week after I arrived in New York, and it ends three months later in October. I was staying at the Commodore Hotel. It's expensive there and I wanted to move to a room, preferably a room in a girls' club or in a hotel for women. Would that I had done so, but I didn't, I moved to a rooming house on 58th Street between Fifth and Sixth Avenues. Phil and George had their room there, and Bobbie also had a room there. At the time, neither of them knew her, and they probably never would have (New York being the way it is) if I hadn't moved into the house. I introduced them, a sad day for Bobbie, as well as for me, though everything could have turned out worse, I suppose. That's a question.

This is all very well, but I'm ready to quit and go to a movie. I have what is called a block, as far as this story is concerned. Both Phil and George have such blocks, and though I could never understand it before, I can now. Merely to look at this typewriter makes me dizzy, and I can understand to some extent anyhow the story they're forever telling about the famous writer who every time he sat down to write would throw up on the typewriter and faint. Then this writer finally got to the last chapter but didn't dare finish it because the main character jumps in the river at the end of the book. He was afraid he'd be so carried away by the poetic writing that he would do the same. Of course, the answer to his problem is to have the main character *not* do it, because why write such a book anyhow? However, I had better start on this story or the reader will conclude that I'll never get to it but will spend the rest of the book writing odds and ends. The truth really is that this one is almost too grim to be written, too depressing and horrible, almost anything would be better, and for that matter a book could be written on the theme of a "writing block," and an interesting book at that because the general public probably never heard of such a thing. For example, a writer has a block and struggles to overcome it, but it looks hopeless, because

8

every time he or she sits at the typewriter, there's an irresistible urge to go down to the Automat for a cup of coffee. This is the basic situation and a plot could easily be worked into it—it's a man and he has a girl friend with tuberculosis, then every time he starts to type she coughs, and the landlady comes in, an Irish woman that drinks beer and is loud and awful—she yells at him for the rent and tells him he can't type because it disturbs her little dog downstairs, and he yells back at the landlady and she threatens to hit him with a broom, then the girl appears ghostly in the bedroom door—she's been secretly writing a novel back there herself, a historical romance, and she's crying now because she's got a letter from the sanitarium saying she has to come back for another six months, her X-ray pictures were mixed up with somebody else's and actually she's in extremely serious condition and might not live, thus might never finish her book. The landlady raises a fuss because the girl is standing there in a nightgown, which means the girl lives there and so on, but of course they could always be married . . . married in secret to keep it from her parents. Perhaps she's an unhappy adopted child and her foster parents wouldn't give her permission to marry because she's under-age. The landlady doesn't know this, but it's really his wife and he's trying to write the book in order for her to go see a specialist that has discovered a cure for her particular type of t.b.—an unusual type. Of course this sounds like soap opera but it would be more philosophical.

Mr. X has just come in with the *Times*. He has a little bag of plastic chess pieces and he's putting them on the mantelpiece right across the room. Of course, this is the game he would play, chess. He's quite a chess player. It's something to see when Phil, or rather, George, comes up here and they sit at the kitchen table and stare at those little pieces for hours without saying a word and no one can breathe—I will have to stop this until tomorrow morning, he's sitting there now in the easy chair by the window, staring idly. When he came in the door and saw me typing he gazed up at the ceiling as usual, to express his opinion, but now he looks as if he might ask me

9

something. I'll return to this first thing in the morning and describe how I met George, which was how it all began, meeting George in that Nedick's and being deceived by his talk, not that he really fooled me—but I must stop this now, he might get curious at any moment and come try to look over my shoulder, and that wouldn't do.

Chapter 2

IT'S ONE THING to write fifty pages of a novel, and something else to write a fifty-page story. The second is much easier. Not only is a novel more complicated, it's much more difficult as far as philosophy is concerned. George or Phil, one of them, was talking about some writer that wrote a book in one afternoon, dictating into a tape recorder rapid-fire like a machine gun. I don't see how the writer did it, even so. Yesterday afternoon I was writing for at least an hour and only wrote eleven pages, and at that rate God knows how long it'll take me to write an entire book, probably at least two weeks even though it won't be an extremely long book, and I really don't have two weeks, because I can't stand it around here much longer, the situation in this flat has gotten so impossible. What I'll have to do is spend three or four days really working, and just go right on through the whole story, put it all down regardless. That is what I intend to do.

Now, I do not believe in premonitions, however I do believe that on occasion we can see into the future and know that if we do a certain thing, something bad will happen—or at least something *difficult*, though, difficult isn't exactly the word. When I think back and remember those awful scenes in the room on 58th Street, those unbelievable, terrible scenes, it reminds me of the way I felt when I first went to that house with George. I knew that trouble would come if I took a room in that house and often since then I have wondered why I did it. Why, indeed? I should never have taken that room, though it was a nice house and the room was what I wanted.

George himself showed me the room, and when he did he said he lived on the top floor with his friend, a nice fellow from Washington, D. C. Little of what he said was true. First of all, the nice fellow was Phil, and Phil isn't nice and isn't even from Washington, he spent most of his life in New Orleans and Chicago. Furthermore, it turned out later that Phil and George don't live on the top floor, they live down the corridor on the same floor. George also said, "Now, next door there's a cute girl, about your age and I think she's from out of town, too. You and her can get acquainted and become real good chums." That was Bobbie next door, and it was true she was in the room there, but this was practically the only true thing he said. He even told me solemnly it was a rule of the building none of the men roomers could visit in the rooms of the girls, not that I believed that one. No New York rooming house cares what goes on in the building, they're indifferent completely.

In any case, when I was standing there looking at the room something told me, *Don't do it, don't take this room, go back to the hotel and find another place.* I thought, *He'll be knocking on the door all hours of the night and day, wanting "a ciga-rette," or "a match," or "to talk."* As I stood there, I could hear him already, tapping on the door at eleven or twelve o'clock and saying something in a low voice. *Don't do it!* warned the inner voice. *Don't take this room! Who is that girl next door? What about that other boy upstairs?* (He wasn't upstairs, he was right down the hall, but I thought he was upstairs, not that a few stairs make any difference, anyhow.) The voice said, *Watch out! This is a situation no good can come from!*

But I decided to take the room. After all, why not, it was all right, and who was this boy, anyhow? He was nothing, it was obvious he was harmless so why not move in there? And if he got in the room, would that be so bad? Not necessarily, yet the very question makes one wonder. The question has not yet been answered. One wonders what is right, what is wrong, and confusion reigns, and all one can say is that history exists. This person has a history, that person has a history, every soul has a

12

history, and all in all this makes the history of the human race. Yes?

Here, we might ask—what is history? I have wondered about this. The Crusades, the Middle Ages, Greece, Rome, Babylon, Macedonia and Ancient Egypt, on back far before that in caveman days, and back even before that thousands of years till the very beginning. Who can fail to be amazed at everything that has happened? History began in an acorn and became a tree, despite the shine in the eyes of walruses, hippopotamuses and alien elements not in line with evolution. Not actually helpless animals in reality, but brute force itself, the powers of darkness as seen in an earthquake, the crash of rocks in a landslide, comets, meteors, fire and destruction from lightning bolts, all-encompassed by a rise from the swamps where life began and begins anew.

Chapter 3

I WAS IN the Nedick's near the Hotel Commodore, sitting at the counter and looking around out the plate-glass window at the traffic on 42nd Street when I felt a hand grip me by the elbow. I almost dropped my hot dog. When I turned around there was this boy or young man, tall and with sandy-colored hair and blue eyes. He was nice-looking and very well dressed— he had on a black shirt, a light blue tie, dark brown trousers and a tan sport coat—I saw this at a glance, and also saw that he was wearing a gold wrist watch with a gold band. For a second, he didn't say a word, then I looked down and saw his hand, the gold wrist watch, the black shirt and blue tie, and looked back up at him. All this took only a second, a split-second. I was about to yank my arm away when he lifted one eyebrow, glanced at the counter and said in a low voice, "Your sleeve's in the mustard."

"What?" I said. He was right. I was wearing a long-sleeved blouse and to this day there's a tiny mustard stain on one of the sleeves. Of course I didn't know he'd put the sleeve in the mustard himself in order to get an excuse to talk to me, but regardless of that, thus I met George, a sad day for me, and it's ridiculous but I liked him at once. I felt as if I'd known him before, he looked very familiar, though I'd never laid eyes on him till that minute. Who knows why this was? Perhaps something mystic? A great deal in life is unexplained, and though I am very much against the supernatural or spooky types of theories, some things really are amazing, and much happens

14

that no one can explain, though George himself, and also Phil, would say the opposite. There are mysterious currents in this world that no one knows about, and now and then for some unknown reason they come to the surface. I was so sure that I knew George that I must have stared at him in a peculiar way, even the tone of his voice was familiar. I think I must have known him somewhere, but who knows how or where, and if this is mysticism, then it can't be helped, it's mysticism, that's all, but I wonder then how I knew already what he was like. I knew that, and other things, mysterious things that science can't explain. I didn't see what a heartless, neurotic brute he really is, how for example he'll talk very nice with some little child he sees in the park, and then ten minutes later say that somebody ought to cut the child's head off, or talk very nice to some old man and later remark that the old man is dying of "a social disease" and ought to be run over by a cab. My first reaction to him was to like him very much, sensing only his good side, but the point is that I was too startled to think any of this consciously even though it was on my mind. Anyone would be startled if they felt a hand suddenly grab them by the elbow, and I didn't even know he was standing there. But anyhow then we got in a conversation. He gave me a paper napkin, and watched while I rubbed at the sleeve of my blouse. I said, "Thank you," and nothing more. This was New York even if he did look strangely familiar.

I put aside the napkin and looked out the window and took a bite of my hot dog. I could see him dimly reflected in the plate glass. He took a bite of his hot dog. For a few seconds, we were both sitting there looking out the window, then he leaned over toward me and said in a low voice, "How do you manage to eat this food?"

"Oh-h?" I said. I didn't know what to answer, and looked around at him. I said, "It isn't so bad."

He glanced at his hot dog as if revolted. "Uh," he said, "it'll take me a week to get over this. Anybody that could digest this can eat duck feathers." He put it on his plate and rested his elbows on the counter, leaning there and watching me eat my

15

hot dog. I could see him reflected in the plate glass as he said, "Do you eat stuff like this as a habit?"

"Fairly often," I answered.

"You do? Well, you won't live long."

"It's only a hot dog," I answered.

"Is that what it is?" he said. He leaned over closer to me and said, "You don't mind if I ask you something, do you?"

I looked around at him. He was staring at me in a very serious way. "No," I answered. "Of course I don't mind. What would you like to ask?"

He said, "You're not from New York, are you?"

"Why do you ask that?" I said.

"I was just wondering," he said.

"No," I said. "I'm not from New York."

There was a pause, then he asked, "Where *are* you from— Maine? Or New Hampshire?"

"Oh, no," I answered. "Not from either. Nowhere like that. I'm from North Carolina."

"Nawth Carolina?" he said. "Well, I'll declare. I could have swore you was from Maine. Your accent had me fooled."

"Really?" I said. He said all that solemnly. This is his idea of *hilarious* humor; and he does this sort of thing all the time, even much worse than Phil. He's constantly joking, whereas Phil is more dry and intellectual. The reader can see the type of character George is—naturally he knew very well I wasn't from Maine, but he asked the question with such a straight face I didn't know, I thought maybe he really thought I was from Maine. He catches you unawares, then thinks it's simply hilarious. So, I said, "Really?" and he grinned and said:

"How long have you been in New York? I bet you-all just got off the train."

I didn't know at the time, but I was talking to a wolf, not that it was a misfortune to me as things turned out, since Bobbie was the one that took him seriously. Yes, I would say a wolf, and in those days he was worse. Any girl he saw that struck his fancy he'd keep after her no matter what, regardless of the obstacles, he'd persist and do anything, go to any lengths,

16

to get them to like him, so he could then walk right out. Such insane conduct, to say nothing of it from a moral standpoint, but when he first started going with Bobbie he had three different girls besides her, and one night it was one and then another, with no one of the girls knowing about the others, and him joking with Phil about what this one was like or how that one acted, what she did or said at such-and-such a moment, and how another one was peculiar in this, that or the other respect, or odd in such-and-such a way. And he still would like to act that way. Let an attractive girl get around him, and he starts it, and of course the girl probably doesn't know what he's up to more often than not, she's vain enough to think he's interested in her whereas that isn't the point at all, and the entire thing is silly beyond words. It makes one wonder if people have any sense at all. Not that he would ever dare do anything but flirt, these days. If he did, Bobbie would take the first bus or train out of town, and he knows it, and though he used to desert them all the reader cannot imagine what it would do to him if *she* should leave him. One time she got halfway down the stairs with her suitcase, and he was carrying on like an insane person and almost collapsed with relief when she finally came back, but that doesn't stop him from acting like a fool—oh no, even now he comes up here and flirts with *me* of all people, not that I give him any encouragement or pay him any attention. *I* like Bobbie, no matter what George and Phil say about her. But getting back to Nedick's—he (George) asked me how long I'd been in New York, and I answered as follows:

"New York? Well, I've been here about a week."

"You-all been here around a week?" he said. "Well, I declare. You wouldn't fool me, would you?"

I wonder: why didn't it make me mad, the way he was mocking my accent? It's his greatest joy to mock at people, I believe, and the better he likes them the more he does it. Does that make sense?

While we were carrying on this conversation (the first we ever had), we were sitting there at the counter, or table or

17

whatever you call it, eating hot dogs and drinking that orange drink. Or rather, I was. He didn't eat any more after the first bite, but sat there talking to me.

I answered, "People don't say *you-all*, or *y'all*, to one person down South. It's always to two people, two or more." This is a point I never could convince Northerners on. I couldn't convince him either.

"We-all sure don't say it up *here*," he replied.

"I know," I said. "You say *youse*."

"Is that any worse than you-all?"

"I couldn't say," I replied. "Up here you don't say youse to one person, do you?" I had to smile at his tone, he was arguing so seriously and yet his remarks were so silly.

"Look," he said. "I'll tell you something. I'm from Philadelphia, but I went to school two years down in Louisiana, and I love the South. I think it's a wonderful part of the country, and do you know why I like it so much?"

"No, why?" I asked.

"Southern girls are so brainy and intellectual," he answered. He had a straight face and looked at me in an honest manner, then added, "That's what I really like about the South. It's the girls down there. But they tend to be too trusting. I mean, they trust everybody. They're the trusting type. I suppose Southern girls just don't expect a man to act wrong or be an old poltroon, because they're used to Southern gentlemen. Do you guess that's it?"

I said, "I think you've got a point there."

"I think so, too," he said. "You're too trusting. What's your name?"

"I don't know what my name is," I said.

"You're much too trusting," he said. "People will take advantage of *you*, I can tell from the look in your eyes. You need somebody to tip you off and warn you. You are the type that believes the best of everybody and won't see the bad side, because otherwise why would you talk to me? Seriously, I want to warn you about this here, Joan. Is that your name?"

"Yes," I said.

18

"It isn't really Joan, is it? You couldn't have a stupid name like that."

"No," I said with a smile. "It's Barbara." This was funny, because Bobbie's real name is Barbara and I just pulled that name out of the air. It was probably psychic.

"That's more like it," he said. "Barbara for barbarian. An unspoiled barbarian, from the South, is that what you are? I think so, but you're in New York now, and you won't be unspoiled long, unless you watch your step."

"Watch my step?" I said. "How do I do that?"

"Well, suspect the worst all the time," he said. "Anybody you meet is a potential Jack the Ripper, understand? Keep that thought in mind all the time. Now for example, there was a man over in New Jersey the other day, who got a little disturbed. He had an idea the neighbors were saying mean things about him. He'd also been poring over the Bible, and brooding over girly magazines, and in his spare time he did some target shooting with a bunch of pistols down in the basement. So one day he went out and clobbered the neighborhood. This is typical of human nature, understand—he shot everybody in sight, this fellow, then was indignant when they hinted he was crazy—he had a good mind, he said. And he was right. He's a perfectly normal chap."

"So what do you mean?" I asked. "You mean I shouldn't talk to anybody, the way I am you, or they might be like that?"

"That's more or less what I had in mind. What did you come to New York for?"

"Me? New York? I always wanted to come here, and I had a friend who lived up here—"

"Well, you're too trusting," he said, "that much is obvious. And in New York of all places. I don't think you can get along up heah, if you don't look out. It's a hard life in these regions and somebody'll take advantage of you."

"Nobody can take advantage of me," I answered. "Don't worry."

"Hmmph," he said. "These wolves up here will play on your sympathies. There's a lot of wolves loping around the streets

19

in this town, and you'd better watch out for them, they'll spot you from a mile off and come tell you a lot of lies about what pretty hair you've got and what a nice smile, and so on, and worm their way in your sympathies. I'm not kidding. You know about Broadway, don't you, and what happens over there? These insincere wolves travel up and down Broadway looking for little innocent girls like you. I happen by sheer chance to be on the level, but if you talk to strange people in places like this, sooner or later you're going to run into an unscrupulous type. One of them will come up, they always do." Here, he paused, a worried look in his eye—he cleared his throat and rubbed his chin the way Lionel Barrymore used to do when playing Dr. Gillespie, then added in a rather worried manner, "They're all around," he said. "Wolves. Loping up and down Broadway." He glanced at me sideways.

"Loping?" I said. "I didn't know they *loped*."

"They all do," he said. "It's their only method of locomotion. If they didn't lope they'd be standing totally still, and did you ever see a wolf stand still?"

"No," I answered idly, and looked out the plate-glass window.

His elbows were still on the counter, or rather, his arms. In the window I could see him lean over, then I heard his voice in my ear. "You remind me of someone," he said. "I don't know who it could be, but you really do remind me of someone."

"Is that so?" I asked.

"I mean it," he said. "Were you ever in New York before?"

This couldn't be a "line," because I was already friendly with him, he already had me in conversation with him. I looked at him and said, "No."

"Were you in Louisiana?"

"No," I said. "Never."

"You know," he said. "I bet you're—are you—?" He smiled, then added, "You don't think all men deserve the electric chair, do you."

"No," I said. "I think they ought—"

20

"I mean men as a sex," he said. "You aren't opposed to men as a group, as a whole, the way most women are, are you?"

"Most women?" I asked. "Are they?"

"You must be as nice as you look," he said. "This is just love at first sight. Where are you living? Let's get married."

"Let's wait, five more minutes," I said. "Hasty marriage doesn't work. You have to know a person ten minutes."

"Where are you staying now?" he asked.

"Somewhere," I replied. "Somewhere in New York."

"Is that so," he said.

Chapter 4

MR. X HAS just gone out to "the library," so I can resume. The dishes aren't washed. He brought in some pork chops, which took him about five minutes, and he thinks that entitles him to walk off. I'll let the dishes sit there until he comes in. I wouldn't wash them for a thousand dollars, I've done it too many times, so he can just get mad. He himself thought up the agreement that he would wash the dishes. I had to listen to him rattle on for half an hour about the equality of the sexes. He really means by that that girls should sleep with every man they meet and pay their share when they're taken out on dates, and he says he's glad to wash dishes, that's only fair since he can't cook and he ought to do something. But he won't wash them, except verbally. Or if he ever does, he groans and mutters as if he's being tormented. It was *his* idea that he'd wash the dishes, not mine. What he's doing is taking *the credit* for washing them, *without* washing them, and he can't get away with that on *me*, not any more. I'll just let them lie there in the sink. Of course roaches like that, and who is it around here that leaves food out on the kitchen table, not me. He is practically impossible, but say one word to him, just one word, and he answers that he saw a cat o' nine tails on sale at Abercrombie and Fitch and why don't I go up there and buy it and beat him to death with it, it would be more merciful than being nagged to death. I don't nag him. I *don't*. He's just more and more impossible all the time. And lately he's been getting curious about what I'm writing. When I started to put away my papers and shut up the typewriter before dinner, he asked, "What are you writing, angel?"

"A book," I said.

"A book, eh," he said.

"Yes, a book."

"Is that so. What's the book about, pet?"

"Nothing," I answered.

"Well, I assumed that," he said. "But what *aspect* of nothing?"

I shrugged and put the papers in the manila envelope I keep them in, but he was staring, so finally I had to say, "Oh, it's just a book. You wouldn't care anything about it."

"Why, *honey* child," he said, "how can you *say* that, you know I'm interested in your writing. Didn't I read all those incredible epics? Everything you write interests me. You have an inexhaustible ability to do it the wrong way, honey. It fascinates me."

"Well, you're not so hot, with those detective stories and all those adventures on Mars, and that 'block' of yours and everything. All *you* can do is just think up silly plots."

"Don't refer to my past misdeeds," he said. "That was youthful folly, a mere tut. And the plots I think up aren't crazy, they're sensible. Those epics of yours are the ones with fantastic plots. Why, if you could catch three or four of them you could open a zoo. People would come all the way from Jersey and pay twenty-five cents general admission."

"Don't refer to your mis*deeds*?" I said. "Huh! But it's your life, it's no concern to me."

"No, it isn't," he said. "So just shut up, please. What's the book about?"

"Oh, nothing," I said. "Down South."

"I see," he answered. "Down South. Ummm. Well, that's your material, like I told you, instead of all that about Canada and Great Britain." He walked to the icebox and opened it and looked for a place to put the pork chops. Then he asked, "How many lynchings have you got in so far?" He has an idea you can't write about the South unless there are lynchings.

"None," I said.

"A Southern epic, and no lynchings? Why, lamb child, is that cricket? You can't write a Southern novel without a couple of lynchings. Put in some lynchings right away. Where are those olives? Where are those goddamn olives they were here last night what did you do with those goddamn olives?" He looked around at me, then peered back in the icebox and found the olives, which were there in front of him. He unscrewed the jar, took out one with his fingers, ate it, and put the olives back and began looking in the icebox for something else. This spoils his appetite and then he complains he has no appetite, but ask him not to eat till dinner and he'll say beat him with a broom but don't try and starve him to death, because it isn't humane. So he found some Roquefort cheese and strawberry jelly, which he took over to the kitchen table. Then he began to cut a loaf of rye bread to make a sandwich. While he was making the sandwich he said, "Honey, in this here book, why don't you have some lint-heads lynch a Chinaman? They've lynched so many niggers in those Southern books it isn't a novelty any more, so this time let them lynch a slit-eyed Chink. I even have a name for him, Wan Sap. How's that. Say he assaults a member of the gentry and the lint-heads are turned loose on him. So he rapes Crimson O'Hollohaney, a beautiful, sexy red-haid that has tried to benefit the pore lint-haids, by teaching Sunday School to them ignorant lint-haids. That's why they love her so much. Besides they've all got a hankering for old Crimson theirselves and nine or ten of them done been in the hay with her. She's a gal that likes the hay, like all them Suthun gals. But when this Chinaman gets through with her she's a broke woman. He's Oriental. The Yellow Peril. And all that, but actually she doesn't know what a Chinaman is, secretly she thinks he's some form of nigger. And so do the lint-haids."

I didn't say anything. He took a bite at his Roquefort cheese and jelly sandwich, and said, "Better yet—use Crimson in another book and have the Chinaman go off his nut and rape a little black goat named Trixie, then the niggers lynch him.

24

Or it's a little white goat named Josephine, and the lint-haids lynch him. The goat of course is symbolic."

This is the way he talks at times. I suppose at this point I might as well say who he is. I can't keep calling him Mr. X throughout the book, and the answer is that he's Phil. Every time I start to write his name I almost write Phil instead of Mr. X, so I might as well say who he is, and besides, because of the similarity between the way he and George talk, the reader might assume he was George, however he *isn't*, he's *Phil*. As for this kind of talk, both of them talk like that—what he says about the goat is nothing, that's mild. I gave no answer, anyhow, so finally he looked over at me and asked, "How many pages of that epic have you got done? Are you going at your usual molasses speed of thirty pages an hour?"

"It isn't an epic," I said.

"Well, what is it, then? It must be an epic. It's bound to be."

"It isn't an epic," I said. "An epic has a hero in the story, and this story has no hero."

"Oh, so I'm in it, huh," he said. "That's what you're doing, writing a story about me."

"I wouldn't write anything about you," I replied scornfully. "Don't you think I have better things to write?"

"I don't know," he answered. "But you've got to have a hero in the story, or it'll be incoherent. An epic is the only thing worth writing nowadays."

I didn't answer. He's so much of a critic that if I talked to him I never would get anything done any more than he does himself. Not that I ever paid any attention to his criticisms, even when I asked him about various stories to get his opinion. He doesn't like anything, therefore he must be wrong part of the time unless everything is worthless. I've heard him and George sit for hours and talk endlessly about how no one was any good—this one, that one, they were all bad. If even the most famous authors are bad, then naturally how could anything *I* write be any good? The only one they think is good is the one that wrote a book no one understands, not even the author, and now Phil has gotten around to the point of deciding

25

that that book isn't really any good either. But they used to read the insane thing aloud by the hour, pages and pages of it and all of it utterly mad, but they thought it was artful beyond words and would argue back and forth about all the things it meant, then they'd argue with Bobbie about why the man wrote it that way, because she couldn't understand the point. They'd say, "Don't worry about this. Just go powder your nose. This is over your head. This is not for you." And so on, like that. However, *now* what does he say? Now he has come to think that all that mad, complicated doodle-woodle isn't so good after all, he has doubts about "the philosophy" of it. I could have told him that long ago, but he wouldn't listen, and even now, if I tell him the man was out of his mind, he says, "Please, don't be obscene. You don't know what you're talking about. You never do, but you always talk, talk, talk all the time. If you only didn't talk, it would be so nice." If *I* only didn't talk? *He* talks constantly. And that's another of his favorite expressions—"Don't be obscene"—yet his own conversation is the most obscene ever heard. If anyone tells him to shave or they'll lock him up as a vagrant, he'll say, "Don't be obscene. These whiskers don't make any —— difference." Or if I say to him that it's his turn to get up in the morning and make coffee, he says, "Don't be obscene."

However, that's the way he acts sometimes and so much for him. I'm so annoyed with him these days he keeps interfering with this story, but no more of him, that's all.

I was in the Nedick's with George, and that certainly seems long, long ago. He was trying to find out where I lived and I wouldn't tell him. But this was the first time I ever saw George, so I'll describe him briefly.

The first thing I noticed about George as far as appearance goes is that he is tall, has sandy-colored hair, blue eyes, and is nice-looking, and very well-dressed. George always dresses well, though lately this has not been the case. He says Bobbie exhausts him. At present, he's almost as sloppy as Phil, and on some days he goes around looking like a hobo even worse than Phil, but on that afternoon some time ago he looked nice.

He had on a tan sport coat and was wearing a black cotton shirt, and a blue tie. A dark brown handkerchief was in the breast pocket of the coat, and he had on brown slacks neatly pressed, and brown shoes. He was not wearing a hat. But unlike Phil his hair was combed and brushed. He looked very nice and neat in every way. Phil is handsomer than George, but George dresses better, or did in those days. Nowadays, as I said, he dresses more and more like Phil.

Naturally, Phil used to criticize George for the way he dressed. According to Phil, anybody that dresses well is a fool, because to dress well is conspicuous consumption. George's answer to that is that Phil's mode of dress is conspicuous non-consumption. They've often argued about that. In fact, they argued about it the first time they took out Bobbie and me, when we were having dinner before going to Coney Island. They sat talking back and forth, insulting each other, back and forth, back and forth, first one then the other, practically for hours, and they wouldn't let Bobbie or me in the discussion at all, every time we'd make a remark, one of them would say, "Wait a minute," or, "Just a second, please," then they'd go right on.

But George did look nice that day. On one finger he was wearing a gold ring that had a tiny black stone in it, and he had a tie clasp with a black stone to match the ring, and he was wearing a gold wrist watch. None of this was flashy or cheap; it was all in good taste. My impression of him was that he was nice, had an unusual manner, was very friendly, pleasant and so on. I guessed he was twenty-five or twenty-six. So all in all he made a favorable impression, but the true character of some people is buried under the surface, and it was that way with him. He kept talking pleasantly about this or that, trying to find out where I lived. For example: "Are your relatives glad you came up to New York to visit them?"

"I haven't got any relatives in New York," I answered. "All my relatives are in North Carolina."

"You're here all by yourself?" He shook his head. "That's bad. Did you say you're going to get a job as a chorus girl?"

27

"Oh, sure," I said. "I am."

"There're some nice chorus girls," he replied. "Some of them spend all their time studying Plato. If you don't think you're the chorus girl type, then that's because you don't know New York and Broadway. They import practically all their chorus girls from Nawth Cah-lina, and they'd spot you a block away, especially in that dress. What do you think you're going to do, get a job as a secretary, or something horrible like that?"

"I'm going to get a part-time job," I said, "and take some art classes or the ballet or something, if you really want to know."

"*Ballet*? But how'd you ever hear of the ballet in North Carolina?"

"We've heard of it in North Carolina," I said. "We've heard of everything down there."

"*Every*thing?" he said.

"Sure," I replied.

"Hmm," he said. "Where do you really live?"

"I told you."

"I mean, where are you staying *now*?"

"I told you where I'm staying now."

"No, you didn't. Where are you staying, with friends or something?"

"Well," I said, "if you must know, I'm staying at the Commodore Hotel."

"You are? The Commodore? Why, you're practically right upstairs, then."

"No," I said. "Actually, I'm staying at the Astor Hotel."

A few minutes before, he had put his hand on my arm accidentally—now he put his hand on my wrist to see the time on my wrist watch. "Two o'clock," he said. Then he examined my ring, which has an opal stone. "This is a pretty ring," he said. "Where'd you get those cute little fingers?"

"Macy's department store," I said. "Let go of them, please."

"Macy's depahtment sto'?" he said. "Well, I declare." At this point, I pulled my hand away and he said, "I didn't know they carried cute little fingers like that in stock, over at Macy's depahtment sto'."

I'd long since finished my hot dog and drink and was just sitting there talking to him, if sitting is the word for those stools—however no one ever sits down in New York, not to eat, ride on the subway or anything, they're too busy and can't waste the time. They run across the street in front of taxis in a race with death, and the taxis would run over them without hesitation if they didn't get out of the way. At this stage, when I pulled my hand away, he reached and took it again, oblivious to the fact that the girl behind the counter was staring at him introspectively. "Please," I said, "don't *do* that." I gave him a cool glance and left, that is, the Nedick's. He followed along. I tried to get rid of him, because I didn't know him, but it was impossible. I couldn't get rid of him. I'd walk along a way and turn and ask, "Will you please stop following?" He'd answer that he was just walking up the block, then we'd walk some more, and I'd turn and say, "You can't follow me like this, I don't know you. Stop it." But he'd answer with some remark or other. Finally we went on over to that park by the library and talked quite a bit. He asked me what I was doing, why I had really come to New York, about my ideas on this and that, and the result of it all was that we went and had coffee in some restaurant, then walked up Madison Avenue and over to Lexington and up 57th Street, then before I realized it I came with him to look at the little room that was empty in the house he lived in on 58th Street.

So I met George. He later said that he put my sleeve in the mustard jar, that he had been watching me for about twenty minutes in the lobby of the Commodore and had analyzed that I was from out of town because I didn't have what he calls a New York look, because of my general expression and manner, though how he did this I don't know. But he determined he was going to follow me around and get in a conversation and take me out to bars and get me drunk, then take me up to his room, so he followed me in Nedick's but I seemed totally unaware of him and he couldn't catch my eye, so he put my sleeve in the mustard jar. If I'd known all this, my life would probably have been changed, but it never occurred to me that he had such ideas in mind. He said that after a few minutes of talking, he decided it would take a long campaign, maybe even a siege. A siege—what a word! And he's an intellectual that reads Freud. And not only reads him, he can criticize what's wrong with him, too. Freud didn't know any sociology, that's the answer. He underestimated the social instinct, and he was monotheistic, arbitrary and dogmatic, besides relying on old-fashioned science like classifying bugs and species, instead of dynamic modern thought like relativity and Einstein, that's what's wrong with Freud. But he picked up most of that criticism from Phil. However they would both say it would take a siege.

Chapter 5

IT'S ANOTHER DAY and Mr. X has gone to work, after leaving last night's and this morning's dishes in the sink. He's in a terrible mood. He looked at me this morning as if he wanted to commit murder then slammed the door when he left. Last night, he was talking in his sleep. Not much that he said was understandable, although at first I thought he was awake. "Where is it?" he said. "Where the hell is it? Mumble-mumble-mumble, where is that thing, here? Uhhhhhhhgggggg-gggah-dammmm-uggghh, where's that thing, ummm-mm."

I asked, "*What?* Where's what?"

"Yeah," he said. "Is that it?"

"What are you looking for?" I asked. I thought he was looking for something in the dark.

"Here," he answered. "Right here. Mumble-mumble-mum-gumgum, pick it up, please."

"Pick up *what?*" I asked.

"Right there," he said. "For God's sake, pick it up. Mummmmmmblegumbbbgumm-mmm."

"*What?*"

"Don't drop it!" he said. "Be careful! Watch out!"

I never could make sense of what he was saying. After a while he turned over and went back to sleep, that is, completely asleep. I couldn't budge him. He'd been half-awake when he was talking about whatever it was on his mind, assuming he had anything on his mind and it wasn't merely the pork chops. I don't think it was just pork chops. For about a week, he has

31

been in an "anxiety state." He says that everywhere he goes, a bird of doom is following him on silent wings. Fortunately he doesn't feel that way all the time, or it would be impossible to endure him. Absolutely impossible. The reader cannot imagine how insane he is. There are no limits when he is in one of these anxiety states, and that includes throwing cups of coffee at waiters, shoving elevator boys out of their elevators, or lying on the floor at the apartment and covering himself like a mummy with the newspaper, and staying down there in utter silence as if dead for *almost two hours*, his eyes shut and not a word out of him, except, "Dead. I'm dead." Such a person as this is very difficult to live with. What can one do, if a person acts like this? There was an *awful* scene here this morning and this cannot continue for another day. Something will have to be done.

To make a long story short, I thought he was all right last night when he came back. He looked tired but was in a good mood and was joking around, but then during the night he talked in his sleep and this morning when he got up he looked horrible. A terrible expression was on his face and at first he wouldn't even get up from the kitchen table and go shave, despite the fact that if he'd gone out to his job the way he was, they'd have certainly fired him, though maybe that's what he really wants. It isn't up to ME to tell him to go shave, but I did and he just sat there with elbows on the table and gazed in his coffee cup and brooded—and all he'd say was, "What a life. What a life." Then when he came out of the bathroom after finally shaving, he refused to wash the dishes. I reminded him he said last night he'd wash them this morning without fail, and told him if he went off and left them I'd never again believe anything he said, so he began to groan and pull his hair. "All the burdens I've got," he said, "with demons of hell wrestling after me, and pixies gnawing at my goddamn liver night and day—and YOU haven't got anything better on your mind than that I should wash those GODDAMN dishes, like a slob on the Bowery. Have mercy, you cruel little fiend. *Have mercy.*"

"Oh, a slob on the Bowery?" I said. "Is that what it is? I thought you said it was democratic—it was *your* idea, not that—"

"SHUT UP!" he said.

"Don't shout at me," I answered. Unfortunately I always get scared when he acts like this.

"To hell with democracy!" he said. "I like *fascism* now. Goddamn it, what are women for, if not to take the load off a man, instead of beating him to death with an old shoe. I'll wash the goddamn insane dishes, but not *this morning*, and if that's medieval then to hell with it, the Middle Ages were a lot better than what we've got now, with women driving men mad on such a scale the asylums won't let you in unless you wait six months. I can't bear all the weight, and keep a cretinous job intended for an idiot, and do everything else, you fiendish little slave-driver. *You* wash the dishes for once. Don't break the goddamn camel's back." He whispered, "Is that what you want to do, break the camel's back?"

"No," I said.

"Then don't lay on that last goddamn straw."

"I didn't lay on the last straw," I said. "But I have things to do, too, and you said you'd wash the dishes."

He asked, "Do you want blood?" He smiled pleasantly.

"No, you're the one that said men and women should be equal," I answered.

"All right,' he said wearily. "Shoot me. Go ahead. I won't wash the dishes so I'm inconsistent and hypocritical, so shoot me."

"No, you said they ought to be equal, you fussed about that. I said I thought women could wash dishes—" Actually he convinced me of the opposite. He always gets me confused in these arguments, because he's a master of arguing.

"Oh, I said that," he answered. "Well, *you* don't think men and women should be equal. I'll tell you what *you* think. *You* think women should wield the whip, *that's* what you think."

"I think men ought to be men, and women women," I said weakly.

33

"Oh, so I'm not a man," he replied. "If I wash the dishes, you interpret it as weakness. Washing the dishes means nothing. The reason I don't want to wash them this morning is because I can't bear the thought—my conditioning is against it—it's rough for me to do it, but it's duck soup for you. Understand?"

"No," I said. "But I'll wash them, go ahead."

"Listen," he replied. "Are you trying to drive me completely mad? Don't be so NOBLE, PLEASE don't be so NOBLE. Don't FORCE me to wash those dishes!" Here, he pulled out some of his hair, at least twenty-five or thirty hairs. "Wash the dishes. It's always something. Go shave! Get up! Do this! That!" He glared at me. "Slave-driver," he said. "You're the most subtle slave-driver in modern times, did you know that?" I didn't say anything. It was impossible to talk, with all this. "*Well?*" he said after a while. "So? What are you thinking now? That I'll give in as always? Anything you say, I'll do? Is that it?" He stood there, hands on hips, then gritted his teeth, and said, "I won't take that job. I refuse. Understand?"

"All right," I said.

"I have other plans."

"All right."

"You don't believe it."

"Of course, I believe it."

"Well, don't look at me like that, then."

"I'm not looking at you, anyway."

"Yes, you are, you're looking at me in a brooding, resentful manner."

"No, I'm not."

"Yes, you are, and if you don't stop it, I'll strangle you. I told you I am considering other plans, and don't ask me what other plans, because a person is entitled to some privacy in this world—stop looking at me like that."

"I'm *not* looking at you any way—what's the matter with you?"

"What's behind that look? What are you thinking?"

"*Nothing*," I said.

34

"I know perfectly well what you're thinking, honey, and it's all right with me."

"Okay," I said. "Good. Let's change the subject."

"You think I ought to take that job, don't you?" he said. "You think it'd be a good idea, don't you?"

"I don't care," I said.

"Oh," he replied. "Of course I might have other ideas, for all you know. In fact, you don't know anything. I might surprise you, that's possible. You can see this stupid job and that eighty-five dollars a week, and that's all, that's what you want me to do, regardless of whether or not it drives me mad. That job could cause a man to attack a mannequin in the window at Macy's, under the illusion it was Betty Grable. Such work as that destroys cells in the brain. But all right, we'll both of us have our work—you sit there and write opuses about the South and I'll figure out phrases to sell ladies' underwear. Ladies' underwear! Heh, heh—some fate."

"What's so awful about ladies' underwear?" I asked, with a faint smile.

"Nothing. Except that it's probably the most horrible thing in the entire world any way you look at it, even when it's on the counter at Altman's and not on some nasty little girl."

"You might as well do that as run an elevator, since the block keeps you from writing those Mars stories. You're not getting anywhere running that elevator," I said.

"Who wants to get anywhere?" he asked. "And what do you mean, *block*, I don't believe in such pollywoddle. I don't write that pulp because I don't *want* to write that pulp, *you're* the author around here. I run an elevator. That's all. I like it, too."

"I never wanted you to take that job if you don't like advertising," I said. "All I said was that it was a wonderful salary."

"Eighty-five dollars a week, wonderful?" he asked. "That's nothing."

"It's twice what you make now," I said.

"Yes," he replied, "but it's below pulp rates."

"But you won't write that stuff because of your block."

"I haven't got any damned block," he said. "People oughtn't

35

to use words like that around you. It's a crime. You get them in your head, then repeat them eternally like a fiendish magpie. I've had enough of it—don't use that pollywoddle word any more or I'll butt my head against that wall."

"You were the one that was always talking about it," I said. "And don't think *I* wanted you to take that job, just because it's twice the salary you make now. The point is that at least you wouldn't go crazy from running up and down in that elevator."

"TRAPPED," he said. "Totally and utterly trapped. There's no hope. Why don't I jump in the East River and get it over with?"

"Why don't you," I said. "It'd be good riddance."

"All right," he said wearily. "I'll go and jump. Arguing with you is a losing game. I might as well. Logic has as much effect on you as snow has on a polar bear. Is there any particular bridge you want me to jump from?"

"It's irrelevant which bridge," I said, "as long as you jump."

"Very funny, VERY funny," he replied.

"I hope you'll do it," I answered. "But I know you're just talking, because it would be too good to be true."

"This type of stupid humor doesn't become you," he said. "But the joke is that you really wouldn't care, that's the joke."

"No, I wouldn't," I said. "You're too mean to live anyhow, so go jump in the river."

"You believe that," he said. "You cruel, fiendish little . . ." Here, he took a deep breath, put his hands on his hips, and stared in a frosty, indignant manner. Then he said, "You don't understand me. You don't understand me because you and I are at variance in point of view. We don't vibrate on the same wave length. It was a sad day the day I met you—I made—don't you dare start to cry!" Anyone would weary of such an argument, but this was the end of it—at this stage he turned with a martyr-like expression and walked out of the apartment, slamming the door so hard it almost fell off the hinges.

That was the scene this morning. They get worse all the time. He was referring in his remarks to a job he was offered

36

the other day, a job with an advertising company at a salary of eighty-five dollars a week, which isn't bad by any means and would be less of a strain than running an elevator or writing those detective mysteries, which he can't write anyhow because of whatever reason. One would think he'd be delighted to take it, especially since he says it's easy as pie—but what conflict that job has brought on, he's been practically out of his mind. His theory is that if he takes it the sky will fall down. Eighty-five dollars a week and all he has to do is every now and then write a little piece on a girdle, or an article on a girdle-making shop or something like that, nothing hard. Of course, those people aren't going to wait forever while he tries to make up his mind. If I'd never said anything one way or the other, he'd have probably taken it. That's another thing about him—whatever anyone says, he always says or does the exact opposite. If I say, "Do you want scrambled eggs?"—then he says, "No, fried." If I say, "How do you want your eggs this morning?"—he says, "I don't know," then if I say, "Do you want them scrambled?"—he says, "No, fried," or vice versa if *I* say fried. Always, every time. If I say, "So-and-so's a nice person, don't you think?"—he says, "No, they're a creep." He doesn't do this *all* the time, but he does it frequently. Maybe if I'd told him not to take that job by any means, that he simply shouldn't take such a job at all, he might have replied like this, "Why not take it? Eighty-five bucks a week for doing nothing? Sure I'll take it." Or maybe he'd have agreed with me. But such a scene as the one this morning has more behind it, much more. He is apparently developing delusions of persecution, that's the only way to explain his peculiar remarks. I've quoted everything he said, even though it didn't make sense. But so much for all that.

Perhaps the reader can understand why I'm not in much of a mood to write this morning. I don't really take such scenes seriously, but anyone would be affected to some extent by all that, and besides, I don't see how I can write this story anyhow. It's far too depressing. The more I think about it, the more I realize the reader wouldn't want to read it even if I

37

wrote it. There are enough depressing things in the world without writing a story that makes everything worse. Why write a story if it's hopeless? What's the point? What do people read books for, in order to become convinced that life isn't worth living? Of course, *he* doesn't like a story unless it's hopeless, and the more horrifying all the characters are, the better he likes it. According to this theory, the most interesting story would be with every character getting killed, going crazy, becoming a drunkard, and all of them being 100 per cent hateful, and the whole thing written in such a way that the reader has no idea what's going on. No idea at all. Four balloons, five little dogs, jump on the ice cream, Alexander in the sherbet, the mule, Suzie, and five cats with little monkeys riding and scratching fleas while Aunt Mary hops on one leg and four Chinamen smile—who would know that's the story of a little girl's first trip to the circus?

But I know what he would say. The point is that I long ago decided to write this story just for myself. I'll throw it away when I've finished, then whether it's gloomy or not won't make any difference.

Chapter 6

THE ROOM IN the house on 58th Street was toward the front of the house. It looked out on 58th Street, as Bobbie's room did—although the doors in the hall were placed in such a way that it seemed as if that room must be on the side of the building.

In New York there are no sides to buildings, but only a front and back because everything is jammed together, a block of houses being built side by side with no space between them. Most of these houses are known as "Brownstones," because usually they are made of a brownish purple stone once popular in New York. Some of these are rooming houses today. Cold-water flats are built in the same way, side by side with windows only in the front and the back, but they usually are not made of brown stone, but of bricks or dark, weatherbeaten granite, and as a general rule are more run-down and disreputable. However, cold-water flats are cheap and you can always fix them up—this one we're in now isn't so bad if you can stand going through the hall to get to it.

The room in the house on 58th Street was tiny, and it seems years ago that I was there, though it was only a few months. The rent was eight dollars a week, which is considered very low for that neighborhood. It wasn't a very attractive room. George said, "It's dark, but on the other hand, it's dreary." Nevertheless, the room was clean and the bed was all right, though only the size of a cot. There was a faded little carpet on the floor, a big pasteboard closet in one corner, and a wash basin by the door. In the window were white filmy curtains that were gray from the soot in the New York air. Fifty-eighth Street was two floors below and the brown steps of the house just beneath the window.

This building was an old one that went back years and years and had once been someone's "town house." The ceilings and many of the walls had carvings that George said cost a great deal of money in its day. Now, it was just a rooming house, but this neighborhood itself is fancy. There is a Longchamps a few doors down, and the Plaza Hotel, the Barbizon-Plaza and Hotel Pierre are not far away. Also, there are many famous shops and stores around the corner on Fifth Avenue, Bergdorf-Goodman's, Tiffany's and so forth. That was the mood of the neighborhood, however New York is always a mixture—in the other direction, no farther away than Bergdorf's, is the 57th Street Automat.

The first night, I unpacked my suitcase and put my things in the bureau, wondering how I'd get my other things put away when the trunk arrived, because the bureau was like a doll's chest. It had a little piece of gray lace on top, a drinking glass and an ash tray. Such is the New York rooming house, but this particular one was not really bad. The rug was worn, but at least it was clean, and there were no "inhabitants" in the mattress or in the walls. A place I moved to later had that, unfortunately. The days I spent in *that* house later were the worst I ever spent *any*where. That was a nice-looking house over on 51st Street near Third Avenue. It was creeping with bugs. And there's nothing like the bite of those things, as I discovered. They bite like mad, and without any pity. It's horrible. First, a bug of this type doesn't bite like a mosquito at all. To be bitten by a mosquito is nothing in comparison. The only advantage is that these don't whine in your ears, the bite itself is far worse. For every bite a mosquito takes, one of these bites thirty times. What they do is get on your wrist or somewhere and take a bite, then crawl a little way and take another, then crawl a little farther and take another, then another and another until there's a whole row. After a while, the first bite begins to itch, but it doesn't exactly itch, it glows. You can feel it begin to get warm and glow, then swell about double the size of a mosquito bite. By this time it is itching so horribly you are out of your mind. If you scratch it, it will make you dizzy, or if you don't, it will drive you mad. By this time, the other bites have begun to glow, and meanwhile two or three others are biting on your legs and there's one biting your stomach, with another biting you on the neck and several biting on your arms, and here, there, and everywhere. There is nothing, or almost nothing, more horrible than to lie in some bed and have these awful things all over you biting you for hours and hours. I hope it never happens to the reader. If it does, get up and read a magazine. Don't just lie there. Sleep is impossible, anyhow.

Of course, this is all depressing, but I mention it partly in the hope that the reader will profit from my experience. I can only add that this is some insect to have in a rooming house that charges twelve dollars a week for a tiny room with paper-thin walls. This particular rooming house is on 51st Street near Third Avenue. When I told the maid about it, she looked blank, then when I told the landlady she said, "We don't have anything like that in this house, unless people bring them in themselves." Imagine paying twelve dollars for that room, then not getting any sleep for six nights. I couldn't even sit in a chair wrapped in a blanket, because they were in the blanket, and it did no good to spray the mattress (no good at all), and I didn't know what else to do, because I didn't know the things lived in the walls. How anybody can sleep while being bitten by these things, I do not know. The other tenants in the house must have been able to do it, because I learned later that the entire house was full of them, and they certainly had them in the room next door, because I knew the girl there. She was a woman, an actress that drank. He (Mr. X) knows all about such bugs, interestingly enough, but *I* didn't know what they were, and that was the worst part, not knowing what they were. Time after time, I'd get up and sit on the side of the bed and turn on the lamp, looking around on the walls trying to find mosquitoes. This sounds ridiculous, but I didn't know what

41

was biting me. Then finally I turned over the pillow and there one of them was, scurrying along very fast, a flat little horrible thing very revolting. May fate spare the reader from ever being bitten by them as I was. And besides all that, I was sick at the time, exhausted to begin with and very unhappy, in a terrible mood—those six days were like six years, and until then I didn't know how awful life can be, how everything can be hopeless and horrible—anyone who has had such an experience is never the same again, the memory is with them the rest of their days, but I'm sure that such trouble is the only way to understand anything, and those who never have it never know what life is all about, and as a result they always misinterpret everything, at least the most important things. Those bugs, however, were the least of my worries then, bad as they were.

This cold-water flat has bugs, too, but thank God not the same type. This place has roaches. All New York is full of roaches, it seems. There really are dozens of them here, running everywhere and stopping and wiggling their feelers. They rush across the sink and down the legs to the undersides, and you can see them under there, upside down with their feelers waving. Horrible things—they're throughout this building, and how the people stand it I don't know. If no food was ever left out in this apartment, at least they'd stay out of here, but unfortunately it seems that food is left out, therefore it does no good to spray, they just come back later. The things are loathsome, and *he* complains constantly, indignant as can be, yet who leaves food out for them, as if they were pigeons?

There never was anything like this down South, not in the South I lived in. In New York, there are as many roaches as there are people, or more. Both Phil and George say casually that the South is where all the roaches came from, but if so there are more of them up here now. The worst thing in the South is that they have a larger cockroach there. What they call roaches in New York, we call water bugs. The Southern roach is much worse. It's two and a half or three inches long, and has big wings and can fly buzzing across the room if you approach it suddenly. Cats catch them and eat them as if they

42

were mice. George and Phil think there's no such roach as this, but any Southerner knows or at least has heard of it. Once George was lying on the couch at the apartment, while visiting one evening with Barbara, and he suddenly gasped and began to stare with glazed eyes across the room, so everyone asked him what was the matter. He saw the great Southern cockroach—there in the window, three feet long, staring at him with huge eyes on stalks and one feeler across the room. It had come up from Birmingham to get him. "Oh," he said. "Those eyes—look, Phil, they're out on stalks. It's the great Southern cockroach. It's climbed up the fire escape. My God, Phil, look at it. Yiiiii!" Very funny, but there are roaches two and a half or three inches long, with wings, in the South. Why would anyone want to say so, if it weren't true? It's nothing to brag about, exactly. They just both like to argue, and contradict, especially *him*.

Chapter 7

I WAS DESCRIBING the room on 58th Street. However, I was only in that room a couple of days before I lived in the room next door, so there's no point in describing it. It was all right.

Even worse than contradiction and argument, is criticism. There are people who criticize everything. The sad thing is that of course this is based on their being dissatisfied with themselves. *That* would be criticized as being too obvious.(!) It's ironic. This is no good, that's no good, everything is terrible. How can they enjoy life at all? Naturally, they can't ever enjoy anything, because nothing is worth anything. Much less the effect on other people, who have to listen to it. For example, this morning, before the argument started, there was a little discussion about coffee. The coffee, incidentally, was perfectly all right, just the same as always. But he looked up with a smile and this is what he said:

"This coffee tastes a little strange, pet. What did you do, dip it out of a manhole, or something?"

"You just taste your upper lip," I said.

"Oh," he answered. "I see. Heh heh, I thought it was the coffee. Tastes to me like it was dipped out of a manhole. Excuse me, dear."

"Oh, shut up!" I said. "You make me sick! Shut up, just shut your mouth!"

He had no answer for a while, but just sat there. Usually it only makes him happy if he's insulted. You can tell he enjoys it. Later when I gave him his eggs he said with a sweet smile they

44

were so firm and nice he could take them down to the shoe shop and get his shoes half-soled. And the toast—it was wonderful, marvelous, because it wasn't crisp. "This toast isn't crisp, pet," he said. "It's marvelous and rubbery. I love toast that'll bounce, in case you drop it."

"Well, you let it lie there ten minutes before eating it," I answered.

"Heat it up again, dear," he said, "will you."

"Heat it up yourself," I answered.

"Come on, angel, be a sweet girl and heat it up. I can't light that oven. It's liable to blow up on me."

"Make some money and buy a toaster," I said.

"Heh, heh," he said. "No getting ahead of you, lamb, is there. Please heat up this goddamned toast immediately or I'll strangle you."

I won't go into this any more. The mailman just slammed the mail boxes downstairs and before I go down to see if there's any mail I'll write a description of the main characters of this story, then go ahead with the main story itself, and no more diversions on him or this apartment. But naturally it's an awful distraction.

The main characters are Bobbie, George, Phil, and Sue, I am Sue. There are several other characters but these are the main ones. Most important are Bobbie and George. The story is about them and it's the story of her troubles. However, I don't mean by that, what the reader might think. When I say trouble, I don't mean in the customary sense—it wasn't that at all. It was more on the order of problems rather than trouble. She made a terrible mistake, there's no other way to look at it—no modern theory can explain how it was anything but a dreadful error even though she thought otherwise at the time. However, I'll tell everything just the way it was and the reader can make up his own mind. I can do that since I know the people very well after observing them closely for three months, and especially do I know Bobbie very well. I lived in the room with her and she told me everything, including the way she felt and what she was thinking.

45

I myself, though a participant, had little to do with it. My own feelings were not involved. Therefore, I can be objective. Now I'm sharing this cold-water flat with Phil, but the story is not about me and him—we were only bystanders. Besides, during those three months, nothing special happened to me, or if it did, it didn't make any dent. I am a more "well-adjusted" type than Barbara. Things don't *upset* me the way they do her. I go along from day to day and never get excited, however the smallest thing upsets her completely. Furthermore, she's romantic, whereas I am not. She's the type that falls in love in a sentimental manner just because she gets a fixation on some particular boy, then she keeps at it even when it's hopeless. I'm not that way, thank God, and I am sorry for people who are.

A brief description of myself, first I'm tall, have blonde hair, blue eyes, and an easygoing manner. I seldom or never get excited, and even when I do, I remain outwardly rational and calm. Phil and George seldom pick at me or tease me. As a rule, I like people of all kinds, but no one ever has much of an effect on me one way or the other, really. If I *don't* like them, I ignore them, and if I do, I enjoy seeing them and that's all. This is the way I am and no doubt I was born like that. A while ago when everything was in such a horrible state, Phil and I were the only ones that remained calm—and even Phil wasn't calm all the time, though that was because of George mostly. But I was always calm, and always sympathetic to Barbara, even when Phil joined in against her and they were telling her she was a "mystic" and "highly neurotic" and "obsessed with guilt" and "having wild fantasies" and all that, then later when they were telling her to marry George and George himself was acting insane—I was always nice to her, though I couldn't quite see her point of view all the time and I still think there's a Puritan streak in that girl, and that's what makes her brood and act ridiculous, and so on. But it's her nature. That's the way she is and neither of those boys understood her. One day when they were nagging at her terribly and she was obviously almost out of her mind, and tormented by all that talk of George's, I told both of them to shut up and leave the poor girl alone, and

46

I also told them other things, especially George. In fact, if it hadn't been for me, God knows what would have happened—however, I don't want to get ahead of the story; I'll come to all this later.

In any case, that's the way I am—a calm, even-natured person. I don't mean to sound vain, I'm only trying to give an objective description, and that happens to be the way that I am. Bobbie herself is very different. Some people do not realize it when they meet her, they think she is even-natured too, but she's very excitable. She takes everything seriously—whatever people say, she tends to believe. I don't mean she's a fool, but merely that she's more temperamental than people imagine, as I know very well from living with her. She's the sort of girl whose feelings are easily hurt, and she will nurse a grudge for weeks, not in a mean way but just the same she'll remember something for weeks, then come out with it bitterly. The way she nurses a grudge always amazes George, because he's the type that gets furious then ten minutes later is pleasant. He sometimes will make a nasty remark to her, and she doesn't answer a word but weeks later when he doesn't even remember it, she remembers it and stares at him and refuses to talk, and he can't understand what has come over her. This is her nature, and in my opinion, she can't help it. Things that wouldn't bother another person reduce her to tears, as I know that from personal experience on many occasions. Not that anything I ever said to her bothered her, but many's the time I've seen her get that tearful look in her eyes because of something George said—especially George, Phil never bothered her very much. Naturally, considering that she was in love with George, it bothered her when he talked to her as if she was a complete fool, until she got used to it. Her eyes would get that expression that meant she was about to cry, and she would look down and shut up and not say a word. I always noticed when this happened, but George seldom ever did, and when he did, it would irritate him tremendously. "STOP it!" he'd say. "Good God—what did I say?" Then her eyes would really fill with tears, and he'd sigh and turn away with a disgusted

47

expression as if he were being persecuted. Childish of her, no doubt, to be that way, but that's how Bobbie is. She was born that way, just as I was born as I am. If Phil says something nasty to me, or if George does, I either ignore it or answer back. It doesn't bother me, I don't pay any attention to it, but it makes her very unhappy. Or it did originally—now, she merely ignores them.

She's also different from me in appearance. She's a little girl with dark brown hair and brown eyes. When she isn't talking, she seems to be very quiet, but then when she does talk, she talks quite a bit, in fact a great deal. Men are always trying to flirt with her and pick her up, because she's very pretty. These days, however, she looks tired. There's one peculiar thing about Bobbie, aside from the fact that she was an adopted child brought up by an old lady and man that had no children. When she was nine, she had infantile paralysis and almost died. She was in bed for a long time, her left side paralyzed, and she still has a numb place on her left arm. It doesn't look any different from her right arm, except to the extent that's natural in anyone who's right-handed, but when she was nine and ten and eleven there *was* a difference, and she tends to imagine that there still is. This is the only "complex" she has, despite what Phil and George said about her "neurosis." She's silly about this and usually wears long-sleeved blouses even now, and is modest about undressing in front of anyone, even girls. I didn't see her undress for three weeks when we first moved in the room together, she always dressed in the bathroom or in the dressing room alcove, then one day I walked in and she was standing there in panties or bra or something, and she acted embarrassed—I didn't know what was the matter, I had no idea anything was supposed to be wrong with her, she looked all right to me, in fact she has a beautiful figure. I thought she was just modest as some people are, but she didn't seem to be that type either. The answer is that it was this complex of hers from having had infantile paralysis. That was long ago, and no one would ever know she'd had it, but no doubt she still has this complex, and probably will never get over it

48

completely. Later that day she told me about it, admitting herself that it was silly. It was in her mind, as I told her, but she was so fixed on this point she said she didn't see how she could ever get married, because she knew she could never undress in front of a man, at the very least she'd fall over in a faint. "You'll overcome that hurdle," I said. "He'll undress you, so don't brood about that." But this idea made her look even more worried, so I told her she had no problem, she could always marry for companionship, sex wasn't everything. But she just looked more worried. About this time I believe she was thinking about George in particular—they were together all the time night and day, with him making no secret about "the ordeal" he was going through trying to get her. Of course he was after her, and what a naive soul she was. One time she said very seriously, "You know, he wants me to sleep with him." She said that in the most naive way, as if it was amazing he should have such an idea. Where have you been all your life, honey, I felt like saying.

George and Phil are sometimes regarded as peas in a pod, but they are not the same. George can be much nicer when he wants to. Phil is all right, but he's more glum and intellectual. He can argue better than George because he has a more logical mind, but George can be more insulting. Phil knows more than George, he's the type that remembers names and dates and can quote facts and figures from memory, and so on. He really argues very well, but George holds his own with him, because he can be more insulting. Few people can be as insulting as George, though Phil can be very insulting, too, at times. They take pleasure in cornering someone the way they did that boy at Betty's. They corner someone like that and argue, first one then the other—when one gets tired the other takes it up. But that boy that time was practically a match for them. It looked as if they were going to get in a fist fight, especially the horrible way Phil was yelling, and especially when George first insulted the boy.

Both Phil and George get in fist fights, and especially George, because he's stronger and taller than Phil. Once I was in a bar with him, and a man down the counter was staring, but not really in a bad way. However, George didn't like it, he stared down at the man, then when the man didn't look away, he walked along the bar toward him very slow and holding his eyes on the man. I followed along trying to stop him but he wouldn't pay any attention. He walked up close to the man and said, "What are you looking at, you ugly —— — — ———." There's no describing the low, horrible way he said that. He was in an utter rage, his face completely white—I was sure any second he was going to hit the man—he didn't even look like himself, it was horrible. I almost fainted, I was so sure he was going to hit the man, and the man thought so, too, he was smiling weakly and asking George to come on and have a drink. Thank God the man was scared, or they'd have had a fight. Phil sometimes does this type of thing, too, but usually Phil is more dry and intellectual. Both of them say they have stopped this sort of business now, but only the other day George insulted a waiter horribly. Bobbie told me about it. The waiter brought something wrong and tried to argue about it, then George told him, "Take this back to the kitchen, you stupid idiot." This doesn't sound typed out one-hundredth as bad as it must have sounded when George said it, because it's his tone—Bobbie imitates him perfectly—I can just hear him saying it, cold and indifferent like he was discussing the weather. "I didn't order this. Take it back to the kitchen, you stupid idiot." The way that waiter stared at George! He *hated* him. Some of these New York waiters are ill-mannered, but the way George talked must have been out of all proportion. And then of course Bobbie was so upset she could hardly eat after all this, and naturally George got mad at *her*. "What's wrong with you?" he asked her. "Eat your soup—do you want me to hold the damned spoon?" This is the way he sometimes talks to her. *I* would tell him "Shut up!" But Bobbie just sits there.

In appearance, George and Phil are similar, but Phil has darker-colored hair and isn't as tall. Phil is handsome in an icy, sarcastic manner, and looks older than George. Considering them objectively, I think George is more attractive, though from a personal standpoint I think Phil is more attractive, of course. George can be wonderful when he wants to be, very nice and sweet, the trouble is that he seldom wants to be. Phil is six months older, Phil is—or rather, *was* taking a degree at Columbia in philosophy, a Master's Degree with money from his father, who spoils him, and also being psychoanalyzed. I'm writing too fast. It's *George* is being psychoanalyzed, not Phil. Phil is against psychoanalysis, the way I said before, I mentioned that—he's against it for himself, but for it for everybody else, though he talks about how "neurotic" he is all the time. But as I was saying, Phil was studying for a master's at Columbia, and George wasn't doing anything, not in those days. George had some money then, the last of some money his parents gave him, and some other money he made himself—he since then spent almost every penny fixing up the apartment for Bobbie. They have an apartment much like ours, a cold-water flat but in a different part of town. Originally, George had been in school in Louisiana for two years, then he was in school in Chicago. One time, he'd flunk all his subjects and the next time he'd make the honor roll, and he slept with a young professor's wife and was caught by the professor's mother, then had to climb out on the shed over the garage in the wintertime in an old bathrobe belonging to the professor, who was out of town on business for the school. He also did some crazy prank besides that, but after he made the Dean's list the Dean said he wouldn't expel him. He decided to quit while he was winning, and because school was a waste of time, anyhow. But that enraged his parents. They gave him some money and his father said, "Get out and don't ever come back! Beat it! Scram!" His parents disapprove of him intensely. They wanted him to carry on the traditions and go into the family business, which is wholesale hardware. When I met him he was playing around gaily, wearing nice clothes. For a while before I knew him, he worked on a trade magazine, but it bored him and he quit, because he and Phil had sold a detective story to a magazine. Both he and Phil, but especially him, wrote stories about travel to Mars, and so on, as well as mysteries, but they hate to do it because it isn't literary enough. It's "hack work." Both of them have also written articles for magazines. These articles they do separately, and George doesn't do them any more at all. These were magazines that pay about ten dollars for long articles, magazines no one ever heard of, but very intelligent according to them, though it's impossible to understand the articles. Phil still writes them, articles like that. George doesn't. George doesn't write anything, he just talks.

These are the principal characters in the story. I myself am twenty years old, Bobbie is twenty, Phil twenty-five, and George twenty-five. At the time the story starts, Bobbie was nineteen, I was nineteen, George was twenty-four, and Phil twenty-four.

Otherwise, the characters in the book are Hugo, a big brute that plays football for Yale, and comes home sometimes— Betty went with him before she met Tom. I never met Hugo. Betty is a friend I met in the Automat—a dancer. Tom is that boy Betty goes with now, the one George and Phil had the argument with, from the South. She (Betty) is from Indiana, a very nice girl. Besides these, there's Jan Mariss, a very famous dancer, Heidi, Charlotte, Jean and Louise, in the Mariss troupe, or in one of the special classes, and also Tami Lang, a boy in the troupe, Doug, another boy, and others. These are most of the characters in the story, assuming they ever get in it. Before Betty got her job on *Dance World* she worked for a while as a doctor's receptionist—that's how Hugo happened to be in it, he was the son of the doctor. There also is another doctor in it later.

However, I've decided to write no more of this book. I can't, it's too depressing a story, too grim and depressing, even though no doubt it could have been worse. But not much worse.

Part 2

An' Chased Him a Solid Mile

Chapter 8

THERE IS NOTHING like the Automat when in a bad mood. I know this from the many times I have gone to the one on 57th Street. Either the Automat makes you feel worse or it makes you feel better, and usually the second. There's something about it. The rush—the crowds—the "characters"—the hustle and bustle—everyone standing and calling to the girls behind the steam counter, ordering this, that and the other— the Automat has the power to change one's mood, and it has changed mine. I've decided really to write this book. I have it planned now and only need to write twenty-five pages each morning and afternoon, and it'll be finished soon. And very easily.

The Automat is very interesting. No other restaurant chain is like it. There're several reasons. The idea of having food in cubbyholes is clever, but that isn't all. All kinds of people go there, including people with money. Some man told me one day there's a wealthy man whose chauffeur drives him there all the time, because he likes the Automat's baked beans. This could very well be true. The food in the Automat is better than in 90 per cent of New York restaurants. Breakfast there is better than breakfast at Longchamps, which is also a restaurant chain but very expensive. The food in the Automat is worth what it costs. If they served it with waiters and tablecloths and so on, they could easily charge three times as much. I'm sure many people are healthy and have a good diet who otherwise wouldn't, because of the Automat. Practically everything there is good. The men that run the Automats are good citizens not just trying to squeeze money out of everyone. They could charge more if they wanted to. And this includes the people who work in them; they're more polite than most people who work in restaurants. A nice type of person is associated with the Automat, with few exceptions, and as far as I'm concerned I often would rather eat there than anywhere else, but as the reader might guess, *he* doesn't like the Automat. He *hates* it. He would eat there maybe, but he can't endure seeing those people drool like pigs while they eat. He goes there, then comes back and says he won't go there any more, because even though the food is not too bad, the people in there slobber in it and all of them need a bath. In my opinion, besides some poor people being there, he doesn't like it because he likes to sit back and have a waiter come with everything, then he can call the waiter an idiot—but no more side-tracking on *this* subject.

Of course an entire book could be written about the situation in this cold-water flat, but that isn't what I started to write or want to write—the real story is on 58th Street, not here, this is no story, there's nothing here but trouble, and it will certainly have an unhappy ending, whereas things on 58th Street did at least seem to end better. But in order to start the real story, from here on, I won't even refer to myself as "I." The reader will know it's me when I say Sue. Since I know these people very well and know practically everything they said or did during the entire time of the story, or learned later what they said or did, it won't be any stretch of the imagination for me to tell it all, every last terrible bit, even the awful, depressing thoughts of some of the main characters.

Now at last, the story. It starts on the afternoon of a double date between George and Bobbie and Sue and Phil, and ends with Bobbie vanishing into nowhere. It'll be obvious enough what happened to her. This story will show step by step how she came to vanish like that without a trace, and then will tell what—but all of that will come out in time.

Bobbie and Sue have been rooming together for a week at

the time of the date. They met in the hall after a couple of days, became friends, and soon after that decided to share the big front room. The day after Sue moved in the house, George got a telegram and had to go to Philadelphia to attend a funeral. His uncle had died and left him a thousand dollars, so he went there to attend the funeral ceremony and to try and get the thousand dollars from his family, who held the money in trust. But his uncle had said according to his father, that when George holds down an honest job for ninety days, give him the thousand dollars, but otherwise don't give the damn fool any money till it snows in August. George went to get the money on the theory that it snows at the South Pole in August. But his father said, "Go back to your wild women, liquor, and the life of a pimp!" He, George, stayed down there ten days arguing with his father and trying to get the money, but he couldn't. It was impossible. His father was fed up with him, writing insane letters to all the relatives and telling them about three-eyed prostitutes, and sending a sex book on marriage to his aunt, and refusing to work, running around, and so on. His mother was nice but agreed with the father that George should reform. So the only way he could get the money was by holding down an honest job for ninety days, and since he never expected to do that, he would never get the money and that was a thousand dollars lost. He came back and shrugged, as though he didn't care. The morning he came back, he went and visited Bobbie and Sue, and told them about what happened—not the whole thing then, but what the lawyers said, that his uncle's estate was tied up because his father was executor. "They won't let me have the money," said George. "My uncle didn't say any such nonsense as that. It's the old man, the damned buzzard. He's a *nasty* old buzzard. You can't reason with the old fool. He envies me because he thinks I run around with a lot of gals, whereas I *don't*. But that's what the old goat thinks and would probably like to do himself. Imagine him being such a cruddy old scoundrel as to hold back that three grand on such a pretext, when my uncle left it to me and wanted me to have it." Such exaggeration is typical of George. It came out later that his uncle left him only a thousand dollars, but that afternoon he said it was three. He seldom can tell the exact truth about anything, especially figures, but always must exaggerate one way or the other. He'll exaggerate even if it makes himself look worse, rather than tell the truth. Yet he calls Bobbie a liar and accuses her of telling fibs and making things up. He never lies, but she does, "because she's a woman," and as everybody knows, women can't tell the truth because it isn't in their nature. No, women will look right at you and tell you the most utter lie, and it doesn't bother their conscience. Etc., etc. Men don't do that, men are honest, they say what's on their mind, if they love a girl they say so, or if they don't want to do something for a reason, they admit what the reason is, whereas a woman will give *another* reason. And so on and so forth.

This was the second time he met Bobbie, that afternoon. Of course, he'd known Sue before, but he hadn't seen much of her because of his trip. That morning, he stayed there and talked, flirting with Bobbie and joking with them both, till Sue had to leave for her job at *Dance World,* a part-time job she got a day or two before. Then he took Bobbie for a walk in the park. Before that, as Sue was leaving, he said,

"Wait a minute, before you leave. What are you doing tonight?"

"Me?" said Sue. "What do you want, a date?"

"I was thinking," said George. "Now that I'm back in town, there's a friend of mine you'd like to meet. I thought maybe we could get up a party."

"A party?" said Sue.

"Some sort of l'il party. We could go to Coney Island, or something like that." He turned around and said to Bobbie, "Would you like to go to Coney Island?"

"Coney Island?" said Sue. She looked bored by the idea.

George said, "Of course, there are other possibilities. Phil has been writing a paper on Santayana—we could always sit around and discuss philosophy over a bottle. How does that strike you?"

58

"Phil?" said Sue. "Who's Phil?"

"My friend," said George. "He shares the place with me down the hall. You must've seen him slinking around the house. A slick-looking type. He saw you, I know, the day you moved in here. Every time he mentions you his eyes bug out about an inch and he drools down on his tie."

"Hmm," said Sue, staring curiously at George. Sue is rather literal-minded. She's a nice girl, and though she has a good sense of humor, her reaction to a type like George is to wonder what's the matter with him to make him say such things. Some other people feel the same way about him. Imagine him sitting there and telling her such things, when trying to persuade her to go out on a date.

"He thinks you're attractive and would like to meet you," said George. "He really does. He's not a bad guy, girls do seem to like him—they think he's brainy. He'll tell you about Santayana before he makes any move at you."

"Well," said Sue, ironically. "Philosophy bores me. I like a man to be direct."

"I'll tell him, and he'll be direct, then," said George.

"Hmm," said Sue. She lifted an eyebrow and turned to go.

"Really," said George, "he's not *that* type, I was just talking. Phil is proper."

"He sounds like an utter bore," said Sue.

"No kidding, wouldn't you like to get up a little party some night?" asked George, in his most pleasant tone.

Sue looked at Bobbie. Her expression was blank and indifferent. "Maybe some time," she said to George, then she turned back to Bobbie. George was no longer on her mind. "Well, good-bye," she said. "I'll see you at one-thirty."

"All right," said Bobbie. "Do I just take the Fifth Avenue bus down the street here . . . ?"

She also is from the South and has a worse Southern accent than Sue. When she said this, George grinned and looked down at the floor and chuckled to himself, shaking his head. In a low voice, assuming what he thought was her expression, he said, "Do Ah jes' take the Fifth Aavenoo bus-s-s-s down the

59

street heah?" Then he looked at Sue and said, "Isn't that nice the way she says that?" He smiled at Bobbie then suddenly reached over and put his hand on her knee. "You're cute," he said. "Heh, heh."

Sue ignored him, and said, "Yes. Take the Fifth Avenue bus and get off at 27th Street. It'll be all right, Betty knows you're coming. Just don't be late."

"I won't," said Bobbie, as she took George's wrist to move his hand away from her knee. He held it there and she couldn't move it.

Sue glanced at George, rather aloofly. "Bye," she said.

"Hey!" he called. "Phil *really* wants to meet you—don't run out. Wait—wait a minute, don't you want to go to dinner tonight at the Stork Club?"

"I don't believe in storks," she said.

"Oh," said George. "No?"

With a blank expression, Sue closed the door and footsteps sounded down the hall and down the stairs.

"Huh," said George. "What's she so withdrawn about? She acts like a paranoiac or something. Where's she going?"

"To work," said Bobbie. This boy made her nervous. His hand was still on her knee.

"I know, but where's that? Where's work?"

"A magazine."

"Dumbjohn is going to chew me out about this."

"Who?"

"Phil. I don't think that girl likes me. What magazine?"

Bobbie paused, then tried again to move his hand from her knee, but she couldn't push it off. She answered, "*Dance World* magazine."

"Daynce Wuhhll mag-zeeeene?" he said. "You are cute, Barbara. Do you know what you remind me of?"

"No," she said. "What?"

He leaned toward her and smiled as if talking to a child five years old. This was to disarm her. He can seem very warm-hearted and friendly when he wants to. "*Ice cream,*" he said.

"I could just eat you up. You don't *know* how cute you are. Give me a kiss."

This is what he said, but when it's typed down it sounds different. As he said that, he leaned over in front of her, and there he was, just about to kiss her and he hardly knew her. He also now had his arm around her waist, and the other hand was still on her knee.

"Why, don't!!" she said. "*I* don't want to *kiss you!*"

"Well," he said.

"Then get away," she said. She shoved at him. "Now, stop," she said.

But he's not the type to take no for an answer. It didn't seem to discourage him, her pushing at him. She was back on the sofa, looking up at him and trying to shove at him. Never had a boy made such a pass as this, so sudden and everything. She was baffled.

Later on, she had still managed to keep him away fairly well. The reader should understand how naive this girl is, because she hardly knew what to do. Anything would shock her, and besides she didn't want to be rude to him. Also, she liked him. Perhaps it was something mystic. More likely, it was her background catching up with her. He upset her and she hardly knew what she was saying. Her knees were weak out of complete surprise. Also, she believed everything he said—not that he said anything except that she was "cute," "sweet" and so forth. In those minutes she was occupied 90 per cent of the time in shoving him away, then finally all of a sudden the telephone rang. It was the wrong number.

"Really!" she said. "You shouldn't *act* like this. Get away, and leave me alone."

He laughed. She amused him. Then he asked, "What does Sue do at *Dance World?*"

"Well," said Bobbie. She swallowed nervously. "Up there? She sorts out subscriptions."

George thought a minute, then lit a cigarette and blew out smoke through his nose. He was sitting on the sofa by her, hands on his lap, with lipstick on his chin where he'd tried to

61

kiss her, partially successfully. He was looking at her now in a sort of speculative way, as if trying to figure her out and try and understand her. Later he said he thought she was trying to fool him. He took another puff at the cigarette, again blowing smoke out through his nose. Then he asked, "Is that where you're meeting her at one-thirty?"

Bobbie nodded.

"What for?" he asked.

"Well," she answered, "I'm getting a job there, myself."

"Doing what?"

"Doing what?" she repeated.

"Yes. What are you going to do there?"

"I'm going to sort out subscriptions, too," she answered.

"Umm," he said, and thought a minute. "I don't think I made a good impression on her," he said. "She was cool."

"That's just the way she is," said Bobbie.

"She was frosty," he answered. "I was too something or other with her, I guess. I'll call her. That magazine's in the book, isn't it?"

"I think so," said Bobbie.

"Well, let's go for a walk in the park," said George. "You don't have to sort out subscriptions for a while yet."

"I can't," said Bobbie. "I have to wash my stockings and straighten up the apartment."

But she went for a walk with him. That afternoon he called at *Dance World* and talked first to Betty, then Sue. He was on the phone about twenty minutes, five minutes with Betty, then fifteen minues with Sue, and the result was Sue agreed to come on a date that night and meet Phil, on condition they have dinner at the 21 Club. Bobbie had already agreed to the date while they were in the park. There was a lot of conversation in the park. He said to her, "You understand I want to take you out to Coney Island and get a gypsy to tell you you're going to fall in love. A gypsy'll tell you, and also who it'll be." They were sitting on a bench by the lake watching an old man throw bread crumbs to pigeons. It was a beautiful day. It had rained the night before and the sky was very blue. He had been telling her what the lines in her palm meant, though obviously he didn't really know what they meant. At the moment she was looking at the boats on the lake, and at the people everywhere, and at the dozens of pigeons gathered on the sidewalk It was nice there, and seemed far removed from New York—she hadn't known there was a park like this right in the center of the city. Tall apartment buildings were all around the horizon, but where they were it was almost like countryside. And though she liked the park, she was so nervous she could hardly talk. He'd put his arm around her there in broad daylight with people everywhere. This romantic line didn't impress her, about it being "fate," and all that. He made her nervous. She was afraid of what he might do at any moment, being so crazy.

"Oh," she said, "such a line. Do you think I don't know how silly all that talk is? I'm not as dumb as you might think."

"Who said you were dumb?" he asked. "You're the opposite of dumb. That's why I like you."

"Why should you like me," she asked, "when you don't even know me? And it's obvious you think I'm dumb, because of the way you talk to me, as if I was a child or something. Now take your arm away, because all these people are looking at you."

He said, "I love you. You're so cute."

"Really," she said, "you don't even know me."

"Sure I do," he said. "I know you perfectly."

She believed him. And it was true. He did know her. He knew what she was thinking all the time, then.

Chapter 9

THAT AFTERNOON, GEORGE and Phil were in their room discussing the two girls. They had been talking about them for quite a while.

"All right," said George. "I'm the one that engineered this, not you, so get off your high horse. I have first choice. Not you."

"Okay," answered Phil. "Make up your mind, then. Which one do you want, the blonde or the brunette? I admit you've got first choice, all I want is for you to say which one you pick. Which is it, the brunette?"

"Umm," said George. He was sitting slumped down in the easy chair. He was in underwear and had a cigarette in his mouth. His eyes narrowed thoughtfully as he gazed into space and said, "Types like that blonde knock me out. They always have, ever since I was thirteen and saw my cousin in a bathing suit. Ever since then, I've never been able to resist —— of —— ——."

"Okay. Do you want her, then?"

"But I'm afraid she's sort of bovine, the blonde," said George. "I mean mentally. It's just that I can't resist a girl with that figure."

"I don't see much difference between her and the little brunette," answered Phil. "I'll take the brunette, if you prefer the blonde. In fact, let's settle it that way, all right? I'll take the brunette, and you the blonde."

"I just told you the blonde is bovine," said George.

"Well, that's your speed," replied Phil.

"Those placid blue eyes," said George. "There's no torment in them. None at all. The blonde is a nice girl but she has a cow's mind." He paused, staring thoughtfully into space. "On the other hand, there's a lot to be said for her, from a physical standpoint."

"That's what *I* always said about her," said Phil.

"But Bobbie has such nice brown eyes," said George. "And she's so cute. If only she had the blonde's figure."

"She looks all right to me," answered Phil. "What's the difference, they're—"

"She's not in the blonde's league," sighed George. "Be realistic. She's cute but she's not in Sue's league, poor thing, not when it comes to —————."

"You didn't pay close attention to her," said Phil.

"The hell I didn't."

"She's nice, she—"

"You want the blonde yourself, dog," interrupted George.

"No, not particularly," answered Phil. "She's hefty for my taste, but that little brunette, a good man —— — ——, ——, and —————."

"I wouldn't especially — —— — ——, ——, —————," said George. "You shouldn't be oafish with a little angel like that. Never be bestial with a sweet little angel like this one."

"Not bestial constantly," answered Phil. "But now and then, bestial. *Very* bestial."

"Never," said George. "Bestial with Sue, but not Bobbie. She's too sweet for bestiality. You have to be nice to her."

"You're out of your mind," said Phil. "All women need a man with beastliness in him. You know that. That's what makes a man a man."

"Oh, quiet," answered George. "I was beastly with women before you were born."

"You've forgotten it," said Phil. "A basic verity. Therefore, I'll take the brunette and bruise her up a little, and you can have the blonde."

"Oh, no," said George. "*I* want the brunette. Calm down, you've got the blonde."

"What?" asked Phil. "You're turning down that gorgeous blonde for that little brunette?"

"She likes me," said George. "Unless I miss my bet, she already thinks she loves me. And besides, I like her. She's sweet."

"I like her too," answered Phil. "Let's flip a coin to see who goes out with who. We have to get it started off right, because once you start going with one of them, there won't be much chance later to change your mind—we couldn't very well switch around from one to the other. And since I prefer the brunette too, we'll have to flip a coin."

"Shut up," said George. "You know you like the blonde better. Stop trying to irritate me. I like the blonde in a way, but Bobbie's nicer. As a girl she's nicer. She's more my type."

This was the way George and Phil talked about girls. They would say the same things over and over, never becoming bored no matter how long it went on. They always made the point somewhere in the discussion that the unhappier girls are, the happier they are. It takes intelligence to understand this theory, but that's their opinion. The truth was they enjoyed talking like this when they got together by themselves, or when they thought no one was listening or paying any attention to them. Whatever girl Phil met, he'd go and talk about her to George, describing her in detail from head to toe, and George would do the same. Later he even did this with Bobbie, he'd spend ten minutes telling her about some girl he met somewhere—the girl was like so-and-so, and so forth, and so on.

Conversation of this type was routine with them. They did it all the time, and the worse things they could say the more they enjoyed it. Anyone overhearing such conversation would be shocked to say the least. It would have been interesting if the girls themselves had heard themselves discussed in this way before the first date, with all that argument about who would take out who. No doubt Bobbie herself would have been amazed, and Sue would probably have been annoyed, especially about George's calling her bovine. She wouldn't have liked that. But she would probably have been pleased that they were discussing her. She was slightly vain about her figure, which was indeed very good. Often she would stay around the room in nothing but panties and a bra, and glance at herself when she walked by the mirror. She did have a wonderful figure, and was vain about it. Once she said to Bobbie, one time when she was standing by the closet totally nude and looking in the mirror, "Don't you think I have a beautiful body?" It was true, many women would give a fortune to have such a figure as Sue, and her face is pretty too, with blonde hair and blue eyes, a sort of pleasant, pretty face, with arched eyebrows and full lips, and pink lipstick since she was a blonde. Bobbie was pretty, too. She wasn't as tall as Sue, and not as noticeable, but her face had more expression and character, her eyes were warmer and she had a prettier smile. They were different types. Bobbie was vain about her own appearance even worse than Sue, in many ways, and in other ways she wasn't.

Earlier that afternoon, Phil had been sitting at the desk in his underwear typing a paper for a class at Columbia. The paper was on Santayana. The class was in modern philosophy and the paper was an evaluation of Santayana's ideas.

At the moment he was lying on the bed, still in his underwear but with shoes and socks and garters on. He'd gotten out his shirt and blue suit. The suit needed pressing. It lay rumpled on the chair. Phil was a dark-haired boy of better than average height, with a high forehead and Roman nose. There was a kind of ironic expression in his eyes, as if he doubted everything. His hair had a slight wave in it, and he always combed and brushed it, keeping it parted. His beard was dark and he had to shave frequently. Phil's chin was rather pointed. His usual expression was one of blankness and reserve. He read a great deal and wore glasses when he read. In comparison to George, he was glum and moody, not that *George* wasn't moody. But Phil tended to be more reserved. He was handsome in a way that George wasn't. His features were regular and he had that look around the forehead and eyes and cheek-bones that make people handsome. He knew this well enough. If he'd smiled a little more, Phil would have been even better looking. Though he was handsomer than George, George often seemed more attractive because of his manner. George was one of those people hard to describe. He was neither this nor that. One minute he looked one way, and another minute the opposite. Basically he looked like an average person of the kind you would see anywhere, but a little taller than usual. He had sandy-colored hair, blondish eyebrows, a high fore-head like Phil, a small cleft in his chin. When George smiled, he looked more natural than Phil, whose smile was more like a sarcastic grin than anything else. Over his right eyebrow George had a tiny little mole not much bigger than the head of a pin, and he had another of these on his temple, and also he had a faint scar over one eyebrow as the result of an auto-mobile accident when he was ten. Phil's voice was pitched rather high and he tended to talk in an even tone. George's voice was lower. He was much less serious than Phil, and usually looked as if he was enjoying life more, but he was given to tempers, when his whole face looked different. He weighed about a hundred and seventy pounds and Phil weighed about a hundred and fifty. George was stronger than Phil. He liked many more people than Phil, and had strange depressions and moods, when he would get a sullen look on his face and refuse to talk. George was also more of a wolf as far as girls were concerned. Phil didn't have George's way of joking, he tended to be more intellectual and analytical, but George would go up to a girl as he did to Bobbie, without any warning, as if everything was nice and he liked her, all the time making a kind of joke of it but very attracted to the girl—that was the thing about him, they all attracted him, at least in those days. Phil's approach was to analyze things and impress the girl with his brains. They were *very* different. They both had a theory that marriage was an outmoded institution. Phil said he never intended to get married, and George said when he was about forty, he'd marry some young girl and have a family.

That afternoon, George hadn't been doing anything. In the morning, he'd gone for the walk with Bobbie in the park, then he went to the library and returned to the room and had a nap while Phil typed the paper on Santayana. George had gotten a book from the library on the New Hebrides Islands, probably to tell somebody all about them in great detail some time, but he was too sleepy to read it.

At present, George was slumping in the easy chair in his underwear, smoking a cigarette and talking to Phil. He'd gotten out his shirt and suit—a light brown palm beach suit, very nice and expensive, and neatly pressed, unlike Phil's wrinkled and rumpled blue serge suit. George was wondering to himself about that night. Could he seduce Bobbie? She was cute. He liked her so much and it would be delightful, but of course she would be a virgin, poor thing. Of course she was scared—the way she'd been so upset in the room this morning, heh, heh. He smiled to himself.

"What are you grinning about?" asked Phil.

"What?" asked George.

"Why the vacant smile?"

"What vacant smile?"

Phil put his hands behind his head and looked amusedly at George. "You were grinning like a zombie," he said. "It must be true love."

"Oh, sure," said George. "That's what it is."

"Is it *(Censored)*?" asked Phil.

"Yes, it's *(Censored)*," said George. "But not right away. It'll take a while."

"How long?"

"Not too long."

Chapter 10

Down the hall, the two girls were getting ready for their date, and they were talking in a different way.

"God" said Sue, "what am I going to do with *this* thing?"

"What's the matter with it?" asked Bobbie. She was standing in front of the mirror, combing her hair, pins in her mouth. As she spoke she turned and glanced at Sue, who had got out the ironing board and plugged in the iron a few minutes before. Bobbie was dressed, but Sue was in panties and a brassiere, and now holding up and examining a dark brown gabardine skirt. This she wanted to press, along with her slip and blouse, which lay on the ironing board.

"It doesn't fit any more," said Sue. "I look like hell in it." She added, "I've put on pounds and pounds since I've been in the city."

"You have?" said Bobbie. "Have you really gained weight?"

"I have," answered Sue. "Tons." She was just talking.

"I don't see where," said Bobbie. "I wish I could *gain* a little weight."

"*Don't*," said Sue. "It's hell to lose once you get it." She sighed, really sounding worried. "I'm going to look like a sailor's girl in this skirt. It's too small for me now, but I don't know what else to wear." She scowled then put the skirt down on the ironing board, a determined look in her eyes. "I'm going to have to buy some clothes and that's all there is to it. All the nice things I have are worn out. It depresses me to look in the closet, much less walk on Fifth Avenue. That's what I

70

can't stand about this neighborhood. You know what I mean? It's like being on a desert and seeing a mirage, except the mirage is Bergdorf's—to look in there makes me feel just tired. If the women that buy there looked nice in those clothes it wouldn't be so bad, but most of them have gotten beyond the point of looking good in anything but a coffin. Doesn't it make you feel the same way to look in Bergdorf's at all those marvelous clothes?"

"Yes," said Bobbie.

"This is certain to be too tight," said Sue, holding the skirt across her waist. She was grimacing in irritation. "I don't dare put it on. I'll look like a sailor's girl."

"Maybe you can get it altered," said Bobbie.

"There isn't time," answered Sue.

"I meant later."

"Later? That wouldn't help now. And besides they charge fabulous prices around here for altering. I'm going to lose a few pounds, then it'll fit. It'll just have to do one more time the way it is." As Sue spoke, she pulled on the skirt and zipped up the zipper on the side, snapping the buttons. Then she turned and held up her arms and looked in the mirror. The skirt was not bad. "Huh," she said thoughtfully.

"It looks nice," said Bobbie. "It's a cute skirt."

"It's just a cheap skirt," said Sue.

"It fits all right," said Bobbie.

"No," replied Sue. "I've put on pounds since I came here. New York makes me nervous and when I get nervous, I become famished."

"I don't," said Bobbie. "When I'm nervous, I can't eat."

"Not me," said Sue. "When I'm upset I can eat anything." As she said this, she pulled off the skirt, then turned and laid it on the ironing board. She smoothed the material then wet her finger and tested the iron. Then she said, "What's-his-name was sort of cute over the phone this afternoon. He had Betty in hysterics. Betty never met him, did she?"

"I don't think so," said Bobbie.

"She's dying to meet him, now," said Sue.

"Is she?" asked Bobbie.

Sue glanced at her, then back at the ironing. "He's a kidder, that George," she said. "He's so goddamn fresh, but he talked nice over the phone. I guess he's irresponsible or something. I knew a boy like that once. He was always playing jokes. That boy would do literally anything to play a joke. He'd go to some nice party and get in a conversation with an old maid, and be polite and proper and everything, then casually use some vulgar expression, to make the old lady think she was hearing things. This George is the same type. Do you like him?"

"I like him all right," said Bobbie.

"I wonder what his friend will be like," said Sue thoughtfully. "This ought to be an interesting date, don't you think—he says his friend is taking a Master's degree at Columbia. You never met the friend, did you?"

"Well," said Bobbie, "I never really did, I only saw him for a minute in the hall. He's nice-looking, sort of quiet. He didn't say anything, just smiled."

"Umm," said Sue. "Bashful, eh."

"I don't think so," answered Bobbie. "I didn't mean that exactly."

"What else do you know about him?" asked Sue.

"Nothing, just that his name is Phil. That's all I know. He's taking a Master's up at Columbia and George says he's very intellectual."

"Intellectual?"

"Yes. George says he's always correcting the teachers. They're afraid of him, he's so intelligent. He has a very logical mind, George says."

"Sounds like a thrilling date," answered Sue. "He isn't bad-looking, though, if it's the boy I think it is. One dark-haired, sort of good-looking boy that's been giving me glances for a week or two in the hall. Is he Jewish, this boy?"

"Oh, no," said Bobbie.

"What's his last name?"

"I don't know."

"The boy I'm thinking about looks as if he might be Jewish. I'm pretty sure he is. He has a little gap between his front teeth and a sort of Jewish face. I like Jewish boys, though. When they're good-looking they're really good-looking. You're not an anti-Semite, are you?"

"An anti-Semite?" said Bobbie. "No," she said.

"It's stupid," said Sue. "I hate people who generalize like that about things, don't you?"

"Yes," said Bobbie. "I think so."

There was silence for a while, then Sue said, "I'll tell you this about George. He impresses me as being slippery. I know that type, and if I were you, I wouldn't pay any attention to anything he says." She smiled over her shoulder, a very nice smile she has at times, then she lifted one eyebrow. "I think he has really evil intentions as far as you're concerned." Sue nodded. "Yes, sir, I think he does. Don't let him grab you when you're looking in the other direction."

"Oh, I don't think so," said Bobbie. "Not really, he just— that's his nature, to joke and talk that way."

"It certainly is his nature," answered Sue. "I know the type. Look at the way he was talking to Betty, and he'd never laid eyes on her, she just happened to answer the phone. I know that type. And he has an eye on you. You're just the sort of girl he'd go for."

"Well, he . . ."

"It isn't any of my affair," replied Sue, "but you know he reminds me so much of my brother Dan. Dan is that same type. His greatest pleasure is to make some girl like him, then the minute the girl is really interested, I mean in love with him, he suddenly becomes a total stranger. Many boys are that way. They can sleep with a girl and it doesn't affect them, but most girls aren't *like* that, if they get involved with a man it tends to make a difference to them. That's true of some girls especially."

"Is it?" said Bobbie. "I think it would be."

Sue glanced from her ironing board. Bobbie had finished combing her hair and was now putting on lipstick.

73

Sue said, "You don't mind my talking like this, do you?"

"No," said Bobbie. "I don't."

"Well," said Sue, "you like him, don't you?"

"I hardly know him," said Bobbie.

Sue looked back at her ironing, slightly embarrassed. "Oh, well," she said.

Bobbie didn't say anything. All the things Sue said about George, she had understood after talking to him for half an hour the first time she met him. She understood much more than that, things Sue didn't know.

Bobbie liked Sue very much as a friend, Sue was sweet and kind-hearted, and had such a pleasant sense of humor. During the week they had shared the big front room, they'd become very good friends, almost like lifelong friends. Sue told her all about her life in every detail. Some of the things she said had been very surprising.

Susan looked like a normal and conventional girl who happened to be prettier than most girls. She didn't look really unusual in any way. But she'd had an incredible life for a girl of her age. She'd had several horrible experiences, yet none of it seemed to bother her, she talked as if it was the weather. It never would have occurred to anyone to suspect it to look at her, but she had certainly had an unusual life. When she was seventeen she'd been in love with the brother of her best girl friend, an older boy, and no one in town knew anything about it all one summer except her girl friend, who was *completely* horrified because this boy was engaged to another girl, an older and very beautiful girl from one of the best families in town. He'd fallen madly in love with Sue and had put off his marriage, and put it off—and put it off, first with good excuses then with excuses that didn't make sense at all, until his fiancée was practically out of her mind. It was a very complicated situation. The boy didn't know really what he wanted. He was torn between Sue and his fiancée, and being human he naturally was influenced by all the fiancée's money, though he really liked the fiancée, and in fact loved her, though he was involved with Sue and was madly in love with

74

Sue. Sue herself was barely seventeen at the time and she refused point-blank to be engaged to the boy, in fact she wasn't even in love with him but for a week, yet she kept seeing him after that. She liked him all right, but didn't respect him enough to love him, so what she did was slip around and meet him at various places under everyone's nose. She wouldn't marry him or become engaged to him and she told him he ought to stay engaged to the other girl, that he ought to go on and marry the other girl. He finally did.

Then, when she was eighteen, she really fell in love, this time with a man that was already married. The man had a neurotic wife and two children both of them spoiled brats. He was eleven years older than Sue and as it happened his wife had a great deal of money. He was a weak character but Sue didn't realize that, she fell madly in love with him (or madly for her) because he was such a marvelous dancer and made wonderful light conversation with a dry wit, and knew the poems of Elizabeth Barrett Browning, and had such nice eyes like a collie, and adored her so. "I couldn't resist," said Sue. "Ah, romance. He used to lay his head on my lap and look up at me like a collie, then he'd recite Elizabeth Barrett Browning and lo and behold—but he was a bad lover though, he was really a pathetic case. I don't blame his wife for nagging at him, but maybe it was just because he was so reverent or something."

This was the way Sue talked, very casual. But then it all came out about her affair with him, and there was a great deal of trouble. Everybody in town knew about it and they're still talking about it to this day. It ruined Sue's reputation. Here she was a pretty young girl, one of the best-looking girls in town and from a good family, and involved in an awful scandal with an older married man. People used to stare at her, little boys would snigger at her, and the girls would turn up their noses. It amused her more than anything, but it also made her feel dreadful, they were all such hypocrites. What finally happened was that she went by herself to Cleveland, Ohio—the reason it had come out was because she was actually going to

75

have a child and she'd told some gossipy girl about it, and that was how it all came out, so they were staring not only because of the love affair but because they knew she was going to have a baby. It was a terrible scandal. Her own family didn't have much money then, so the solution came by her going to Cleveland, on money she got from the man, which he got from his wife, and when she came back, the man and his wife and their two little girls had moved to California to take him away from Sue, not that she wasn't through with him anyhow, he had acted like such a worm.

She had lost all feeling for him, and realized he was weak. As for the trip to Cleveland, the first few days had been rough, but she got over it and none of it seemed to have bothered her a great deal, whereas it would have practically killed many people, circumstances being what they were. Her family didn't even know she was going to Cleveland until she'd already gone, and even then they didn't know her address. Her brother came there and looked in the hotels, but couldn't find her because she was staying with a girl she'd known at boarding school, a Cleveland girl that she wrote about it all, a girl a couple of years older than her, who'd been her student councilor when she was a sophomore, and this girl had told her to come to Cleveland and she'd help her do something about the situation. So that's why she went to Cleveland. "It wasn't bad," she said idly. "What you have to do is just say to yourself that it's hellish, then try and live through it. I had a lot worse time back home than I did in Cleveland. By the time I got there, it was settled. My dear lover had told me all about how it would be nothing, just a little unpleasantness." She laughed, very amused. "I'm glad I didn't know what it would be like. *That* I didn't know till the actual occasion, and there was nothing I could do about it then." She laughed again, then shook her head. "I'd sure be on edge if I was in that boat again. Believe *me*, it was no picnic. I never had such a rugged half-hour."

"It's a wonder you lived," said Bobbie. She stared thoughtfully at Sue. "Didn't you feel bad about the child?" she asked.

"Child?" said Sue. "It was only the second month. You could hardly call it a child. Besides, what was I supposed to do, have it and bring it up without a father, or have it and turn it over to an orphan home? When I have a child I want to keep it and I want it to have a father."

"I know," said Bobbie. "But you could have been killed."

"It's nothing like that," answered Sue. "It's not much, the only trouble is it's painful. The pain is absolutely killing." She paused, thinking. "All that about the dentist's my dear lover was telling me. Not as bad as the dentist's, he said. He was petrified for fear I'd have the child, but I didn't even dream of having it. I was no fool, *he* was the fool. No dentist could possibly be as bad as that in a million years, and I once ran into a crazy dentist, too. He was a *maniac,* that dentist, really insane. A sadist. He wouldn't give anyone novocain, and I can't understand why he had any patients. I fainted in the chair one day, and never went back after that. What that man did to my teeth! Grrrrrrr, that thing grinding at you. . . . But don't let anybody tell you that operation is like going to the dentist. If you ever get in that fix—and God forbid—I'd bet ten dollars the boy will smile pleasantly and tell you that. They all say that, and a lot they know about it. Naturally they'll say anything in such a situation, but it's idiotic to compare it to the dentist. It's more honest to tell the girl it's going to be terrible, but then I guess the only way to know is to have the experience, at that."

"I couldn't ever," said Bobbie. "I'd never have the nerve in a million years, and besides, I'd feel bad about killing the child." She shook her head. If Sue had had the baby it would now be about a year and a half old. Besides, despite what she said, it could easily have killed her. Bobbie sighed. "I don't see how you did it."

"Thousands do all the time," answered Sue. "Hundreds of thousands. Millions. There're doctors everywhere that do that, but let's change the subject, this conversation is too morbid—just take a tip from me and don't *get* in that fix in the first place. Only a fool gets in a mess like that. It's ridiculous to be that silly."

"Well," said Bobbie, "I'm sure you're probably right, but human nature isn't always perfect."

Sue stared. "Take precautions," she said. "That's all."

"I don't mean to criticize *you*," said Bobbie, "you know I don't—I don't think you're *bad* or anything like *that*. You thought you loved those boys, but—"

"I slept with one when I didn't think so," said Sue. "If you want to know the truth."

"Did you? I know—you didn't love him at all?"

"No," said Sue. "Not a bit. He disgusted me."

"Even so . . . what I meant was, it seems that for most people, if that's the way they feel, it would be best if it works out that way, for them to get married. Don't you think so? I don't mean I think it's a sin and anything old-fashioned like that. Don't you think you should marry a man, if that's the situation?"

"Not necessarily," said Sue. "Why ruin your life?"

Chapter *II*

At six o'clock, George knocked on the door. He said to Phil, "Now act your age."

"Act yours," said Phil.

They waited, then Bobbie opened the door. She said, "Hello."

"Hey," answered George. He smiled pleasantly and glanced over at Sue, who sat on the couch smoking a cigarette. "Hey, theah," he called to Sue.

"Hey, theah," answered Sue.

"Come in," said Bobbie, standing to one side.

George came in, eyes on Bobbie, then he glanced over at Sue, and then back around at Phil. He said to Sue, "This is my idiot cousin here. His name is Philip. Ah-h, come on in, Philip, and speak." Phil had a rather self-conscious, sarcastic expression as George introduced him. "Well?" said George. "Speak, Philip. Say hello. This is Bobbie, and that beautiful girl over there on the divan is Sue. Just because you have an incomplete nervous system, don't stand all night there with your tongue lolling out. *Do* something, *say* something."

"Aw, shut up," said Phil. He smiled self-consciously at Bobbie and Sue, and pulled down nervously at his coat sleeves and walked on into the room. Sue moved over on the couch to make space for him to sit down. Meanwhile, George had walked over to the mantelpiece and was leaning there, looking at Bobbie.

He said, "We were going to go get a bottle of wine or something. But we realized if we did we'd be late."

"Would you like a drink?" asked Sue. "We have something here, don't we, Bobbie?"

"Drink? I don't know," said Bobbie.

"We can go to a bar," said Phil quietly. "The Wyndham's only a couple of doors away."

"I was hoping you might have some corn here," said George to Bobbie. He looked at Sue. "You don't have a jug of corn around, do you?"

Sue said, "Where do you think you are, Tennessee? What would we be doing with corn whiskey?"

"Why, they drink it in No'th Car'lina, don't they?" said George. "I mean, they-all do, don't they?"

"Well, so what?" asked Sue.

"Ah don't know," said George. "But Ah thought you-all would have some. Ah have a cole in the haid."

"I've got a cold in mah haid, too," said Phil thoughtfully.

"Keep yo two cents out of it, Yankee," said George.

"Pardon me," said Phil. "But as a matter of fact, *I* was really born in the South."

"You weren't born, they found you in a garbage can," said George.

"That sounds like a slur on Mammy," said Phil. He was sitting on the couch by Sue, one hand along the pillow and a cigarette in his other hand.

Sue said, "I think we've got something to drink here." She put her cigarette in an ash tray and got up and walked over to the bureau and pulled open a drawer. "We haven't got any corn, but there's a bottle of Seagram's Seven Crown here somewhere, I think. Did you see it, Bobbie?"

"No," said Bobbie. Phil's intellectual manner made her feel nervous. She felt he would say something, and she wouldn't know what to answer. Besides, though she had drunk beer, she had never drunk whiskey. Her foster father drank it himself, but felt that women shouldn't.

"Seagram's Seven Crown," said Phil. "Is that fit to drink? Let's go to the Wyndham bar."

"It's all right," answered Sue. "Besides, where are your manners? Weren't you born in the South?"

"Yes," said Phil. "But I didn't stay there long enough to get any manners."

"You wouldn't have any if you stayed ninety years," said George. "What's wrong with Seagram's? It's better than that radiator fluid you drink on your periodic excursions to the gutter in the Bowery."

"That's true," said Phil.

"I actually had a fifth of Ballantine's," said Sue, "but I left it on the bureau, on top I mean, and every day it would go down a little bit. It was the maid that cleans the room. Every day it went down and down till finally there wasn't anything left but a little, then she let that sit there intact for about three days. She must have gone through hell resisting finishing it. Her sense of ethics, or something, I guess."

"Whiskey-stealers have their standards," said Phil. "They rarely polish off a bottle totally. It isn't etiquette."

"She did eventually though," answered Sue. "She polished it off, all right, but she resisted three full days and that's pretty good, you have to give her credit for that. I suppose when I left it sitting there she must have figured I wanted her to kill the bottle. Anyhow one afternoon I came in and it was empty."

George said, "Why didn't you fill it half with water, then next day she'd have grabbed it thinking it was a new supply. The water would have been such a shock she never would bother your liquor any more. Heh, heh."

"Oh, I don't have enough liquor for it to matter," answered Sue. "But that *is* an idea."

Meanwhile Sue had found the bottle and put it out on the bureau. Bobbie went to the pullman kitchenette and got glasses.

"Get some ice," said Sue.

"Well," answered Bobbie. She carried the glasses over.

George took the bottle of whiskey and held it in the air and looked to see how much was in it. It was almost full. "Mmm,"

81

he said, and poured out about three inches in each of the glasses.

"I'll have mine on the rocks," said Sue. "How do you want yours, Bobbie?"

"The same," said Bobbie.

Sue put two ice cubes in each glass, then handed Bobbie a glass. She took one to Phil, and another to George.

"Well," said George. "Here's how." He drank his whiskey at one gulp and set down his glass on the mantelpiece, then took out a cigarette and glanced at Bobbie. He showed no effects; it was as if he had drunk water. However, she learned later, though not that night, that George could get incredibly drunk. "It's slightly raw," said George. "But not too bad."

Bobbie took a swallow, and almost strangled since she was unaccustomed to it. It burned, and fumes rose in her eyes and nose. How he had been able to drink it all down the way he did was beyond her. "Mmm," she said.

"It's definitely not up to corn," said George. "Did you ever have any really good corn?"

"I don't know," said Bobbie. She could scarcely talk, the whiskey was burning so. It was as if she had swallowed a mouth of fire. She could feel it glowing in her stomach.

"Do *you* think it's up to corn?" George said to Sue.

"Real corn?" said Sue. "Don't be silly. Nothing is up to real corn."

"Don't mention that stuff," said Phil. "I had some once. A hillbilly in a filling station gave me half a dipper of it and I've never been the same since. It tasted like carbolic acid and rotten eggs blended with compost, radiator fluid, chlorine and nitroglycerin, then the whole thing stirred up with a dozen pair of dirty socks that had been worn at least six months. One mouthful practically lifted off the top of my head. It must have been about hundred and fifty proof. My hair turned temporarily white after drinking that dipper, and I had double vision for two weeks."

"Go on," said George. "You're making that up. You-all never tasted corn."

82

"I had that one drink," said Phil. "Just like I said. That was enough for me."

Sue was smiling. "I had some once too," she said, "and I know what you mean. It's terrible. No wonder the South has problems drinking such stuff as that."

"Well, this isn't bad," said Phil, referring to the Seagram's Seven Crown. "Considering the price, it's all right. I used to drink a hell of a lot of it, back in school. It really brings back memories. I used to drink it all the time."

"So did I," said Sue. She glanced upward, as though thinking wearily of those days when she used to drink so much.

George meanwhile had sat on the sofa by Phil, slumped back. This was his usual position when sitting anywhere. He always slumped as much as possible and locked his hands together over his belt. Throughout most of this conversation, he had been staring at Bobbie, who now was sitting in a chair by the fireplace, holding her drink. She hadn't drunk any more of it. What she'd already drunk had caused her stomach to feel as if there were a fire burning inside her. He kept staring at her, in a friendly manner, that made her nervous. She hardly knew what to say in this conversation, since she didn't know anything in particular about liquor, and the boy kept looking at her.

"Where shall we eat, anyhow?" asked George. "Are you hungry?"

"Give us a chance to finish those huge drinks you poured out," said Sue. "After all, it's our liquor and at least we ought to be able to drink it."

"Where would you like to go, though?" said George. "Let's decide, then we won't have it hanging over us."

"21 is all right," said Sue. "That's what we decided over the phone—let's stick to that."

"Well," said George. "But I have an idea. Let's choose between the Stork Club, 21, and the Sixth Avenue Delicatessen."

"What was the last place you mentioned?" asked Phil.

"La Petite Sixth Avenue Delicatessen."

"All right," said Phil. "Cut it out, now."

83

"That's where we're going," said George. "We'll go to 21 some other time."

"Disillusioned again," said Sue. "I thought I was going to 21."

"Well," said George. "Let's go to the Stork Club, then. Or 21. I don't care."

Phil looked at him. "Calm down," he said. "My old man isn't rich."

"We'll go on me, then," said George. He thought for a second. "Of course, at the Stork Club they probably wouldn't let us in, so we better go to the delicatessen instead."

"They'll let you in, if you look all right," said Sue. "It's a myth that you can't get in there."

"It isn't any myth about the prices," said Phil. "A meal in there is more than my old man can afford. We better go to the Sixth Avenue Delicatessen, which incidentally is one of the best restaurants in town, no—"

"The idea has come to revolt me," said George. He was staring moodily across the room at the fireplace. "I can't face the glitter and the raucousness of it."

"You're thinking about Lindy's," said Phil. "Not the Sixth Avenue Delicatessen. Lindy's is where the well-heeled Broadway Jews take their blondes. Phil turned to Sue. "He gets all this from me, then turns around and says it as if he originated it, but he always gets it wrong."

"Oh," said Sue. Neither she nor Bobbie had any idea what they were talking about.

"I can't go there," said George. "I'd almost rather go to the Automat."

"What's the matter with the Automat?" asked Sue. "It's not so bad—in fact it's good. If you're so broke, let's go there."

George and Phil both shuddered.

"I wouldn't mind," said Sue. "The food's all right."

"You call that food?" said George.

"It isn't so bad," said Sue.

"It'll shorten your life span by twenty years," said George.

Sue said, "You probably don't like it because the common herd eats there."

"I resent that," he said. "Just because I can't stand unwashed humanity in the bulk, you insinuate that I'm a snob."

"I agree with him about this," said Phil. "The Automat goes too far."

"Why?" asked Sue. "What's wrong with it?"

"All those people drool in their soup," said Phil.

"You're not kidding," said George. "Slup, slup, slup. It's enough to wear a man down to listen to it."

"It wears *me* down," said Phil. "I can't endure the place."

"*You* can't endure it?" said George. "I'm the one around here that can't endure it. The other day when I had lunch in there, this character across from me was eating beef pie and I thought he was going to devour the crockery, I thought he was going to crunch it up and then eat the silverware, and then go on and eat the table, before he got through. Did he assault that helpless beef pie! I never saw anything like it—slobble-obble-gobble! I sat there in fascination, transfixed with awe by the horror of it all. If I'd had a recording machine and had made a recording of that noise he made, and played it over a radio station and broadcast it, it would drive millions of people raving mad to listen to it. I never saw anybody attack a beef pie the way this character did. And every now and then he would look furtively around, his beady little eyes shining, he'd dart nervous, hysterical little glances at me, like an old dog when you get near him when he's eating. You know?" George shrugged. "But he needn't have worried. I didn't want to take away his beef pie. After watching him, I can't even eat beef pie again in my life."

"You're sure about that?" asked Sue. "I think maybe you wanted that man's pie, and that's why he looked up."

"No," said George. "I didn't want it." He glanced at Bobbie, who was laughing at this story, then looked back at Sue. "Why don't you finish your drinks," he said. "All this talk about eating has worked me up an appetite."

"Okay—let's go," said Sue. "We'll get beef pie at the Automat."

Chapter 12

HOWEVER, THEY WENT to a delicatessen. They took a booth in the back and had another drink, this time with ginger ale, and then the waiter brought the chopped liver. Bobbie had thought it was a joke, that there wasn't really any such thing as "chopped liver," but there it was, ground up liver with bits of hard-boiled egg in it.

"Is that what this is?" she asked. "Chicken liver?"

"It's probably 90 per cent beef liver," said Phil. "But they call it chicken liver."

Bobbie stared at her plate. "What's that yellow stuff on it?" she asked.

George said, "Chicken fat."

"What?"

"*Essence de Poulette.*"

"When are you going to start a pogrom?" asked Phil.

"Any day," answered George. "And you'll be the first one that gets it in the neck, buddy. If they wiped out all the Jews, it'd be worth it, as long as you're included. But you'd probably be omitted."

"Well, shelve the idea temporarily, then," said Phil.

"Okay," said George.

"This looks like nothing but grease," said Bobbie.

"What does?" asked George. "You mean the chicken fat?"

"It looks greasy."

"Well, how else can it look?" asked George. "It *is* greasy. Now don't be backward, honey, go on and eat it. It'll put hair on your chest."

86

"Eat it, no matter what George says," said Phil. "It's good for you."

"There are conflicting theories about that," answered George. "My Grandpappy was raised on it, and he died of indigestion before he was fourteen."

"Aw, shut up," said Phil. "*My* Grandpappy *really* was raised on it. Yours wasn't, but mine was. When he came over from the other side, over yonder, all the polecat had was a barrel of chicken fat and a knapsack of dried herring. The miserable polecat pretty near starved. Furthermore bilge rats nipped at him all the way across."

"Would that he had starved," said George. "Then you wouldn't be around to blight the scene and disgrace nature."

"I don't disgrace nature," said Phil. "And I don't blight the scene, either. You-all do."

George leaned across the booth and said, "Yo' Pappy was a son of a bitch, yo' Mammy was a son of a bitch, yo' Grandmammy and yo' Grandpappy and Great Grandpappy and Great Grandmammy was all sons of bitchs, and *you yo'self* is a son of a bitch."

Sue said, "That's some accent, isn't it, Bobbie?"

Bobbie said, "I never heard such an accent in the South."

"You didn't?"

"I never heard such an accent in my entire life," she said.

"Not in your entiah life?" said Phil.

"Don't impugn my accent," said George.

"I'm not impugning it," said Sue. "And neither is Bobbie, it just isn't authentic."

Bobbie said to George, "Is he really a Jew or is it a joke?"

They turned and looked at her. Phil said, "What does she think I am, an A-rab?"

Bobbie turned to George. "He isn't, is he?"

"He is," said George. "But he'll excuse you if you're not."

"She thinks I should have horns," said Phil. He turned to Sue. "Of course, she's right, most of us do."

"Is he?" asked Bobbie. "Really?"

"I don't know. Maybe," said George. "It's a question."

"In fact, we all have horns," said Phil, "but I had mine taken

87

off. The old man has never forgiven me, that's why he sends me only two hundred and fifty a month. 'Boy,' he says, 'is that any way to act? Is *that* any way to treat your Momma and Poppa, after we raise you up nice and send you to college? Is that any way to act, going against your traditions and cutting off your horns? How is anybody going to know you're a Jew? If you go down South they'll probably think you're an A-rab.'"

Bobbie said, "Well, you look English or something." She stopped, not knowing what to say. There weren't any Jewish people in her hometown, but Jews were supposedly dark-haired. Phil's hair was almost as light as George's and he had blue eyes. She said, "Were your people converted to the Jewish religion? Or something like that?"

"That never happens," said Phil. "We're so good we never let nobody join with us. Besides, gentiles could never stand the pressure. They'd die like flies of nervous anxiety in a week if they became Jews."

"Well!" said Bobbie. She started eating again. "I never would have known you were a Jew."

"Well, I'm a white Jew," said Phil. "It's all right. You can sit here at the same table with me."

"He's lying," said George. "He isn't a white Jew, he's black."

"A hell of a lot you know about it," said Phil idly.

"I know plenty," said George.

"You don't know anything," said Phil.

"I know that Galitzianers are aristocrats, and you aren't one, you're a low Polack."

"Oh, shut up, for Christ's sake," said Phil. "First, no Jews are aristocrats, and second, Galitzianers are the worst crumbs alive. They're worse than Litvaks, who have no culture at all. And Polacks aren't even Jews, they're Polacks. Shut up, or talk about something you know something about. Aren't you already anti-Semitic enough as it is?"

"Galitzianers are the cream of the crop," said George, "and you're a lousy Litvak."

"Shut up," said Phil.

88

"What are they talking about?" asked Bobbie.

"Who knows," said Sue.

"You haven't finished your drink, Bobbie," said George. "Down the hatch then we'll have another one."

"They're plying us with liquor already," said Sue to Bobbie.

"I know," said Bobbie. "But it won't work, I'm already drunk."

Sue said, "Isn't it early? Wouldn't it be more dignified if you waited a while, before you start to ply us with liquor?"

"We aren't doing that," said George."

"Oh, no," said Bobbie, "you wouldn't."

"Well, I'm famous for my capacity," said Sue. "It won't work on me, I'll tell you that. I never get drunk, no matter how much I drink."

For several minutes, George had had his hand on Bobbie's knee. Now he put it over on the other knee. She ignored this, though it distracted her. Then the waiter came, and he ordered more drinks. This was the third drink, including the first one back at the room, and by this time everyone was affected to some extent—even Sue looked sleepy. Bobbie herself thought she was affected far less than she actually was. She thought she was all right, but during the meal she was almost drunk and hardly knew what she was eating. After the liver, they had soup made of beets—it was very red with a potato in it and white cream, which was sour.

"This is sour," she said.

"It's meant to be," said George. "That's the whole point."

She hardly tasted it. She felt as if pleasant, invisible cotton was all around her. Even her hearing seemed affected and everything was slightly hazy. She knew what she was doing, but the drinks had made her dizzy.

Then they were analyzing clothes. The subject came up and George and Phil began to talk about it. The talk kept coming back to this subject all through the meal. George and Phil argued violently about it.

"You don't understand what the man was trying to do," said George. "The idea wasn't to lay any blame."

89

"Not to lay any blame?" said Phil. "What's the matter with you George? Can't you understand anything? The entire work is a polemic against waste and uselessness."

"It was not a polemic at all," said George. "No one but an adolescent would call it a polemic."

"What's a polemic?" asked Bobbie.

"It was no polemic," said George. "Your saying so just proves that you're a nitwit. Don't you know an objective study when you see it?"

"What *is* a polemic?" asked Bobbie.

Sue shrugged. She looked slightly uncomfortable and obviously didn't understand what they were talking about. During the conversation, she kept looking at Phil in a blank manner.

Bobbie nudged George. "We're in this conversation," she said.

"Just a second," said George. Phil was looking coolly across the restaurant at the other booths and tables, as if George bored him. "What do you think he *was*?" asked George. "A crusader? He was a scientist."

Phil answered, "You don't understand."

"What don't I understand?" said George. "I understand perfectly! You're the one that doesn't understand."

Phil said in a detached but friendly tone: "George, what you're doing is maintaining there's such a thing as scientific objectivity in the social sciences. The fact is that once your data becomes complicated objectivity is out of the question. If your problem is simple you can approach objectivity, that is, you can limit your field of observation—but the main characteristic of social problems is their complexity. It isn't like dealing with ingredients in test tubes, George, not in social science. In social sciences, a man must have a point of view, or he's bound to wander around in an aimless quagmire. This has long been recognized in social sciences. You really don't know what you're talking about. Ordinary middlebrows such as the Lynds demolished that nonsense about objectivity. Of course there's no such thing. Read the introduction to the second Middletown book. They explain the idea very well, and I'd explain it to you now, but it gives me a headache to wrangle on such a childish level."

George said, "Listen, if you try and tell me Veblen was doing anything more than describing a situation as it existed, you're full of bunk. Don't try and impress these girls, you know damn well what I mean and you know I'm right. Veblen wasn't prejudiced one way or the other."

"I never heard such nonsense in my life," said Phil.

"Veblen was filled with indignation," said Phil thoughtfully. "And the sort of thing that revolted him most was characters like you. Gaudy, chattering sparrows, dressed in the hues of the rainbow by the sweat of other people. Silly idiots consuming the wealth of society in order to feel superior to other idiots. Look at these shops on Fifth Avenue—millions and millions of dollars down the drain forever, and for stupid finery for idiots to drape on themselves in order to snoot other idiots that haven't got it. And look at you, in that sport coat. You're a laugh, George. Look at that gaudy silk tie and that silly handkerchief in your coat pocket. Ridiculous! How many people sweated so you could deck yourself out like that? And for what? In order for you to look *snappy*." Phil pulled at his own coat sleeves, and added, "If I can't dignify a suit of clothes I have on, to hell with it. If I need a sport coat to get by, things have come to a pretty pass."

Meanwhile, George was looking mildly at Phil. He didn't seem affected by all this, though one would think he would be worried by the argument. He said, "Phil, anybody can go around dressed like a tramp. That doesn't take any brains. The most ignorant Bohemian fool can do that—they do, in fact. Why don't you get a pair of dirty overalls and a toothpick, then at least you'd have some status among people who make judgments on such a superficial basis as clothes—that is, you'd have status in the Village. Other Village creeps would look at you and say, 'Mmmmm, he must be brilliant, sees through all the phoniness—a poet no doubt.'" George leaned over and smiled at Phil, who sat in turn listening calmly. "Phil, don't

91

you know *I* understand you? This is George you're talking to—you can fool these girls, they don't know you, but you can't deceive *me*. Phil my boy, at heart you're a teen-age intellectual, chronic type. A perpetual undergraduate, the perennial freshman. You probably suspect the Bible isn't literally true, don't you—your brilliant, probing mind has come to focus on the question and you've come up with the answer. But if *I* try and adjust reasonably to this society in which I happen to find myself, like a civilized human being, then I'm exploiting poor people in workshops, who happen incidentally to make damn good dough making coats like this, you son of a bitch. I like the goddamn coat and I'll wear it if I want to, and if you don't like that you can lump it."

"He's getting worse all the time," smiled Phil to Sue. "Of course, nothing he says has any connection with what *I* said, but it sounds good if you don't analyze any of it and just sort of absorb the flow."

"Why do you wear that STUPID-looking, unpressed, cheap suit?" asked George. "Answer that." Phil didn't say anything, he continued eating, an indifferent expression on his face. Now that the conversation had got on this subject, Phil had lost all self-consciousness—he had lost most of that anyhow, but now he was in his medium. "WELL???" said George angrily.

Finally, in a very quiet voice Phil said, "You really want the answer? I mean, are you interested, do you want to continue the discussion?"

"Sure I want the answer," said George.

"I wear the suit," said Phil, "which incidentally doesn't look as bad as you say, because I don't care to throw my money away on conspicuous consumption to impress children like you."

"Conspicuous consumption?" said George. "What's the difference between conspicuous consumption and conspicuous non-consumption, may I ask? They're both conspicuous."

"One is cheaper," said Phil.

"That's true," said George. He glanced at Bobbie, then asked, "What do you think about that?"

"I don't know," answered Bobbie, "but—"

"Are you interested?"

"Yes, I'm interested," she said.

"There's no reasoning with that fool, is there?" said George. "Let's have some coffee and get out of here."

Phil nudged Sue. "Now he wants to quit the argument."

"We've been here an hour and a half," said George. "I'm tired of this dump. Let's have some coffee and get out of here."

"Are we going to Coney Island?" asked Bobbie.

There was a pause, then George and Phil looked at her.

"Coney Island?" said Phil. "What put that idea in her head? We'll get a bottle and go back to the room."

"What's the matter with Coney Island?" said George. "Why not go out there? That's a good idea."

"I don't think so," said Phil.

George said, "What about you, Susan? Would you like to go to Coney Island?"

"Sure," said Sue. "I don't care."

"Not Coney Island," said Phil. "There are limits. Manhattan Island is bad enough. Forget the idea. We'll have coffee, then go back to the room and listen to some records."

"That's too tame," said George. "We need the excitement of Coney Island after all this boring dribble from you. Anyhow the girls want to go there, so you're overruled."

Phil explained to Bobbie, "It's only a lot of junk out there— gambling games, gimcracks, popcorn stands, plaster dolls— you wouldn't like it."

"*Millions* like it," said George. "And what about the roller coaster? You're a wet blanket, a complete wet blanket."

"The roller coaster," said Phil. He glanced up at the ceiling. "Roller coasters," he said. "Good God."

"I'd like to ride one," said Bobbie. "My cousin came here once and went out there and rode on one. She said it nearly killed her."

"The death urge raises its head," said Phil. "Coney Island is probably saturated with it."

"What?" asked Bobbie.

93

"You just want to ride the roller coaster to see what it's like, don't you," said George.

"Yes," she answered. "Of course, if it crashed, we'd all be killed." At this point, she was so drunk she could hardly talk, but none of them knew it.

"Ah," said Phil, "see? The death urge, like I said."

"Don't be stupid," said George. "How could she have a death urge?"

"I know they never crash," said Bobbie, "but you think they will, that's the point. I rode one one time. It was nothing in comparison to what they must have out there, but I was terrified. My cousin says the one at Coney Island is horrible. She said she thought she'd never live through it. But there're probably lots of different rides out there. Don't they have a parachute jump?"

"She wants variety," said Phil. "She wants to think she's going to be killed in lots of different ways." He turned to Sue. "Are *you* like that?"

"I don't know," said Sue. "But why not, it's a good way to be, isn't it?"

"Do we *have* to go to Coney Island?" said Phil. "Must we go out there?"

"Yes," answered George. "We must. I want a gypsy to tell Bobbie's fortune."

"Get a Manhattan gypsy. We don't have to trek out—"

"There are no Manhattan gypsies, and they both want to go," said George. "Women rule this country, so shut up. They want to go and we'll take them."

"It'll be boring," said Phil.

"No, it won't," answered George.

They left the restaurant around eight o'clock, and walked over to 57th Street and took the subway. Coney Island was indeed interesting and they didn't get back to 58th Street until two o'clock, and didn't get to sleep until six.

94

Chapter 13

INTERRUPTED YESTERDAY AFTERNOON, but it's just as well, I was tired anyhow, and hadn't even gone out for lunch. I had an idea it was around eleven, but when the interruption came, it was three-thirty. I'd been typing right on through since eight o'clock, which is seven and a half hours, or seven, allowing half an hour for time spent making coffee. That means yesterday it took an average of an hour to write nine pages. It took that long because a lot of it was conversation, and you just can't write conversation, you have to rack your brain trying to remember it. I have a good memory for what people say, but it's difficult to remember all that conversation, and when I started to write it I was afraid I wouldn't be able to. Though I could make up some of the things Sue says, or Bobbie, I could never make up the things Phil and George say. However in reading it over, I believe I have quoted them very well, in fact I believe they would be flabbergasted to read it, especially to read what they were saying in the room. Anyhow, though I don't feel much like writing after last night, I don't see why I can't go ahead and finish the rest of the book. I find that if I concentrate it all comes back—I can hear George talking about that man in the Automat, and if I can remember that I don't see why I can't remember some of the things he said later in the story, especially the things he said in in the room, to say nothing of all Bobbie told me he said to her.

But today I don't feel like writing. If I hadn't been interrupted yesterday I'd have gone ahead and written about Coney

Island—the roller coaster, baseball game, side show, crazy house, this, that, the other, including the parachute jump, which isn't one-tenth as bad as the roller coaster.

Coney Island was interesting, though it's nothing but a huge carnival. The rides are genuine enough, but practically all of the games and shows are nothing, or practically nothing, but—then this is true of all carnivals. That's all Coney Island is, aside from the beach and the ocean, which doesn't make any difference at night or not much. You can't win any of the games, and the shows hardly live up to their advertising. The baseball game consists of throwing scrawny-looking baseballs at wooden milk bottles—three bottles, and if you knock them all over, you're supposed to win a big doll. George knocked them all over, but it turned out you must not only knock them over, you must knock them off the stand as well.

"Impossible," said George to the man. "Who're you kidding? Walter Johnson himself couldn't knock those jugs off there. You can knock them down but they still won't fall off the stand—that's obvious."

"You have to have a square hit," said the man. "Put a little muscle into it. Here, try your luck again."

"Muscle, hell," said George. "NObody—"

"You get three more shots for nothing," said the man, "since you knocked them all down that time. Here, try your luck, the charge this time is only a dime instead of a quarter, and maybe you'll clean them off."

"I thought you said nothing."

"Only a dime. Three balls."

It was impossible to knock the milk bottles off the stand. When they were knocked over, they wouldn't fall back far enough to go off. They were weighted with lead and when the balls hit them they would go, "Thunk." No one could ever win that doll. The only result would be that sailors and boys such as George would throw the balls hard to impress their girls, but they wouldn't win anything. George argued with the man, but ended up spending a dollar or so, and Phil did about the same. He spent fifty or seventy-five cents, and also knocked them down but couldn't knock them off.

Another game was based on the same principle. This was a game in which you paid a quarter to shoot an air rifle that fired a cork at shelves of cigarettes and other objects. The girls, as well as George and Phil, shot at these. Many of the cigarette packages had dollar bills on them and several had ten-dollar bills, but if the cork hit a pack, it would go thunk and bounce back. According to George, the packs had lead cigarettes inside, and furthermore you couldn't aim the corks, they might go anywhere. You always won a prize in this game, as the barker said, but it was a worthless trinket. The trinkets were the only things that could be knocked off the shelves.

Such were the games. The reader has no doubt encountered them but perhaps this book will be translated into some foreign language, and they all want to read about America and this is what the games are like at Coney Island, not that Americans are "idiots" as Phil says. After all, he played the games himself. He kept shooting the popgun at the pack with the ten-dollar bill on it and cursing when it knocked down something else, and so did George. In my opinion, the reason people play those games is merely in order to be doing it, not to win. How could you expect to win the ten-dollar bill? The man running the game would be foolish if he would let you have ten dollars for a quarter. Obviously all Americans are not idiots, anyhow, because what about the man running the game, he was no idiot. Everything George and Phil said to him, he had an answer, and the result was that they kept shooting the popguns and winning plastic tie clips and other worthless things.

I'll write a little about the side show, which was more interesting.

However, I don't really feel in a mood to write this today. I was in the mood yesterday, but I certainly am not today. The situation around here in this flat has gotten worse. In fact, it has gotten so bad I hardly know what to do.

He has an idea I have designs on him. If it wasn't for the

apartment shortage, I'd make him get out of here. He thinks he can talk as he pleases. One minute it's one thing, and the next minute something else again. Life is too short—far better to be dead, dead in body rather than a degenerating soul, above ground in the flesh but underneath in mind and spirit. Isn't that true? All people quail before spiritual death, even the so-called intellectuals, as a matter of fact they're worse. And now he really knows I am just about at the final stage. . . . I'm not even interested now in what he says when he talks in his sleep. This shows how you can get in a mess! Obviously the reader knows I don't simply exist in the same apartment with him, but the general idea was that we'd share it on a cooperative basis. It certainly hasn't been very cooperative. He won't wash the dishes at all—last night, of course, he was too sick.

The situation here has gotten impossible and I don't know what will come of it, but something will happen soon. Yesterday afternoon, I was typing, and suddenly the door opened and there he was. He looked terrible.

"I'm sick," he said.

I asked, "What's the matter?"

Now before going on, is there anything wrong with what I said? When someone tells you they're sick, isn't it customary to ask, "What's the matter?" What's wrong with asking that? I asked it in a perfectly nice way, not dripping with sympathy, but just to know what was wrong with him. However he let out a groan as if I'd said something horrible beyond words.

"What a question," he whispered. "I'm sick as a dog, and she wants to know what's the matter. Ohhh-hh, God." He walked over and sat in the easy chair, a miserable look on his face. He really did look bad. He was really pale and there was sweat on his forehead.

"Don't get near me," he said. "Any shock will precipitate a crisis."

"Are you nauseated?" I asked.

"No," he said.

"Do you want a glass of soda?" I asked.

98

He winced, holding his stomach and shutting his eyes tight. "Ohhhh," he said. "Mercy."

What could I do? He was sick but also in an impossible mood. I went back to the desk and put away my papers and the typewriter, while he sat there motionless, eyes shut and his face white. He really did look terrible. I asked, "Did you leave the job?"

"No, I'm still there," he said.

"I mean you got off early?"

"No, I'm still there running the car. Ask me another one."

"I'm merely trying to be civil," I answered. "What did they do, let you off?"

"That's brilliant, but you can do better," he said. "Ask me something really obvious, such as if it's snowing outside."

"Is it?" I asked.

"No, it isn't," he said.

"This is typical of the way you act," I said. "You're sick and you want someone to be sympathetic, and yet you don't want them to be."

He didn't say anything. He just sat there. I thought he might have ptomaine poisoning and asked if I should call a doctor, but he said, "Don't bother. It's just psychological."

It turned out he was terrible sick because of some fried chicken he'd had at the place he worked. The chef had given it to him, but he had been feeling bad that morning anyhow. It had started about the middle of the morning. He decided that if he went up in the elevator one more time it would be the end, something would crack and he'd never be the same again. He had endured it for eight weeks, but now he was through, it had got him. But he stayed on till lunch then went back in the kitchen and had the fried chicken and that was really the last straw.

I said, "Well, I suppose running an elevator must be boring." "Ohh-h-h-h," he said. "*Boring?* Ohhh." What's the point, he doesn't want sympathy. At this stage I stopped talking and I got a book and sat in the chair by the table and read. Every now and then, he'd say something, but I wouldn't reply. He lay there in the chair, all slumped down—he was sick all right, but what could *I* do about it? Every now and then, he'd make another remark, such as, "If I were dying, would you read that book?" I paid no attention. This went on for at least fifteen minutes. He wants to suffer—though of course women are supposed to be the ones that like misery. So he lay back in the chair and I read the book. I thought he was asleep, he was so quiet, then he said, "Listen . . ."

"What?" I said.

"I'm sick. I feel awful."

"Well, I'm sorry."

"Honey," he said.

"What?"

"I'm *sick.*"

He really was sick, though of course later when he felt better it was different.

Chapter 14

"LET'S GO IN here and see these marvels," said George.

"No," said Phil. "Let's go ride the roller coaster and get it over with."

"Yes, let's go ride the roller coaster," said Bobbie.

"But look at that," said George.

"Oh, come on," said Sue. "We all want to ride the roller coaster."

"Wait," said George. "Look at the illustration of that alligator man."

Bobbie and Sue were staring at the illustration. "He couldn't look like that," said Bobbie. "It's just to rope you in."

"No, it's genuine," said George. "He's a freak. Let's see this, I always did like freaks."

"That's natural," said Phil.

"Let's see this," said George. "Maybe they'll offer Phil a job."

"Hmm," said Phil. "How about it, Barbara, do you and Sue want to go, or is George enough of a freak for you already."

"I don't want to," said Sue. "Things like that make me sick. Let's pass it up, and go on and ride the roller coaster."

"We can ride that later," answered George. He turned to Phil. "Come on, persuade her. Doesn't everybody want to see the alligator man? Look at his fangs." He was pointing up at the big, colored canvas painting. They were standing on the sidewalk outside the store. There was no sawdust, it was a regular sidewalk and store front. The canvas illustration that had attracted George's attention showed the various freaks and exhibits that were inside. The illustration covered the entire front of the building and left a little rectangle down at the bottom for the doorway and the box office. This was about twenty feet away. A fat woman with rings in her ears sat there.

"Those are some fangs all right," answered Phil. "He'd be rough on women, that character. I suppose he and the pig girl are love birds." Phil took Sue by the arm and said. "How about it? Do you want to go in?"

"Well . . ." said Sue doubtfully.

George asked, "How about you, Bobbie, would you like to see all these monsters? We can ride the roller coaster right afterwards."

"Well," said Bobbie. "I don't care if Sue wants to."

"Freaks depress me," said Sue. "But if you insist on going I guess I can stand it."

"Let's go, then," said George. "They aren't all freaks, anyhow. See, one's a magician. And look at that one, he eats fire." Part of the illustration showed a man who looked like Satan and was dressed in a tuxedo, with his head tilted back and flames pouring out of his mouth.

Sue stared, then said, "That makes me nervous."

"Come on, Susan, don't be obstinate," said George. "Haven't you got any curiosity about the horrors in this world? Everybody wants to go but you."

"Well," answered Sue. "But it's all silly. These shows never amount to anything. That baby won't be alive—wait and see, it'll be some sort of thing in a bottle, and who wants to look at that?"

"You might give birth to one of them some day," said George. "You ought to be prepared for the possibility."

"Is that so," said Sue.

"It doesn't look to me like it's in a bottle," said Phil, staring up.

"Of course, it isn't in a bottle," said George. "How could it be? Look at the illustration."

The illustration showed a two-headed child. Both the heads were girls, curly-headed little girls. One of the hands held a red rubber ball, another a candy cane, another a doll, and the fourth hand was playing with a yo-yo. There were two legs and one middle. Both heads were smiling. Sue shuddered. "If that's alive," she said, "it's much worse."

George answered, "Don't call them it. They're two little girls. What you ought to say is them."

"No, *her*," said Phil. "Essentially there's only one of them."

"There are two," said George. "What's the matter with you, boy. You would address those people as them."

"There's only one of them," said Phil. "Fundamentally."

"What do you mean, fundamentally—look at those two heads. Each of them would talk at you and argue with you, wouldn't they?"

"Oh, shut up," said Sue. She glanced at Bobbie, as she lifted one eyebrow ironically.

"I'll explain," answered Phil. "Now, suppose—"

"Wait," said George. "Don't go into it."

"I—" said Phil.

"It's too murky," said George. He added, "Hmmm, what would that be like? Four arms and two heads, but one of them from the waist down. That would be real wild."

"It'd take a better man than you," said Sue.

"Oh, I don't know," said George. "I might rise to the challenge." George rubbed his chin, studying the illustration thoughtfully. "It *would* be a challenge from every standpoint. Imagine they're about nineteen and a man gets mixed up with them, a double, I mean, triple date or something. He falls in love with them, or it. Now suppose one of the heads wouldn't feel in the mood, let's say. It would tell you it wanted to get some sleep, whereas the other head would want love. Then the two heads would turn and argue back and forth. It would be a terrible situation. If you stroked the head that was romantic, the other one, the tired head, would probably rise up angrily and bite you. One set of arms would be pulling at you and the other would be pushing. It would be a hell of a

103

situation. It'd really be more fun than a barrel of monkeys, wouldn't it Phil, those heads in conflict that way."

"The heads would get together about that," said Phil.

"No," said George, "the heads never would get together."

"Listen!" said Sue. "You've digusted me and Barbara thoroughly, if that's what you're trying to do. I know I'm not going in there now."

"Aw, it's nothing but a thing in a bottle," said George. "What's so bad about that? You don't have to look at it if you don't want to. There's a lot else in the show, for instance Porky Peggie up there. See her?"

Bobbie and Sue looked at the canvas illustration in the upper right hand corner where George was pointing. They saw a picture of a fat girl with dark skin in an evening gown. She had a little kinky hair and human eyes, but otherwise looked like a pig.

"Oh, lovely," said Sue. "If the thing in the bottle is depressing, that'll cheer us up."

"Sure," said George.

"Really," said Sue. "People that go and stare at such things are depraved. Don't you think so, Barbara?" Bobbie felt slightly dizzy. It was the effects of the liquor, which had worn off during the subway ride, but had left her feeling slightly odd. When George was talking about the two-headed girl, it had given her a very peculiar sensation. The idea of the two heads arguing with each other, or him patting one of the heads and the other head biting him—all this gave her a peculiar sensation. Nevertheless she wanted to see the show. Years before, she'd gone to a carnival and seen a man put a spike up his nose and hold a blow torch on his chest. She'd also seen a man who was born without arms throw knives with his toes, outlining a girl with them. She was thinking about that when Sue asked her if such shows were depraved. "They *are*," said Sue. "I'll go if you want to but the whole thing's silly."

"It's starting now," said Phil, "and we might as well go, or George will complain for a month."

So they finally went. As Phil said, the show was starting and a large audience was waiting inside in a big room. There were no seats, just a large empty room with a small stage at one end, with drawn curtains. George and Phil forced their way up to the front, as the lights got dimmer, then the curtains opened and they saw the show.

Porky Peggie was a colored woman who was very ugly but didn't look like a pig. She sat there on the platform in an evening gown for a few minutes then the curtains were pushed shut and there was nothing to look at. Then a man came out from behind the curtain with two or three crackerjack boxes under his arm. They looked like crackerjack boxes, but were not, they were just small boxes containing taffy candy. The man looked at the audience. He cleared his throat, looking down from the platform at the people standing three feet below, mouth together and a thoughtful expression in his eyes. The audience waited. They were mostly sailors, soldiers, girls, and other couples, with a few middle-aged people. Most of them seemed bored, however they waited for the man to say something. It took him a long time, then suddenly his eyebrows went down and he said: "Good evening, ladies and gentlemen."

"In these little boxes," the man said, "which we do not sell, we have various prizes ranging from five-dollar bills to ten-dollar bills, and even twenty-dollar bills, brand new from Washington."

The man talked on about twenty or twenty-five minutes. It became very tiresome. He kept selling boxes and selling boxes. Somebody behind the curtain kept handing him six-box units and he kept selling them, talking along and whetting the audience's interest. One sailor bought five six-box units, one after the other, he kept buying them, and didn't win anything, except worthless trinkets that he threw away after the show, such as plastic earrings that wouldn't work, tiny little cotton flags of the United States about as big as postage stamps, worthless rings and pins, plastic cuff links, and so forth. The man would sell a whole batch of boxes, then start

105

all over again and deliver another speech with a new approach, and sell more, this time green boxes instead of red boxes, the green ones containing even more valuable prizes. The people kept on buying. It was amazing, but they kept trying them, and it went on and on, then finally at last the place was covered with empty boxes and taffy candy, and the man couldn't sell any more, so he went back behind the curtain. No one had won anything except a few people—and they were all in the employ of the management, according to Phil and George.

"Well," said Sue. "I hope you enjoyed that."

The rest of the show was not much when it finally came. A man put a cotton wad in his mouth, struck a match to it, and it burned for a while with a bluish flame, then he shut his mouth, opened it again, and the wad was still burning. That was all he did. No great flames poured from his mouth, much less from his nose as shown in the illustration. He didn't look like Satan and had no mustache or tuxedo. Then, the alligator man, who had a loathsome skin disease and looked awful and sat on a chair in a pair of purple trunks. He was skinny and bony-looking and his arms and legs were covered with rough scales. The audience gawked at him, then the curtain was drawn. The man had been sitting there smoking a cigarette indifferently. He had no resemblance to an alligator except for the skin disease, and even that didn't look like an alligator. After that there was another colored girl, with a huge tumor growing from her forehead. This was supposed to be an elephant trunk. It was fifty times bigger in the illustration than in reality and it didn't look like a trunk, it was just a deformity or tumor of some kind, and horrible-looking. When she shook it back and forth, one girl with a sailor turned away, her face white, and the sailor had to take her out. This was horrible-looking, but otherwise the girl looked normal. Then a man did card tricks, the same man that had sold the boxes. He made a deck turn into three of spades, and so forth, but he did only three tricks, then pulled a series of colored handkerchiefs out of his hand, made knots disappear, made coins disappear, meanwhile prattling on and amusing the audience or at least holding their attention. In the illustration, there were pigeons flying out of a hat, cards suspended in the air, a goldfish bowl on a stand, and so on, and the magician also was drawn to look like Satan, but he didn't. Finally, a man came out in an undershirt with tattoos on his arms and chest. This man stuck pins in his arms, about fifteen altogether. He was supposed to be invulnerable to pain. He did stick the pins in his arms and at first several people gasped as he did so, but it didn't seem to hurt him. Then came the last thing, the two-head child. The curtains opened and there in a jar of alcohol was a putty-colored little baby with one eye bulged out and terrible marks on the side of its face, and its mouth open. It had part of another head, but the eyes on this head were shut tight and the features were mashed together. The baby had what seemed to be little arms growing from a lump on its chest. It was a pitiful-looking thing and had a horrible hunchback besides. A gray-haired woman was standing there, the same woman with the rings in her ears that had been out front in the box office, and some people in the audience whispered, "Is that the mother?" But she was not the mother. She gave a short lecture and pointed at the baby with a ruler, and in the lecture she said that although the institution from which it had been obtained for twenty-five thousand dollars had never divulged the identity of the parents, it had had a normal father and mother.

"Normal, hell," said Phil. "They must have had syphilis."

"They were *loaded* with it," said George. "Look at that thing. Gad."

"Well, I hope you've enjoyed this lovely show," said Sue.

"It was great," said George. "Very educational. Don't you think so, Barbara?"

"No," she said. "I think it's pretty disgusting. They ought to bury that baby, instead of keeping it in a bottle to frighten people."

"Well, that's a straight answer," said George.

"She's absolutely right," said Sue.

Phil laughed. "Well, tell them about it," he said.

Chapter 15

THEY RODE THE roller coaster, later that night after wandering around trying to find the one called "The Blue Comet" and in the meantime doing other things. If it hadn't been for the safety bar, Bobbie would probably have been thrown out and killed, because she fainted. For that matter, she would have probably been thrown out if she'd been by herself, but as it was, George held her. It surprised her to faint more than it did anyone else, she had never dreamed she would faint since she never had in her life, however she had never ridden a thing like this before. When they were standing in line waiting their turn, they could hear it roar in the distance and they could hear women and girls scream and shriek, there were even men yelling, but it didn't look so bad. However, it was horrible. The people had plenty of reason to scream.

Bobbie and George were in the first car. They sat down and the man put the safety bar in place. Then there was a clanking and the cars started, very slowly. They went straight ahead, then around a long curve, then there ahead was a long, steep slope stretching far up. It began to climb up this slope very slowly, the machinery groaning and chains clanking. "Hold on," said George. "We're going up." He had one arm around her, and she was holding on to the bar. The seats were tilted far back and they faced toward the dark sky which was lit like a pale bowl from the reflection of city lights from Manhattan and Brooklyn in between. Once Bobbie glanced around over her shoulder at Phil and Sue, but it made her dizzy and she looked around again—Phil and Sue were almost directly beneath her and George; she'd looked down almost on top of them. As the thing kept climbing up and up and up, tilted back that way, she became more and more nervous. It kept climbing and climbing, the gears clanking, and the people in the rear of the car laughing and making comments. As it went up, gradually more and more of Coney Island became visible, as if they were coming high on a Ferris wheel. Looking over the side they could see lights, the streets and the hot dog stands far below. The people on the ground were getting smaller, and far over to one side was the parasol-like parachute jump with lights all around it and one of the swings at that moment going up.

"When will this get to the top?" asked Bobbie.

"In a minute," said George. "Hold on when it does, it comes down faster than it goes up." He held her around the waist with one arm, and was holding the bar with his other hand.

It still hadn't reached the top, though they were up higher than a Ferris wheel at an ordinary carnival. The palms of her hands were wet with nervousness—but then finally the track came to an end—it led so far, and there was no more. The half-lighted sky of New York was spread out beyond.

"Here we are!" said George cheerfully. "This is it—now hold on, don't let it throw you to your doom."

The cars clanked, then stopped completely for a moment as the front car tilted over. In that second, they were high over Coney Island, high above the ground and tilted over tracks that went almost straight down, and it started, first slowly, then roaring down with tremendous speed. It was impossible to breathe. There were terrified screams in the air —"HOLD ON!" yelled George. The thing was lurching insanely from side to side, going straight down at horrible speed, and when it got to the bottom it was going at truly dreadful speed, and one girl in the back or somewhere gave a terrible scream. The tracks clattered and the whole thing roared down and suddenly zoomed upward. It was at this point that Bobbie fainted. Her head fell on George's shoulder, and he held her the rest of the way. The remainder of the ride was a blank for her. The next thing she was lying on a bench near the ticket office, and George, Phil, Sue and three or four other people were looking down, including several sailors and the man that operated the controls. "What's the matter?" she asked.

"You blew a fuse," said Phil.

"Be quiet," said George to Phil. He leaned over.

"All I said was she blew a fuse," said Phil. "I almost did myself. That thing isn't civilized."

"How you feel?" asked George.

"All right," she said.

In about fifteen minutes she was really all right and wanted to ride it again, but none of them would. And so much for the roller coaster.

Chapter 16

THE REST OF the night on 58th Street, after the ride back on the
B.M.T., from 2 A.M. till 6 A.M., with Phil and Sue in one room
and Bobbie and George in the other, would be difficult to
describe.

At six o'clock, Sue still hadn't returned to the room. It was
bright day outside, in fact the sun had come up long before.
Coney Island seemed far in the past.

"Well," said George, "Let's go get some breakfast in the
Automat."

"All right," answered Bobbie. She jumped up and put her
arms around him. "Isn't it wonderful to be up early in the
morning?" she asked.

"Lovely," he said, "especially after such a night."

She hung around his neck in such a way that her feet were
touching his toes. "You think I have the strength to hold you
up?" he asked. "Cut it out, you're heavy." He now looked
sulky.

She laughed, then asked, "Don't you love me any more?"

"I don't like that word," he said. "It has no meaning."

"You said that last night—don't you remember?"

He stared away into space. She laughed—it all amused her
very much. "Let's go for a walk in the park," she said, "after we
have breakfast. All right?" He didn't answer, and she stood
on his toes and put her hands in his hair. He picked her up
and put her down back on the floor, and said:

111

"Don't pull my hair, honey. Put on your shoes and we'll go get something to eat."

So, they went to the Automat, which at that hour had just opened and was not at all crowded. Then they went for a walk in the park. In the park, he said, "Where I made my error was in not looking up a helpful gypsy at Coney Island. That was the whole point in going out there, in the first place. The gypsy would have made everything clear to you."

"Oh, I don't know," said Bobbie. "What makes you think I'd pay any attention to a gypsy?"

He laughed. "What would you pay attention to, then?"

"Many things," she answered.

"Many things?"

"Yes."

"What kind of talk is that?" he asked. "Many things—what sort of things? You puzzle me, Barbara. I can't quite analyze how your mind works. You don't altogether make sense, honey. Now—"

"There's nothing at all to analyze," she said. "What have you got to worry about, really? Just enjoy yourself."

"Huh," he answered.

"Isn't it a beautiful day? Is there anything to analyze about that? There isn't. New York is nice in the morning, don't you think, it almost isn't like New York at all, especially in the park. Don't you think it's beautiful?"

"It's lovely."

She laughed—he amused her. She was in really good spirits, though by all logic she should have been tired after being up all night.

They got back to the room at eight-thirty, just after Sue came in. Sue looked tired and sleepy. "Hello," she said.

"Hello," said Bobbie. She listened as George's footsteps went down the hall, then heard the door down the hall open and close.

"You're looking cheerful," said Sue.

"Am I?"

Sue sat on the couch. She was wearing only her slip, her

112

clothes and underwear were on a chair. "It was a long night, wasn't it," she said.

"Yes," said Bobbie, "it was."

They talked on for a few minutes, about Coney Island the night before, and so forth. Sue had a rather tired look in her eyes. She asked, "What sort of line did George give you last night?"

"None," said Bobbie.

"I'll bet," said Sue. She stared curiously. "You mean you just didn't swallow it."

"He did say it was fate, and why did I resist, and all that."

Sue lifted up one eyebrow. She looked very tired. There was no lipstick on her lips. Then she smiled and said, "Maybe he really likes you. Otherwise he never would say anything so corny. He's too smart."

"He is, isn't he," said Bobbie.

"I have a hunch you can cope with him," said Sue.

"Oh, I don't know," answered Bobbie. "After all, *fate* and everything." She looked over her shoulder at Sue, with a smile.

That was the first date. The scene moves ahead two weeks to that Saturday night they went to Betty's.

Part 3
Then, Po' Fella Lay Down

Chapter 17

On the afternoon of the party at Betty's, George was waiting for Bobbie around five o'clock in the afternoon on the corner of 57th Street and Sixth Avenue. She had been working at the *Dance World* office from ten that morning on, straightening out back issues of the magazine in the loft with Sue and Heidi. It was filthy up there, very dusty and everything covered with grime. Also, there was almost no light, except one hanging, dim bulb. But the job had to be done, and quickly. Betty supposedly had promised Miss Lanahan (the Managing Editor, an old maid, rather masculine and skinny with a mole on her chin, and very energetic in regard to everything connected with the dance) three weeks before she would take care of it, but she hadn't.

Miss Lanahan was threatening to fire Betty and all the girls that worked around there part-time, including all the ballerinas and hangers-on and friends of Betty's, such as Heidi and Sue and Bobbie. She wouldn't fire Betty, because Betty was too smart and capable and did practically all the work on the magazine—that was partly why Miss Lanahan had these tantrums now and then, out of anxiety because Betty did more and more of the work, calling writers and getting information, fitting the copy for "make-up," handling illustrations, ads, everything, even including pacifying Mrs. Coshon, who financed the magazine for art and lost thirty or thirty-five thousand dollars every year on it. Miss Lanahan had gotten neurotic and discouraged, with terrible foot trouble and other worries,

117

and she no longer put her heart and soul in *Dance World,* she let Betty do more and more and more, hence her anger. Also, she was getting more and more homely. The older she got, the skinnier and bonier she got, her chin pointed and sticking out like a sharp spade. They said she was interested in girls.

But no, she was just unfortunate enough to be born unattractive to men, most of whom naturally go by the usual standards of prettiness and don't care what a woman's soul is like. That was her curse. She was very sweet even if miserable and neurotic, and had awful trouble with her feet, such terrible trouble she had to spend hundreds and even thousands of dollars on doctors and special shoes, and even then she could scarcely walk and went through agonies, her feet warped and twisted all around. Miss Lanahan did get crushes on some of the girls around there, but she wasn't really abnormal. She first got a crush on Heidi, then she got a dreadful crush on Bobbie and acted so weird around her, as if she was a hard-boiled man and wanted to advise her. "Barrbahrah!" she would say, and go, "Harrrrumph-rumph-rumph," clearing her throat, frowning and touching sort of nervously at her hair, then she would give some advice, about taking ballet lessons, eating health food. "Why don't you int'rest y'self in the dawnce, m' dear?" she would ask. "You have tha figgah." Or she would scold—"What are you doing? *Wat* are you doing, Barrbahrah? Dreaming? What in the worrrld do you see out that windah? The inehfficienceh around this office . . ." etc. But the giveaway was that then she would sometimes get a miserable, pitiful look in her eyes, such awful unhappiness she would have to turn away to hide the fact that she was crying, and it was only too obvious she wasn't a man and couldn't act like one, but was just an unhappy woman who had no affection. Heidi and Bobbie and all of them were too naive to understand her, but it was Bobbie's nature to feel sorry for people and beside that anyone could admire Miss Lanahan for the years she had spent or devoted to the dance, working on the magazine against all odds and every year persuading rich old Mrs. Coshon to put up more money and support it. Mrs.

Coshon had three poodle dogs and a chauffeur and dyed her hair red, and jumped on Miss Lanahan constantly. This was another thing that had Miss Lanahan in a nervous state, always having to pacify Mrs. Coshon. She would be utterly exhausted after Mrs. Coshon descended on the office with all those poodles, threatening to sell the magazine, throw it away, it was a disgrace and put out by amateurs, nothing was done right, and so on. This had gotten worse, along with Miss Lanahan's having more trouble with her feet and her not being able to work on the magazine and letting Betty do more and more, and as a result of all this, Bobbie was sorry for Miss Lanahan and friendly to her, which seemed to touch her very much because after all, Bobbie was a young, pretty girl and why should she be interested in her, a woman who was no longer young and whom no one liked or respected. That's what she said one time when she thought Bobbie didn't understand something she did—the truth was that Miss Lanahan knew they all said she was unnatural, all of them were always telling Bobbie to not talk to her, give her a wide berth, and all that, and Miss Lanahan herself knew how they talked, but then one day she called Bobbie in her office and sat by her on the sofa, very frightened and nervous and gulping, trying to tell her something about the ballet but looking and trying to see what was in Bobbie's mind, then suddenly dropping all her manner of being a business executive and starting to cry, dreadfully, as if her heart would break. Poor Miss Lanahan! There are many people like that in the world, miserable and unhappy underneath the shell they put on for others to see. Who knows what could make her happy, but she likes children and should adopt a child and find an outlet for her affections, but it should be a boy, not a girl, and she should see that the boy was taught at school by a man, and thrown around some man, to teach him carpentry at an early age or something like that. This way she could have a purpose in living other than the magazine, which alone is obviously not enough or she wouldn't be crying and unhappy and thinking she loves some little girl or other that she hardly even knows.

119

But so much for Miss Lanahan. Around the office, she was a veritable tyrant, screaming at everyone, throwing all the papers off her desk, screeching and choking with rage, her eyes popping out as she intimidated the office boy and both the porters, driving Betty crazy and tormenting Miss Page at the switchboard. And that afternoon she had a terrible fit about the back issues. For years they had stayed there in the loft, not organized according to any system, most of them mixed up, etc. When orders came in, the boy had to go look and find the issue that was wanted, and it sometimes took him half the morning. This was stupid, said Miss Lanahan, and the back issues had to be sorted out intelligibly, in *order*. And it had to be done right away. Or otherwise Betty and everyone else would be fired. Small loss at seventy-five cents an hour, but according to her work there on that magazine was sacrosanct.

At the *Dance World* office there was no soap, except Octagon for cleaning, and no hot water, just a messy bathroom. When Bobbie got off the bus at 57th Street, her hands and face were dirty. Ordinarily, she wouldn't have got off the bus there, but would have ridden on to 58th Street and gone up to her room, but there was George waiting on the corner so she got off, grimy and tired, her hands dirty and soot and dust on her face. She was weary and out of sorts. The work had gone on without interruption from ten that morning till four-fifteen, and Heidi had been sick and used it as an excuse to be unreasonable, as though it meant she couldn't read, see, or think or anything. "I can't *see* these damn magazines," she'd say. "Ohhh!" she'd sigh angrily, slapping down a magazine. "There isn't any *light* here!" Heidi, a small brunette girl with glasses and a nice smile, danced in Jan Mariss' troupe beside her part-time job at *Dance World*—she was a marvelous dancer, with a great deal of talent though not much creative ability of her own. She'd never been interested in that side but she worked very hard and was able to do very difficult things, almost like a con-tortionist and much of modern dance is this way—she was not a ballet dancer, but a modern dancer, and also did Hindu dance, though not with Jan, with Madame Remier. Heidi could

120

do perfectly what others told her, that is, interpret other people's work, such as Jan Mariss, who was extremely neurotic and very creative. He was definitely not normal, but none of the men dancers were. They were all effeminate. Anyone from outside New York would have been amazed and astounded to hear the way they talked, just like a group of women, exclaiming shrilly about this or that, fluttering their eyelids, holding their hands in a funny way and turning their profile around, grinning in a coy manner—and all of them extremely handsome, with wonderful, graceful physiques, certainly much more handsome than 99.9 per cent of all men. Shop girls and secretaries at the 57th Street Automat would stare at them when they came in there, and lean over and whisper among themselves, but it wasn't reciprocated. They couldn't stand girls. The very idea repelled them. Their way was to look very aloofly at girls, as if a girl were a post or something, but some girls they liked better than others. None of them liked Sue much, and they were all very frigid to Bobbie, especially on first meeting her. They "adored" Betty and would kiss and hug her and jabber away with her all about linens, dishware, recipes, and so forth, though not all of them talked in this way, some of them talked almost normal and seemed almost normal but they weren't. There are many of them in New York and their word for themselves is "gifted." One of them will say, "Is he gifted?" That's a funny kind of gift. They come here to New York because they're interested in art or the dance, and also because if they're from a small town people are intolerant of them. No one cares in New York, but detectives sometimes catch them and beat them up.

"Hello, angel," said George. He smiled, a rather pale expression on his face. "You're looking cute."

"Am I?" replied Bobbie. "Is that so. My hands are dirty, my face is dirty, and I'm tired and don't feel well. Heidi has been complaining all afternoon and we didn't even get the job done, which was straightening out all the back issues there ever were of the magazine. I'm in a terrible mood. Miss Lanahan was so hateful and mean I could have choked her. She yelled and carried on like an insane person. And after all that scene, Heidi was so ill-tempered and irritable it gave me a headache, complaining all afternoon as if it was *my* fault she was sick, snapping at me about this, that and the other. It isn't my fault if she's tired and been working too hard. In short, I'm not good company today, and furthermore I don't want to go to Betty's party tonight. I'm very angry at her. She bawled out Heidi just like she was Miss Lanahan, then talked to me as if I was a little fool, and I don't want to go to her party. I don't care if it hurts her feelings, she can't act like that to me. She isn't neurotic. It's bad enough with Miss Lanahan, without them all acting like that. Where are you taking me?"

George had his right arm linked through hers and was guiding her down Sixth Avenue, staring at her in a sort of love-sick way, smiling in a sort of absent manner, as he had been doing more and more the last few days. He had stopped telling her he loved her, though, because it was obvious she saw through him. That's what happens when you're insincere all your life. Now George was really sweating blood, because he couldn't carry out his plot to seduce her. She had him where he hardly knew what he was doing, but it was all for his education or so she thought. He sighed and said weakly, "You're looking sweet." Then he sighed again and glanced around, and added in a businesslike tone, "We'll get a drink down here at the Park Circle. God knows I need it."

They walked on down the sidewalk and she said, "I thought you were worried about money, George. Why don't you do what you say one time? Drinks in bars cost money, don't they?"

"Money?" he said. "That's the least of my worries." He looked over at her in a slightly bitter manner, as if she were to blame for not falling in with his plot to sleep with her. "So," he said, "what's the matter with that goddamn little Heidi? What's she complaining about?"

He hadn't even listened. "I told you," said Bobbie. "She's not feeling well so she took it out on everybody else."

"Not feeling well," said George. "Rheumatism?"

122

"No, she's tired," answered Bobbie. "But the real trouble was that she was mad at Betty."

"Why was she mad at Betty? What did Betty ever do to her, and what's she got to be tired about? It must be rheumatism."

"Rheumatism?" said Bobbie. "What do you mean, rheumatism?"

"Solar rheumatism," he said. "I mean, lunar rheumatism, like you had a couple of weeks ago."

"Oh, *George*," she said, "how can you *talk* like that, that isn't a nice way to talk. George, you aren't funny, why do you talk like that? What do you expect people to think of you if you talk like that? A lot of people would be very embarrassed if you talked like that. Heidi just was tired and has a headache, and don't you *dare* say anything to her tonight, and furthermore, I don't want to hear any more such expressions."

"I'm sorry, honey lamb," he answered in a meek tone. "I meant all the time to put it more delicate, but I thought that was real delicate."

"Why always *think* about such things?" she asked.

"I don't know, hon'," he answered. "I guess I'm just a lowly type and no damn good." He pulled her over to the doorway of the Park Circle Bar and said, "Come on in here quick. I need that drink bad, very bad." He took her by the arm and they walked on in and back to an empty booth. "Well, well, well!" said George. "Another day, and I certainly need a drink after living through it. Gad, do I need a drink." He slid in beside her in the booth, then put his left arm around her and leaned over and said in her ear, "You're so sweet and such a little angel I can't even eat. I haven't had anything to eat since day before yesterday."

"The waiter will see you," whispered Bobbie. "Sit over on that side."

"I want to sit over here," said George. "I have something to tell you."

"The waiter's going to see you."

"Oh, to hell with the waiter, I have something I want to *tell* you."

123

"He's going to come any minute."

He sighed mournfully and kissed her on the cheek. "Your face is dirty," he said. "It makes you look very attractive. Turn around here and give me a sweet kiss."

"George!" she said, wriggling away. "Be nice, now go over there and sit on that side."

Slowly, unwillingly, he took his arm from around her and slid out of her side of the booth and took the seat across. He had no idea at all what she was thinking. She could always fool him, after about the first two or three days, actually after the night they went out to Coney Island. In a sulky tone, he said, "You're just a mean little thing, underneath all that exterior. I know what you want me to do. You want me to push a peanut all the way down Broadway from 135th Street to the recruiting booth on Times Square, with my nose."

"Oh, I don't want you to do that," she said.

A few seconds later, he was all over his sulkiness and there he was taking off his shoe, wriggling one foot out of one shoe and putting the foot in her lap while pretending to study the menu, then acting as if it wasn't *his* foot but was somebody else's. "You say there's a foot in your lap?" he asked. "Hmmp." At least he had on clean socks. She reached down finally and lifted the foot and moved it over to the side and told him, "If you want to take off your shoes, at least don't wear purple socks." By the time the waiter came with the second drink, he had leaned back and put both his feet in her lap, or tried to, still studying the menu to try and decide what to order for dinner. She moved the feet and there they stayed, on either side of her, bright purple socks, with George slumped back in the booth as he sipped at his little glass of whiskey, an amused look in his eyes. He still thought he could seduce her. After all, it had only been a few weeks.

Chapter 18

JAN MARISS WAS a tall black-haired man with sideburns and sunken cheeks and cavernous brooding eyes. In profile, he looked vaguely like John Barrymore, the Great Profile, and it was said that he had the most beautiful physique of any man in the world. Not the strongest, but the most graceful and aesthetic. It was also said that he was born with a natural style and grace that affected every move he made and everything he did. It was true that he seemed aware of the least movement or gesture. When he reached for a cigarette, he did it in a way no one else would have. He would reach over with a little gesture, and when bringing the cigarette back, his wrist would curve in a graceful arc as lovely as the letter S, except that he didn't smoke. He remained in perfect trim, like a seasoned athlete, which was what he was, even though he was at least fifty and according to George, he was seventy-five.

George said, "Mariss is at least seventy-five years old. He's been doing that moon-worshiper's dance since Nicodemus was a pup. He's seventy-five. All his teeth are false and he has an aluminum plate in his head, and half the bone in his right leg had to be replaced with crystal gypsum."

He said that to annoy Betty. Early that night he was in a foul mood and tried his best to insult Betty and everyone else, and also to express his annoyance with Bobbie. He was very nasty to Betty's friend Tom, but in all fairness to him he didn't act that way all evening. He had gotten Betty absolutely furious by talking as if he was prejudiced against Negroes,

125

teasing her and accusing her and Tom of being insincere liberals about colored people, the type that thought they were noble because they were against prejudice verbally, whereas he himself was against it fundamentally and not just verbally. Verbally, he was in favor of it. Any Negro worth a damn would be disgusted by them, he said, but he himself wasn't a bluffer and a nice-talker the way they were. This was all very unfair to Betty and Tom and the only result was that George talked in such a crazy way that any colored person hearing him would have been more than insulted, but he claimed he wouldn't talk like that in front of any colored person, but only to knock the props out from under stupid white people, though at that colored people were deeper philosophers than white people in this country, and knew more about how to live in a minute, than the white people would ever know. George's conversation gets utterly insane at times. He hasn't got a logical mind like Phil. And he was terrible, early that evening at the party, in a dreadful, foul mood, talking like that and trying to offend Betty and obviously trying to insult her boy-friend, and inbetweentimes glancing over coldly at Bobbie to see the effect on her. But he did stop it later, after he'd had more to drink. Then he took Betty aside and explained his position to her, or tried to. It took him fifteen minutes to get back friendly with her—she'd been practically ready to kick him out of her studio. He also talked more friendly to Tom, but by then Phil and Tom were having an intellectual argument that was really nasty.

Jan Mariss, who at the time of the party was at his summer home up in Massachusetts, was actually in his early fifties, according to Betty, who knew him well and loved him very much and was in a better position to know his age than George, who not only didn't like him, but didn't like the dance either. "Jan is *wonderful*," Betty said. "He's a very wonderful person. There's nobody like him, either as a person or as an artist."

"Oh, he's only another fag," said George.

"I don't especially like that word," Betty answered coldly.

126

"And you don't have the least knowledge of Jan. He's generous to a fault and the most sympathetic, understanding person I've ever met. He'll do anything for his friends. I've never known Jan to do a mean thing to anyone, and as far as his personal life is concerned, I'm sure that's his affair, not yours."

This argument came during that party that night. At this point, George was cold sober, though later he got drunk, but at that by no means as drunk as he seemed. Bobbie also got drunk, or slightly tight. Phil didn't get drunk; he rarely ever did—he didn't like the sensation of having his brain dulled. Sue got tight. That is, tight for her, very sleepy-looking and affectionate to all the men around and especially to Phil, who by this time she liked very much. Betty got dignifiedly tight, keeping her wits about her and being the hostess, but getting words slightly twisted later in the evening, and also getting tight enough to excuse George for the way he talked earlier. Her boy-friend drank a great deal but the only effect on him was that his accent became even thicker and thicker—he had a very pronounced Southern accent that sounded funny even to Bobbie, though after a while people didn't notice it.

The party had come up because Betty had met this boy and wanted George and Phil to meet him. They'd argued with her once and subdued her, and she wanted them to meet this boy and get in an argument with him, and that's exactly what happened. Several days before, Betty had said, "You two come to my place Saturday night if you're not doing anything, and bring those two boys. We're having a little party, Heidi and I, and you can meet this boy I met the other day at Andrea's. His name is Tom and he's from Mississippi. He doesn't look like much but you ought to hear that accent."

"Southerners are so dumb," said Sue.

"I know," said Betty, "but he went to school and got book-learning and everything."

"Well," said Sue, "I think it's a pity to take those poor boys like that and put them in school and make them wear shoes."

"Oh, I approve of shoes," said Betty. "The fact is, I think his people had money. You know, those Southerners, when

127

they have any money at all, they have piles and piles of it. In fact, he's very intelligent. He teaches a class downtown and taught last year at some little college up the Hudson, and writes for those Southern magazines, wonderful articles. Tom's mind is very logical. I think he could hold his own with that Phil in an argument, maybe even get the best of him."

"I doubt that," said Sue. "Phil's really very intelligent."

"So is Tom," said Betty.

"Phil really does know what he's talking about," said Sue.

"Well, we'll have a little party, and they can get together," answered Betty.

So the conversation went. That night they were all at the party, if it could be called a party. The ones there were Heidi and several other girls from Jan's troupe, with one or two boys they picked up somewhere—most of the time they were all in a group of their own in the back room. Also at the party were Betty and her friend, this Tom from Mississippi, and also Bobbie and George and Phil and Sue. These last formed one group in the studio room. This room was large and was used as a dance studio, one wall consisting entirely of mirrors. Along this wall was a movable bench, very low and with a red plastic top, and nearby, a large oak table. And scattered around, there were straight chairs, usually placed against the opposite wall but now out here and there on the floor, which was hardwood and waxed and polished very highly. They were all sitting at one end of the room, gathered more or less around the oak table, most of them drinking beer, but George and Sue were drinking whiskey and later everyone was drinking whiskey. For a while, they had listened to a recording of a string quartet that Betty liked very much and played for everyone on her phonograph, a portable one that she put on the table. Then she put on some other records, jazz records of Bunny Berigan, Louis Armstrong.

"Where're you from, Tom?" asked George. "New Hampshire, or Maine?"

That same old trick. Tom gave him a look and said, "Neither. Vermont."

"Oh," said George. "Maple syrup. I wondered what that was." Tom looked at him in a sort of beady, black-eyed way, then took a sip of his beer and turned and said something or other to Betty, a remark of some sort about the music they'd played.

But George wasn't satisfied to let it go at that. In a thoughtful manner, he stared at Tom, then said, "North Vermont, or South Vermont?"

Tom looked back at him. He certainly was not very handsome, a rather tall, strange-looking man with black hair prematurely thinning on top and pronounced black eyebrows and a big Roman nose, with a sort of contemptuous, critical expression around his mouth, as if he had no use for the human race. He was several years older than either George or Phil. It was obvious that he thought George was a sap. He said, in his rather thick Southern accent, "Theah is no South or Nawth Vuhmont. It's all just plain unvahnished Vuhmont, understand?"

"Oh, Ah see," said George.

"What's yoah name?" asked Tom, drawling. "Ah didn't get it a minute ago." His beady, black eyes were staring intensely and sarcastically at George. By this time, Phil was listening to the conversation, and so was Betty and Sue and everyone else.

"My name?" said George. "It's a good old Alabama name. *Gawge* is mah name."

Tom smiled thinly and said, "Your name's George, eh, all right, George, what amuses you so much about a Southe'n accent? Do you mind if I ask you that?"

"Ah don't mind the leas' bit," said George.

"I happen by accident to have been born in Mississippi," said Tom. "It's a geographical and biological accident—my mother happened to be in the state of Mississippi at the time of my birth—"

"You mean you-all was bawn and wasn't found in no alley?" asked George, eyebrows raised.

Tom continued: "—she happened to be there at the time of my birth, and as it turned out, she kept on living there

129

after the happy event of my successful delivery. I'm sure you can understand this, George old man. I was wondering if you wouldn't be a really good sport and sort of cudgel your brains for a minute, and try and tell me what it is about these rather mundane, ordinary, uninteresting geographical facts that amuses you so. Speech intonations and rhythms are slightly different in the South than elsewhere in the country, a normal thing entirely to be expected. What about it amuses you so?"

"What makes you think it amuses me?" asked George.

"Well, since you were making witty about where I'm from, I assumed it amused you."

"It doesn't amuse me at all," replied George. "On the contrary, it depresses me intensely. I keep wanting to ask you to get that pile of mush out of your mouth."

"I see," said Tom.

"Glad you do," said George.

This was their first "brush." Betty laughed nervously and pacified them, then for a while George was polite. They were discussing art. No one said much about art that anyone disagreed with, then Betty mentioned Jan Mariss and that started off George, first on that and then on colored people. She said, "Well, you know when I first came to New York, I expected to . . . I thought that Jan Mariss would naturally—I thought naturally it would be almost impossible to see him, I didn't think just anyone could go—just like that—go up to his studio, walk in and speak to him. I suppose I had some idea you'd have to send a letter asking for the privilege of sending another letter asking for an appointment, but actually you *would* think as famous as he is, that at least there'd be a secretary or two. That was four years ago, just four short little years . . . but it seems to me that I've really known him forever. He is *such* a wonderful person. I just *adore* him . . . but everybody does."

"*I* don't," said George. "Do you, Phil?"

Phil shrugged, and Betty smiled coolly at George, then said, "Bobbie said you'd never met Jan. Is that true?"

"No, I never met him," said George. "Thank God."

130

Betty smiled. "Well," she said, with a kind of laugh, and glanced over at Tom, as if to say, "See what this person is like." Tom was staring expressionless and rather meditative at George, his thick eyebrows making his eyes look rather solemn, like an owl.

"I never met the fool," said George. "And I never want to. I know damn well I wouldn't like him. He's a heel."

"A heel?" smiled Betty. "Oh . . . hardly a heel." She smiled even more. "That would be the last word you'd ever apply to Jan."

"Is he really that nice?" asked George, as if really considering the possibility that he was mistaken.

"He's very nice indeed," said Betty.

"Well, he's a fag, though," said George thoughtfully.

"Jan is *wonderful*," answered Betty. "He's a very wonderful person. There's nobody like him, either as a person or as an artist."

"Oh, he's only another fag," said George.

"I don't especially like that word," Betty said coldly. "And you don't have the least knowledge of Jan. He's generous to a fault and the most sympathetic, understanding person I've ever met. He'll do anything for his friends. I've never known Jan to do a mean thing to anyone, and as far as his personal life is concerned, I'm sure that's his affair, not yours."

"Well, you can defend him if you want to," said George. "But as far as I'm concerned, he's nothing but an old, decrepit fag."

"He isn't old," replied Betty, biting her lips together with annoyance. She added, "He has the spirit of eternal youth."

"Aw, hell," said George. "Mariss is at least seventy-five years old. He's been doing that sun-worshiper's dance since Nicodemus was a pup. He's seventy-five. All his teeth are false and he has an aluminum plate in his head, and half the bone in his right leg had to be replaced with crystal gypsum."

"This jay bird talks a lot, doesn't he," said Tom to Betty.

"He talks entirely too much," replied Betty, her eyes angry and a flush in her cheeks as she stared indignantly at George, whose expression was bland and innocent. "Listen," she said coldly. "Jan is a very dear friend of mine. If you want to make ridiculous and untrue remarks about him, don't do it around me. Nothing you've said is true, either in fact or in principle, and you might think you're funny, but *I* don't think so, it doesn't amuse me in the least to listen to you slander Jan."

"Do you deny he's a fag?" asked George.

"A *what*?" asked Betty angrily.

"A fag," said George.

"I told you I don't care for that word," replied Betty.

"What's the matter with the word?" asked George.

"What's the matter with it? I'll tell you what's the matter with it, if you really want to know, and you might as well get that idiotic grin off your face, you're just making a fool out of yourself. It's *obvious* what's wrong with the word. The word is a stupid, prejudiced word, it's what an ignorant, narrow-minded person would say, and you know it every bit as well as I do. The word implies moral disapproval of something a person can't help. It's prejudice, that's all, a word like that, and it belongs in the same class with such words as *nigger* or *sheenie* or any such word as that."

"The hell you say," answered George. "But what do you mean, something they can't help? Why can't he help it? Nobody makes him be a fag, do they? Is anybody standing over him with a whip telling him to be one?"

Tom said, "Yes, essentially, they are. Homosexuality is the expression of a deeply embedded neurotic pattern inculcated in the earliest days of childhood."

"That's a tumescent statement if I ever heard one," answered George.

"Do you disagree?" asked Tom.

"He doesn't know whether he agrees or disagrees," said Betty.

"I not only disagree," answered George, "I say flatly your statement is nothing but pure, utter bunk."

"Yeah?" smiled Tom. "Well, I suggest you read a little modern psychology. Seriously. I mean it. Your sensitivity on

132

this point is revealing." Tom smiled at Betty, who smiled back, rather relieved that he had taken over the discussion.

"What do you mean by that turgid comment?" asked George. "Just because I say a fag is a fag because a fag wants to be a fag, does that mean *I'm* a fag? Are you kidding?"

"No, I'm not," said Tom solemnly, his eyes staring owl-like at George.

"Okay, I'm not, then," said George. "It was my imagination all these years that I thought I liked women."

"Probably so," answered Tom, with a tolerant smile. He looked thoughtfully at George, then added in an explanatory way, "You see, the neurotic pursuit of women, the Don Juan pattern, is an expression of a deep-seated fear of homosexuality that drives the so-called Don Juan on and on, from one girl to another. He doesn't like any of them, and only utilizes them to gain a temporary sensation of virility. Furthermore, his conquests are an expression of a deep-rooted fear of women, a fear and a dislike. He really wants to pollute them all. From what you say, I'd guess you are this type."

"Well, to hell with *you*," said George. "For two cents, I'd grab you by the neck and throw you out that window. A lot you know about my attitude toward women, to go spouting off that college sophomore version of Freud—what are you trying to do, make Betty? Do you think that jabberwocky will get you anywhere?"

"Just a *minute*," said Betty. "I don't like that kind of talk, if you don't mind."

"Well what did he say to me?" asked George. "He just accused me of not being human, and if I didn't know he was a jackass anyhow I'd resent it."

"Listen, this is *my* house," said Betty.

"Well, you invited me up here," answered George. "And you're being some damn hostess."

"Oh, please, please," said Tom, grinning. "Relax." He turned seriously to George. "I don't mean my comments to be personal," he said. "You're right, I was too personal, and I apologize."

"Don't apologize to that fool," said Betty.

"Fag, fag, fag," said George. "Nobody can prevent me from saying it. And it doesn't make me one, either. Any more than it means I don't like women. Fag, fag, fag."

The tension relaxed slightly, as more drinks were gotten and so on, but then in a light manner Betty said, "Well, George, you really are quite a Philistine, whatever else you are. I haven't heard anyone talk like that since I had a date with a Rotarian back in Indiana. Only this one used a cruder word than you did. I suppose I ought to be grateful for that, anyhow."

"Yes," said Tom. "It's something to be grateful for." He chuckled.

"Heh, heh, heh," said George. "So you people are ready to sell out the human race in order to be liberal." He stared at Tom. "I bet you're opposed to all sorts of things. You probably think Negroes are as good as white people. You probably think they ought to be allowed in the Stork Club."

"As a matter of fact, I do," said Tom. "Don't you?"

"As ah mattah of fack, Ah do. What a disgrace to the South!" said George. "You, a Southerner, betraying your background like that! God! Will the horrors never cease?"

"He thinks that's funny," said Betty, nudging Sue, who was sitting listening, chin in hand. Phil meanwhile looked as if he had gone to sleep; he was slumped back in the chair and watching Tom. "Very humorous, this friend of yours," said Betty to Bobbie, who had kept out of this argument.

"Letting niggers in the Stork Club," said George. "A fine thing."

Betty said angrily, "Listen, there are limits. Don't you know nigger is a very ugly word? I don't care whether you think you're joking or not—that's a filthy, stupid word and I don't want to hear it."

"Nigger, nigger, nigger," said George. "Oh, nigger-nigger-nigger-nigger."

"Well," said Betty. "You give me a pain. What are you trying to prove, that the word *isn't* ugly? It *is*. Suppose you were colored, how would you feel if somebody used the word around you?"

"If I was a nigger and they called me a nigger," said George, "I'd slug them in the jaw. That is, if I was up North. Down South, I'd bide my time, and say nothing. Those Southerners don't know any better than to use the word."

"Well, you're using it yourself, *sap*," said Betty. She turned to Tom. "Did you ever hear such talk?" She looked back at George, and said, "*This* character gives me the *creeeeps*. I'm going to ask you to take him out of here soon, Barbara. He might think he's joking, but his remarks are simply vicious and I don't like them. That kind of talk sickens me."

Phil cleared his throat, a thin smile around his eyes. "George," he said, "tell them how you led that lynch mob that time, when you were going to school down in Louisiana."

"I didn't lead the mob, I frustrated it," said George. "I helped a boy hide in the back of a car during my sophomore year. A bunch of tough high school kids were on the verge of beating hell out of him and he came running my way and I signaled him in the car and threw a rug on him, then the kids ran by and didn't bother to look in the car." George paused thoughtfully. "There was another time, though that I was in on a hanging. The janitor at school had been peeping through the ventilator at the co-eds in the shower, so a bunch of us guys took him out and removed his manhood and strung him up on a poplar tree. His eyes bugged out as the rope tightened around his old neck—I guess he was eighty, which was all the worse, his peeping on the girls like that, especially considering what a group of those girls must have looked like in the shower—practically like a scene out of Dante, I imagine, enough to curdle a man's blood permanently. That's the only reason *I* got in on the party. I don't have any use for lynch mobs, as a rule, and don't care what horrible crime anyone did, I don't want to see any lynch mob handle it. It's okay to get a few regular guys together, the way we did, and make up a little posse and go get the son of a bitch, but I've got no use for a typical lynch mob. How about you there,

Tom, do you agree with me. Or has your Southern blood turned to clabber up here in New York? Are you a real Southerner, a real lynching son of a bitch, or are you one of these neutral Southerners, the pale gray type that leaks out of the South in a sleazy stream to the North, East and West, and spreads a misconception about the true Southerner, who according to *my* experience, is a lyncher from way back."

"I think you might have a point about that, George," said Tom, pleasantly.

Chapter 19

"You don't understand George," said Phil, with an amused smile. "He's not rational. It isn't up his alley. You wouldn't any more expect George to be rational than you would an amoeba to sprout wings and fly around like a bird. What George is, is a sort of elongated sounding post," said Phil thoughtfully, leaning back in his chair and frowning a little bit as he analyzed it in his mind. "I tried for months and months on end to make him think, but it's hopeless. Thinking dredges up his anxiety so he avoids it at all costs. If you try and get him to think, he launches off on one of those verbal sallies like that and you can't do a thing with him."

"I'm the only rational person in this room," said George.

"No, George, you're not rational," said Phil.

"You give me a pain," said George. "Your saying that like that doesn't make it true—do you think you're an authority or something?"

"I think I see what you mean," said Tom to Phil.

A few minutes later, the argument between Phil and Tom started. This time, Phil did most of the arguing, and Tom answered him, much more than he had answered George. Tom obviously had no use for George at all. George irritated him. Phil irritated him too. From the look on this Tom's face, practically everyone irritated him, even Betty. He had a sort of angry expression in his owl-like, beetle-browed eyes, a constant sarcastic look around his mouth, and a nervous manner of slicking down his hair with the palm of his hand, again and again and again, as he sat there, staring owl-like and impatiently at whoever he was talking to. With the other hand, he constantly flipped ashes off his cigarette, tapping it with his index finger over and over, even when there were no ashes to knock off. This was a tense, intellectual person, very bitter, argumentative, scornful and funny-looking though rather disconcerting the way he stared with those owl-like eyes. He certainly wasn't like the usual Southerner, though there is no such thing as the usual Southerner, as anyone knows who has lived down there. All they really have in common is the accent and some of them don't even have much of that. But this Tom did. He had quite a thick accent that was strong enough at first but got even thicker the more he drank. It began to get very thick indeed about the time he got in the argument with Phil. Just before that, he'd taken a huge, enormous drink of rye whiskey that Betty gave him, and though it had no apparent effect and he kept staring on with those owl-like eyes, his voice got very Southern and he began to talk louder.

"Well, look heah!" he said. "All Ah said was that fundamentally the man was a minah poet no mattah how brilliant he was. Today the man has tuhned to the solace of religion and embraced the theory of the aristocrat, and besides that—"

"You-all's an aristocrat yourself, ain't you?" said George slyly. He wasn't really in the argument any more and was in a good mood now, but he said this. Now he seemed to like Tom.

Phil said, "Come on, George, be quiet a second. I want to hear this."

Tom had stared around at George, his eyes owly and his long neck craned, the black hair on top of his head thinned and showing a white scalp through, visible because his head was tilted downward slightly, as if in politeness to listen to George.

"Oh, Ah'll answer the question," said Tom to Phil. "If George here wants to know. But Ah'll make it brief. The answer is this. Due to the economic struchah of the South, everybody down theah is necessarily an aristocrat of some sort if they aren't totally impoverished. Of course, theah is a new group of middle-class people caused by industrial development in the South of the past three decades, but they don't count and are culturally on a basic minimum level, therefore practically speakin', they remain in the minority, Ah'd say." He cleared his throat. That took care of George. "And naow to retuhn to what Ah was sayin' about Mellon. Mellon not only has lost all his distinctive quality as a poet, the man has tuhned to an outmoded concept of society, nothin' but nineteenth or eighteenth century snobb'ry, and European snobb'ry at that as far as Ah'm concerned, and also he comes out in favor of official fawms of religion and practically becomes a Cath'lic—that's what he really would like, Ah guess, and naow mah point is that this all indicates what's happened to the bes' brains of modern times, whah they wear themselves out an' grind to pieces on the millstone of the times. The pressah on the artist today is fantastic, how any man could be a poet's beyonn' *me*—"

Then the argument *really* started.

"Yes," said Phil, "but nevertheless what you're saying doesn't actually tell us much about the real nature of the human problem today."

"Whah—" said Tom.

"Just a second," said Phil. "Let me talk a while, you had the floor, you and George, now let me say something. My point is this. It's interesting enough to cite special cases such as Mellon. I think his case is significant, certainly. But I doubt if he ever was very different in regard to formal ideas, and I absolutely disapprove of turning to *poets, painters, novelists,* and *musicians* for authority on the nature, structure, meaning and function of various forces in society. I think that's totally absurd. What does a *poet* know about society? He can write great poetry and still not know a thing about society from a structural standpoint. It's *ridiculous* to expect A. K. Mellon to be an intellectual. Why, Mellon has no analytical brains. The man's a fool, an utter jackass, from an intellectual viewpoint."

"Ah'd say he is a *very* capable thinkah," answered Tom. "But very reactionary. And Ah don't mean politically. Ah mean socially."

"Reactionary? Sure," said Phil, "but more than that, stupid too. He can't think. That's my point."

"Ah wouldn't say that," answered Tom.

"Well, in any case, my basic point, getting back to what you said before, is that a case such as Mellon's doesn't tell us much about the stress and strain of our time."

"Mellon is symptomatic of the time," said Tom.

"Oh, no, he's *not* symptomatic, that's just the point."

"Whah, how could it be othahwise?" asked Tom, indignantly. He turned to Betty. "Our greatest poet has no significance, acco'din' to this boy."

Betty smiled. She was very fascinated by everything Tom said, and obviously thought he was winning the argument with Phil. Sue thought Phil was winning.

"Boy?" laughed Phil. "What do you mean, boy? Who're you, Methuselah?"

"Ah'm sorry if Ah sounded patronizin'," replied Tom. "But yo' remark did shock me. Ah really can't see how you could say that a poet of Mellon's stature has no significance . . . that confuses me."

"Good night man!" said Phil angrily. "Why should he have? He's only one individual, poet or no poet, great or not."

"But do *you* maintain," said Tom angrily, "that the man means nothing? My God fellow, what's the matter with you? Mellon reveals the troubles of the age. Do you disagree with that? Do you say we are in a period of hope? Is that what you say?"

"No! I never said that," answered Phil. "It's a hopeless period. I never said there was any hope."

"No hope," said George to Bobbie, who was sitting back on a divan beside Sue, listening silently to all this argument. She smiled at George. While sitting there, she'd made her decision about him. He caught some expression in her eyes and immediately sat up in his chair, like an old fire horse that lifts its ears when it hears the bell. But now she wouldn't look at him. She looked at Phil in a solemn way, as if listening to the argument.

"In fact," Phil continued, "this era is completely and utterly black. Our civilization can't last. It is doomed. We all will be destroyed." He paused, staring thoughtfully and worriedly into space. "It's a terrible era. But—nevertheless Mellon's case has no particular significance as far as I can see."

"Ah wouldn't say that doom was absolutely inevitable," said Tom.

"The hell it isn't," said George. "A thousand years from now, where'll you be? Where'll we all be? Doom is so inevitable it isn't even funny. But of course that doesn't matter *now*. Right now, life is fine, in fact it's wonderful and this is good liquor. Both of you are sons of bitches."

"Be quiet just a minute, George," said Phil. "You're drunk. Why don't you go sit over there in the corner and talk to Bobbie instead of getting obnoxious." To Sue he said, "Does this conversation bore you girls?"

"Oh, no," said Sue. "It doesn't bore me."

Betty sighed. "Not at all," she said, eyes respectfully on Tom.

George was still trying to catch Bobbie's eye. "Does it bore you?" he asked

"No," she said. She glanced at him, then looked back at Tom. Tom, for several minutes, had been smiling in a very amused, tolerant manner at Phil, and now he was chuckling to himself, as he lit a cigarette and stared across the room, his eyes owl-like and his eyebrows raised. This had finally gotten on Phil's nerves. He said:

"Excuse me—what's funny? What are you chuckling at?"

"Oh, nothing," said Tom. "Ah was just thinking of what you said about this civilization. Of course they've been—but never mind."

"Well, go on, say it," replied Phil. "Whatever it is you have on your mind, go ahead and say it."

"Nothing."

Phil stared. Politely, he asked, "What did you have in mind? I'm curious what could be so funny."

"Well . . ." began Tom, tolerantly. "Ah was just thinking

141

about the way in every culture since the beginnin' of time, they sat around and predicted doom."

"Well?" replied Phil. "They've been right, too, haven't they? Every civilization up till now has perished."

"Ah know," said Tom pensively, staring at his cigarette. "But not really. Cultures ebb and flow. You can't judge too rigidly. Even in the Dark Ages, Greece and Rome weren't really lost—they were only temporarily laid aside." Tom had stopped smiling about Phil's remark that the world was doomed. Now he was serious. He said, "Actually, the world today couldn't be ruined. That is, so-called Western civilization is too dispersed to be obliterated. Of course, *we* could be obliterated, and we probably will be."

Later on they practically got in a fist fight as the argument continued.

Chapter 20

ON THE CEILING colored lights were going around and around, red, yellow, orange and blue, around and around and around, changing on the walls and reflecting from the mirror, blending with the amber light from the floor lamp in the corner. The lights above shined from a revolving crystal that came with the studio. Heidi and Betty hadn't bothered to move it or take it down, and it worked automatically if the overhead light was turned on. Without the floor lamp it gave a really weird effect, glittering and shining with one different color after the other, like a masked ball at the Mardi Gras. It had some of that effect even with the floor lamp on. Later that night they turned off the lamp, when the people in the other room came in the studio part of the apartment, but that was after George and Bobbie had gone out for more liquor and fresh air, an errand from which they didn't return because of what happened to George.

The party itself went on and everyone became much more intoxicated, especially Heidi, who at such times would do things no one would ever expect, to look at her. Later that night when they had only the dim-rayed colored lights on, she changed into an outfit that was meant to be for Hindu dancing, an elaborate beaded costume with long sleeves, pantaloon-like trousers and a brocaded silk vest. She came out amongst great applause without the vest, giggling and smiling, without even a slip or brassiere or anything, her breasts completely bare, and did a Hindu dance, moving her fingers and arms and not caring in the least if a whole roomful of people were looking at her. Then they tried to get her to come back and do the whole thing over again, minus the long-sleeved jacket and pantaloons this time, as well as the brocaded vest, however she wasn't that drunk and probably never would be. In Bali of course they don't wear anything there and no one thinks anything of it, but New York City isn't Bali. Heidi is very pretty and must have made quite a sight. The next day she giggled nervously about it. She was only nineteen and had never had any love affairs with any men, but two boys were after her and about a month later she fell in love with a third boy. Nothing much else happened at the party; it continued on until around three-thirty, and then broke up.

The room was filled with smoke and very stuffy and hot, and it was obvious George had had too much to drink. He had sat over on the floor by Bobbie, his arm across her legs and one hand on her knee, a drink in his other hand and turned in such a way that he faced partly toward her and partly across the room. A girl in a tan-colored leotard was standing over by the doorway. She was a dancer from the other group in the back room, a girl with long black hair and bangs across her eyes. George saw her, and said to Bobbie, "Look at that girl over in the door. What's she doing standing there?"

"Nothing, I guess," said Bobbie.

"Isn't that a sweat suit she's got on?" asked George. "What's she doing looking in here?"

"Just looking in, I guess," said Bobbie.

"That one's a lost waif," he replied. "Look at the moody expression. She seems to be interested in those colored lights on the ceiling. Did you ever see such moodiness? Or is it those bangs? And look at the figure. If she was a pinball machine, her forehead would light up tilted."

"Are you really getting drunk?" asked Bobbie. She looked at him from the side, a smile in her eyes. "Or are you just pretending to be drunk?"

"I'm already drunk as hell," he answered seriously. Then he added, "Nah, I'm not really drunk." He peered up at her, a smile in the back of his eyes just barely hidden. She looked back at him, and raised one eyebrow. With that, he smiled and set his drink down and put his hand on her other knee. She said nothing. His expression was now once again very hopeful and pleased, once more like the old fire horse who hears the bell. For a while, he'd been discouraged, she'd been ignoring him and listening to the argument. When she raised her eyebrow like that, a happy look came in his eyes. But also he was slightly amused, as if to say, "Ha ha, I knew it all the time, but you're sweet even if you can't fool me." She knew exactly what he was thinking, but not vice versa.

George thought he wasn't drunk and he thought she believed he was really pretty drunk. The truth was that he was drunker than he himself realized. George couldn't drink very much. Despite all the thoughts he was having, at the same time there was a kind of dreamlike, confused, bewildered look on his face, which actually brought out his better side. It was this that made Bobbie lift her eyebrow and smile at him. She couldn't help but think of the difference in the way he looked now and the way he'd looked when he'd been teasing Betty and wrangling with that Tom. Then he'd looked almost as hateful as Tom.

In some people, liquor brings out meanness—sometimes the normally well-behaved, reserved type becomes loud and awful and snarls at everyone, looking for fights, staring roughly at women and doing all kinds of obnoxious things, such as insulting everyone in sight, spitting on the floor—there's little that a so-called mean drunk won't do. And this person, when sober, is often a very mild type, a well-behaved man who wouldn't dream of going up to a strange woman and making a rough, nasty remark, much less shoving a smaller man at a bar, as a drunkard once did at the Park Circle when they were in there one time, though it wasn't any of them, but someone else the drunk pushed. On the other hand, there is the opposite type. This type when sober will sometimes act like the mean drunkard acts when drunk, except even worse because he's got his wits about him and knows what he's doing. But then when he gets drunk, or more or less so, he relaxes and gets confused and mixed up, and becomes friendly. Not that George, who is this second type, acts like that all the time when he is sober. By no means, but liquor does make him more friendly, or it did in those days. Nowadays it has a terrible effect on him, most of the time. However, that has nothing to do with this story. At the time of this story, he reacted to liquor by being much more friendly. It probably all depends on a person's state of mind, in the last analysis, but in any event it put him in a good mood that night, at least while they were still at the party. He even tried to patch up things with Tom. Phil and Tom had gotten into a very complicated argument about philosophy, and they were arguing violently right in the middle of it when George reached over and tapped Tom on the knee. Tom was saying:

"I don't see *his* significance at all! Ah—? Pardon me?" Tom's eyes were cold as he reached down and moved George's hand away. "Excuse me," he said frigidly. "Don't do that."

"Tom," said George. "I'm sorry I called you a lyncher."

"Don't give it another thought," said Tom. He turned back to Phil. "A theory of history doesn't—"

"I didn't really mean you were a lynching son of a bitch," said George, "any more than I would say that about my own Grandpa."

"Forget it, George," said Phil. "We're in the middle of an argument."

Betty had gone for more soda and another whiskey bottle. This was when she learned they were getting low on whiskey, a whole fifth of it seemed to have gone. Sue and Bobbie were just sitting there as before, listening. The discussion was too deep for them, so they just sat there. Sue really was listening. She didn't know all this, and Phil impressed her very much. As she said, she'd never known such an intelligent person. She seemed to be in love with him, though she didn't talk as if she was. He obviously didn't love her, and naturally she knew he didn't. One time he said in front of them all that he wasn't the lovey-dovey type and had respect only for a reasonable approach to the meeting of human needs, and romanticism was

146

for adolescents and adults of the sort who needed a prop in life. Sex was okay, fine, swell, healthy, but love was a mystic unreality that caused 90 per cent of the grief in the world. Go to the movies for that, it didn't exist elsewhere, though of course there were relationships based on mutual respect and understanding, real adult relationships that were sensible and honest about instincts. All this agitated George and put him into a mood. He wouldn't agree with Phil, yet didn't know what to say, rubbing his jaw and glancing around in a blank, nervous manner, and scratching his nose in a way he had when he didn't know what to say, which was seldom with George. Later he told Bobbie that Phil was fundamentally correct, but expressed it all too cynically, especially for someone accustomed to old ideas, and of course there were stronger relationships than Phil was talking about, but nevertheless there was a great deal of truth in what Phil said, and in the last analysis Phil was right.

"Maybe so," answered Bobbie. "I suppose, growing up, I got a sentimental viewpoint."

"Of course you did," he replied. "All girls, or most of them, anyhow, grow up with that viewpoint. It's movies and novels and everything. The only trouble is that it doesn't stand up against reality. It's pretty thin, the morning after."

"I can see that," she answered.

As for Phil, he had been spoiled and favored by his parents because of illness as a child and because they thought that was the way to raise him, anyhow. Especially had he been spoiled by his mother, the hovering type according to what he said. He could hardly stand her and wouldn't write her, even though she was going through a terrible time, almost a nervous breakdown with the change of life. She had spoiled and babied him and treated him with great importance from his earliest days, and also screamed at him, a very nervous, tense woman who wanted him to be a genius, and took his I.Q. all the time, as if brains were the only thing in the world that mattered. With that type of atmosphere, and being sick on top of it all when he was three and four, the result was

147

that naturally Phil grew up unable to see how other people felt, an inevitable result with his parents telling him all along in millions of small ways that the most vital thing was his own ailments and his I.Q. All this would seem ridiculous to him, but the truth remains the truth, and George is nearly as bad, except that at least his mother and older sister used to get mad at him and slap him and throw glasses of milk in his face, and they never took his I.Q. But they used to dote on him terribly all the same, and then get frightened when he would have a tantrum. They gave him the idea he was so smart, doting on his remarks. He started talking when he was about six months old, and by the time he was two they couldn't shut him up, except his father, who'd be his best friend one minute and hit him in the head the next, all of which accounts for the way he acts himself, but on the other hand there's no accounting for him. He can analyze most of that himself, and it doesn't mean anything. But Phil was certainly spoiled, or mostly spoiled, whatever the truth about George. George's mother was unusual, and not like Phil's, to judge from the letters she wrote him telling him to reform.

"TAWM, you old dawg!" yelled George. In a low voice, he said, "Come on and shake, Tom."

"Cut it out," said Phil.

"I want to shake with Tom," said George.

"Okay," said Tom wearily. "Shake, then."

"Mmmm," said George. "Thanks, boy, you're a good old sock." They shook hands, then George asked, "What part of Alabama are you from?"

"I'm from Mississippi," said Tom.

"What part of Mississippi?"

"The back part," replied Tom.

"No?" said George. He stared, as if trying to figure this out, then blinked and rubbed his chin with one hand. "No, seriously," he said. "What part of Mississippi are you from?"

Tom looked coldly at George, who had sat back against Bobbie's knees, his legs crossed and elbows on his own knees, chin in his hands. Then Tom turned back to Phil and resumed the argument. He said angrily:

148

"Getting back to what I said. I intended *fully* to characterize the remark as stupid. *I* knew what I was saying. Theah's no othah way to characterize it. What *you* said—"

"I know what I said!" answered Phil angrily. "You don't have to tell me what I said! Good God, you don't even understand *Moody,* much less *Rico.*"

"I understand Rico PERFECTLY!" yelled Tom.

"The hell you do," answered Phil, gritting his jaw and glaring. "*Listen* to me a minute. The point is that there's a tremendous difference between Formsy and Rico and Moody, and particularly between Rico and Formsy. A *crucial* difference, and I'll tell you what it is. Remember this. In Formsy you've got a completely status quo thinker. He's not released from the tensions of his age—"

Tom had a thin, acid, superior smile. "Who is?" he asked.

"ANY GOOD HISTORIAN!" screamed Phil. "Not LITERALLY, for God's sake, but you know damned well what I mean! It's a matter of degree, fellow! Good God, Formsy mentions some things that exist in our present society, and treats them as if they were fundamental elements of ANY society, and that isn't SCIENCE! Obviously, many of the things he cites are by-products of our own social forms and customs. Let the man study a little anthropology, for Christ's sake."

"Anthro*pology*?" asked Tom, smiling ironically.

"Of course anthropology. That's one of the better and more fruitful of the social sciences. Why in hell shouldn't he familiarize himself with the best work done in the field, if he pretends to be a great historian and wants to analyze all the cultures of the present and the past?"

Tom shook his head with amusement. "Well . . . really, I just can't see how you can say he doesn't know the best work in anthropology. He quotes Myrtle Mitchell."

"MYRtle MITCHell! *That* popularizing fool? Let him quote Thomley! Blake! Masterfield! Whitley! Jesus Christ, this is too much."

Tom said, "Personally, I think the trouble heah lies in our different estimation of Fawmsy's integrity. You're cold-blind determined to question the man's honesty as a scholah—why

I don't know. All I can say is that it boahs me, in fact it makes me goddamn tired. You appeah to think highah of Rico than you do of Fawmsy, and by God *that* would baffle ANYbody. Listen to me for a minute. Just because Robert Ramsey was influenced by Rico, don't let that turn your head. Ramsey was an artist, not a thinkah. Ah'm telling you once and for all, you're sadly underestimating Fawmsy. He's no middlebrow even if the middlebrows took him up. He's a damn good man, Ah don't care how populah he is, he's a hell of a good man and don' make any mistake about that. My God, but yo' dogmatic assertions have wore me out!"

The argument got even more violent and angry later. But before it ended, Bobbie and George left. They went out to get some more liquor, and if there were no liquor stores open they'd borrow a bottle from Jan Mariss' studio. Betty had a key to it and no one was over there, Jan was away in Massachusetts. As it turned out, just as they were going, Betty found another bottle where some boy had hid it in the sugar can for a joke, but Bobbie and George decided to go anyhow and get more. There were all kinds of liquors over at Jan's and besides, it was a chance to see his studio, which according to Betty was the most fabulous studio in all New York. In the hall just outside the door of Betty's apartment, George said:

"Nobody's there?"

"No," said Bobbie. "But it's all right. He left this key with Betty, and he wouldn't mind."

"Nobody at all is there? This fabulous, exotic studio is totally empty?"

"Jan's away for three weeks," said Bobbie. They were standing by the door of the elevator, waiting for it to come to Betty's floor. George had had another drink, or perhaps two more. He was decidedly under the influence, and had put his arm around her and was smiling, his hair over in his eyes. She added, "We'll get Betty another bottle and see what Jan's place is like, then come on back."

"Will we?" asked George. He kissed her on the cheek. "Whatever you say, honey lamb."

150

"You'll have to pick out the bottle," she replied. "I wouldn't know what to get."

"All right, angel child," he said. "I'll pick out the bottle."

"George," she said, "there's something I want to tell you. I think you might as well know it, so stop leaning on me and listen."

"Okay," he grinned. "I'm listening. What have you got to say, honey baby?"

"I've got *this* to say. George, you can *stop* all this, what you're trying to do, understand? You might as well know right now that I'll *never* sleep with you, George. *I mean every word of that.* If you were the last man left in the world, it would be impossible. I'll never change my mind about that, either. Do you understand?"

He stared at her blankly for several seconds, then said, "Aw, honey child, don't talk like that." A truly unhappy expression was in his eyes. In a low, uncertain voice he said, "Nobody wants to sleep with you, exactly."

"I've made up my mind, George," she said. "And it isn't because of inhibitions, either. The whole thing is just completely impossible and you know it."

"Well," he said, feebly. He was crushed.

"But I'm sorry if I've hurt your feelings," she said. "I know you like me, and I wish I felt that way about you, too, but I don't."

"Oh, that's all right," he said. "There isn't any law, or anything." A gloomy look was on his face. She really had shocked him. He opened the elevator door and she walked in, glancing at him out of the side of her eye.

Chapter 21

THEY WERE WALKING down 57th Street, hand in hand. She was in a very happy mood. He took her in a bar and grill first, when they left Betty's building, because she was very hungry. In the bar and grill, he had two more drinks and she had a sandwich. At first, he was very glum but after a while he got in a slightly better mood, after telling her solemnly that she didn't understand him at all, not in the least, and nothing had ever depressed him so much as the way she misunderstood him, the very thought of it was practically enough to make him cut his throat, and so on.

Now he was teasing her about some statue that Jan Mariss was supposed to have paid a thousand dollars for.

"Tell me what it is," she said.

"Nah, nah, nah," he said. "You wait and see it, then just remember all Betty said about him being so wonderful and me being so dumb and wrong about him and everything. Not that I don't think it's humorous, but imagine paying a thousand bucks for such a thing."

"But what is it?" she asked. "I'm curious."

"You'll see it," he replied. "It must be up there in his studio somewhere. It's a nice, lovely piece of statuary, carved out of the trunk of an ebony tree, and just *wait* till you study those graceful outlines. Boy, you'll go for that statue. It's right up your alley."

Actually, it had been George's idea originally to go over to Jan Mariss' studio. He had later gotten so tight he'd partly forgotten it, but he wanted to leave the party and take her over there, rather than to the room on 58th Street. It was obvious why he wanted to take her there, rather than to the room. A few nights before, at the room, around one o'clock, it had all gotten so terrible and difficult that the only thing she could think of to say was that Sue might come back. It wasn't entirely honest of her to say that, but it was his fault for acting the way he did and making everything so difficult. In such a situation, there was nothing she could do except blame it on Sue. So, he thought if he could get her somewhere else, it would be all right. That is, all right according to his way of thinking. So early at the party, he mentioned Jan's studio, knowing perfectly well that she knew why he mentioned it. That was why, later in the evening, he acted the way he did, when she herself took the lead about their going there. All of this was an undercurrent, such as his pretending later not to know that Jan was out of town and the studio empty.

"Much earlier in the evening, he had said, "Let's duck out on this and go over there."

"Leave the party?" she said.

"This is a dull party," he answered. "Anyhow, I'd like to see a real sure enough 57th Street dance studio. Why don't we get Heidi or Betty to give us a key and walk over there and look at it?"

"We can't do that," said Bobbie.

"Why not?" he asked. "Mariss is at Esau's Mountain, so what difference does it make, nobody's at his studio. And besides, I want to get out of here, this place is giving me the willies. Go ask Betty if she has a key, or Heidi. One of them must, they rehearse over there. I'd like to see that studio and besides we need some fresh air. Let's go."

"I don't think Betty has a key," she answered. "It would be like housebreaking. Let's don't go, let's stay at the party. What do you think about this argument? [She meant the argument between Phil and Tom, which had just started about then.] Who do you think is right?"

"Right?" George stared at Phil, then at Tom, then looked

153

back at Bobbie, peeved. He shrugged. "They're both wrong," he said. Then he leaned toward her and touched her forehead with his, grinning and staring into her eyes, at such close range it was impossible really to see. "This trick drives Eskimos mad," he said.

"It does?" she said.

"Yes, they do it for hours. Listen—" She had leaned back. "I'll tell you something serious." He sighed. "I've never seen such pretty brown eyes. I can't even see the bottom of them— what's going on in that mind of yours?"

"Nothing," she said. During all this, he had been trying now and again to kiss her, with all the other people there in the room, but she moved away each time, until at last she got tired of dodging him, so, he kissed her right there, and this Tom boy raised his eyebrows sarcastically. The truth was that she had practically no control over herself whatsoever, as pathetic as that is. If George had known the real facts it long long ago would have turned out differently. Her feelings were amazing, even to her. Little did he know. Fortunately, she still could fool him, but the least thing upset her. Her brain disappeared and she couldn't think. Perhaps there is no love, but Phil never felt this way. Her thoughts were so obsessed with this particular boy that she hardly knew what she was doing, and naturally it wasn't rational. He complained all the time, but it was even worse for her, actually she had much more to worry about. What did he have to worry about? Nothing.

Unlike the common idea, love would seem to be stronger in most women than it is in men, but perhaps this would be difficult to say. It is true that nature can be frustrated to a certain extent, but sooner or later that causes all sorts of trouble. The needs of the spirit are greater than the needs of the body, but the former are expressed through the latter, even in the case of the most beautiful saint many times. In any case, Bobbie herself had no such ideas, she didn't know what she thought and was only trying to act in the right way as far as he was concerned, which was very difficult. She thought only in terms of love, because in her belief it would have been

154

ridiculous otherwise. There would be no point, none at all unless perhaps the man, uneducated and childish and afraid of the opposite sex, would pay ten, fifteen, a hundred, ten thousand dollars, whatever amount—and this, of course, is assuming the girl herself is heartless and not only cares nothing about other people's feelings but has almost none of her own, or is in some dreadful situation. If she just acted that way as a matter of course, she'd be so far gone nothing would matter to her really, but then some women seem to be like that, and others seem inclined in that direction, perhaps because so many men are the buying type. It's amazing when you think about it that things aren't fifty times worse than they are . . . look at those burlesque shows and those women in the magazines on newsstands. Is it any wonder the divorce courts are full? How can any woman stay married, when the burlesque girls are calling, "Come on, honey, look here!" and the husband unfortunately runs after the burlesque girl and gives up some woman that really loves him, for something that lasts no time and that's that.

Little does the average reader know how the mood of an author is affected by current surroundings. Most people in reading a book, at least if they are like the writer of these lines, merely read it and assume the author wrote it just like that, and that the book itself is not influenced by anything happening to the writer at the time. Of course when one thinks about this it becomes obvious that it couldn't be true. Naturally, a writer would be bothered, and his or her work influenced, by adverse or difficult circumstances in the world, at the time he or she is writing. The nature of the book might change dramatically from one to the other extreme, in accordance with changes in the life of the author.

Suppose someone is writing a book about a happy marriage, a beautiful story of true love winning over the many difficulties of life—two people who manage despite all the hazards to succeed—say, a nice man, a professional man of some sort, the type that is very friendly, smokes a pipe, has a pleasant sense of humor, rakes the leaves, putters around the house,

155

and so on, and a lovely wife, a good sport and even-tempered, rather pretty and a wonderful bridge player, a fair golf player, a rather athletic type and very good-looking if not beautiful, and also a good mother and efficient housekeeper—all in all very nice, a very good wife, well-suited to the man, and kind-hearted, witty, with a number of good friends of her own, and so forth. Suppose they have two children, both still young, a boy and girl, with the boy just starting school and the girl a year or two younger. They have a car, their own house on some pleasant street. He teaches at some school, a college somewhere, and is about to get his Ph.D. At present he's an instructor, and makes a good salary and extra money (for vacations, the car, and so on) by writing occasional articles for magazines, articles on some economic problem such as "The Influence of the Hoover Dam," or "Water Development of Southern California"—any number of possible topics, interesting non-fiction articles. The whole problem of the book is his finishing an economic study he is making of New England, that, and the troubles he has in his department, because he wants to be friends with the students and teach in a different way. The wife tries to help by talking in a nice way, casually one time at a party, to the Dean's wife, but that makes it worse. Then the wife talks to the Dean and they become friends, so there's peace for a while. Now suppose all of a sudden the husband starts having an affair with an immature sophomore girl in one of his classes, and the wife finds out about it and is shocked, miserable, loses all her poise, separates from the husband making him go and stay at the faculty club because he can't give up this girl. She cries bitterly and heart-broken, as she tries to answer the children's questions about what's going on, there's nothing to say, it's a tragedy and it'll all come out and get in the tabloid papers and John (her husband) will lose his job—so, what has happened? This was supposed to be a happy story about a good marriage, not all this with the husband being drawn despite himself to this cheap little blonde tease who also is having an affair with a football player, and also another teacher now and then, and a

156

boy back in her home town, and incidentals here and there—not all this, with the husband acting that way like a man in the grip of insanity, so stuck on this little superficial, silly blonde girl just because she's attractive physically—not all this, with the wife finally almost taking her own life, before she goes for a walk in the woods and sees the autumn leaves, the gold autumn sky, and thinks of her children, and somehow finds faith and decides to live, even if life (she believes) will always be gray and unhappy for her, now that her marriage is destroyed. So, what happened? That's easily answered—what happened was that the author in writing the book happened to come home, let's say, and heard voices through the door, and it's a man's voice (say the author also is a man), a strange deep-voiced man is in there and shouldn't be there, so he goes up to the roof, climbs down the fire escape silently and peers through the window into the living room, and there, sitting on the sofa or the divan, smoking cigarettes and smiling and talking, his wife and another man, both of them not wearing anything at all, and even as he looks the man puts his arm around the wife, so the author rushes back and changes the book, having the schoolteacher go out and get a young, no-good co-ed.

But enough of that. Life goes on. Back to the story—what happened did happen, whatever it means or whatever has happened since, and the scene now is Jan Mariss' studio that night.

Chapter 22

On 57th Street on the island of Manhattan, in the midst of very expensive and fashionable shops, art galleries, office buildings, and so on, stands a very, very old building, with ceilings literally eighteen feet high. The rooms in it are enormous. In the past, it was designed throughout for gas lighting. That was in the 1890's, in another century and another era, though perhaps the building goes back even farther than that. Again and again, this building has been condemned by the city authorities on the building code. The floors slope in the hallways sometimes as much as six inches from one side to the other, and the elevator rises inch by inch in a grillwork iron cage, all open and exposed along a cracked marble staircase that once was elegant but now is all broken down and dirty and covered with years of grime.

The building is made up of gigantic studios. Originally, years ago, it was very, very fashionable and the rents were high. The most famous artists had studios there. Then it went into a period when it was not fashionable, but now it is again very fashionable, despite being rundown and the hallways sloping and unswept and dirty. Once, the rents were as low as seventy-five dollars for studios in the back, but now on sublets the studios rent for as much as three hundred and three hundred and fifty dollars, because in these times such high ceilings and wonderful space cannot be found anywhere. Also, the building just "became" fashionable. Several movie stars have studios there, though they are seldom around. Otherwise, photographers, artists, and so on, fill the studios. The enormous, tremendous rooms in this fantastic old building, plus its location in the center of mid-town Manhattan Island, made it ideal for a dance studio. Of course some of the people actually live there, in fact many of them live there as well as work there, at photography, painting, the dance or music, whatever they do.

One of the most surprising things about this building is its height. It's only six floors high, or perhaps seven, yet those six floors are as high as twelve or thirteen floors in a modern building. This is because of the height of the ceilings. Three floors up in this building seem as high as seven or eight or nine floors in an ordinary building. The entire impracticable old thing would long since undoubtedly have been torn down, but for the war and the situation in regard to building materials, and so on. This was the place where Jan Mariss had his studio.

So, to this strange and eerie and weird building, all dark and deserted, they came. She felt gloomy now, all of a sudden, the minute they went through the door, a premonition came over her, the old lobby was so empty and dark, with the high, cracked ceiling ghostlike in a naked electric bulb. George by this time was even more drunk, and his good mood too had disappeared. Something happened then, that amused her, anyhow. He was in a very gloomy mood and very irritated with her.

They were in the lobby downstairs, waiting for the self-service elevator to inch down from an upper floor. George was looking around, staring at the gilded grillwork of the elevator shaft and the long greased supporting shaft the elevator came down on. "Look at that old monster," he said. "It works by hydraulics, for God's sake. Look at it." The elevator was coming down, inch by inch in utter silence. He said, "That thing must go back to the Civil War. It's the granddaddy of all elevators, isn't it?" He took her by the arm. "Look around at this place. Look at all those shadows. Doesn't this remind you of a Frankenstein movie? That ceiling must be twenty-five feet high. Do you guess there are vampires and bat-eared monsters with fangs, upstairs? How in the hell has this place survived on 57th Street, anyhow?"

159

"George," said Bobbie. "I don't think I want to go upstairs. Let's go back to the party. They'll wonder where we are."

He whirled around at her, a grim look on his face. "Oh, so that's it!" he said. "You think so, do you. Well, you're wrong, understand? You're wrong." He gritted his teeth angrily, glaring at her.

"Let's go back to the party," she said nervously. "I don't want to go upstairs. We shouldn't—do you think we should?"

The elevator had arrived. George had opened the door and was holding it for her as she said this. Now he suddenly reached forward and grabbed her around the waist, and slid his arm down and around her legs, and picked her up. Naturally she wriggled and said "George!" at this treatment, but he wouldn't let her down. "Stop it!" she said. She had one arm around his neck, to avoid falling. He was really angry and all this exertion had got him out of breath. Also, he was much drunker than he seemed. He said, "We're here at this damn place and you can go up there, and I don't want any goddamn back talk out of you." By this time, they'd gotten in the elevator.

"Put me down," she said.

"Hell, no, I won't put you down," he answered.

"George, put me down," she said.

"No!" he answered.

"You're twisting my arm," she said. "Put me down, now."

"Oh, hell," he said. "Fooey on everything." He put her on her feet and sat down on the floor of the elevator and folded his arms, a tight-lipped, grim, angry expression on his face.

"What are you so mad about?" she asked.

"Fooey on the whole world," he said.

"Do you want to see Jan's studio as bad as all that?" she asked.

"Fooey on Jan's *studio*," he answered. He cast her a furious look and slumped down even more, till he was practically lying on the floor of the elevator and naturally getting his clothes dirty and everything else.

"George, now don't be so silly," she said. "Get up off the floor, you look ridiculous down there."

160

"I'll get up in a minute," he replied. "I'm resting. I just hope the world is covered with a tidal wave soon, and everybody drowns."

"George! Will you stop being so silly? You're not that drunk."

"I'm drunk as a dog!" he yelled. "Nobody gives me any credit, even for being drunk!"

"Don't talk so loud!" she said nervously. "Now, get up."

"*Why* should I?" he asked. "After you've treated me so *mean*, as if I was Jack the Ripper, when all I wanted to do was be nice to you, and see that you got along all right in this city, when you can't even look after yourself and haven't got any sense, and act just like a child, wandering around here without even knowing what you're doing, as if you're back in Nawth Car'lina. *That's* my reward. You turn on me as if I was a brute, when anybody else around here would have taken advantage of you. I hope the world blows up."

She laughed. But he said nothing, so then she sighed and said, "Well, the studio's on three, shall I press the button or not?"

"You said you didn't want to go up," he answered.

"George, *why* don't you get up off the floor?" she asked.

"Listen, Barbara," he said. "Relax. Don't worry. I'll get off the floor when I'm good and ready, and you don't have to risk a fate worse than death by going up to that deserted studio, either. Just understand this. I'll never in my life touch a hair on your head. Not me. Just understand that. You don't have to worry about *me*, honey child." She had pressed "3" on the panel, and the elevator had begun to rise, very slowly. He stayed there on the floor. "Just don't ever worry about me," he said. "I seldom ever attack helpless little girls that don't like me. I think you have practically nothing to worry about, honey lamb." He continued to sit there, as the elevator went up inch by inch through the grillwork shaft, but now he wasn't quite as angry as before.

She said, "All I told you was that I didn't especially want to go upstairs, because everything is so dark and spooky."

He stared up at her. "Well, just wait," he said. "Maybe the Mr. Hyde in me will suddenly come out. In fact, there's prob-

161

ably a magic potion up there that will bring out the Mr. Hyde in my character. If so, I'll drink it, and then what will happen to you shouldn't happen to . . . to . . . it shouldn't happen."

"You're just bluffing, George," she said. "You're not really mad at me."

"Wait till I get in that studio," he answered. "If there's a potion up there, that'll be just too bad for you."

"Well, this is the floor," said Bobbie. The elevator had stopped. She opened the door. "Come on," she said. "We're here."

With a rather sullen expression, he got up and brushed off his clothes, then followed her down the tiled hallway, which was very dark, gloomy and depressing. After some trouble they found a small card thumbtacked to one of the doors— on the card in spindly writing in blue ink was "Jan Mariss." Then, with a glance around at the dark hallway, she put in the key and opened the door, found the switch inside and turned on the lights. At once, they were in a completely different atmosphere. It was like an Arabian palace in there, with warm light and beautiful colors and carpets of animal skins and amazing, surprising decorations of all kinds. Even George was impressed; he stood there staring for a minute and looking around, then said, "My God," and went into the little music room or lounging room off the main dance studio and over to the bar by the phonograph, where he proceeded to pour out an enormous glass of "magic potion" to turn him into Mr. Hyde, a drink from a bottle of Vat 69 whiskey, mainly, with gin, Old Crow whiskey, Rhine wine, vermouth, and a few drops of vodka, Don Q rum, bitters and three or four other things. It was practically a whole glassful. He glanced over at her coolly, and drank about half of it, then stood there waiting to turn into Mr. Hyde, but instead he sat down by her on one of the couches and put his head on her shoulder and said many nice things, getting drunker and drunker but fortunately not being able to find the magic potion where she'd hid it under the coffee table. Finally he put his head in her lap and in no time he was sound asleep. Really sound asleep.

162

Chapter 23

THE STUDIO WAS furnished and decorated in a manner that would have puzzled many people. There were two sections; the personal section, and the business part. These two were divided by an enormous Japanese fish net hung from the ceiling, with tapestries and bits of driftwood attached to it, and beautiful egglike, colored stones picked up on the beach at Cape Cod, in smaller nets hanging here and there. There were other things as well. It made a very unusual wall indeed.

This net divided the big studio room from the rest of the apartment, the business side from the living quarters, where the kitchen, bedroom, bath, and music or sitting room were. The little sitting parlor (it was little only in relation to the enormous main studio room) was actually part of the main room off the foyer. It was formed by the division of the big hanging net. On the music room or parlor side, up to about eight feet high, the net was hung with dark brown burlap to make it opaque. The burlap was supported by a rope at least three inches thick, of the type used to hold boats to docks. The burlap was splashed with gold paint here and there, streaks of gold and occasional smaller streaks of red. It had colored pieces of broken glass sewed in it. There were also two or three photographs, apparently of Italian towns or scenes of North Africa, Morocco scenes, framed in thin-edged black frames and covered with glass. The burlap was drawn tight as a drum, fixed at the bottom to a two by four. How they did this was a mystery because the net above hung

163

loosely. Beside that, there were many other things here and there on the burlap, some pieces of gray driftwood, an old-fashioned water pitcher, a shaving cup with "FATHER" on it, a woman's old shoe with a rusty spoon in it, a lady's red wig, dead butterflies here and there, some red and yellow autumn leaves, a filmlike silk scarf, a lady's fan, and other things. Although it sounds jumbled up, it all was placed on the burlap in a manner to catch the eye and look interesting, as well as be surprising. Jan himself did most of it, according to Betty, but some of the most original touches were from Billy, his friend.

On the walls, all of which were different, with panels, tapestries, monk's cloth, there were many paintings, almost none of them of anything in particular—they were abstract paintings, swirls of bright color, forms, lines, cubes, paint dripped here and there in curlycues, some of them like linoleum, a few with vague figures that could have been people or animals or almost anything. The frames of these pictures were not homemade but they didn't look like ordinary frames, some of them went far out, others receded, and they were in all kinds of colors, painted or made of strange wood.

In the studio itself, the studio proper, there was a great deal of crepe paper, purple and gold and pink, hung on the walls, the ceiling, over the door, and so on. There were also light tan, polka-dot draperies all along the window side, full length. These alone must have cost a fortune for the material, aside from making them. The studio was completely bare. The floors there seemed to have been built in, on top of the original old floors, because they were of perfect new hardwood, scraped and sanded down very smooth, but not waxed very much. Also, there were enormous mirrors all along the right-hand wall.

The kitchen, though of an old-fashioned type, had every pot and pan known, many with copper bottoms and all hanging from hooks on a huge timber or beam that went across the room over the old, huge stove, once a wood stove but now somehow fixed up with electric burners. There was an enormous refrigerator made of plain varnished wood, not white enamel, and a big marble table. On a large shelf was a collection of at least a hundred spices. The entire apartment, incidentally, smelled of incense and a subtle kind of perfume of some sort. A green statue of Buddha was in one corner, with a place for burning incense, and there were countless jars and Chinese figures, fat porcelain figures of Chinese men. Speaking of statues, there was one carving hidden behind silk curtains, with record albums and books, out of sight in a recess in the wall—this was the one George had heard Heidi or some of them talk about, carved out of black wood as hard as rock. It was some statue. Part of it was unfinished. Probably some friend of Jan's did it. The statue itself was the same sort of thing as the pictures in the bedroom upstairs, but not finished and very crude, obviously cut out with a hatchet. It seemed to be of four men, or perhaps three men, all wound around and around the trunk of the tree, like snakes almost.

The bedroom upstairs was something else again. There actually was no real bedroom in the studio. In reality, the studio contained no bedroom, but in this case one had been cleverly made by cutting off half the height of part of the kitchen and the music room, and having a carpenter make a big framework of two-by-eight-inch beams, then building a floor across that. This made the height of the ceiling in that part of the studio (the music room part, where the phonograph and little white organ were) and the height of the ceiling of the kitchen only about seven or eight feet high, and the height of the ceiling of the bedroom upstairs even less. A narrow little flight of stairs made of hand-hewn beams went up to the bedroom. It contained nothing at all except a huge rosewood bureau eight feet long and an enormous mirror against one wall and another enormous mirror on the ceiling, and a tremendous giant bed almost eight feet square, or perhaps even larger. It was unbelievably big and luxurious, with colored sheets, silk and satin pillows all over, etc. On the other wall were photographs, and on the wall across from that was a kind of railing or banister waist high that looked out on the fish net and down into the dance studio. The photographs were all of men, most of them obviously dancers. Some of these photographs were rather amazing. Many people probably wouldn't believe there were such photographs, especially posed so "artistically," that is, dreadful, yet posed very elegantly—for example, some horrible picture, yet the dancer or whoever it is, some man, is delicately sniffing at a flower, despite the picture. Such pictures as this are really too much, but ordinarily Jan never lets anyone up there in the bedroom and at that none of them are as bad as such pictures could be, or so Betty says, and Heidi. They would certainly shock the average person.

The music room downstairs was furnished very strangely, with bamboo mats on the floor and a pair of huge couches as big as normal double beds, but very low on the ground, only two or three inches from the floor. Each visitor to Jan's has to take off their shoes at the entrance and go in stocking feet the way they do in Japan. It's impossible really to describe this apartment, however. A whole book could be written about all the details in it, but the reader at any rate can take the writer's word for it that such an apartment as his is not seen often. At the doorway, for instance, somehow they had gotten an enormous wrought-iron gate, at least seven feet tall. This was in the foyer and painted black, just standing there for a decoration, with bits of aluminum paint flicked on it here and there, very tiny little flecks of silver, and also a few of red. Who would ever have thought of such a thing as that? It served no purpose, but it looked very interesting. But there were many other such things, including the polar bear rug and the two smaller black bear rugs in the music room, and the enormous phonograph made to order and filled with albums, a huge piece of furniture all along one wall and matching the bar, the same height and made out of the same wood, and also there were weird lamps and lamp shades, a funny-looking, old-fashioned little desk, and along the living room ceiling a kind of gulley made of black wood with the grain showing white, with indirect lights behind it shining up

166

toward the ceiling, which was made of purposely crude knotty pine boards that had at least ten coats of varnish and were a deep golden color. Everything was in a soft, warm light, with the pretty red lamp shade in the corner and the little yellow lamp shades on the phonograph, or rather curled out over it on black goosenecks. It really was an amazing studio. Not the least thing was a coffee table made of an old, weather-beaten barn door, or what looked like a barn door. That was right by George, where he was sleeping on one of the low couches, oblivious to his surroundings. He'd hardly even looked at the place or noticed it at all, and now he slept on, while Bobbie looked around admiring everything, or practically everything, and wondered what exactly to do, whether to go to sleep herself on the other couch, to try and wake him, or what. She didn't feel sleepy in the least. The pleasant light and everything in the apartment had changed her mood, though she did feel a little bit fuzzy-minded from the drinks at Betty's. So, what to do? She sighed and looked over at George, chin in her hand.

Chapter 24

IT'S EASY TO know what's going on in your subconscious mind, afterwards. But at the time, no one knows. She literally didn't know what was going on in hers, or not exactly. She had no idea, until she turned those crazy pictures around. Then she was so shocked she almost fainted from sheer amazement, not that that made the least bit of difference. Anyone who thinks nature isn't more powerful than they are is crazy.

Far below, dim and barely audible, there were horns and the sound of cars and buses; it wasn't late for New York, and there still was a lot of traffic on 57th Street. The studio itself and the building were dead quiet—the floors and walls were built so thick no noise came through from other studios, whether there was any sound or not. She sat there on the couch, thinking about the party and about everything, feeling rather tired and a little bit depressed, or gloomy, the place now seemed so empty and silent.

Somewhere far in the distance, she could just barely hear music, perhaps from another studio in the building. She glanced around at George, annoyed at him for being asleep, not that he wasn't better off asleep, drunk as he was. She sighed, then got up and looked through the record albums and finally found a Beethoven symphony that she'd heard long, long ago at her friend Mrs. Prentice's house. She used to go over there all the time, when her aunt was in a temper or had migraine, or just to visit. Mrs. Prentice loved all music, and had operas, everything. This was the Seventh Symphony, which she and Mrs. Prentice liked better than any others, except the Third, the Ninth and the Fifth, though the Sixth was wonderful, too, and even the others were good. It usually changed her mood to listen to music like this, but not that night. She took the records out of the album and put them on the record changer, after figuring out how it worked. Then, the sound boomed up tremendously from the speaker in the wall before she could turn it down, suddenly Beethoven was thundering in the room, terribly loud. George slept on, hair in his eyes and head on his arm. She'd put an angora-like blanket over him, a sort of large, pretty-colored shawl that was draped over one of the chairs, and he was breathing regularly, dead to the world, his lips slightly apart and so relaxed it was obvious nothing would wake him up. But she had jumped nervously when the sound suddenly boomed forth like that. It gave her an awful fright, thundering into the room so suddenly, and for a second or two she couldn't find the right dial to turn it down. Also, she'd never heard such a powerful speaker or phonograph as that one. It sounded almost like they were at Carnegie Hall it was so loud, and all the instruments were crystal clear, once she could even hear a vague hum, perhaps Toscanini himself, humming the melody as they say he does sometimes when conducting great music. But the tremendous, sudden noise was too much. The whole thing made her weak at the knees, as much because of the noise as because of possibly waking him up. It was legendary the way he slept, anyhow. Phil sometimes had to wake him, yell at him, push his head down in the pillow, ring the alarm in his ear, pull off the cover, shake him back and forth and shove him here and there, and nothing would have any effect, George would sleep on unaffected by it all, especially if he'd been drinking the night before or had been up very late. George himself said that once his sister poured water on him, and he didn't even wake up. And he said that once in school, after he'd been studying all night for an exam, they couldn't get him up, absolutely nothing would rouse him, so four of them carried him all the way down the hall by his arms and legs,

169

with him still asleep, then they put him in the shower in his pajamas, so he woke up there and got on his hands and knees, but he was still half asleep and wanted to crawl back down the hall and go back to bed. All of this is probably a little exaggerated, George-style, but he was a heavy sleeper all right. Besides that, at present he was dead to the world because of that last enormous drink. He actually drank over half of it, on top of everything else he'd had, and it was a mixture of practically everything in the bar, his idea of a magic potion and certainly enough to make anyone totally drunk. So, he was unconscious. Even Beethoven's Seventh Symphony wouldn't wake him up.

But for curiosity's sake she sat down by him on the couch and leaned over and stared at him. He certainly seemed to be dead asleep all right, if anyone ever did. Actually, all this amused her, she liked to sit there and look at him with him oblivious to the world, his lips apart and breathing in his sleep, hair in his eyes and his arms limp. It gave her a chance to see what he really looked like. George didn't have a bad face—asleep he looked just very tired, so tired and sleepy, and much younger because the muscles of his face were relaxed. He was really sleeping away. It was practically as if he was dead, except that he was breathing so steadily.

"George," she said, "are you having a dream? Hmmm?"

No answer. He breathed on—*Hummmm . . . Hummmm . . . Hummm . . . .* every four or five seconds, another breath . . . *Hummmmm . . . Hummmmm . . . Hummmmm . . .* and now and then a long sigh, *Hmmmmmmmmmmmmmmmmmm,* and then a longer pause than usual before the next breath. She took his wrist and held up his hand. His arm was completely relaxed and moved here, there or anywhere. How could he have gotten so *completely* asleep, when he had been so awake and carrying on in the elevator? But he was.

"Well!" she said. "All right, if you don't want to wake up and talk to me and be nice, I'll just have to find somebody else, that's all."

He didn't say anything. *Hummmmm,* he went. *Hummmmm.*

170

She laughed and took a handful of his hair, and pulled it. No effect. Then she felt his chin. He could stand a shave, even though his blond whiskers didn't show. She leaned over and put her lips about two inches from his mouth and said, "Kiss me." No answer. All of this amused her very much, especially the thought of what he would think or say, if he knew what she was saying, but he didn't. She leaned over, her arm actually around his waist, and said almost in his ear, "George, wake up right now, and I'll sleep with you." He didn't wake up, and she said, "Well, you missed your chance."

But this one-way conversation got boring. She decided she might as well lie down and see if she couldn't get some sleep herself for a while. So, she took the cover off him and crawled in by him, then covered them both and snuggled up against him, staring at him to see if he would wake up. He didn't. It was nice, lying there, but after a while she decided against it. If she went to sleep, she might not wake up till morning, and it would be better for her to go on home and leave him there, and sleep in her own bed, rather than in this strange studio in her clothes with George. It wasn't comfortable lying there dressed, in that strange apartment with George drunk—it was ridiculous, she could go home, take a bath, and sleep in her own bed without having someone breathe liquor in her face all night. She sat up. It hadn't had the least effect on him, she had to laugh at the idea that anything less than the atomic bomb would wake him up. He was simply drunk, and no wonder.

She sighed. It was gloomy, there in that studio with him. She sighed again and made up her mind to go on home. So, she tucked the angora shawl or blanket, whatever it was, back around him, and got up and went in the bathroom and washed her face, with lavender-scented soap and hot water, filling the antique basin. The bathroom was an elaborate affair containing a black marble bench, a glass-enclosed shower and an old-fashioned tub at least seven feet long but built-in and decorated all around with black and gold mosaic tile. Nothing in this studio was ordinary, not even the bathtub. As she dried

171

her face, she suddenly got the idea—why not take a bath? Indeed, why not? No sooner had the thought come into her mind than she closed the bathroom door, turned on the water, pulled off her clothes and laid them on the marble bench, and there she was, completely naked before it even occurred to her that maybe she shouldn't be taking a bath there at all. This was when she walked over to the shelf to get a jar of bath salts, and turned and saw herself in the mirror on the bathroom door, totally nude, with nothing whatever on and her skin all white and naked-looking, with a tiny little red line across her stomach from the elastic on her panties, and the same dents up above where her bra fit. She felt cold and shivery, standing there without a stitch, in a strange apartment, the studio of a dancer she hardly even knew and a weird man besides, and even though he wasn't in town, it was his apartment, not hers to be taking baths in, and beside that, there was George asleep not ten feet away. He could wake up, and suppose he did, and came in the bathroom, she'd feel silly then. She stared at herself, looking at her body in the mirror. Gloom overcame her. Not only didn't she have enough of a figure, she looked foolish with goosebumps on her arms and legs. "Hmmph," she said. So much for all that, there was no use worrying about it, and as for taking a bath, she might as well, the tub was already a third full and she had all her clothes off. Besides, why not? Jan Mariss certainly wouldn't care, and as for George, he was totally unconscious. Indeed, why in the world not take a bath? She was tired and had had no chance to really wash after all that day with those dirty magazines. All this was exactly what she was thinking. But then just as she was reaching for the bath salts, the phone rang.

At first, she thought this was the doorbell, and that really petrified her. But as she listened, it rang steadily and she knew it was the phone. Actually, it was only Betty, calling to see what had become of them, but she didn't know that then and the whole thing made her very nervous to say the least. However, it wasn't her nature to just stand there. She took a deep breath and grabbed a kimono hanging by the mirror, put it on, and went out of the bathroom in bare feet and hurried across the sitting room past George, who was sleeping just as before, and picked up the telephone from the desk and said, "Hello?"

Just when she said that, there was a click as whoever was on the line hung up, undoubtedly assuming that no one was there. She learned the next day that it was Betty. With that, she shrugged, hung up the phone, looked over at George, who slept on unaffected, and went to the front door and bolted the chain, just in case anyone did come there, by some chance. Then, she went back to the bathroom, took off the kimono and hung it up, turned off the water in the tub, which now was full, put in bath salts, felt a draft and glanced around and shut the bathroom door, which was still open, then she got in the tub and had a wonderful bath and even shampooed her hair. It was wonderful. She pulled out the plug, all warm and hot from the bath, got up, stepped out on the bath mat into the cooler air and dried for a long time with an enormous purple towel at least two yards long and a yard and a half wide. Then she rubbed the steam from the mirror and looked again at her reflection, and what a difference, she looked beautiful now, her skin was warm and a nice color, not white-ish as before, and there was nothing wrong with her figure at all, and furthermore, she *felt* wonderful. That's what a bath can do. So, with a towel wrapped around her head, she put on the black kimono, went outside to George, shook him and pulled his hair for about ten minutes till he finally woke up. He was groggy and hardly even knew where he was or anything else, but she got him in the bathroom and made him wash his face, then she took off his shirt and shoes and socks, while he sat with his eyes closed on the marble bench. She had decided to put him in the bed upstairs to keep him from catching cold on the couch in the sitting room, but it was almost impossible to get him up the stairs. But finally she got him up there, somehow or other, and pulled down the covers. He had collapsed across the bed, sound asleep all over again. With the greatest of difficulty, she got him turned around and

173

straightened out and under the covers, after finding him a pair of pajamas in the rosewood bureau, though she couldn't get them on him. That was too much, and it wouldn't hurt him to sleep without them, anyhow. Then she reached up to the wall and turned around several of those pictures, the worst ones, because she didn't want to wake up and see them, and then, her heart beating loudly and an empty feeling in the pit of her stomach, she took off the kimono and dropped it on the floor, and slipped into the bed with him, and put her arms around him, and lay there, her body tight against his and so weak she was almost fainting. She squeezed him in her arms, listening to her heart pounding in her ears, and a long, long time went by, she had almost gone to sleep when she felt him kiss her. He was hardly even awake, but he knew it was her. And so it was. They stayed there till four the next afternoon, sleeping then waking up, talking in low tones, laughing about this or that as he gradually became more and more sober. It was one time, he said, when he didn't have any hangover, and the only time he'd ever seduced a virgin and been so drunk he hadn't even known it, till he woke up three hours later and saw it wasn't a dream, there she was asleep with her head on his shoulder. He was very happy and told her many, many times that he loved her. She too was happy. Only the slightest worry was in the back of her mind, and she didn't think about that then.

Part 4
An' Cried Like a Natural Child

Chapter 25

MOST OF THE rest of this story is so horrible some of it will have to be censored. Many awful things happen in the world, but that is no excuse to write about them in books—life is hard enough, anyhow. A book doesn't need all the gloom and horror in the world, there's enough of that in life without buying a book or paying money to take it out of a rental library, only to get more of the same. Of course the truth must be told, and naturally there are horrible things, but everyone knows there are such things, it isn't news. And yet some authors write about horrors as if there were some point. What's the point? There is no point.

For example, there was recently a story in a magazine, all in artistic language, about a little boy whose mother gave him a cat for his birthday. It was called, "The Birthday Cat." The little boy, an utter little toad of a monster about eight years old, smiled very nice and kissed his mother on the cheek and said, "Oh, thank you, Mommie dear, for the lovely kitty," but when she went out shopping, he grabbed the kitten by the tail and dragged it out in the back yard and chopped its head off with a hatchet. First he tied it up on a stump so it couldn't move. Next he told the neighbor's dog to eat it, but the dog only sniffed at it curiously. All of this was in artistic language. Then the little boy kicked the dog in the ribs and took his older brother's hatchet and chopped off the kitten's head and buried it under the garage, then cried brokenhearted to the mother when she came home, and told her the neighbor's beastly dog had grabbed the poor kitty in his mouth and taken her off somewhere and must have eaten her. Of course the mother never doubted this story for a minute. A lovely child, this one, and a lovely mother to raise up such a child. She undoubtedly had spoiled him completely, which shows that spoiled children are sometimes terrible. But why write such a story? Suppose this writer writes it all out very clever, what the little boy says, what the mother says, a good description of the kitten, and the neighbor's big mastiff looking puzzled and interested at the cat and sniffing at it and wagging his tail—suppose it is written very well and holds your interest, even fascinates you because this little boy is such an utter fiend and you wonder what awful thing he will do—at the start of the story you see, he was thinking about "them," and what he is "gonna" do to "them," how the truck will back over and over "them," and when he sees the cat he says to himself, "A prisoner," so you know right away something is going to happen. But even so, what's the point? Why write that? To prove that mothers shouldn't spoil their children? Who doesn't know that? No sensible person would spoil their child, and if some person foolish enough to spoil their child read the story, they wouldn't understand it anyhow, they'd say the little boy was just born mean. Anyone knows that the worst spoiled children are cruel, and the worst of them would do just this type of thing. The writer knows of an almost identical case, a horribly spoiled little brat who later beat up a girl with his fists, and that same evening wrecked a car and killed three people and was sent to the penitentiary for drunken driving. When he was eight this little brute would cut the tails off his white mice. And he did other things so utterly dreadful to those mice it can't even be written—one wouldn't think the human mind could be so fiendish and cruel. Now suppose a story was written describing the gruesome tortures this awful, fiendish little beast inflicted on those mice, what earthly good would that do?

But the rest of this book is worse than that, in a way, because it involves people, not animals. Therefore, some of it

178

will have to be censored. Of course it cannot be entirely censored or it would be impossible to tell the story. It'll be depressing enough to write any of it, God knows. It's easy enough to write about weird apartments, love, intellectual arguments, walks in the park, trips to Coney Island, but the rest of this is something else again. That's why this part is called, "Death."

Besides that, the situation in this flat continues. During the past week, the occupant here has gotten moody beyond all words. If Part 2 and 3 of this book seem to vary in mood, then it's his fault. Or if it doesn't make sense at times, the writer is sorry, but it's his fault. No one could write anything with him around and not be influenced, with him acting one minute one way and the complete opposite the next, being very nice for a while and then sitting there in utter silence for two hours, or suddenly getting up at three in the morning and stalking out into the rain without a hat and raincoat, then coming back at six in the morning, soaking wet, hair in his eyes and now in a good mood and cheerful, but two hours later in a bad mood that gets worse and worse until he has to leave for work, dead-tired, naturally, after being up all night and walking God knows where in the rain. It's weird the way he's acting. He sits at the kitchen table and puffs on cigarettes, forehead all wrinkled, a moody frown in his eyes, as if he's thinking and thinking and doesn't like what he's thinking but can't get rid of it, and every now and then he glances around in a morose manner, then sighs and looks up at the ceiling. There are probably three things worrying him, though now he doesn't say anything about any of them. One is this job, the other is the better job he was offered, and the other is his older sister, who is having another child, her third. He never worried much about her before in that way, but it's obviously on his mind now, even though her other children were born readily and she isn't even due to have this one for six months. He broods about that sister as if it were a catastrophe, and other things seem to be bothering him as well. Who knows what, but he certainly is acting peculiar, especially

179

these silences. It isn't like him. When he stops talking, it's abnormal. Also, he is acting nervous, and lately he has begun to ask strange questions, all of a sudden. For example, last night out of a clear sky he said, "Suppose we were on a desert island. What would you think of that?"

"Think of it?" I said. "What do you mean?"

"Oh—ah-h," he answered. Then nervously he grabs up *Time* magazine and looks through it and says, "It . . . they say here . . . a little story. This is funny. Where is it, it's in the 'People' column." He's swallowing and blinking, almost like a nut or an old professor or something. "Heh-heh," he says with an artificial smile. "This is funny." Now suddenly he's frowning. "Listen to this, lamb, this is cute. Ah-hhh—they asked Madeleine Carroll—uhhhh, where is that thing? They asked her, somebody or other, who—ahh she'd like to be stuck with on a desert island, I mean, stranded with, what man, or rather, who. If she had her choice. This is cute. What do you think she said? Heh heh. *An obstetrician.*"

"What?" I said.

"An obstetrician," he answered gloomily. "That's what, I mean, that's who she'd want to be on the island with. Isn't that cute? Madeleine Carroll is beautiful, don't you think? A very sensible, ahhh, type of looking woman."

"Yes," I said, "she is, but what put all that in your mind?"

"Nothing," he answered. "Nothing at all. I was just thinking about a desert island—reading that story, or anecdote or whatever it is. And she has a point. It'd be hell to get caught on an island like that, stranded and everything, with nothing but coconuts." He put his chin in his hand and stared across the room, then looked around and said, "Jane's having another one, according to my mother. But the women in my family seem to have babies like chickens have eggs. An aunt of mine felt uncomfortable and went in the bathroom for a dose of soda, and the baby was born so fast she couldn't even get back to the bed in the bedroom. Jane's last baby was practically born in the car on the way to the hospital. But if you think most women are like that, you've got another thought coming.

180

They go through hell for days, and then the baby gets born the wrong way, especially the first one, which is naturally the most fiendish of them all. The reason for that is because women were meant to run around on all fours, and *not* to stand up, any more than men are, and that's why it's practically impossible for a woman to have a baby unless she's spent her whole life digging potatoes, or something like that. It's the most strenuous thing. But getting back to that desert island—now imagine being stuck there with some woman whose heredity wasn't like my sister's, some woman who'd never had any child. You, for example. You're little and it would probably be impossible for you to have a baby, or very difficult—or someone—how wide are your hips?"

"It isn't the *hips*," I said. "That isn't it. It's the pelvis, not the hips. Didn't you know that?"

"Yes, I know, but take some girl with a narrow pelvis, or hell just take any girl, they're all the same. Say, a very pretty girl, the type men whistle at, and suppose you're on a boat, say a cruise in the Caribbean, and there's a storm and the boat is shipwrecked and you and the girl are clinging to a piece of timber, with sharks and barracudas all around, but somehow you wash up on a tiny little island—say it's out in the middle of the South Pacific and it was a private yacht and you're ninety thousand miles from nowhere, not even on any steamship lanes, just marooned on this tiny little island with a few land crabs and coconut trees and a bird or two. Now, imagine that. *God*, but would that be awful! Horrible is the word! At first, sure it would be idyllic, a pretty girl and everything, and of course you'd sleep with her, there wouldn't be any question about *that*, no matter what the girl thought or what kind of upbringing she had, nature would take care of that, it would be inevitable, and I will admit, at first it would be very pleasant on that island. And even nicer if it was some naive girl. She would realize there was no avoiding it, after all, on an island like that and everything, so even if you chased her around a coconut tree once or twice that would just add to the fun—she'd never jump back in the water and join the barra-

181

cudas, that's for sure. In fact, she might even chase the man around the coconut tree . . . that has been known to happen, hasn't it. Huh. But for that matter, no man ever seduced a woman, anyhow. So, she'd chase him around that coconut tree, and she'd catch him. Then it would be idyllic. Am I boring you?"

"No," I said. "I'm listening."

"You look funny."

"No, I'm listening."

"Well, the point I'm coming to, is this. There they are on the island. It's very sinful. They've just sinned all over that island, having a wonderful time. You know, tropic breeze in the moonlight, coconut trees, love. They just have a wonderful time. Hawaiian guitars in the background—a phonograph has washed up with them, let's say, and the batteries are still working. The amount of sin that goes on on that island is fabulous. Let's say they're even in love. Now this is a lovely picture, isn't it. We agree on that, but there's just one fly in the ointment, and that's what Madeleine Carroll had in mind. *Normally*, when the girl started to have the baby, she could go to a hospital, and everything would be all right, *but not on that island*. Hell, no. Just imagine what it would be like, imagine her going into labor and having the baby, or starting to have it, and the man not knowing what in hell to do. It would be a catastrophe. Suppose the girl died and the man was left there all alone, marooned forever, and maybe with a live baby. There wouldn't even be anything to give it to eat . . . but I suppose you could give it coconut juice."

I said, "If the girl died, the baby would probably die, too, because if she died, the chances are the reason would be because it couldn't get born, and then it'd die, too, naturally."

"Good God," he said. "Let's change the subject, this conversation is entirely too morbid."

Five minutes later out of a clear sky, he says, "Back in Philadelphia one time, this woman got run over by a taxicab and killed. She was pregnant at the time and was just about to have a baby, so this interne did a Caesarean section on her

182

right there in the ambulance just after she was dead. It was horrible. He didn't have any real instruments with him, so he stopped the ambulance outside this barber shop, ran in and got a straight razor, rushed back and right through the woman's dress he made a cut about a yard long, and just opened her up like she was an animal or something. He had to work fast. So there she was, cut wide open. Then he cut through her womb and reached down with his hands and pulled the baby right out of her, and do you know, that baby lived? Isn't that fantastic? Angel, isn't that the most horrible thing you ever heard in your life? There is no horror story to equal it. It's terrible, and the answer is that they shouldn't have taxis and automobiles. Something like that could only happen in modern civilization. In cave man days, people stayed on the ground and walked, they had some sense. Maybe it took them longer to get there, but for Christ's sake, at least they got there, and you didn't have these insane cars running down the street killing pregnant women, and then some smart interne cutting them open half a minute after they're dead and pulling a bloody little baby out of their stomach. Why, the entire world ought to blow up! Imagine how that husband must have felt. I can just picture it. He goes to the hospital and sees his wife, all cut up and covered with blood and dead, then they tell him to brace up, and they show him this bloody little baby and tell him, 'You're a father.' That type of thing happens all the time in the world. That type of thing goes on constantly. Pregnant women get killed continually. You'd think chance would favor them, but it works just the opposite. No sooner do they get pregnant than they're run over by a truck, or they fall out of a window, or a fiend rapes them and garrotes them with a scarf and throws them in the river. Some such thing happens. It never fails. Or it turns out the woman has one kind of blood and the man has another kind, so the baby is a total idiot. Besides all that, the pain of childbirth is so dreadful it drives women out of their minds, and do you think they care in those hospitals? In 90 per cent of hospitals, you find gathered the most insane fiends and sadists in the

183

entire population. They chuckle when patients are in unbearable pain, or worse than that they just don't even care at all. Those nurses are hellcats and most of them ought to be tied down and whipped within an inch of their lives, and the doctors are worse, a bunch of fiendish bastards—don't think they care a damn about humanity. But even if you find an exception to this rule, and find a *decent* doctor and some *kindhearted* nurses, it's *still* a hell of a situation. Looking at it philosophically, I'd say that any woman who'd have a baby in this day and age ought to be shut up in an institution. Why have it? It'll only get blown up by an atom bomb, and why go through something so dangerous as that, for nothing? It's much too dangerous, infinitely too much so, and furthermore there're too many children in the world, anyhow. In fact, why not let the human race die out? It's no damn good, anyhow, with all these wars and bombs. Ninety per cent of the population ought to be in the insane asylum, anyhow. Walk out on the street and you never know but what a nut might pull out a gun and shoot you, just like that. I say let the damned insane human race die out, it isn't worth a goddamn and it would be good riddance. Let the honey bees take over. That would be a hell of an improvement. Imagine how nice the world would be, without the human race running all over everywhere in their automobiles, crashing airplanes, derailing trains and plotting to blow the hell out of everything with atoms. It would be a peaceful world, if all the goddam people in it would drop dead. And don't give me any of your optimism. You don't know what life is all about, because your head is up in a cloud. It's all very well to think the world is lovely and everybody is nice, until you start trying to base your life on it, and all *I* have to say is thank God one of us has some sense. If I acted like you, forty of those lecherous old goats you're always jabbering with in the Automat would be up here raiding the icebox, sleeping on pallets on the floor, and peeping at you through the keyhole when you take a bath. Why do you think those filthy old goats talk to you? Don't you know that the contents of one of those senile old goats' mind would make

184

a vial dipped from the Paris sewer pass for Chanel No. 5? You sit there and jabber away at one of them and think they're talking to you just to be friendly, but they're undressing you mentally and *slobbering* at the very idea. I know what those old bastards are like, but do you know? Oh, hell no. You just go traipsing on your way, strewing buttercups in every direction. If a drooling fiend walked up to you with a knife, you'd smile and toss him a buttercup, under the illusion that he intended to peel an orange. It's—now what's the matter with you? Eh? What did I say? What's the matter? Where are you going?"

"Out for a walk," I said.

"At this hour in this neighborhood?" he replied. "That's pleading with fate for rape. I'll get my coat and go with you."

"I don't want to go with you," I said.

"Oh, you don't," he answered. "You don't like what I said, so you'll retaliate by going out on dark, dangerous streets late at night by yourself, to make me sit up here and worry. All right, that's fair enough. I slandered your senile boy-friends at the Automat."

"You *shut* your vulgar mouth," I said. "You know what you said about those poor old men is a dirty lie, and you only said it because you're *mean as a snake*. If I was as mean as you, I'd curl up and die. *You* ought to die out even if the human race doesn't. You think you're *smart* to talk about poor old men like that, who haven't got any money and can't get any jobs and have nowhere to go but sit there and drink coffee, and it's because you're a cruel, heartless, mean brute. I'll talk to *any*body I want to, *any time* I want to, and as *long* as I want to, and if you don't like it, you can lump it! And furthermore, it's none of your *damn* business what I do! And you listen to me, if you think you can talk to me like that *any more*, you're wrong, because I won't stand for it, do you hear? I'll slap your face! If you think I'm afraid of you, you've got *another think coming*!"

"Why, *angel* lamb," he said. "You're all in a *huff*. *I* didn't say anything. What are you so mad about?"

"And as far as my going out on a dark street late at night,

185

it's nine-thirty and I'm going to walk on Fifth Avenue, and this neighborhood isn't dangerous anyhow."

Here it should be said that the first part of this book is not entirely accurate, because of the way it started. There seemed to be no reason to go into any of it, however now the truth might as well be told, though at that there isn't really any need to go into it. But the truth is, of course he isn't merely living here in the apartment, though of course on the other hand he does sleep on the cot in the kitchen, since there's no "love" around here, due to all the scenes. Of course at times he sleeps on the cot, and at other times he stays up late and reads the newspaper. But naturally all this has nothing to do with the situation that is developing on 58th Street, five or six weeks after the party at Betty's. The first month after that party was very happy, but now impossible is the word for the situation there, and the worst has just begun.

Incidentally, two friends of ours, a couple who have been living together for quite a while, got married yesterday, which was slightly surprising, since the fellow was opposed to marriage for intellectual reasons, not long ago. Of course his father will increase his allowance, and in these days a marriage license is just a scrap of paper. I ought to know. I've noticed it.

Chapter 26

LIGHT CAME UP from the street through the Venetian blinds and made a pattern on the ceiling. There was an outline where the plaster had cracked and ceiling paint had begun to flake, a leak that had come down through the floor from the room above. The outline looked like an octopus with four or five short, stubby arms. Against the opposite wall was the mirror, shining in the darkness, and under it the two bureaus. She could see the draperies hanging on either side of the double windows, and not far from there, by the telephone table and the floor lamp, was the easy chair. Next to that was the desk lamp and typewriter, and piles of books and magazines. Beyond the desk was the other couch made up with a corduroy cover and big pillows. Everything was in dim shadows and could just barely be seen. She had looked at it all again and again.

Until very recently, she had not thought very much about anything. For the first two weeks he had been very worried and had quizzed her constantly—"How do you *feel*? How are you *this morning*?" Etc. The last three or four days of those two weeks, he was really getting worried, and he gave a sigh they could hear all over Central Park when she told him everything was all right. "Well, thank God," he said, and he added he had aged five years. If he aged five years that week, later on he aged a thousand years. As for her, however it had seemed, she knew all along deep inside that everything wasn't "all right," but her attitude was, why think about it, why say anything? Everything would be awful soon enough, and besides, she hadn't known what to tell him anyhow. The truth was that the whole situation was impossible. From the way he reacted, she knew that, if she hadn't known it anyhow.

But now what time there had been no longer existed. That afternoon, she had taken him aside and told him. He stared at her, then said, "That's impossible." And now she had to think, and decide what to do. But there was nothing to do. The feeling that bothered her was something vague, an uneasy feeling that gave her an emptiness in her stomach and a terrible restless sensation, as if something dreadful was going to happen, but she didn't know what. The feeling was like in school at the age of nine, while waiting to be called on to recite a memory gem, but a thousand times worse, an awful sinking feeling, as if one would fall and fall and reach an end so horrible it couldn't even be pictured at all. This, he says, is anxiety. It isn't anxiety, anxiety is nothing. This is *terrible*. The way he talked that night, with Phil and Sue and everything, acting as if she was out of her mind and letting Phil say all sorts of things, that wasn't the least of her worries. And then coming around and wanting to kiss and all that, then lying over there indifferently and almost going to sleep. If he had been the intellectual type like Phil, who was good for practically nothing except to analyze things, then this is what you would expect.

Now she was lying on the bed propped back on the pillow, which was doubled up, an old pillow like most of them in this house. A sheet and light cotton blanket were over her. It was impossible for her to sleep. For hours she had laid there in the bed, staring around the room, wide awake, a butterflies feeling in her stomach that got worse and worse as time went by. This, then, was insomnia. No wonder people couldn't stand it, and took pills. It seemed that hours had gone by and it was almost morning. She finally switched on the bed lamp and looked at the Baby Ben, but it was only two-thirty. The clock was ticking, it was the right time, and only an hour and

188

a half had passed. All this time, he was peacefully asleep. He had no troubles or worries.

He slept on, one arm around her and his foot over her ankle, his other hand in her hair. There was a clammy, hot feeling where he was against her, and she'd reach up and pull that hand out of her hair and try and slide over a little, then he'd slide over too and fumble around and get his hand back in her hair, waking up enough to do that. How could she go to sleep with him holding on to her hair like that, to say nothing of lying half against her with his arm around her as if he owned her, breathing against her neck and making her entire right side all clammy and hot and unpleasant, and also he needed a shave, his chin on her shoulder was like sandpaper, and to make it even more complete, the hair on his chest tickled. Furthermore, he hadn't had a bath that day and he smelled vaguely like a men's locker room, with shaving lotion from the day before and an acrid male smell that ordinarily she liked but now annoyed her intensely, faint though it was. She was very sensitive to smell. Ploughed earth, a lickory stick tree in blossom, the salty, warm smell of the ocean, a newborn puppy's breath, ozone from heat lightning, old harness, the smell of cut grass on the golf course . . . she dreamed of all this, smells like that, not the thousand scents of flowers or the murky, overpowering, unnatural odors of man-made perfumes bought in some department store. Love to her smelled like all those things, but now she was left with nothing like that, but instead something shameful and depressing and abnormal, a stupid perfume-ish type of odor, synthetic and medical and unnatural. She was so depressed she could hardly endure to lie in the bed with him. She was sick at heart and filled with dread, everything was a mockery, she had been a complete fool even worse because she'd known it all the time. So now she'd slept with him and had the illusion of love, and next the consequences. Anyone can borrow money, but not everyone can pay it back. Neither of them could, including her, but the thought that worried her the most would have surprised him indeed, if he had known it.

This was the thing that made everything really sad, and as unpleasant as the arguments that night had been, it had nothing to do with that, and nothing to do with her own feelings either. The sad thing was that he loved her—she knew it, or she never would have slept with him, and the thought made tears come to her eyes every time. What she'd learned was that love alone, was not enough. Love alone is blind, and something else must be behind it, something he didn't have and would never have. But about that last, she wasn't sure.

Chapter 27

THAT NIGHT AT the Automat, in the middle of dinner, he said, "Bobbie had a dramatic idea this afternoon, speaking of surprises the fair sex gives the dumber half of mankind. I was bowled over all right, but of course she gets the best of me constantly. That's nothing new. I'd be discouraged except that I realize a twelve-year-old girl has enough built-in stuff to baffle and confuse the most experienced old roue, which I am not. And besides, Bobbie here is nineteen, not twelve, which means I have about as much chance with her as I'd have Indian wrestling with a mountain gorilla in his prime—*not* that that metaphor exactly fits my little angel lamb, the joy of my life. I don't mean there's anything sadistic in the way women—"

"What dramatic idea?" asked Sue.

George glanced around at her, then said, "She might get mad, if I told you. But it was very dramatic. I had to hold on to my jaw teeth there for a minute."

"What dramatic idea was it?" asked Sue, curiously.

"I didn't have any dramatic idea," said Bobbie. She was staring coldly at George, from the minute he started talking. At first he had avoided looking at her, but now he stared up at her, a rather cold look in *his* eyes. It was obvious what he was thinking, and her heart sank.

"You certainly did," said George. "And now that I've thought about it a little, I don't like it the least bit. The truth is that

191

it's neurotic as hell and for two cents I'd jolt you right out of it."

"What *is* he talking about?" asked Sue to Phil, and Phil shrugged. She turned back to George. "What are you talking about?"

"For two cents, I'd tell you," answered George. This was right in the middle of dinner. They were sitting near the front, near the plate glass windows looking out on 57th Street and the sidewalk with people passing by. That night they were all supposed to go to a movie at the Little Carnegie Playhouse. In the past weeks, they'd all gone out a great deal together, and tonight they were supposed to go out. By this time, Bobbie and George practically lived in the big back room, over at the house, and Phil and Sue in the front room. Clothes and everything were all mixed up. Now, Phil and Sue stared curiously, Phil with a blank look and Sue with a slightly bothered expression in the back of her eyes. She obviously thought it must be a joke, but she wasn't sure. "Maybe I really should tell them," said George thoughtfully. He glanced over at Bobbie. "It really might be a good idea, at that."

"*Tell what?*" asked Sue, irritated. "What is he talking about?" She looked at Bobbie, who had stopped eating and had decided to get up and leave the Automat, then she looked back at George. "What are you teasing her about?" she asked.

"I'm not teasing her," said George. He ate for a few seconds, an annoyed frown on his face, then he said to Sue, "You don't know anything. Why don't you just shut up and eat."

"Don't tell *me* to shut up," said Sue. "You've got a nerve." She turned to Bobbie. "What's he talking about, honey? Do you want—is there anything wrong? Don't let him spoil your evening."

"Never mind," said George. "Everybody relax. It doesn't amount to anything."

"Yes, everybody relax," said Bobbie. She got up and walked out then. He didn't follow her, until twenty minutes later when he came over to the house. Why humor her? Women become hysterical, when they're humored, and the thing in common between a woman and a dog is that they both appreciate a firm hand and like to have their tail rubbed, and any man that says otherwise doesn't understand women and might as well rely on orange juice, because he's such a fool he doesn't know the difference between his elbow and home plate. To hell with *her*, if she wants to get up and stomp out like that and not even eat her dinner, let her go off and cry and boo-hoo up in the room, women aren't truly happy unless they're weeping anyhow.

"Why good God," said George in a peeved tone. "There's nothing *wrong* with her. I know for a fact that there isn't. If there was a chance of anything being wrong, it'd be different, but this is just some goddamned mystic female urge that has no connection with reality, and I'll be damned if I'm going to pamper her. I've pampered her enough already. You don't know how I've pampered her. Why, say boo, and you hurt her feelings. You have to nip this mysticism in the bud. Next thing, she'll have me sitting off in a corner with my legs crossed and arms folded while she burns incense. Then wouldn't I look silly."

"Well, no sillier than you already look," said Sue.

"You don't look so hot yourself," said George. "If I had those rheumy blue eyes of yours and that blonde straw for hair, to say nothing of a warped peanut for a nose, I'd go hang myself. You're not so hot. You're the psychopathic nose-picker type, and if you think I'm going to let little Barbara make a fool out of me, you're wrong. Why hell, the next thing, she'd want us to go down to Sixth Avenue and get our horoscopes took. I'm telling you, this is the only way, firmness. A woman's instincts have to be governed, and that takes firmness. A woman is just like a dog, fundamentally. They both need a firrrm hand, then when you pat them on the head they wag their tail. All of them are mystic. And as for *her*, don't kid yourself, *she* has a mystic streak a yard wide—and I'll tell you something, now, just like in all women, sex brings out this mystic streak, see? They start getting all those emotions and sensations, and my God, it's mystic to them."

193

"I never heard such silly talk in all my life," said Sue.

"It's silly to you because you're a woman," answered George. "And you're more levelheaded than Bobbie. She's *wild*, there's a *deep* mystical streak in that little girl, don't let her looks fool you! I know her, and you don't. It's all right when she's just prattling on and giving her ideas about life and this and that, but when it gets obsessive, I say it's time to call a halt. I say it's bad, and I for one am not going to humor it, whatever you think. Goddamn it, I'm thinking about her own good. All this idea of hers is completely irrational. She had her period three weeks ago and she couldn't be having any baby. It's a mystic notion." George stared first at Sue, then at Phil. "The only time she could have had any baby, is before then," he added.

"Well, she's sensitive," said Sue.

"Sensitive? My God, the word doesn't even begin to describe her. Say boo, and you've got a problem the U.N. couldn't solve in thirty years. There isn't any word to describe her. And do you think you can *argue* with her? Do you think *reason* makes any dent on her? Oh God, no, she's above such things as that. Especially on a point like this. It's mystic, that's what it is. She knows. You can't tell *her*. She's going to have a baby, and she knows it in her bones. And you can't argue with her knowledge about it, either, not this super type of knowledge that comes up from the bones. Hell, no. Just try it and see how far you get. I say to her, 'Now Bobbie hon, you realize you couldn't be having any baby—you realize that, don't you?' She says 'I am.' I say, 'Angel, it isn't really possible.' And she says, 'I can tell. Things aren't the way they look. I am.' That's utter certitude. *Ut-ter certi-tude.* Now, you can't argue with that type of thing. All you can do is ignore it, or treat it lightly and hope for improvement." George shrugged, and looked around, eyebrows raised quizzically. "Isn't that right?"

Sue said, "*Could* she be pregnant?"

"No!" said George. "Not like she thinks—it would have to be in the last three weeks if at all, and it couldn't be that. She

194

thinks it goes back to that night of Betty's party. That could have been, but she's had her period since then, and the odds are a thousand to one, or ten thousand to one, against it *since* then."

"Sometimes out of the nine months, you have the first period, or even the second," said Sue.

"Almost never," said George.

"I heard of a case," answered Sue.

"And so did I," said George. "And don't tell me I could run into two such cases in my life, either. The odds against that are astronomical and you know goddamn well that isn't true, it's so unlikely it's ridiculous. Bobbie couldn't possibly be pregnant, the odds are ten thousand to one against it, *fifty* thousand to one. And furthermore, if she is, she couldn't possibly know it. You realize as well as I do, a woman can't possibly know until there's some obvious indication. Why do they have tests for it, if women can tell?"

"Okay," said Sue, "but they say that after six weeks, some of them can tell. And I don't see why not. That's conceivable —the body certainly knows, if not the conscious mind, and maybe some women are able to know it in their mind as well."

"Good God!" said George. "You sound just like her!" He laughed, then said, "Listen, don't try and worry me. I feel fine, thanks. You know damn well the trouble with Bobbie is that she's upset, that's all."

"Well," answered Sue. "All right. I agree. But if she's upset, I don't see why you aren't more patient with her, then. You know she hasn't had much experience . . . this doesn't mean anything to you, but she takes it very seriously. She's insecure with you emotionally. That's the answer as far as I'm concerned."

"She isn't the least bit insecure with me," answered George. "And how do you get off saying it doesn't mean anything to me? You don't have the least understanding of my character."

"The hell I don't," said Sue. "I understand you perfectly. The only one around here who doesn't understand you is Bobbie."

195

"She loves me," said George. "And it's real love, too. You can just talk right on, but Bobbie loves me."

"Huh," said Sue. "Worse luck for her, then, if she does."

"Oh, yeah?" said George. "We'll see about that."

"We certainly will," said Sue.

"You're damned right," answered George. "And not the way you think, either. I wish she was pregnant. I'd marry her, if she was, and I might marry her anyhow, very possibly, one of these days."

"I like the way he puts that 'very possibly, one of these days' on there," said Sue. "A sort of safeguard, don't you know. After all, the little boy doesn't want to commit himself."

"Why in hell should I commit myself to *you*? Who the hell are you? And where do you get off, ragging and picking at me like that? What did I do to you?"

"Okay," she said. "So I've got you all wrong. We'll see."

"All right, we'll see then," said George.

Chapter 28

THE FOLLOWING LETTER was written on October 16th, and mailed three days later on the 19th. Sue saw it in the bureau drawer and copied it down with some idea of showing it to George, though later it happened that there was no point in that, and in the meanwhile she'd changed her mind anyhow. Not that the letter had any real significance. It was only a letter Bobbie had written in an unhappy mood to her aunt.

This aunt was not her real aunt, but a woman of no kin who had adopted her when she was very young. She was a strait-laced, strict woman, very unusual and eccentric in character. A whole book could be written about this aunt. She was a schoolteacher and her husband had been the Principal, a very strict, religious man twenty years older than she was. She married him in early middle age herself, then ten years later he died.

The aunt had adopted Bobbie when she was three and a half. Her husband, who was known as a very religious and severe person, died seven years later when Bobbie was eleven. They were very strict with her. She had lived before with an unmarried girl, a friend of her mother's. This girl supposedly had died. The aunt took Bobbie away and no mention was ever made of the girl. Bobbie as a child remembered her, and asked about her, but they said she was dead. "The lady died," the aunt would reply, and the uncle would say, "We will not discuss it any more. Be silent, child, silence is golden." Then if she said any more, he would say, "Silence!" If she said anything else, he would have to do his duty. Doing his duty meant she got a whipping with switches from the hedge, and then for fifteen minutes, thirty minutes, or an hour, depending on how serious it was, she had to stand with her nose in the corner, holding the family Bible in her arms, and the Bible was one of those huge Bibles that weigh about twenty-five pounds. He thought this was good for her, and often said, "Nobody ever did their duty by the child, but I do it." He did it, all right. All his life, he never called her by her name, the only thing he ever called her was, "child." He resembled an old turkey, with wattles hanging down and a red nose, and rimless glasses with a silk cord dangling from them. Mr. Prince was his name. He was the terror of the high school. However, at times he was kindhearted, and he always did exactly what he thought was right. The aunt was the same way, except that she was far more nervous and more prone to illness—he had never been sick, until he dropped dead of a heart attack, whereas though she had no heart attack, she was sick constantly.

They never would tell Bobbie anything about this girl or woman who had had her the first three and a half years of her life. She had half-thought until she was eighteen that this girl might be her real mother, though she hadn't called her mother—she called her by her name, Jo Anne. But when she was eighteen, she saw for herself on the hospital records that her real mother died when she was born. There was no name given for her mother, just a line drawn with a fountain pen, and either no one would tell anything about it, or no one could remember back eighteen years. All they knew was that she came to the hospital, died in childbirth, and a few days later a girl came and said she was a friend and took the baby and said she would give it to the mother's family, which was supposed to be in some other town, but she didn't do that, she kept the baby and stayed there in the town. And that was that, till the aunt stepped in the picture and took the baby, after three and a half years, away from the friend. Perhaps someone might find out the truth about what happened, some

198

day. All it said about Bobbie's mother was that her name was —————————————— and she had brown hair, brown eyes, weighed 129 pounds on admittance, no marks or injuries, height five feet two inches, age approximately twenty years, and general condition fair. Who was she? Where did she come from? What was her story? Considering that she weighed anywhere between fifteen and twenty pounds more than normal because of the baby, her description was much like Bobbie herself. And where did the name "Bobbie" come from? (The aunt started calling her "Barbara"—Jo Anne and her sweetheart never called her anything but "Bobbie," never Barbara.) Was that her mother's name? Very probably. Sometimes they would call her "Little Bobbie," as if there was another one, though maybe it didn't mean that—she must have been just a little version of her mother, who had such a tragic end and died as a young girl. Her mother lies in the graveyard without even a tombstone to mark where she is. She could remember Jo Anne talking about that and how terrible it was, and how the hospital did it, put this poor dead girl in potter's field and not treat her with any respect, because some man got her in trouble, and she couldn't get out of it. How many sad things there are in the world. Probably she was a nice girl from poor people somewhere, maybe her parents had turned her out, or maybe they couldn't take her baby, or maybe Jo Anne had got attached to Bobbie and wanted to keep her herself—who knows the answer? As a child, she spent many hours imagining a thousand stories of what had happened, some of them very complicated, about her family, and a man, and she and Jo Anne leaving, but her not wanting to live, and the man tries to find her but he's too late, and she dies, then he comes the next day and finds her grave, she's dead and he will never love anyone else. It used to make tears come to her eyes just to think about it. The aunt once said that she was a girl from a smaller town sixty miles away, either there or another town forty or fifty miles past there, some mill town, and her people were poor but she was going with a well-to-do boy who got her in trouble and ran away, or intended to marry her and then didn't—the aunt once said that was the answer, she'd heard it from Jo Anne, but the aunt also said her mother was a bad girl. She couldn't have been very bad at the age of twenty, and with such a girl friend as Jo Anne, who the aunt also said was bad. Jo Anne wasn't bad, but just the opposite, a wonderful, good-natured girl very humorous and very pretty and warmhearted, and always smiling and having a good time. It was impossible for her to have been bad. If she was bad, why did she keep her friend's baby for three and a half years, when she could have turned her over to the orphan home? The only thing Bobbie could remember about her as far as facts are concerned was that she worked in a roadhouse, but it was a roadhouse, not any house of ill repute, she wasn't that type of girl. However, she did go with this married man, and probably because of that, they took the baby away from her, the town board of society ladies. Who knows what it was? There must have been some trouble about the man, who according to the aunt was a bootlegger. If so, all right, but he wasn't a bad man, it was the depression and the great Mr. Prince himself bought whiskey from bootleggers, that's why he had a red nose. The man was very nice, whatever he did. His name was Jim, he was always polite and quiet to everyone, loved to play jokes, and looked like the movie actor Henry Fonda. Bobbie remembered him perfectly—he used to bring her presents all the time and called her his "little girl" and used to put her up on top of the jukebox, and anything she wanted, he would do it. He couldn't refuse her anything. He loved Bobbie more than his own children. Whatever happened, to him and Jo Anne? Both of them just disappeared. The rumor according to the aunt, was that both of them were caught driving a car of whiskey with the baby in the car for camouflage, and were sent to jail, but if that happened, she'd have remembered it. And what if they did use her for camouflage? Why not? So what? Liquor isn't as bad as some of the people that drink it. Including the sheriff, an old drunkard. He goes to the house of ill repute, he fell drunk down the steps and broke his arm and everybody in town knew it, and it wasn't that roadhouse by any means, it was a white frame house over in the colored district and everybody knows that, too. A book could be written about that town and it would be some book too. But anyhow what happened was that after three and a half years the town Orphan Board of society ladies that with one or two exceptions do nothing but play bridge and go out once a month to the "Open Door Home" and look down their nose at the dirty little orphans, they decided that it wasn't a good home for her, so they took her away and gave her to the aunt and the uncle, who were good people at heart but didn't have the least idea what to do with a child. Is it any wonder that she stopped talking for a year, or practically stopped talking. It wasn't because she didn't have any sense. She thought if she stopped talking, they'd have to send her back. Before, she'd talked all the time. People don't know that a child that age understands everything. They know exactly what's going on and they can remember anything they want to. The only thing she couldn't understand was what in the world had happened to her friends. But what must have happened was that they moved away somewhere, to get away from his wife, to California or somewhere like that, and if they ever wrote to her or sent her any presents or asked about her, which they must have done beyond any doubt, the aunt wouldn't tell her, not that "bad influence," not that bad girl and her married man. In any case, they never came back. Once those ladies took her away, she never saw them again. Even if they had gone to jail the drunkard sheriff could have kept them there only a short while, and they could have seen her once they got out assuming no one stopped them, but once she'd gone to the aunt's, she never saw them again any more. Maybe they were in an accident, or maybe they can't come back because of his wife, or maybe some day one of them or the other will come back to the town and look for her to see how she is, but who knows, there are many mysteries in life and one doesn't have to know all the answers, because who knows the answer to life itself?

As for the aunt, obviously she was a nice woman, but a very strict person who had no doubt of what was right and wrong. The type that thinks such things as holding hands and going to movies on Sunday (or most movies any time) is a sin. Since she will never live to read any of this, it can be said that she undoubtedly thought that *sex* was the most horrible and embarrassing thing in the entire world. She told Bobbie the facts of life when she was fourteen, and warned her against men, and almost died of embarrassment, it was all so dreadful, yet she said love was beautiful and it was God's plan. She talked for about five minutes against lust. "Resist lust," she said. "As you grow older, Barbara, men will seek to arouse up lust in you. You don't understand that now, my dear, but in times to come, you will understand it. My dear, that is God's plan, and don't break that plan—you must be a *good* girl, and not let lust ruin *you,* the way it does so many. Never let the least thought of that type come in your mind, never, nothing of that type at all. Read the Bible, Barbara, read the Bible. All the wisdom of the world is in that great book. It's the only protection and guide that we have, the word of God. Make it your own. Attend church regularly. Think good thoughts. Help others. And if temptation comes, pray for aid, never be too proud, my dear, to pray for aid, because human nature, in God's wisdom, is very weak."

The aunt was very sincere, and in her heart a good woman, but she had another side to her nature, she never smiled, went through the world in misery, and was cruel to people who were helpless and wouldn't or couldn't resist her, such as the children she taught at school and Bobbie when she first came there. She also was so religious no one else was religious enough to suit her, and only when she rose above herself did she practice what she preached, but who else does except then, and also she was very cultured, much more so than most of the people in town. She had always been religious, but before she married Mr. Turkey Gobbler the Liquor Drinker who disapproves of liquor and bootleggers and bad girls but stares at girls like an old fool, before she married

202

him, she had read many books, Dickens and Thackeray and many others. It was after she married and got older that she became so strict and determined in her ways, and no wonder, married to Mr. Turkey—how in the world could she ever *sleep* with *him?* That would be enough to disappoint anyone, though the poor man couldn't help looking like a turkey and probably couldn't help it if he was an old hypocrite. But she respected him as a man, or pretended to, then a year after he died, when she was fifty-two, she had a terrible nervous breakdown and was almost out of her mind for weeks, though few people knew it. She would pray all night. Only Naomi the colored cook, and Mrs. Prentice, a neighbor and wonderful person who'd studied music for two years in New York, Bobbie's best friend later on when she was older, only those two kept that house going that summer, but by fall when the school term started, the aunt had come out of it and went on her way, hat on her head with the false cherries and driving her old Buick coupe, grim-lipped and determined no matter what. At heart, she was a noble and brave woman, and kind as the day is long. The letter to her follows word for word.

But on second thought, first there were some scenes that led up to the letter. The letter really comes a little later. It was actually the turning point, and by the time the aunt's answer came, Bobbie had made up her mind what she would do. But that is getting far ahead of the story—though maybe not so far ahead at that. And what *should* she have done, in that situation? What was the right thing? Perhaps the reader might say, "The answer is obvious." But when you're in love and afraid to die, what then? There is when something deeper, must come to your rescue, and make you stand and meet your fate, regardless of what the consequences might be.

Chapter 29

GEORGE TOOK HER hand and looked into her eyes, his face serious. He said, "Now listen, honey, you've become very neurotic about this, and it isn't any joking matter any more. Now I want to have a serious talk with you. It's very important. Unless you get some perspective on all this, it'll get worse. That's the way neurotic ideas are. They get worse and worse. Now I want you to listen to me, understand?"

"I'm listening," she said. She was staring out the window, at the building on the other side of 58th Street. They were alone in the front room.

"All right, then," he answered. "Look at me." She looked at him. "That's right. Now honey, do you know what a neurosis is?"

"What?" she asked.

"Don't be so listless, honey, this is important. Answer what I ask you, and try and cooperate, angel. If you won't even listen, we can't ever get anywhere. All I want to do is try and make you realize some things that are so obvious anybody can see them. That is, anybody except you. You can't, because they're things in you, inside your own mind."

"All right," she said. "A neurosis is a nervous breakdown, then. They used to call it a nervous breakdown but now they call it a neurosis. I haven't got either one of them."

"Not exactly," answered George. "That's more or less true, but not exactly—a nervous breakdown might *come* of a neurosis, but more than likely a neurosis, at any given time,

204

wouldn't be in its most acute form, which is a nervous break-down. See?"

"Yes," she said. "And I'm perfectly normal."

"A neurosis is *unconscious conflicts*, understand? Conflicts that the person isn't aware of. The pattern goes all the way back to *early* childhood. That's what a neurosis is. First, it leads to irrational attitudes, then it leads to irrational be*hav*ior. The irrational be*hav*ior tends to get worse and worse, until either the neurotic becomes an out and out psychotic, or in other words crazy or mentally ill, or until they have a nervous breakdown, or get in serious trouble of some type. *Unless*, they get an *insight* into the unconscious conflicts that are bothering them. See?"

"Yes," she said. "And you're the one that's crazy. I'm normal."

"All right, good, now just a minute. Relax, angel, *I* know you're normal, *of course* you're normal. Nobody said you were crazy. You're a perfectly normal girl—as far as this culture is concerned, but the culture sort of goes against human nature, and implants neurotic fears that are unnatural, then when human nature asserts itself despite the culture, the person thinks they've done something wrong, or 'sinned,' or whatever you want to call it, and as a result they punish themselves with neurotic obsessions or anxiety, insomnia, and what all else. Now you have an obsessive idea, with a little anxiety—not much, but a little. Understand? Now it's all completely obvious. Believe me, this is all completely elementary. Your case is so obvious it's practically a classic example. You see, neurotic fears implanted in you at any early age, have flared up, since you lost your virginity. This is just subconscious guilt, that's all it is, and in your case it's made worse by the fact that you were so bold about it, getting in that bed with me like that, even if you thought I was utterly drunk."

She said, "I knew you would get sober some time. Don't think I didn't know that. Furthermore, I decided long before that. I made up my mind at Betty's party, but then you got drunk and went to sleep."

"Umm, yes," he said. "Of course you remember what you told me right after we left Betty's party."

"That doesn't matter," she said. "I changed my mind."

"Uh-huh," he said. "Well, let's don't get sidetracked. But let's go back to that night. Now what I want to impress on you is that what happened then was against all your upbringing— it was *completely* against all the things you were told as a child, entirely against the moral standards of your background, and according to those standards, which are the standards of the whole country pretty much, even today, according to those standards, what you did was a sin, a shameful, bad, wicked, immoral thing for a nice girl to do, to get in bed naked with a man like that, knowing very well that she would lose that dearest possession of every good girl, her honor. The treasure beyond rubies and diamonds, that little piece of silly membrane that separates the goats from the sheep, the pure of heart from the soiled and the deflowered, *holy* virginity. You lost it by your own action, and all girls do, but most of them can claim they didn't do anything, the man did it all and they couldn't stop the cruel brute he was so insistent, but you can't even claim that. I was dead drunk. In fact, I hardly even remember it."

"You don't have to tell me all that," she answered. "I know it. Everything you say is true, but I thought there was a chance you might not wake up, you were so drunk, and furthermore, I didn't even dream of getting in that bed until the very last minute. It was late and I was tired and I wanted to lie down. Furthermore, when you woke up, I told you not to. Naturally you didn't pay me any attention."

"Naturally," he said. "I was a cruel brute who wouldn't take no for an answer."

"You certainly wouldn't."

"Listen, honey, you don't understand," he said wearily. "I don't blame you for that, for God's sake. Just the opposite. It was wonderful to wake up and find you there, a sweet little girl in the bed with me, it was like a dream come true, and as far as I'm concerned, it just proves you're not a hypocrite like

206

many girls, but honest enough to act more natural without pretending. How many times I've had to tell girls I'm taking off their pants so they'll be more comfortable! A man gets tired of such goddamned silly hypocrisy—'Just take 'em down, dear, you'll be more *comfortable*.' If you told 99 per cent of them the truth, just why you're taking the pants off, which is as obvious as ANYthing in this world can POSSIBLY be and BOTH of you know it, then they'd freeze up on you and you wouldn't be able to get the pants off with a can opener. Instead there has to be this constant phoney approach. It was the most wonderful thing that at least that night, you weren't like that. You were honest and I admire you for it. Not one virgin in a million would have done what you did—or not many, anyhow, very few. Maybe some would have. But you know I don't blame you for it. The only point I'm making is that according to the standards you were brought up by, it was bad. People like that aunt of yours would probably collapse from sheer horror."

"You were *dead* drunk," she said. "You were *completely* drunk. How did *I* know you were going to wake up, as drunk as you were? I thought you'd sleep till noon. You were so drunk you didn't even know where you were. I admit that what I did was silly, but I didn't know you were going to wake up, and if I *had* known you were going to wake up, *believe* me, I never in this *world* would have gotten in that bed. I thought you were just going to sleep on, and I didn't see any reason why I shouldn't lie there in the bed for a while. It was a very nice, big bed and there was plenty of room, and I'd just had a bath—I didn't see any reason not to get in the bed. You were *completely* unconscious. And it would have been perfectly all right, but I went to sleep. Then you woke up around four and I was so sleepy myself and everything—and besides, I loved you. It isn't immoral if you love the person, and my aunt wouldn't say a word about it. It would shock her but she would understand it, at least deep inside she would. And as for people who would blame me, that doesn't mean anything. You have to live by your *own* conscience, George, not by somebody *else's* conscience. I don't care what people say. I didn't do anything wrong, and if I had the choice to make again, I'd do the same thing."

"We're sidetracked," he said. He sighed. Then he said, "Look, let me make my point. It got lost somewhere back along the line. Forget about that night. It doesn't mean anything. My only reason in mentioning it was to make my point. Now *listen*, Bobbie, listen to me, listen to what I *say*, be *reasonable* —you know perfectly well that according to the standards of your background—"

"The girl that had me the first three and a half years of my life lived with a man she wasn't married to," said Bobbie.

"I know, but that was still against the standards. Be quiet for a second. For God's sake, let me make my point, then I'll give up. *Please* let me make my point. I'm asking you, honey, *let* me make the point, won't you? Be a sweet girl, don't interrupt. All right?" She sighed and looked up at the ceiling. He repeated, "All right?"

"I'm listening to everything you say," she answered. "What more can I do? Agree with you about things that I know aren't true?"

"Look!" he said. "Goddamn it, *before*, you said you knew you'd lose your virginity when you got in that bed, and then you said you thought you wouldn't. Now why don't you be consistent? I don't want to argue with you about that, but don't act as if everything *I* say is so ridiculous, when you yourself make about as much sense as a sign in Chinese."

"I thought maybe so, but I didn't know," she answered. "And if you don't leave me alone about it, I'm going to wish I never laid eyes on you. In fact, I practically wish that already."

He sighed very wearily, and was quiet for a while, then he said, "Okay, I'll make my point. I'll make it despite all the odds. Look. In this world, nice girls don't sleep with men unless they're married to them. That's the rule. It's changing but it still is the basic belief in this society. You can't disagree with that because you know it's true. *I* don't support that theory,

208

and I don't criticize girls that act otherwise, but many people do. Now, you broke that rule, and since then, as a result of sub-conscious fears implanted in your early childhood about sex, your neurosis has flared up. Now honey, you can see this for yourself, it's so obvious. I know you can and that's why I'm trying to talk to you about it. You're not a dumb girl, you're very intelligent, in fact you've got all sorts of insight, and you can see this. I'm not trying to argue with you, Bobbie. I'm only trying to make you see why you've got this fixation about hav-ing a baby. Now, do you remember telling me that night, or rather that morning, that you were going to have a baby?"

"Yes," she said.

"Well, to assume it like that, even though it was possible, was slightly neurotic."

She leaned back against the pillows of the couch and stared across the room. "I don't see why," she said. "What's neurotic about having a baby?"

"Nothing," said George. "But it's slightly neurotic to assume in such a mystic way that you are, merely because there's a possibility. Your attitude was as if it was certain. Furthermore, it's neurotic, definitely neurotic, to weep guiltily about sex. Sex is nothing to weep about, and though I know how you felt, the truth is, you wept mystically and told me you were going to have a baby, which is all very well as long as it's nothing but emotion, but it's something else when it develops into a full-fledged obsession. Do you know that there are women who get a fixed idea that they're pregnant, because they want a child, and they go to one doctor after the other, *insisting* that they're pregnant, when actually they aren't?"

"I didn't cry mystically," she said.

"I know you didn't, but it had a mystic edge to it. Listen, honey—a certain amount of fear of pregnancy is normal, that's what's *really* behind this, probably. So you feel guilty about everything and punish yourself by imagining that you're in trouble, and play on your fears of having a child. But—"

"I'm not afraid to have a child," she said. "I like children. I've wanted a child ever since I was nine or ten, or even before

209

that. Any normal girl does, but of course it's probably neurotic, according to Freud."

He was silent for a moment, then said, "No, it isn't, but you didn't know what you were thinking or anything. You probably only had a dim idea of the facts of life at that age. What you really wanted was a doll, or something to play with."

"I wanted a *live* baby," she said, "not a doll. Naturally I knew it was impossible *then*, but I thought it would be nice to have one, anyhow, some day."

"It's perfectly normal for a girl to want children," he said. "Of course that's normal. It's how the human race survives. If girls didn't have that instinct, the human race would die out. But for God's sake let's get back to the point. You still haven't answered the point."

She said, "I answered the point. And I'd think it would be neurotic for a girl to be afraid of having children, not vice versa. But *you* say it's neurotic for her to want them, so I guess I'm wrong again."

He gritted his teeth. Perspiration was on his forehead. Then he smiled. "Look honey," he said, "we're not getting anywhere, because you keep sidetracking the discussion. *Listen* to me. I don't say it's necessarily neurotic to want a child, and of course fear of having a child can be neurotic—very much so. The point is—"

"Which is neurotic?" she asked. "*Wanting* a child, or *not* wanting a child? They can't both be neurotic. It has to be one or the other."

"You simply don't understand neurosis. By God, I'd like to see a psychoanalyst come up against you. You'd drive him totally out of his mind in ten minutes. In fact, if you ever decided to get analyzed and starting going to analysts, they'd be coming down on the sidewalks of Park Avenue like human hailstones. It'd be dangerous to walk on Park Avenue, for the psychoanalysts jumping out of their windows."

"You'd drive them crazier than I would," she answered.

"Now listen," he said. "For the last time, *please* listen. You haven't listened once so far. You haven't even *tried* to listen, and I've been as patient as can be, with all these incoherent sidetracks and skirmishes, but now I'm asking you in all seriousness, honey, to listen to me. Bobbie angel, be a sweet girl and listen, won't you? I realize my point doesn't make any sense and isn't worth making in the first place, but give me the satisfaction of making it, won't you please? I implore you. I beg you to be a nice sweet girl and try and hear what I'm saying to you. Won't you do that, as a special favor to me? I know it goes against the grain for you to do that, but try and pay attention, won't you, lamb? Instead of being emotional, try and *think* for a moment, just for a little while. Emotion isn't everything, honey, you have to analyze things in this life if you want to get by. Your nature is very emotional and I know you don't like to analyze everything, and that's just what I like about you. Who can stand intellectual women, anyhow? Women aren't meant to be like that."

"Well, who can stand intellectual men?" she asked. Then she added rapidly, "But I'm listening to you."

"All right—I think you are. Now here's one good point. The fact that you *are* emotional, makes it even more important for you to understand, and analyze your emotions. Otherwise, you'll have troubles many other people never have, simply because they aren't sensitive enough to be bothered very much by anything. You'll have real troubles."

All this had absolutely exhausted her. She was so depressed at this moment that she hardly wanted to live. "I have troubles all right," she said. "I agree with you about that." For several minutes, tears had been forming in her eyes. He had been trying not to notice, but a slightly nervous tone had come in his voice—it always drove him wild for her to cry.

"Bobbie, will you stop feeling sorry for yourself?" he asked. "You haven't got any real troubles at all. Self-pity like that is a *typical* neurotic trait—are you crying? What's the matter with you? Are you crying? Look at me!"

"No," she said. "I don't want to."

"You *are* crying—now stop it! Stop it this minute!" He took a deep breath and added in a low tone, "If you don't stop that right now, I'm going to pull out my hair. I'm warning you. Stop it *right* now, understand. Don't you dare cry when I'm trying to talk seriously to you." Her lip was trembling and the tears were about to fall. Suddenly he changed his tack and put his arm around her and said in a nice, gentle voice, "Honey, don't cry. Please don't cry. I can't stand to see you cry, especially when you haven't got a thing in the world to cry *about*." Here she began to weep very unhappily, her head on his shoulder, and he groaned. He kissed her cheek and patted her on the back. Then ten minutes later went out and asked Phil and Sue if they wouldn't come around that night, and try and reason with her. He himself was too entangled, but perhaps they could do better.

Chapter 30

"WELL," SAID PHIL, "you admit the whole idea is unlikely, since there's nothing to back up what you say, except this sort of hunch, or feeling that you have. Therefore, the question becomes—why do you have such a feeling? What purpose does it serve? Let's look at it teleologically for a moment. Did it ever occur to either you or George to wonder about it in terms of a means to an end, rather—"

"That won't work," said George. "You're not using the right approach. She—"

"Shut up," said Phil.

"Be *quiet*, George," said Sue.

"I'm quiet," said George. "But that approach won't work. It has as much future as a snowball in hell."

"Stay out of this," said Sue, "won't you please? You're the irrational one, around here, if you ask me." She looked over at Bobbie and smiled. Bobbie was sitting in the chair, without any expression on her face, but actually indignant beyond words. Sue said, "You don't mind talking about it, do you? I know it isn't any of our business, but George is carrying on so—if only to make him calm down. You don't mind, do you?"

"No," said Bobbie. "But what is there to talk about?"

"That's what I was coming at," said Phil, "when George interrupted me." He looked analytically at Bobbie, his hand on his chin and elbow propped on the arm of the easy chair. "I was saying that I think the key to all of this is pretty simple.

213

If you look at it in terms of a means to an end, rather than in terms of cause and effect, it's simple."

"Of course it's *simple*," said Bobbie. She looked away, annoyed.

"See what I mean?" said George. "Your approach is no good."

"Just a minute, we're making headway," said Phil. "Listen, Bobbie, we don't want to embarrass you or anything. Just like Sue said, we know it isn't any of our business, but we're friends of yours and George, we all live here in the house, and this *is* a serious thing and it could lead to other things even worse. Now look at it the way I suggested. Look at it in terms of a means to an end."

"What are you trying to say?" asked George. "Is she supposed to understand that? I—"

"The agreement was that you'd shut up and let me talk to her," said Phil. "Just sit there and be quiet, I'm trying to get her to see it from a certain point of view." He turned back to Bobbie, his face solemn. "All I want you to do is this. First, you've admitted that your idea is basically irrational. Now the question is why you have this irrational belief. I can suggest *two* answers, and you can either accept them or reject them, as you please. I can't force you to believe anything I say, but I can give you my opinion for whatever it's worth, and at least leave you something to think about. That's all I want to do. Now the *first* answer is in terms of cause and effect." He glanced at George. "This is Freudian psychology. Freudianism is a psychology based on a theory of cause and effect. This answer would go as follows: the pressure of your superego, on your ego, due to the misbehavior of your id, causes you to throw up a defensive screen mechanism and at the same time punish yourself for the bad conduct of your id, by creating in your own mind an irrational belief that you're pregnant, which simultaneously makes you feel that you are really, a quote, good, unquote, girl, because it is a noble thing you do to propagate humanity, and also frightens you and punishes you, because, after all, you're not married and this

214

will lead to the disclosure of your id's wickedness, and further-more childbirth is a frightening thing. That's Freudian psychology, simplified of course. You see, your superego is the repository of your ideals of good conduct, and those ideals have been violated by impulses arising from your id, the instinctive side of your nature, and thus your ego is battered and bruised, and to defend itself it marshals up the battalions of the subconscious, and plants this obsessive idea that you're pregnant, as a pure defense mechanism. It's all very well, a pattern like this, but it's irrational and life tends to punish us sooner or later if we're irrational. One irrational concept tends to breed others, to protect itself, and others in turn, until a maze of conflicting irrational concepts run around helter-skelter in the individual's mind, and when this reaches its final stage, nervous collapse occurs, nervous breakdown. The individual is in a corner and cannot get out, so he or she ceases to function. Understand? All this, in the language of the street, can be expressed in these terms: you got laid, and you're afraid people are going to find out about it and think you're not a good girl, so you develop this obsessive idea to defend yourself. Of course, it's not a real defense, but neurotic reasoning by its very nature is not rational. Now according to Freudian psychology, you can perhaps rid yourself of the obsessive idea by having its mechanism explained to you, but in order to rid yourself of the *need* to develop such mecha-nisms, you'd require depth analysis, to rid you of the conflicts and tensions that underlie it all. I can't possibly do that, naturally. All I can do is show you how the machinery of the thing works, and thus demolish this particular obsessive idea. Of course, as long as the underlying neurotic condition pre-vails, another obsession will crop out somewhere else. It does no permanent good to treat symptoms. Now, why not just admit that you got laid, and liked it, and want to get laid some more, instead of indulging in all this nonsense? I'm deliberately trying to shock you now, Bobbie, and get you mad. What you have to accept is that sex is not sinful. It's simply a biological drive. Understand?"

"Sure," said Bobbie. "An instinct. A monkey could understand that. Thanks for the lecture. Did you talk like that when you were five years old?"

"Not an instinct," said Phil, with a faint smile. "That's a pattern of behavior. Like a bird building a nest. A rigid, formal pattern. Sex is a generalized drive that can take any number of forms of expression. You might not think so, but it can. Some people, for example, are attracted to leather boots. There are men who become dizzy with passion when they see a good-looking pair of leather boots."

"I hope the boots don't mind," said Bobbie.

George cackled with amusement. "They don't," he said. "Furthermore, they don't argue back at you, either."

"Well," said Bobbie, "since I'm such a neurotic, and you just sit there and let Phil tell me how neurotic I am, you obviously agree with him, and now you tell me just because I don't agree myself that I'm crazy, that you'd rather have a pair of leather boots. All right, that's fine with me. Never again as long as I live in this world can you ever touch me, and if you think I don't mean that, you're wrong. If that's the way you feel, don't you ever dare come near me again."

"The threat of withdrawal of love," said Phil. "We're making real headway now. This is getting down to fundamentals, to the basics." He settled back in his chair, a thoughtful frown on his face, cigarette between his lips as he looked over at George. He said, "But now let's take a look at this teleologically, not in Freudian terms, but in *Adlerian* terms."

"I'm not going to look at it in *any* terms!" said Bobbie. "You make me sick, with all your jabbering! You haven't got the sense that God promised a grasshopper." She glared at George. "And *you* make me even sicker."

"See the results we're getting?" said Phil. "We're getting it down to the basics." He said gently to Bobbie, "I know you're mad at me, Bobbie. In fact, right now, you just *hate* me. That's my intention, I meant for you to react like that."

"I've had enough of this," said Bobbie. "All of you think you

216

can bully me, but if this goes on any longer I'm going to leave the room."

"All right, but at least have the courtesy to let me say one more thing," said Phil. "I'm not here for my own amusement. I'm here because George asked me to talk to you, and you can listen for two more minutes, without flying off the handle. None of this is personal. I don't intend it to be personal. Now —do you want to know why you have this idea, from an Adlerian standpoint? This will really shock you. It's obviously completely subconscious—you haven't even dreamed of it, consciously." He smiled at George. "It'll probably surprise George, too." Then Phil paused, and stared into space for a while. At last he said, "This is much simpler. Adler departed from Freud much more radically than most people realize. He looks at things in a very different way. I myself feel he is superficial from a therapeutic point of view, but this entire business tonight is bound to be superficial anyhow, and with Adlerian psychology you can sometimes get remarkable results, and hit the nail right on the head, uncovering things you'd never uncover with Freud. So—what would an Adlerian ask, on learning of this obsession of yours? He'd say, 'Well, what *purpose* does it serve?' You see, they think neurotic behavior is a means to an end. For instance, say a young man doesn't want to get married, he's afraid of the responsibility, or a girl doesn't want to get married, she's afraid of the duties and responsibilities, and afraid to have children, and so forth. So, such a person develops anxiety, heart palpitations. A Freudian would look back in the past and ask, 'What causes this?' But an Adlerian would say, 'Let's look in the present, and see what *purpose* this neurotic behavior serves.' You can see the difference there. You get dramatic insights from Adlerian psychology, and today the Freudians are taking over much of it, without giving credit of course. But anyhow, let's look at your case, with this in view. What's your obsessive idea? Namely, you're pregnant. Now, pregnancy means what? A child. Now, what kind of fellow is George? If a girl was in trouble, a nice girl that he liked, what would you say he'd

217

do? Marry her, wouldn't he? Bobbie, your obsession is just a desire to get married. You love George and want him to marry you and all this idea about having a baby is a subconscious urge on your part to put pressure on him and make him do it. What you're doing, is *hinting* to him to pop the question. Of course, you use the tensions and conflicts of your childhood, to whip up your own very real anxiety, just as we uncovered with the Freudian method, but it all serves the purpose of getting George in a vise and putting pressure on him. That's why he's so upset. Naturally George would be upset. He isn't the marrying type any more than I am, and besides, all this is so stealthy and surreptitious, I suppose it scares him, it's something he can't put his finger on even if he senses that it's there. Now I'm telling you this not to be brutal, but because I think you ought to face it yourself. Remember: I'm not saying these are conscious urges on your part. You've changed a great deal, all of us know that—just since you've been in New York. You were a pretty naive kid when you first came to this house, but you've learned a lot. You've gotten laid and mixed with bright people, you've seen the sights of the big city and combed all that North Carolina hay out of your hair—besides, if you were the conventional, I-wanna-get-mahwid type of moron girl, you'd never have had the curiosity to do such a rash thing as leave Nawth Cahlina, anyhow. This is all subconscious on your part. It relates back to basic insecurities as a child and this is where we'd have to turn to Freudian therapy again, after making our discovery of your motives by the aid of Adler. All you have to do, to get over this idea and calm down and have fun the way you were before, is get it all out in the open, realize that nobody is going to put you in jail just because you go to bed with George, and—what the hell, *laugh* about it all. You know you don't want marriage and children and all that mess, certainly not *yet*. You're only nineteen, live a little bit before you fall into all that. I wouldn't tell you this, unless I was sure of my ground, and sure that what you really want isn't that at all. And one more thing— we *are* your friends, Bobbie, after all—Sue and I and George.

It isn't as if you're surrounded by enemies." He smiled pleasantly, then asked, "Now, is what I've said really so bad, and are you still angry at me and George?"

Bobbie didn't reply. She sat there in silence, just as she had done during the time he was talking. As he talked, she thought of writing her aunt and what she would say, not that she didn't hear every word he said. So, now there was a silence, and it continued. She said nothing. None of them said anything, until finally Sue remarked, "Well . . . I'm sure that must have been *completely* unconscious."

"Of course," said Phil.

George cleared his throat. "Hmmmp," he said. "Hmm-hmmp-pp. Well. Well . . . I, ah, wonder, I don't think that's—"

"Listen, I have an idea," said Sue. "After all, you both are assuming that you're right, but there is a chance Bobbie herself might be right, even if it is unlikely. But why in the world not find out, that's simple enough. I think the main thing is that she's just worried, that's all—it's understandable, anyone might be worried about something like that without necessarily being neurotic and everything. My God, it only costs ten dollars to have a test made. Why didn't you think of that long before? George, take her to a doctor and get a test."

"*Sure*," said George. "That's a *good* idea. Now that's *very* sensible, and I was going to say that myself."

"Listen," said Bobbie. "I've got something to say to George." She stared at him calmly, then said, "I wouldn't marry you if you were the last man alive, and *this* time, I mean it, understand? Now just remember that in the future. Don't ever come asking me to marry you."

He looked at her, then blinked. "All right," he said. "We won't worry about that. I'm not worrying about it. As far as I'm concerned, what Phil said was nonsensical."

"It's what you thought all the time," she answered. "Don't you think I knew what you were thinking? But you just don't know how wrong you are. I'd never marry you, much less try and make you marry me. That's the most ridiculous, conceited idea I ever heard of. Who are you? What person in their right mind would want to marry you? Besides, haven't I listened enough to your theories about marriage, to know how you feel? What do you think I am, dumb?" At this point, she was so angry tears were in her eyes. "Maybe I *was* dumb," she said. "I thought you were different from what you are, at least I thought you had some feelings, but believe me I've learned better, and as for marrying *you*, I'd never in this world consider it, and don't forget that. Later on, don't come pleading with me to marry you, because it won't do you a bit of good. I'd never marry you, George. Never."

"All right!" he said. "I heard you the first time, you don't have to keep repeating it like a goddamned parrot, and I didn't think what Phil said and you know it. It never entered my mind. You're just mad because nobody will take your neurotic carryings-on seriously. *I* don't agree with what Phil said. It's Puritanism pure and simple. That's all it is, Puritanism. The South is full of it, and now it's catching up with you. It's the curse of this entire country, neurotic Puritanism. That's why in Europe they think all the Americans are crazy. Imagine a girl in France or Sweden or Norway acting like this! No wonder they can't understand this country, with that utterly neu*rotic* Puritan business here, there and everywhere, and on top of that, a 'sane' attitude toward marriage. By that I guess you mean a job at the Bankers Trust and a home in West-chester. Don't think that affects *me*. I understand what you're doing. You're just projecting all your neurotic guilt on me, that's all. It would depress me, if it wasn't so goddamn ridiculous. What do you jump on me for, *I* didn't say all that to you, *Phil* did. Why blame *me* and accuse *me* of being conceited? But I'm not going to let you inflict your neurotic resentment on me, we're going to end all this nonsense. Don't think this is going to drag on for days, because it isn't. The first thing in the morning, honey child, you're going to a doctor, and we'll find out the truth."

"We're not going to the doctor," she said. "We don't have to. I've already gone."

"Oh, yes we are!" he said. "You're not going to pull that on
—*what?*"

"I've already gone," she said. "Do you think I thought you'd
ever believe *me?* Oh no. And this just proves what I knew
about you all the time."

George was staring in a blank manner. They all were. A
sudden silence had come over the room. Finally, he said,
"Bobbie, this is no time for humor. Are you kidding? Have
you *really* been to a doctor?"

"*Yes!*" she said angrily. "*Of course* I've been to a doctor,
and I had a test, too! If you still think I'm crazy, then look in
my pocketbook and see what it says on the lab report."

No one said anything. George stared at her. He kept staring,
his face blank, then finally he said in a low voice, "Okay. Why
in the name of God didn't you say so, in the first place?"

"You told me I was neurotic the minute I opened my mouth,"
she answered. "Why should I tell you anything? You flew up
and hit the ceiling and said I was neurotic and mystic and
out of my mind. I couldn't even get a word in, you were so
busy analyzing me and explaining Freud. Why don't you
apply Freud to yourself? Ever since you met me, you've
treated me as if I didn't know anything, but all the knowledge
in this world isn't in books by Freud and Adler."

"Well," said George. "All right. I'm an idiot."

"You certainly are. And that's not all you did. It's none of
Phil's business. What did you bring him in it for? Why did
you go and get Phil and Sue? It's none of their affair. And
why did you sit there and let him say all those things, if you
didn't think they were true? I'm just giving you a dose of your
own medicine, for a change. Why, not only did you let him
say things that made me look like a fool, you let him say
things no man would let another man say about a girl, if he
loved the girl. And don't think I blame *him,* it's nothing to
him, he's got his theories and naturally he wants to show Sue
how smart he is—what does he care how I feel, but it should
have made some difference to you. And don't think I care
what expressions he used, either. It was his tone of voice. He

221

tried his best to make me look like a silly fool, and you sat there and didn't even care. I'll never forgive you for that. Never."

"All right," he said.

"I didn't really mean it that way, Bobbie," said Phil. "So help me."

"Besides," she said, "I wanted to see how long you'd keep this up, about Freud and Adler, and not even once think to ask me if I'd been to a doctor. The only one of you that has any sense at all is Sue. But I'm telling you now, anyhow. I'm going to have a baby, understand? It isn't mystic, and it isn't neurotic. It's a baby."

Silence. "All right," said George.

More silence. Finally, Phil smiled and sat back in his chair, hands folded under his chin. "Well," he said, "score one for North Carolina."

"Hmm," said Sue, "you're not kidding."

George looked sick.

But all this was a hollow satisfaction indeed. She'd known for three days, known beyond all doubt, and hadn't had the nerve to tell him, and when she finally did, this was his reaction. Little wonder she stared at the walls that night and couldn't sleep, her thoughts turning over and over on this and that and everything, as she lay in the bed, and *he* slept on, as if all this could be solved. How could it be solved? She couldn't even make up her mind one way or the other about him, much less about anything else—after all that, such weakness! Not only had she wanted to forgive him, she had cried bitterly and convinced herself all over that he really loved her! She had done the forgiving more than he did, and it seemed to her that she had no strength of character and was helpless and would fool herself all the time, unable to face reality. And yet she *had* to face reality. There was no avoiding it, but what could she do? It seemed to her that there was no possible answer.

Chapter 31

A WOMAN WAS run over by a bus at 57th Street near Sixth Avenue one afternoon a few days later. It was dreadful. The woman was a middle-aged lady who had been shopping on Fifth Avenue. She had a package lying by her that was broken open, showing a wool suit with a Lord & Taylor label, new and in the mud and ignored by everyone. She'd never wear that suit. She had been killed at once. Probably while crossing the street against the lights, the way they all do in New York, and it's a miracle more people aren't killed, with taxis going sixty miles an hour down Park Avenue and the traffic terrible everywhere. This woman was knocked down and the huge tire of the bus passed over her, crushing the life out of her and breaking her back and legs and killing her immediately. It was horrible beyond words. Phil and George almost saw it all—they were in the Automat having coffee and heard the scream of brakes and shouts and noise, and went outside and saw a crowd gathering on the other side of Sixth Avenue, so they went over and saw the woman lying there in the street, legs twisted awry and her dress up, showing pink underpants and a girdle, and blood all over everywhere, unbelievable amounts of blood and the most brilliant red. Both George and Phil came in white-faced and shaken. This accident, coming literally in the very middle of everything, and terrible as it was, bothered George especially. He couldn't eat and looked persecuted and five years older, was pale, worried, frowned all the time, wouldn't let Bobbie out of his sight, kept smoking cigarettes and staring into space. It was right after this that he said that under no circumstances whatever as long as he had breath in his body would he possibly allow her to have an operation. That was out. He'd call the police. Never in this world would she have that operation. It was much too dangerous and inhuman, anyhow. The men that did it were anti-social swindlers and medical misfits out of necessity, charging ridiculous fees and bribing corrupt detectives, and what did they care if some girl died because of their butchery. He had been absolutely out of his mind even to discuss it or as much as mention it, and so on. He talked to Sue and Phil as if they were criminals, with great cursing of Phil, who had found the name of this doctor who did such operations, with help from Sue and Betty, and then after almost having an actual fight with Phil and after calling Sue names, then he'd go over to Bobbie and pet her. With the accident and everything, it at last seemed to dawn on him that they were in a difficult situation. Who knows what he'd thought before, but as late as that morning, he'd been calm enough.

That morning after breakfast he had said, with a sigh, "Well, we'll just have to get married. You're against murder, and I agree with you. We'll get married. There's no problem."

Then at lunchtime he had sat quietly with her, eating his food and looking around absent-mindedly at the people in the Automat and saying little. When he spoke to her, he was super-polite (unlike him) and smiled in an absent-minded way. At the revolving door, he took her arm and helped her in, then crossing the street, he again took her arm. It was not customary for George to do such things. Maybe these were signs of why he had such a fit that afternoon. At the house after lunch he said that he wanted to talk with her seriously, and when they got in the room and sat down, he looked sad for a moment and then said, "Honey, I really want to get married. You don't understand that, but I really do. Let's get married." She didn't reply. "I mean it," he said. "We can't go on like this, and I want to get married anyhow. I need to get married, it'll do me good."

"That's a romantic proposal," she answered.

"I can't be romantic," he said. "I'm not the type, but so help me, I mean it. I want to get married. Let's get married."

"No," she said, "we can't get married. And besides, I don't want to marry you."

"Honey," he said. "Please, don't act like this. You know you really would like to get married. Every girl wants to get married. It's an instinct with women. And besides, you know you love me. You can't hide that, so why tell me lies? You just think *I* don't want to, but you're wrong, I do. I honestly and truly want to. Any mixed feelings I have are no more than any normal man would feel at such a prospect as wedding bells. I love you and I want to marry you, and if everything else I've ever told you is a lie, then that isn't. I mean it from the very bottom of my soul. Now don't keep arguing."

"You're just afraid of what people would say if you left me in the lurch," she said. "You couldn't go up to them and explain that you were drunk when it happened, that's the only thing that's bothering you."

"You know that isn't true," he answered. "For God's sake, isn't there any way I can convince you?"

"You don't want to marry me, any more than I want to marry you. And I'll tell you why I don't want to marry you, George. I don't really love you."

"Yes, you do," he said wearily.

"I don't," she replied. "That's your conceit, George. I don't love you and never have."

"It isn't my conceit. I'm not conceited to the point of utter madness."

"In a way, you are," she said. "You think I love you, but I don't. I'm only attracted to you, that's all, and that isn't love. I thought it was at first myself, but it isn't, it's just something physical, because it's gotten less and less, as time goes by."

"Huh," he said. "The hell it has. You know *that's* a lie."

"Maybe you think otherwise, but *I* know," she said. She sighed. "There was a boy back home that I *did* love—only I didn't understand enough at the time to know how deeply I

225

really loved him, and I had all those ideas from Mrs. Prentice about going to New York, and hearing Toscanini at Carnegie Hall, and seeing the world, getting away from North Carolina and my aunt, having adventure and all that." She sighed ironically, a smile on her face, wistful. "At the time, I simply didn't know what love was. And that boy wanted to marry me. He still does."

"Now, Bobbie, cut out the goddamn nonsense," said George. "This is no time for such idiotic talk. How could you ever marry some Southern yokel? How can you even talk such drivel, at a time like this? You're going to have a *baby*, don't you *realize* that? And it's *my* baby!"

"Oh, George!" she said. "I know it! And that's the tragedy— I don't love you!"

"Listen, goddamn it, you're pregnant," he said. "You're going to have a *child*, don't you understand that?" He reached over and put his knuckles against her stomach. "Why, it'll show in a few more weeks, right *there*. This is no time for theatricals. Do you suppose all this argument and strain is good for either you or the child? You can't keep this up forever, can you?"

"*I'm not* arguing," she said. "You're the one that's arguing. And why are you so concerned about me and the child? The other day you were saying maybe I should have that operation. A lot of good that would do the child's health, or me either."

He blinked, frowning. "I never completely suggested that," he said. "Sue and Phil were the ones so hot for it, not me."

"Well, you said so too, and then you let them do the arguing for you, which is even worse," she answered.

"All right, angel, so I thought of it in a weak moment, under the illusion it might be better for you and me and everyone—"

"Especially the baby," she said.

"Oh, hell," he replied. "But I'm not talking about an abortion *now*. We've given that idea up, since you don't want to do it. Now we're talking about getting married."

"You are, I'm not. And you said why not have the operation. Sure, go on and have it, it's nothing. Have it. Then when you've once had that maybe you can never have any other children. If you live through it. To say nothing of no anesthetic and the fact that it's against the law and costs four hundred dollars. You love me and you want me to go have that operation. What a laugh." She smiled. "You're funny, George," she said. "I'm amused at you."

"Will you stop that goddamn sarcasm? You have no idea how unbecoming it is, from you. Besides, I'm tired of all this nonsense. I've had enough of it. Now listen to me. I'm asking you for the hundredth time to marry me. Will you or won't you? I can't keep on asking you forever."

"Thank goodness for that," she replied. "I can't go on saying no forever, too."

He sighed—"Well! All right! That settles that, at last you're getting some sense in your head. We'll go get blood tests, then go on down to City Hall and take out the license." He rubbed his forehead with the palm of his hand. "*That* is *that*," he said, with a grim smile.

"You misunderstood me, George," she said. "I didn't say I'd marry you. All I said was that I can't go on saying no forever. And I can't. I've got other things to do with my life."

"Well, good God almighty," he said. He stared at her for several seconds, hand on his chin and his eyes narrowed. "Well," he said finally, "I think I understand how you feel— I know what you're thinking, and I agree. All this would hang over everything. It isn't the ideal way to get married, with a shotgun in the background. I realize that, but—"

"I don't *want* to marry you," she said. "It isn't a question of whether it's a good way or a bad way. I don't want to marry you. Can't you get that in your stupid head?"

"Are you halfway serious?" he asked. "You couldn't mean that." He stared at her, thinking, then added, "Honey—what *else*? You won't have an abortion, what else? And as far as an abortion is concerned, you've paid no attention to anything I said on that score. I never said it was a moral thing to have such an operation. Of course, it's something else to call it 'murder,' when you're concerned only with the first, faintest glimmerings of life—you have to get theological to call that murder. I've thought a lot about this. I'd say that it *isn't* moral, in this sense, that the purpose of pregnancy is to have children, and to interfere with any pregnancy is unnatural in every way. Also, there's danger in it, danger to the woman— not much. There isn't much. That's proven by the numbers of women who have the operation and survive it perfectly well. Furthermore, it's a very simple, minor operation that only needs sterile precautions and the operating skill that any professional abortionist has, out of practice and out of necessity. They don't lose patients. They can't afford to. They lose one patient and they're out of business and in the penitentiary. In fact, if a girl feels that she doesn't want to stay hopelessly 'in trouble,' that she's not prepared to have a certain child at a certain time, and if she's early in pregnancy due to some bad luck, and if she has no moral feelings that she's committing a crime, why shouldn't she have an abortion, and why shouldn't she do it with a clear conscience? Is it such a dreadful crime? She can have other children, when she's ready to settle down to diapers and squawling howls at 3 A.M. and baby-sitters and the laundry and all that—why should she throw away her youth, if she doesn't want to? Now you can feel whatever way you like about it, that's your privilege, but is it so *bad* to have an abortion? Just because it's illegal, is it bad? Prohibition was no success, isn't this similar? Most broadminded people think abortions should be legal. Some don't, but most of them do. Imagine some girl *really* up against it, with a man who's run out on her—my God, your own mother! Look at her—would it have been wrong for her to have an abortion? She might very well have died in childbirth partly as a result of her whole situation—maybe not, but she certainly was in a terrible predicament, anyhow, an impossible predicament, a young girl with a baby and no way to take care of it, no money. Think twice about this. And let me say something else. In life, you have to face reality, not avoid it. In life, there's no such thing as the third alternative. This is something everyone has to face, sooner or later. We tend to get in situations all

228

the time, situations that have only *two* alternatives, and both the alternatives are bad. In other words, due to bad luck—"

"Is that it? Bad luck?"

"Listen to me. Just for a minute. You get in such situations, due to bad luck or a mistake—in our case, the reasonable thing to say is bad luck—you get in such a situation—why look at us—bingo! right away, bang! You're pregnant. Just like that! Bang! How often does that happen? Why it's pathetic— the first time you sleep with a man, and right away, you're pregnant. It's ridiculous. How many girls have that happen to them? Do you know that people try for *years* to have children, and can't, and go half-crazy wanting a child? Yet you come along and pop, you're pregnant, and you don't even want to be. Don't tell me that isn't bad luck."

"All right, it's bad luck," she answered.

"Anyhow—to make my point. You get in such a situation, and life had been simple up till then, but suddenly now you find that you have no *good* alternative. You can do one of two things, and both are bad. For instance, if we get married now under these circumstances, it will be bad. Or if you have an abortion, that will be bad. Now, the stupid person in such a situation just throws up their hands and says a curse on both your houses, neither of the things is acceptable or tolerable, therefore, do nothing, just sit. But *that's* no third alternative! There *is* no third alternative! You have to do one or the other of the first two, and the real question you have to decide is— which one of them is the *least* bad? Many people get in all kinds of awful difficulties because they refuse to choose be- tween two evils. That's basic. Look around you and see. You *have* to choose between evils in life. Situations come up all the time when you have to do that, and naturally it takes a pinch of moral courage to force yourself to see it, and much more than that to force yourself you do something you don't want to do. Understand?"

"Yes," she said.

"All right. Now you never would listen to the idea of an abortion, and that's all right with me. I'd never ask you to get one, and in fact—" He stared wearily at her. "In fact, I know how you feel, and I don't even really and truly want you to do it myself. In your case, it just doesn't seem right." He sighed gloomily. "I don't want to see you get anything like that. Not you. The only thing we can do is get married, that's all." He smiled. "And what the hell, that won't be so bad. I'll be sweet to you, honey. And you'll make a nice wife, won't you? I like the idea—why I was going to suggest it, anyhow. Why should we live in this place? We'll get an apartment somewhere and set up house. Can you cook, angel child?"

"Well," she said, "that's a little nicer proposal. But marriage is a stupid institution, George. It's outmoded and doesn't work any more in modern society. And it probably always was artificial. Human nature isn't monogamous. Both men and women like to play around."

"Bobbie, don't be sarcastic with me when I'm really asking you to marry me. Don't you know I mean it?"

"But this is what you said yourself. I'm just quoting you. I learned this when I came here and met bright people, an ignorant little girl. George, nowadays women are equal to men, and that means the normal, uninhibited woman likes to have affairs with many men. She wants to have a good time just like men do. Marriage doesn't—"

"All right, that's enough," said George. "Being pregnant seems to make you mean as hell."

"Oh, I still have a long way to go to catch up with you, George, when it comes to meanness. But let me make my *point*, my all-important *point*. *Listen* to me. Be *reasonable*, George, don't be such a *mystic*. Why, you'll be *neurotic* pretty soon, George, and that gets worse and worse and worse till you collapse, and then we have to bring in *Freud* and *Adler*."

"All right—"

"Will you let me make my *point*? I know it goes against your nature to think, but won't you try, just as a favor to me? George, don't interrupt me! Shut up! Shut your mouth, you ignorant fool, and maybe I can educate you! All right? That's right, just sit there and listen to all my wisdom. Marriage

230

doesn't *work* any more, and the real answer is nursery schools!
Nursery schools, George. Women will have babies by any man
who comes along—oh, they'll get laid, that's what they'll do,
they'll get laid. That's very good for them. It keeps them from
being neurotic, but *of course,* on the other hand, it brings out
their neurosis, too, Freud's already written all about that. But
in any case, there won't be any such thing as fathers any more,
and won't that be good! Old-time marriage will disappear, and
good riddance to it. And romantic love will disappear, too.
Everybody will be indifferent to each other and they'll all get
laid. You see, romantic love causes 90 per cent of the misery
and trouble in this world, it prevents people from living normally and getting laid all the time, by strangers they meet in
the subway and anyone else they get a yen for. Why suppress
an instinct, anyhow, that's bad, even Freud says so, but he
also says you have to, which is so brilliant it's amazing. But
with romantic love gone, people will have a healthy attitude
toward normal sex and getting laid and liking it, then we won't
have vulgar movies and cheesecake, because people would
be above the need of constant titillation. And also prostitutes
would disappear."

"You can be a real little viper," he said. "To think, that you
could suddenly become such a little viper. It doesn't suit you
in the least. I could throw up, to listen to you distorting everything you ever heard, just because you're angry at me right
now. What the hell, do you *want* prostitutes? I wasn't talking
about *real* love, and I never said people should get laid in the
subway, or there shouldn't be any fathers. Phil was telling you
about some ideas of planned nursery schools to free women,
a wonderful idea, and you distort the hell out of it. And I never
talked to you that way, either. You know I've always respected
your intelligence. There *were* and *are* some things you never
heard of, but I'm not patronizing you when I say that. I've
never patronized you and you know it. Good God, how could
I, when ever since the first day I met you, it's been one damned
crisis after the other, with me getting a beating out of every
one of them. Why, you could drive a man to drink. You're the

most outlandish little brown-eyed viper I ever heard of. Bobbie, you're as unreasonable as the day is long. You're practically impossible! Little did I know, what I was getting into, when I got involved with you."

"You're not involved with *me* at all," she replied. "I'll go off and have the baby in an alley somewhere and throw it in a garbage can, then come back and live with you if you're around. Or if not, I'll find somebody else. Everything is casual. When you try and make things too serious, you take the life out of it, and nobody likes to get laid any more." She smiled. "You're not involved, George."

The argument continued on and on the same way. It made her sick but she kept it on. On and on, as she was trying to make up her mind what she would do. And thinking of something dreadful. In the midst of hopelessness, such plans are formed and death covers the scene like a cloak, falling in darkness over everything and turning love to hate. The end of life, though the body and the mind go on. Cruelty, meanness and pain that leads to nothing and has no purpose except itself—not just these arguments, they were only a reflection of the plan that was in her mind, the plan that didn't come completely in her thoughts until she got that answer from her aunt, and even then, not until she had another argument worse than any before, with George. In such a mood and with such a view of things, all one can say is that death conquers all. All struggles are doomed to failure, no matter how one tries. There is no point in anything and life itself has no meaning whatever, the universe is an endless and pointless reaction between molecules and atoms in a tremendous nothingness. Such was life behind the illusions people had to create to support their animal instinct to survive. It was all pointless. Death and extinction were around the corner for everyone, and that was all.

Chapter 32

"ALL RIGHT!" HE yelled. "You think I'm going to just let you sit there and look at me like that and not say a damned word? What the hell do you think you are, a statue of the Lord God Buddha in a female version?!! I'll swear before all the Holy Toad Frogs of East Ethiopia that you beat anything I ever heard of since I was born into this treacherous swamp of a world without even being asked if I wanted to get the hell out of limbo—you're unreasonable to the nth degree, I'm not joking with you the least damn bit! Not a bit! And furthermore it isn't just temperament or personality, it's a sinister hidden streak in you that's disguised by that little girly look, a streak of sheer stubborn fiendishness, the most incredible bitchiness, meanness and hostility. You don't like men. You're against the male sex, it's like cats and dogs to you, and God pity the poor pathetic wretches in this world who just like me won't be able to see beyond that surface of innocence, who'll look at you and not know that beneath the pretty little girl there lives a goddamned maelstrom of whirling, moiled neuroses of every stripe. You don't like men any better than you would a horned toad crawling in the bed with you, and it enrages you profoundly because fifty million years of patient evolution of the race make your body disagree with your judgment—every moment you spent in bed with me you're going to take out of my hide. Thank God you don't have me on a rack, or you'd pull me limb from limb. I know I'm talking irrationally and I'll keep on talking irrationally because everything I say is true in the deepest sense. You're really a cruel little girl, that's the only explanation for the completely insane way you're acting. You sit there and think to yourself that the reason you won't marry me when I've practically begged you on my hands and knees, is because *I* don't *really* love you and don't *really* want to marry you, but that isn't the reason at all, the reason is that you don't really want to get married yourself. You're such a hostile little mixed-up insane bitch that you're incapable of it. I don't mean to curse you, exactly, but you infuriate me beyond endurance."

"Cursing is nothing," said Bobbie. "What about that girl you slapped that time?"

"What girl?" asked George thoughtfully.

"That one out in California."

"California?" He scratched his head. "I never slapped any girl in California. In fact, I never slapped any girl. They slap me, I don't slap them."

"That girl in that motel," she said.

"What motel? Motel? It must have been some story I just told you in passing. I never slapped any girl in any motel."

"You said she cursed you and tried to make you give her the address of this boy you were with, and then she spit on you and pushed you, so you slapped her and almost knocked her down, then she behaved."

"Oh, Christ, what an improbable tale. I never slapped any woman, not that I wouldn't love it and cherish the memory ever after. I must have been drunk when I told you that. You know I didn't really mean you were a little bitch, honey, a minute ago. I just said that because you drive me to desperation. Will you marry me, honey?"

"No."

"Oh, God! Listen! Do you read in the papers about these guys blowing their top and shooting women with shotguns and all that? Why do they do it? Because the women act like you. Now what do you want me to do, go crazy? What are you trying to do? If you don't marry me, I'm going to throw you in the East River and jump in after you. You've *got* to marry me. I'll drag you down to City Hall bodily if necessary. Do you want *that*? Won't *any*thing convince you? The truth is, you don't *want* to be convinced. *Nothing* would convince you. You have an *idée fixe* on this point, you're obsessed with this idea and what can I do? The reason, and there's always a reason, is that deep inside you *loathe* the male sex, and don't want to get married. What you want is to be mistreated by a man, so you can bolster up your dislike of men. You're putting me in the position of betraying you, forcing me to do you wrong, so you can say to yourself, 'Men are no good, look at what that louse did to me. They're all like that.' That way, you can avoid responsibility all your life. It'll be a pattern of you giving one man the business for what the last guy did to you, then another guy giving you the business so you'll have the usual excuse to take it out on the next one, and none of them will become a real relationship because that's what you don't want in the first place. Don't you understand this? Bobbie, let the better side of your nature come out. Don't be so eternally and unreasonably stubborn. We're going to get married and you know it and why in the hell not go ahead and do it? Now this is too much. I insist, and if you say no one more time, I'll blow my top and strangle you. Will you marry me?"

"No," she said.

"All right, I'll strangle you. This is the end. I'm going to strangle you and then jump out of the window."

"I think that's a good idea," said Bobbie. "Why don't you?"

"I am," said George. "In just a minute, as soon as I get the energy."

"Go ahead. It would solve everything."

He got up from the chair and went to the divan where she was and sat down on the floor on the rug, and sighed and put his head and arms on her knees. "After a while," he said.

So, time went by, with him sitting there on the floor, his arms and head on her lap. The seconds passed on in silence. Almost three days of this type of thing had gone on, ever since the afternoon the woman was killed by the bus over on 57th Street. Now he was even worse than she was, if anything. He was talking in his sleep, pale and nervous, smoked all the time and

235

carried on constantly. Also, he hadn't eaten anything whatever since that accident, and was living on coffee and cigarettes and now and then a bowl of soup, because food gagged him, he couldn't eat with her acting like that. Much of it was put on, no doubt, to make her do what he wanted, or thought he wanted. In fact, practically all of it was put on, he didn't fool her. However, that accident had horrified him. Now he said in a low voice, "I wonder how that woman got run over. Maybe it was psychological. She might have subconsciously meant to get run over. Some accidents are like that, but then maybe this was just an accident. Did you ever see anything horrible like that?"

"I saw a lineman electrocuted on a telephone pole once," she answered. "He touched the wrong wire and was killed."

"You saw that?"

"Yes. Me and some children were playing in a lot near there, and we watched him climb the pole, then he was working with a big wrench and the next thing he was covered with blue flames and sparks. He turned red and couldn't move or make a sound and by the time they got him down, he was dead. They couldn't revive him, but the fire department and police cars came and they tried for about an hour. He was dead. He was a middle-aged man with a wife and a lot of children, the oldest one in the second year in high school. All he had was twenty-five hundred dollars' worth of insurance."

"Insurance," said George. "There's no security in this world, insurance in this world is impossible no matter if it's for five hundred thousand. This life is so hopelessly insecure you might as well be dead and get it over with. Let's jump out of the window." She didn't reply. He lay there a long time, then finally sat up and looked at her, his face now serious. For several seconds, he stared in her eyes, and now for the first time, he really and truly looked worried. He said, "Listen, honey, I've got something to say to you. Will you listen to me? I want you to listen, because I'm going to be very honest with you. Understand?"

"All right," she said.

236

"Bobbie, you've *got* to understand the way I feel. I'm sure you've got yourself mixed up, because of things I've said before, and it's my own fault. A lot of times I don't mean the things I say, but I'll tell you honestly and truly how I feel about marriage. Honey, I've felt for a long time, that marriage and all that, was not for me, that there's something almost sordid about it. I've seen so many miserable marriages—my own parents for instance. They've stuck together, but God almighty what a hell of a struggle. And not just them, but uncles and aunts of mine, the same goddamn thing. And in these days it's even worse. You jump on me for saying marriage is an outmoded institution, but look at the goddamned miserable, wretched marriages around on all sides, people tied up together in a Gordian knot, bored to death with each other, hating each other—it practically never works, just look around and see for yourself. That's the way I've felt about it. You know that, because I've told you. My attitude has been that people ought to be more sensible than to get married. It takes the fun out of life to tie yourself up to some person like that. It's not a natural thing—at least this is the way I've felt about it all along, but so help me God I've changed my mind. I think the truth is, there are some good marriages, even if they aren't always ecstatic, and frankly running around after a lot of women isn't any good. You never get to know any of them so it's a bore. I mean all of this. And besides, there's another point. If there're going to be children, you have to have marriage or something like it, and you can't have nursery schools and no fathers, because that's too mechanical and furthermore children need a male image, that is, a man to identify with for the boy, and a man to get an idea of the male world, for the girl. Besides that, every girl is brought up to look on marriage as her *goal*, and as a result it's hard for her to see it otherwise. Now, I've changed my point of view radically, in the last few days. It isn't just that there's no other choice in this situation. I *want* to get married, so *let's* do. I'll take on the responsibility. I'll get a job and all of that, if it takes years off my life. And I'll be nice to you always, I'll always love you, and furthermore, I'll be nice to the baby. I won't beat it. I'll be nice to it, I'll jiggle it and crawl around under the bed with it. I swear all this on my word of honor and I hope God strikes me dead if every word of it isn't the truth. The only difference is that all this predicament has made me come around to this point of view sooner than I would have otherwise. It was practically on my mind already, so help me God, and in another month or two it would have been certain to happen. Now honey, that's the truth. Will you marry me?"

She said nothing.

"Don't be foolish, Bobbie," he said. "I want more than anything to get married."

"I believe you, George," she said. "I really think you do. I admit I didn't think so, but I think you really would like to marry me. What you say and everything sounds very honest and I believe you mean it, but the truth is, I really don't want to marry you. I know you don't believe it, but it's the truth. You can't believe it, because your vanity would be too hurt, to think that a girl you wanted, doesn't want you. But you've got to face that sooner or later. I'm not trying to make you prove anything to me. I simply don't love you and don't want to marry you, and that's all there is to it."

"Please, honey," he said. "Don't talk like that. I'm asking you on bended knee to marry me."

"No," she said. "I told you a thousand times already. It wouldn't matter *how* you asked me, can't you understand that? I simply don't want to marry you."

"Do you really mean that?" he asked. "Are you crazy? Are you going to keep saying no like that forever? This can't go on. You've got to stop it. It doesn't make any sense. *Let's* get married. We'll go to Connecticut right now and get married this afternoon."

"No! No! No!" she said. "How many times do I have to tell you? You're dumb, George, you're dumb as an ox. I wish to goodness you'd shut up and leave me alone, if all you can do is call me names and talk like a crazy person and ask me again and again and again to do something that's impossible and that I don't want to do, anyhow."

"Impossible? *Why* is it impossible?"

"It just is," she said wearily.

"The only thing that's impossible is *you*," he said. "You're just so ultra-super-sensitive that you won't believe anything I say. You have determined the way you think it is, and nothing will convince you otherwise."

Then she said what she'd been meaning to say to him for several days. Now she said it, and in a very calm voice. "Listen, George," she said. "There's something I've got to tell you. I wasn't going to, but I think you really do feel the way you say, and therefore I owe it to you. What I have to tell you is this. I'm going away in a little while. I don't know where, because I'm not sure what I ought to do, but I still have almost five hundred dollars and I can go where I please and do what I want. I think I'm going back home, but maybe I'll go to Chicago, or Boston or somewhere like that, far away. You won't know where it is, or anything else, and it'll probably be neither of those cities. I still have to make up my mind and I will in the next week. But I've already made up my mind about one thing, and that's you. This is the end. I'll be here at least another week while I decide where I'm going, but I'm through with you, George. I don't ever want you to come in the room again, and I'm not going in your room any more. I mean I don't want anything at all to do with you any more, and if you think I'm just saying that, you'll find out otherwise. The truth, whether you believe it or not, and I don't care *what* you believe, is that I don't love you any more. All this has ruined any feeling for you that I ever had. In fact, I guess I never really loved you in the first place, and it's obvious you never loved me, until now that you realize you're losing me. I'm sorry for you because of that—if you'd loved me before maybe I'd have felt different myself, but right now we might as well be honest. George, it's going to hurt your vanity very bad, you think you're attractive to girls and may be so to some girls, but not to me, not any more. I hate to say this. But you absolutely revolt me physically. *That's* why I can't *marry* you. How can you be married to a man you can't stand to touch

239

you? The last few times you've touched me, it's been all I could do not to shudder. I'm really sorry to say this, but if I don't you'll just keep on forever with that insane business of my marrying you. Since I've gotten to know you better, my old feelings about you have simply changed, that's all, and I can't endure such things as kissing you, not now. The very idea makes me feel nauseated. With me, all that is impossible just by itself. I have to love a person, it's just the way I am, and since I've been so repelled by you physically, I've come to realize that I simply don't love you. God knows that's true. You come and put your hand on my knee, and I can hardly stand it, then all this silly, crazy talk about me really loving you and not admitting it, because of some other wild theory of yours—don't you realize that all this talk just makes me dislike you as a *person*? Don't you realize how vain and conceited it is to keep insisting I love you, when God knows I don't have any feeling like that for you at all?"

He stared at her in silence, then scratched his head and looked down wearily at the floor. He sighed, and looked up at her. "Well, you don't feel that way about me," he said.

She shrugged and looked out the window. There was silence as he stared up at her. Finally in a low voice he said, "Bobbie . . . you're lying. You don't feel that way. You couldn't. There wouldn't be any solid ground in the whole world, if you did." Another long silence. Then he stood up from the floor, hands on hips, still staring at her. She continued to look out the window, and didn't move when he sat down by her on the sofa. "Bobbie," he said, in a low voice, "honey, don't make us both miserable. It isn't like you think." She said nothing, and then he said, "If you don't care about yourself, don't make *me* unhappy. I love you." Then, he put his hand on her shoulder. She didn't say anything, so after a while he took it away. But a little later he put his arm around her.

"Will you please leave me alone?" she said.

"Aw, honey, for God's sake—"

She turned and put her hands on his chest and shoved him, hard. "Get away from me!" she said.

240

Chapter 33

DEAR AUNT:

I have tried many times to start this letter, which will be an awful shock to you, but the only thing I can say is the blunt truth. Maybe in a way you won't be surprised, because you always predicted it. I can hardly bring myself to say it, but the very thing I never dreamed in my life would ever happen to me of all people has happened. Yes, Auntie, almost like fate itself—I am going to have a baby and am not married, exactly and identically the same thing has happened to me, that happened to my mother. The only explanation is that it simply must have been in her nature and in mine as well, and even much worse in me, because I was always sure that would never happen to me, and I wouldn't make her mistake and think some man loved me only later to be deserted. You know I never did any least thing back home, but just let me say a word, and all those people who were supposed to love me and wish me well and who said, "Isn't it nice, a girl with such a sad background, doing so well at school and being such a nice girl, you'd never think she had such a background"—all those people, if I so much as said a word, they'd shake their head and say, "The apple don't fall far from the tree." Well, they're right, to my surprise—the apple doesn't, maybe it can't. All the very worst has happened, the very worst thing in the world, for me. As for the boy, the father, he is here and everything, but he refuses to marry me. I don't love him and actually detest him now completely, but I thought I should marry him because after all he is the father of the child. However, he won't marry me. He has made the most lukewarm proposals, as you can imagine, saying in a sullen way, "All *right*, I'll marry you," and so on like that. If it came right down to it, he wouldn't.

Auntie, I am sorry to shock you like this. I know how you must feel to read this letter—it must seem like a nightmare to you. But believe me, I feel worse. There was an accident here the other day, a woman killed on the street, run over by a bus and killed at once, and I felt as if it was me, that's how my mind works these days. I never knew life could be like this. I don't want to sound self-pitying because I realize all of this is only what I deserve for having been such a fool as to think it could turn out any differently—I must have been completely out of my mind, looking back I can't even begin to understand how it could possibly have happened. But I am paying for it now and will continue to. There's no describing the minutes and the hours of the day—I would think that anyone feeling like this, would not even be able to breathe. It's the most dreadful torture to eat, I must force myself and it takes all my will power and even then I can hardly eat anything, yet I have to. And sleep is impossible, but so much for all this. I have no sympathy for myself really. If I hadn't known any better it would be different, but as it is I simply asked for it.

Now, Auntie, since I found out for sure what the situation was, I have been racking my brain to try and decide what to do. I have thought about it constantly night and day, and have decided what I am going to do—I hope I have decided, because it's the only thing, and I'm writing you to tell you and let you know. What I'm going to do is leave here, since I still have most of my money. I'll go to some strange town and get a job till I can't work any more, then I'll stay in a boarding house and wait till I go to the hospital, and then have the baby. The money will be enough to make this possible, but I will probably die when the baby is born, I am afraid. Maybe I won't—don't worry about it, I'll go to a good hospital and of course in this day and age very few women die in childbirth. The chances are 100 to 1 that I will be perfectly all right. This doctor I have seen says I am ideal to have children, so it's undoubtedly just my imagination that I won't live through it. I almost certainly will. But naturally there's a chance that I won't—that's true of any woman having a child, it still is the valley of the shadow of death for a woman to have a child, even in modern times in the best of hospitals. So, all I want to do, is anticipate the possibility that something might go wrong, as it did in my mother's case. If all goes well, then most of the rest of this letter will not apply at all. But in case it should happen, I want to make some provision about the baby, I even have to do that, because of the circumstances and everything. I don't really think I will "probably die" or any such thing, that's silly—you understand I am under a nervous strain now and such things slip out. So remember that in reading all the rest of this, and remember that all of this is written just on the chance that something does go wrong, unlikely though that is.

What I will do, if everything is all right, is send you a letter at once and let you know. However, otherwise, here is what my plan is. I will leave at the hospital a letter saying for them to hold the baby *for three weeks*. Now Auntie, you are too old to take on any new baby, if it should turn out that anything happens to me. I don't want you to have the baby, because of yourself and because of the baby as well. If you try and go and claim that baby, I will curse you forever, but I know you won't, you will realize it isn't right. I wouldn't send you this letter unless I was sure you would understand— I know you are a wonderful person but it wouldn't be right for you to try and take a newborn baby, and besides my plan is something else.

Of course, none of this applies if I am all right. If everything goes well as it very probably will, I'll get a job and keep the baby with me, then decide what to do and whether or not to tell the father, or how to tell him, and so on. I can take care of all that, but if anything should by any chance happen to me, it will be up to you. You're the only person I can turn to, about this. I have to turn to you, because he will come to you. But what I have planned is this. I'm going to leave them a note, saying they should hold the baby there in the hospital, with the money I have on deposit, and they are not to let *anybody* have that baby except the father. Now, if the father comes and asks for the baby, they can give it to him, and I will also leave a letter for him, if he comes for the baby. Otherwise, if he doesn't come, they are to burn my letter and resign the baby into the hands of God, and let some couple without any children have it.

This is the way it will be, Auntie. I will disappear, and this boy won't know where I am, or what has become of me. He expects me to try and leave, but I have it all figured out how I can fool him completely and just when he thinks I would never leave him, I will go. There will be no way for him to find out where I am, because nobody will know where I am. However, he knows my home town and your name. If he comes down there, Auntie, and he will, then what you must do is this. Read very carefully. I am trusting you with my very soul, and remember I love you. Please do what I say to the last word. If you don't, it will be on your conscience forever. I know you'll do what I ask, and I say this only to convince you it is important. Auntie, you must do what I say. Now, if he comes down home looking for me, this is what you say, and it's very important.

Tell him, you heard from me some time ago. But you burned the letter. Above all else, do not tell him anything, but what I say to tell him. I know him, and you must do exactly what I ask—don't say anything except this. Tell him you heard from me, and burned the letter because you were so indignant. Tell him I said I was going to have a child and I was leaving to go to some charity place and have it, but I didn't say where or in what city. Tell him I would have stayed with him, but he had gotten to be such a bore and annoyed me so much, I couldn't endure him any more, and besides, I didn't want to be burdened with a child, I'm too young and don't want such

244

cares, I want to live and enjoy life and I'm going away to have the child then I'll give it to an orphan home when it's born. Tell him I said the child would interfere with my getting married, that that's the reason I don't want to keep it. Now he'll ask you in a rage what I said about him, he'll question you very close, but you be sure and tell him only what I said. That he was such a boring person (use the word boring) that I reached the point where I couldn't endure him another minute. The last thing he thinks he is is boring, so tell him that, I want him to know just what I think of him. Besides, he got me in trouble and I resent him for that; he practically ruined my life. He really is a very unpleasant boy and I never would be able to endure marrying him, he's so fantastically ugly and homely and doesn't bathe and has B.O., is an ill-tempered, slouchy person, and childish, disgusting, mean, tiresome, and unpleasant in all his mannerisms, expressions and general appearance. Also, he's thoroughly neurotic. You tell him all of this, memorize it if necessary—especially tell him that he ruined my life.

Now, he'll have to leave, because there won't be any point in his doing anything else. *You must not show him this letter.* As soon as you have read this letter, *burn it.* You *must* do that. If he ever saw this letter, I would never forgive you, *never.* Absolutely *never.* No matter what, *burn this letter.* Don't leave it around, *burn it.* Do that *as soon as you have read it.* I am trusting you, Auntie.

Now, if you do it the way I say, he'll assume I am back in New York somewhere, maybe, and he'll leave. Maybe he will look around and try and find me, but he won't be able to. However, before the baby is born, he might come back down home again still looking for me. I doubt that, but he might. If so, tell him the same thing. And now the point is this. By the time the baby is born, seven months will have passed. That is a long time. And here is the most important part. He will know, after seven months, that the baby must be born, and if at that time he comes back again, then you are to give him another letter that I will send you later. This is after seven months, and after you have heard from me that the baby is born, or heard from the hospital—all this is assuming of course that something has happened to me, you understand that. This is if things turn out as I fear. I'll send you this letter to give him, but don't open it, it will be for him. If he never comes after the seven months, then burn the letter. I'll tell you what the letter will say—it will merely tell him I hate him for all he has done. But maybe he won't believe the letter and will ask you, "What *else* did she say?" This is assuming he comes at all after the seven months. You must be able to judge what is in his mind. If he just curses and is angry, tell him nothing, and above all else, do not tell him anything has happened to me, not unless he says he doesn't believe the letter. If he still says that after seven months, and *insists* that you tell him the truth, then perhaps despite the fact that I don't love him, perhaps his feelings for me are really true after all, indeed they would be true, so then you tell him where his baby is because he would want his own child. He can then go to the hospital and get the baby and also a letter from me. Now Auntie, this is assuming the worst, that you get a letter mailed by the hospital. It has to be this way, because otherwise it would just be the baby of some girl he once knew, and far better for it to be adopted by strange people, yet if he does love the mother he would love the child. Auntie, do all this right, if you knew how unhappy I am, you'd do everything I say. I am trusting you to do it even if you don't think it's right, but believe me, it is right. If there were any other way, I would do it, but there isn't. There's no other alternative. Just hope I have the courage to do this.

I wish you knew how sorry I am to write you this letter. Not because of your being shown to be right about me, but because of what I know it will do to you to get such a letter. Let me say that you were always an angel to me, both you and Uncle when he was alive. I didn't understand before what I do now. I never knew what life is really like, and now feel completely different about everything. I know now that only some things matter in life, and other things mean nothing at all. I realize

246

how all this must seem to you, it's just what you predicted. All I can say in my defense is that this came about because of a mistake in my ideas—not because I was being wanton, yet I know you must think I was just immoral and so on. You were really right in a way, in saying that a person must live according to his or her own conscience, which must come from God and not from their own ideas, because once you do that, you always deceive yourself about what is right and wrong.

I have come to feel that little did I appreciate all you did for me, though I wasn't your child and came from a background different from all your ideals. You were sweet so many times throughout all your troubles, and now I realize it. Even Uncle James, though he died before I could understand him— Auntie, I wish he was here so I could tell him, but if there is a heaven and he is there, I know he forgives me for the mean, hateful things I thought about him as a child, merely because he did his duty as he saw it. Uncle James was not a bad man, and he always was convinced he did what was right, whether he did or not—in his own mind, he thought it was right, and I would send him my love if he were still alive. Auntie dear, I ask your forgiveness and ask you to do me the last favor of what I say in this letter—that's all I ask, I know I can't come back home or anything like that, but please do me this one favor and I'll always love you. I know you will, and know you'll forgive me too, as you always have.

Yours with love,
B.

October 22

My dear Barbara:

I received your letter and have thought about it throughout most of this day, and now I rise from a sick bed, in weakness of the body but in resolution of the spirit, to write you as best I can. First, it is not up to me to forgive you, that is in the province of the Lord; but I have only pity for you in my heart. Second, it is written in the temple of the Lord, "Thou shalt not sin." My child, who came to me and brought light and love

247

to my home and cheered me on the dark path of life, do you not know of all people that hell is the reward of those who ignore God's word? Let us pray, "Oh, Lord, in thy tender mercy, behold a girl fallen, into the pit of corruption a little flower has been cast. But Lord, let her hang her head in shame, for Oh Lord, she has sinned and is dishonored, her name and memory ruined for those who loved her and wished her well, she has fallen and must suffer, as her poor tired aunt who loved her must suffer, her sick tired old aunt, who adopted her from an unknown past to save her little body and soul from sinful adultery and drunkenness, to give her a home and a respectable place in life, an education, opportunity, culture, and Thy Word. Her old aunt has said to her 'Thou shalt not sin.' Oh Lord, forgive this child but do not withhold thy divine punishment. Let her soul grow in wisdom from her expiation. Praises to the Lord, amen."

I must be severe as the occasion demands. Let me therefore say that I expected this out of you, Barbara. Your mother was crazy and your father died drunk in a jail, and as the slut goes to the street, so goes the daughter of the slut. It is written in the Bible that so pass the sinners of this world, in an unstately and tragic procession. The foul and dreadful letter you wrote fills my soul with horror for your fate. Barbara my dear, hell beckons like a yawning, fiery pit, for those who are subjugated by the power of the passions of the flesh. A terrible and eternal pit of fire and flame eager to receive in eternity not you but your immortal soul! My daughter, for you are my daughter in the spirit, absolve yourself from this dreadful youth who has captured your soul in his meshes. Renounce the passion of the flesh, which so eats at the very fabric of your God-given soul.

I say to you, Barbara my dear, you must renounce this man! Leave his door! You are sinning, sinning all the time, day by day, constantly sinning in the most dreadful way a woman can sin, for you sin wilfully, and dreadfully with your own body of your own free will—*how* can you write me such a letter? *How* can you live such a life? *How* can you with the upbringing I have given you, lie like the Babylon whore in the arms of this corrupted youth and in that hour lose your soul? How can you *do* it, Barbara? I cannot conceive how you could ever have done such a thing, and can only conclude that this wretched youth who spurns your love, must have a dreadful power over you, a cunning design to trap and ensnare your affections. I *ask* you, do you not *know* that every touch of his hand, though it leaves no mark on your pitiful body, must soil, blacken and corrupt forever your soul? I beseech you, forego such weakness! You, with your upbringing, can conquer the unfortunate inheritance of your parents! You need be no sinful girl, lying in sensuality in a hypocritical youth's embrace, a wretch who obviously has no respect for you yourself or the word of God or the law of man! I implore you! If he won't marry you, give him up, don't waste your love on him and ruin your soul!

You are out of your mind to write me such a letter as this, and I can't even answer it, every page is equally and utterly dreadful. I loved you and took you in my home, but even as a little child you cast aspersions on the word of God, and questioned His Love. For that, you must now suffer. Your dearly beloved Uncle James—would that he had been sterner with you—spare the rod and spoil the child—yet you behave as if dear Uncle James corrected you out of cruelty or meanness of spirit, a deed the poor man was quite incapable of. And now you have the atheistic audacity to question not only the existence of Heaven, but whether or not Uncle James is there —he is there, good and decent man that he was, never fear, and of course he forgives you. What you do not realize and never realized, was that Uncle James, though an elderly man when you came to live with us, loved you very much. In your long and terrible illness, often he wept because of your suffering, that a child should lie in helplessness near death, and any moneys he had he would give readily, and did give. You do him a great injustice. Short-tempered, severe, yes, but he loved you and simply was not the man to show his feelings, even to me. Would that he had been even sterner with you. Would that he had, for then your soul might have been saved!

Why, you could have stayed down here and married Dr. Gleason's boy, but you said he bored you, a nice boy like that. Bored you! What ideas Julia Prentice put in your head! That woman! That wretch! That thief, to turn my child against me and fill her innocent head with ideas of New York and luxury! Didn't I predict it? But *now* who do you turn to, Julia or me? You turn to me, because in your heart you know I am the one who really loves you and has your best interests at heart. Why, Barbara I am overcome to think what an error I made, ever to allow you to leave, to even give you money for the purpose! It is a sin on my soul, and God forgive me! I knew not what I was doing. You could have stayed here and married Jimmy, or if not him, someone else, and been an honest, good woman and the mother of fine Christian children, but alas, you now will meet an altogether different fate, which God in His wisdom has seen fit to bestow. Ah Barbara, my dear, sow the wind, and reap the whirlwind, the reward of sin is death. Continue to sin, and death is your mete. Darling, the passions of the flesh have overcome you and turned your mind from sanity to insanity. You write me like a hypocrite, entirely out of your natural character, and speak of my virtues, but they are virtues you never had the gratitude or the kindness to appreciate or the spirit to understand, not till now, when it's too late and your soul is lost! Or will be, if you continue to err! You say I am right, but when it is too late, too late! You speak of my patience with you in all your strange and changing moods, of my effort all in vain to counsel you and give you spiritual guidance, yet not a month ago you sent me a postcard of dreadful tormented statues that had no meaning, as if I have no appreciation of culture. Modern art indeed! Barbara, you pride yourself on your interest in art, literature, music and the opera, but please recall that you acquired your tastes in my home. Our home was and is a cultured one. I appreciate, as did Uncle James, the true world of art as found in the days of Greece and Rome. There is no art in the modern era, and you need not lecture me and send me postcards of twisted railroad ties as a sample of art.

What you have really forgotten is that God comes first, there is no art without God. But yet you seem also to forget all your harsh words to me when you departed from my house on your mad, doomed flight to the most sinful and corrupted city in the entire world, the Babylon of false and lying tongues, New York City, where every day is Golgotha and the nighttime a revelry of sin and waste. If you had to go, you could have gone to Charlotte or Atlanta, but no you had to go to New York, a Northern metropolis and a sinful city as the entire country knows. Little wonder at what has happened, though it could have happened to you anywhere, even in Charlotte. Do you think these old eyes have not seen the way you have always stared and smiled at little boys, pimple-faced boys? Do you think I cannot recognize the dawning in a child of beginning passions that later will rend the soul of the grown woman if unchecked? Do you think I did not see and warn, and see and warn again, and see and warn again? I remember when you were fourteen—fifteen—sixteen—and each year it was worse. More stares at little boys, surreptitious stares, then shy smiles, flirtation and on and on. Barbara, if a girl is born man-crazy and cannot be decent, she at least can turn to God and pray, because He and His wisdom understands all and forgives all—and I implore you now, to turn to God. Take Jesus in your heart and accept Him, and whatever happens your soul is saved.

I must end this letter. I cannot write more. I've been very sick and things haven't gone well. The bank is always tardy with the pension checks and Mr. Johnson is always rude, a smart young man, and besides that poor Timothy has been sick, she is getting old, I am not the only one who feels the hand of time. Also, Taffy has had a set of puppies, seven all told, and I have been busy cleaning them up, brushing them, and thus and so. There is much detail of this type I could write you, but am too weary and it wouldn't be suitable here in any case. Now Barbara, I have spoken to Mr. Alfred at the bank, and he has arranged to make me a cash loan of six hundred and fifty dollars on the west lot on the Pierce property.

This will enable me financially to make the proper arrangements for your care, when you come home. Of course you will come. Why darling, I love you as my own child, and naturally you will come—what else can you do, in your unfortunate situation? As terrible as all this is, my heart warms at the thought of having you back again . . . I have been lonely, very lonely and sick as well, and need you just as now you need me. Naomi is a constant spirit, she will be in delight to hear you are returning, and of course the Negro thinks less of such things as all this. She won't blame you, and neither do I. You always were the sweetest child despite everything, and I send you my love as always. Come on back home and you can have the baby here and we will keep it a complete secret. We will make a lovely home for it and if anyone finds out, we won't care what *any*one says, because if all the sin in the world were known there would be few who would not hang their heads in shame, for the flesh is weak on this earth, and only the love of God is strong.

Always with love,
Aunt Louise

October 23rd

DEAR SUE:

Explain to George that there's no point in his looking for me, if you can. By the time you read this, I'll be far away from New York City, farther away than any of you can imagine. And I'll never return.

Yes, you were right to say that he loves me. I didn't think so, either, but the way he's acted the last couple of days makes me agree with you. And that's why I have to go away. The truth of the matter is, this mess is even worse than anyone thought. At first, I didn't want to marry him because I had no intention of marrying a man who didn't want it himself and didn't love me—such a marriage would be hell on earth, to live with someone under such conditions. He knew this, too, and you know how he tried to convince me it wasn't that way. Throughout all that, I thought I loved him, and I couldn't convince him that I didn't any more than he could convince me—naturally I couldn't convince him, because I didn't believe it myself. No matter what I said, he wouldn't believe it.

However, I decided that I *had* to make him believe it. And I partly succeeded in that, by not letting him get near me, and you know how he reacted to that. This is all such a dreadful, impossible mess I hate to even think about it much less write you this letter, but I think I owe it to George to leave some explanation behind, and since I can't bring myself to write him, I have to write you.

I think perhaps you all were more right than you realized, in describing me as "neurotic." If that means you don't know your own mind, I certainly am neurotic all right. God knows I don't understand it myself. Maybe some day I will. But I'll tell you just exactly what has happened in the last few days, and maybe since you're a girl you'll understand it and can explain it to him. I can't myself—it puzzles me more than anyone. But this is what has happened.

You know yesterday afternoon the argument George and I had, with him acting so crazy and wild as if he was out of his mind. Well, he convinced me that he loved me, that was the result of it all. So I thought—well, thank God at last it's all solved! The nagging worry in the back of my mind, I refused to think about. It was just a feeling, as if something was wrong but I didn't know what it was. I thought everything was solved, and you know this morning I went and got the blood tests with him, took out the license, and all that. But the truth is this. Last night in the room with him, though I didn't admit it to myself, I knew that *I didn't really love him.* After all this, what a finish to everything, for him to try and convince *me*, and me thinking I was lying to him, when actually all the time I didn't love him at all. I guess I am simply crazy, or maybe it's just that he's the first man I ever knew—you might understand it, but try and tell him, anyhow. I'm horribly depressed about him but what can I do? I simply don't love him and this time it's no lie to spare him from marrying someone he doesn't want to marry!

Because here is the final thing that makes it completely clear to me what my real feelings are. Sue, I never was pregnant at all! The test said so, but it was wrong! I'm not absolutely sure about that as yet, but almost 100 per cent and I'm seeing the doctor again this afternoon for another check-up, then I'll really know. But the test must have been wrong. I asked the doctor about it before, whether the test could be mistaken, and he said very rarely, it was correct 97 per cent of the time. You see, right now I am due to have my period, rather yesterday, and I assumed I wouldn't, but this morning it seemed as if I was, and now there isn't any doubt. The doctor told me before that women sometimes have the first period, but almost never the second. All of this hullabaloo has been about nothing. I'm not pregnant at all, and this afternoon I'll know for sure. I'm going to see the doctor and get another test, which takes forty-eight hours, then I'll phone him when he gets the answer. But something tells me that all this has simply been the craziest tempest in a teapot. You have no idea how exhausted I am, and how relieved. There'll still be some uncertainty for another two days, but believe me I am like a different person!

Also, this turn of events has made it completely clear to me how I feel about George. I couldn't admit to myself last night that I didn't actually love him—it was too ridiculous and crazy, after all the scenes and troubles. For me to not love him, after all that, was just too much. Besides, I still thought I was in trouble and subconsciously I'm sure I must have been afraid to face the real truth, then also there was the child to consider. But now there's no reason for *me* to fool *myself* any more. And thank God for that. You can imagine what a terrible marriage it would have been, with him loving me and me not loving him. That would have been poetic justice indeed. You have no idea what a horrible sensation it gives me, to think how close I came to that actually happening. But at times like this, everything becomes completely confused—when you're worried and afraid, you simply don't know your own mind, and *I* certainly didn't. This is the most amazing and bewildering experience I have *ever* had. I had no idea that life could be so complicated and utterly confusing. Little wonder that people go crazy and lose their sense completely—when you get in such complicated situations where your mind turns around and around, and you don't know what to do, or what you think, how you feel—God knows, anything can happen, then.

But I have been lucky indeed, and actually, so has George. I know he'll feel bad, but it's fortunate for him that fate has given this twist to all our difficulties. So, rather than stay around, and—what in the WORLD could I say to him now? You can understand how I feel. Maybe I'm a coward not to tell him to his face, but I simply can't do it, it's too much. The only thing I can do is simply leave and go away. It's best for all of us, better for George and better for me. He'll be hurt but I think he'll get over it—George has a kind heart underneath for all his mannerisms, and he'll forget me and find some other girl. I think all this was good for him, in a way, though God knows what he himself will think. He'll get some other girl, and find happiness some time, I'm sure. He has my very best regards, in any case, but it's best for he and I never to see each other again.

I hope you and Phil continue to get along so well, and it was wonderful knowing you both. Thanks for everything, and

Best love,
Bobbie

P.S.:
I'm only taking a small suitcase of necessary things. Please have railway express send my trunk home. My aunt's address is on it. Thanks *very* much—you can understand how it isn't possible for me to take the trunk myself now, having to slip out this way.

One other word. Tell George he can't possibly find me. I'm not even going to be in New York, and it would be utterly impossible for him to ever find me. I'm not saying where I'm going, but for a long time, no one will know where I am, not even my aunt. I realize this is all very melodramatic, but I simply can't face George after all this, I haven't got the nerve. Besides, though I'm reasonably sure I don't love him, my emotions are still so confused because of all this trouble that I have to get away. I want to be by myself for a long time. Around him, I can't think. He still upsets me terribly. What I really want to do is get completely away from him for a long time, at least for six months or more likely a whole year, and see other men and put him out of my thoughts. I think he should do the same. It's too bad in a way that our relationship was ruined by all this, but troubles some time have a good result, by forcing the truth and making people be realistic. Tell George that my feelings about him *are* mixed, and I *am* terribly sorry to run away like this. I'll send him a postcard or something some day, perhaps, but he should just forget me and put me entirely out of his mind and find another girl. Well—so, I guess that is really all . . . it has been quite an experience, all of this. I never thought I'd get in such a mess the minute I arrive in New York! But at least it's all over now. I'll send you a postcard and let you know for sure how that second test comes out.

Love,
B.

October 25th

DEAR SUE:

Right!!! Everything is fine. It was just like I said, but I went to another doctor under another name—you can imagine why. I'm leaving New York now, and good-bye and thanks for everything.

Love,
Bobbie

Chapter 34

AND SO IT was that Bobbie decided to have the operation and kill the baby. The real reasons were that she was afraid to go away by herself and have it, afraid to go to some town and have the baby all alone and perhaps die like her mother. So, a fine end to her resolves, and little wonder things turned out as they did. It doesn't take mysticism to understand that. The shadow of death is blacker than midnight when hope is gone, because in it there are no stars and the dawn never comes.

That was the reason, she was afraid, and also there was George. But why should she try to do the impossible? She couldn't go away like that, she had thought of it but she didn't have the courage, and besides, this was the more sensible solution. With things as they were, she couldn't marry him. It was impossible, she couldn't do it, not that she hadn't thought about it until it almost drove her crazy. Something deep inside told her that she couldn't. But even Sue, who was always critical of George, asked her why she didn't go ahead and marry him. "I'm sure he loves you," said Sue. "I know he does. You don't have to worry about that. You know how I've always felt about George, I never believed he was serious about anything and I even warned you against him, but my God, I have never seen anyone so crushed. You've got him half-believing you don't like him, and look at him. Why even I'm sorry for him. He looks like he's lost his only friend. I think you're silly not to marry him. You seem to know just how to handle him, why not marry him? Why not? The only thing wrong with George is that he just never applied himself. Bobbie, I honestly think you're just being too sensitive."

Sue meant well and believed what she said, but she wasn't in the situation and there were things she never had thought about. If she had been the one, and her future was in it, and she had been through it all and knew what it was to be suddenly deserted and have those you love leave you, maybe she would have felt different and not have given such pleasant advice. Maybe he did love her, but Sue didn't understand his good side any better than she did his bad side, she wasn't involved with him. Naturally she would shift from seeing all his faults to seeing all the better side, because she'd never understood him in the first place. Perhaps he did love her, but let him get free of it all and out of any obligation, then let six months pass, and if he loved her he'd still feel the same way, then they could get married and have a chance of happiness. Otherwise, he would always think deep inside that she had been very sly to trick him into marrying her, as if she'd *meant* to get pregnant that first night and trap him even though he was against marriage, whereas she had never even dreamed of any such thing.

Thus she thought, and she was sure she was right. So, on with the story, there're only a couple of more chapters to this book, it is coming to its conclusion. And the story has been truthful so far, so it might as well be truthful to the end, including everything that happened and all the things she was thinking, no matter how depressing any of it is.

The doctor that Bobbie went to see on October 24th, the one that Phil and Sue had located through friends of Betty's, can be called Dr. Charles Groats, though that isn't his real name. The first time she saw him, sitting behind his desk with huge fingers touching at their tips as he stared across the room at her, a fat man like a graying banker and not like a doctor at all, but with something blank in his eyes, and a flat line for a mouth, with babyish dimples in his cheeks and a deep cleft in his chin, like a fat, balding, middle-aged Cary Grant but much shorter and with a big nose and tiny blue

258

eyes—the minute she saw that man, her heart sank. She felt like turning and walking out of there as fast as possible.

This Dr. Groats, to look at him realistically, was a fat, angry-expressioned man with a diamond ring on his finger and a flower in his coat. He really looked nothing at all like Cary Grant, except that he had a cleft in his chin. His work in life was to destroy unborn babies. He did that for a living and had no other practice, he did only that. His office was in Manhattan, a nice place somewhere between 36th Street and 57th, and Madison Avenue and Third Avenue, in other words, right in mid-town, a nice office very well-furnished, very proper and everything, with his name on the door and out on the front of the building in brass, like any other doctor. The only thing was that he did nothing except operate on pregnant women night and day. All the operations were illegal and his price was very high. The same operation if done legally under an anesthetic in a hospital, costs seventy-five dollars and the price of a hospital room for a day, less than a hundred dollars. He charged five hundred and kept his patients there after the operation for around three-quarters of an hour, on a cot in the anteroom, then whether they could walk or not, or even stand on their feet, out they had to go, because by then another woman or girl exhausted and covered with sweat and blood and half-fainting had to take her place—that was the way it worked, like an assembly line. Terrible, but true. How many women go through it? Enough so that it doesn't matter? Betty herself had done it, not in New York but in Chicago, Illinois. However, a friend of hers had gone to this same man, the fat doctor in New York, and it was exactly the same as it had been in Chicago, the same "routine," the same "instructions," the same attempt to get more money, the same browbeating, the same type of hard-boiled nurse, the same dismal little room with a cot afterwards. And Sue also had done it. How many others? And how many more in the future? Of course there are things that are worse in life than this, and merely saying it's bad isn't saying that it should be legal, or illegal either, though if done legally there certainly is little comparison as far as the girl is concerned, but so much for all that. In any event, her heart sank, the minute she laid eyes on this man.

That was in the interview. The doctor, when she finally got to see him, was a fat man with a gray mustache and eyes in which there was no trace of any feeling, just a flat stare, bored and peeved-looking. He talked with a New York accent, pronouncing his words in a nasal way, and said "anywheres" instead of "anywhere," and so on. Such as, "Can't you get any more cash anywheres?"

He didn't look in the least like a doctor, but he was a doctor, and obviously was a good one. He had gone to school in America and Europe as well, according to the diplomas on his wall, and had an enormous case of shelves full of medical books that must have cost a fortune. Why he wanted those was a mystery. Probably for camouflage, but if it was true he gave money to the vice squad detectives as George said, then why have camouflage? And he certainly didn't need medical text books to check on anything he didn't remember from medical school, because this single operation was all he ever did. And he didn't look as if he could do an operation—he had very large hands, with huge fingers and matted black hair over the top of his hands and on the joints of his fingers and up all over his wrists, white skin showing through. He was of medium or short height, and getting slightly bald. His clothes were very expensive, and the furniture in his office was also expensive, with wall-to-wall carpeting, oil paintings, modernistic lamps and many magazines. No one would have dreamed he did nothing but this operation, and that he did five, six seven or even more every day, often on into the night. The money he made must have been fantastic. He agreed to charge her only three hundred dollars, which was all she had except for about sixty-six dollars that she had to keep, and at that she had to cry to persuade him, because his usual fee was five hundred, he said, and it didn't pay him to take any less, he was doing an illegal operation and could go to jail at any time.

If the way he acted with her was any indication, he usually

got the five hundred. As far as she was concerned, it was a miracle he agreed on the three hundred, the way he reacted. And he certainly wouldn't have taken any less even if she'd gone right out and committed suicide. As it was, she cried and told him she would have to do that, if he wouldn't help her, because she had nowhere to go and couldn't go back to her family, because though they were nice people they would be absolutely impossible about a thing like this, and if he wouldn't help her and lower his price just once, she'd have no choice except to kill herself, because life for her would be impossible. He listened with a stony eye. No doubt it was old stuff to him, to hear girls talk like that, about killing themselves and so on. He even said, "That won't get you nowheres, dear." It would get her in the river, that's where it would get her, but little did he care. He asked her to go and get her boyfriend to give her some more dough, but she said the man was a lieutenant in the Royal Air Force of Great Britain, and she hardly knew him, it had all been an accident and she had thought she loved him, but he suddenly left her after telling her he was stationed here for a year, and now, he was over in England and she couldn't get any money from him, she didn't even know his address. All this with tears and sobbing, but did it affect that man? No, he just looked at her with a stony eye, and obviously was only thinking whether or not she really couldn't get any more money.

So, weeping and crying and hoping to God she could convince the cruel money-mad fiend, she asked him please to help her, wouldn't he lower the price just this time? She told him she would always be grateful if he would, because under the circumstances she just couldn't have the baby, it would ruin her life. It was a wonder he didn't ask her to sleep with him, but he probably judged she would prefer death, and besides he was only interested in money, this man.

He said, "All right, dear, but can't you raise four hundred, at least? I can't help you for three hundred. I never have taken that low a fee in all my medical practice. This is an illegal thing you're asking me to do, you realize that, don't you? I'm sorry you're in trouble, dear, but you should have been more careful, it isn't *my* fault. And I can't help you for three hundred. Can't you get any more cash anywheres? I don't even see how I could do it for four hundred. But that's a sad story you tell me and I'd like to help you out. I'm sorry for girls in your fix or I wouldn't do the operation at all. I'd just stick to my reggalah practice. You'll have to raise another hundred."

"I can't!!" said Bobbie.

"Sorry. You'll have to."

"Oh, Dr. Groats! I can't! Please!" said Bobbie. She was weeping pitifully, but he just looked at her.

"You know you can raise another hundred, dear. What's a hundred bucks? That's not much to get you out of your fix."

"I can't get it!" she said desperately. "I can't! I don't know anybody that would give it to me!"

"Well, you'll have to find it somewhere, dear, and that's my last word. I couldn't touch the case for three hundred. I have my expenses to consider, my nurse and office and everything. Besides, this is an illegal thing that you're asking me to do. Now I've come down a hundred dollars, I'm meeting you halfway and I can't do a cent better than that and that's final. You'll just have to raise another hundred if you want me to risk my neck and help you out. Go see if you can borrow another hundred from your friends, and when you get it come back and see me and I'll try and help you, but now I'm a busy man and I'll have to ask you to—"

"Oh, doctor!" she said. "Don't you want to help humanity?! I can't get any more money, I swear I can't—please help me!" She was half-afraid he wouldn't, though she could tell from the look in his eyes he was just after money and probably would, if he was sure she couldn't get any more. Lucky for her she didn't let him fool her, not that it makes much difference about that.

"I wouldn't be a doctor if I didn't want to help humanity," he said. "But you'll have to raise that other hundred if you want me to risk my license and a jail sentence on your account.

Go out and hustle up that money and then come back, and I'll get you out of trouble. See another boy-friend, ask him to help you—you know some other fellows than just that English lieutenant, don't you?"

"No!" she said. "I just got in New York!"

"Well, I guess you're no New Yorker at that. Where're you from, dear, Georgia or Mississippi?"

This was the only time he sounded even halfway human, and not much then. She said, "I'm from North Carolina."

"North Carolina," he answered. "Well, wire down there for money."

She said she couldn't, it was completely impossible and her parents would rush up here and put him in jail or at the very least drag her back home, and they could never know about it and never would. On and on and on it went. He said again for her to borrow it from another boy-friend, she knew she had more boy-friends, and she said there wasn't any boy-friend but the English lieutenant who was gone over to England and hadn't even written her or anything. And the doctor said— well, his usual patients were married women for whom a pregnancy was physically undesirable, he didn't like to do such operations anyhow, and though he himself was not a Catholic, sometimes he really thought those Catholics had some grounds to be against it, especially for those who didn't really need it, and she was a healthy-looking girl. Was she sure she really wanted the operation? "Oh, yes!" she said. So finally he sighed and looked at her a long time and said, "Well, I guess I'm a sap, but I'll help you out." "Oh, thank you!" she said.

It wasn't her tears that made him agree, but his belief she had no more money and couldn't get any more. He was a cruel man and a hypocrite. God knows, if she had had any more money there wouldn't have been any argument, but if she handed over to him the other sixty-five dollars where would she have been? She had to have something to live on till she could get a job. Already she'd spent almost fifteen dollars, for food and a week's rent in advance for the room she'd taken, to say nothing of the fact that she had almost no clothes and couldn't get the rest of her things for who knows how long. And this man, trying his best to get another hundred dollars out of her, and even hinting for her to make it fifty more, as if two zeros make one, when she'd already told him she couldn't get another cent anywhere. Think of the money this man made. He probably got more than three hundred dollars from most patients, the average must have been much higher, but even saying he got only three hundred, and had only five patients a day, that was fifteen hundred dollars a day, seven thousand five hundred dollars a week, and three hundred and seventy-five thousand dollars a year, with two weeks off for a vacation. And he was doing his utmost to squeeze fifty or a hundred dollars more out of a girl in trouble. What a man—how does he live with himself? But imagine the money he must have made, even if he took long vacations, had to pay detectives off, and didn't work all the time—he must have made at least half of that, which is a hundred and eighty-seven thousand and five hundred dollars. No wonder he had expensive clothes and a diamond ring and a huge black Cadillac no doubt, and blonde mistresses, with oil paintings on the walls, but such things must be empty indeed and it's no surprise he would think he hasn't got enough money and must torment some poor girl into giving him more, his own life is empty and meaningless and he must feel he is poor indeed. And yet who would judge him, it was true he could go to the penitentiary, and other doctors must look down on him as if he was vermin, not that he isn't vermin. The worst thing about him was being such an utter hypocrite. But so much for him, his place in this book is only incidental and no doubt he is merely typical of doctors who would rather do this and make a lot of money, than try and run a real practice.

"Your appointment is on Friday evening at eight-thirty," he said, now completely bored. "You should pay half the fee now, but since you don't have that much with you, give the nurse fifty. I hope you understand that I'm doing you a special favor, taking all this time with you and accepting a fee much below my regular fee. If you ever send any friend of yours to me, just tell them they needn't come if they haven't got my regular fee [Betty's friend had paid $375], which is a minimum of five hundred dollars. I won't bother with them and the only reason I'm helping you is because you're from North Carolina. Understand? Now, the nurse will tell you what to do. She'll give you your instructions. Do what she says, and show up here Friday evening at eight-thirty. Furthermore, don't tell those parents of yours a thing, I don't want them arriving here and causing me trouble."

"Oh, *no*," she said.

"All right. The nurse will tell you what to do."

What the nurse told her was: "Don't drink any liquor or anything, understand? If you come in here with liquor on your breath, the doctor won't touch you. Not a drop. You don't need liquor, it isn't painful, and we give you a pill anyhow. Don't eat lunch, I can't have you throwing up all over me and doctor, you just eat a roll and some tea or something, or—wait, you're down for evening, so eat a light lunch that day but just take tea and toast for supper. Understand? And one more thing, if you have a chance, an hour before you come take an enema, and have you got a razor? You shave under your arms don't you, dearie?"

"Yes," said Bobbie.

"All right, shave down there too, dearie, and wash with soap and hot water, and you needn't blush or look as if it's the end of the world, it'll grow back, dearie, don't worry, but if you haven't got time to do any of these things, if you have a job or something, don't bother, we'll do it here, but it'd save time if you did. The *main* thing is not to eat anything except tea and toast or something like that, and above all else don't come in here tight. And don't take any aspirins or Anacins or anything like that—we give you something to dull your pain, and don't you dare take anything of that kind, or the doctor won't touch you. Now, do you understand and remember everything I've said?"

"Yes," she answered, in a weak voice.

"All right, dearie, now one other thing. Don't be late. Be

here at eight-thirty sharp or you won't be taken. In fact, you'd better be here by eight, just to be on the safe side. We have a schedule around here and the doctor can allow only so much time for each patient."

"All right," she said.

"One more point," said the nurse. "Bring the other two hundred and fifty dollars, in cash. No checks. Cash. This is payable in advance and don't try and come in here with a cent less, or the doctor won't as much as touch you. He'll kick you right out of here, understand?"

"Yes."

"All right, dearie, now cheer up and don't worry, everything will be hunky-dory, the doctor is a wonderful surgeon and your worries are as good as over."

So then there were two days while she waited, alone in that room, almost never going out for fear of accidentally running into George or Phil or Sue or Betty or someone. The room was tiny even though expensive, and she couldn't sleep there. At night she sat in the chair by the lamp, shivering with cold though it was still early fall and warm weather, sitting there and thinking and thinking and thinking, in the depths of misery. Life was dark to her then. The hours she spent in that room were the most unhappy of her life, and she was living only to go and keep that appointment and get it over with, then she wouldn't care any more. What was George thinking? What was going on over at 58th Street? Were they looking for her? Sue and Phil would believe it, but what about George? Wouldn't he be almost out of his mind? She had sent the postcard to Sue on Thursday, and it would arrive there on Friday morning, the day of the appointment. Then they'd think she had left New York, probably to go back to North Carolina. All this had her in constant tears, and now she thought of the times George had been nice and sweet, and she would weep dreadfully because it was all so tragic—but maybe in a minute he would find out where she was, and come and knock on the door and everything would be all right. Though he couldn't possibly know where she was, the least footstep of other roomers in the hall set her heart to pounding—maybe that was him and he'd found out where she was! But no, the footsteps always disappeared on down the hall.

So, now the scene is a cafeteria on Lexington Avenue near 54th Street. The time has almost come. It is Friday and twenty minutes till eight. She should leave now, and in fact had left the room in order to take a cab to the doctor's, but she has had nothing to eat all day and has decided she has to eat a little.

So, fifty minutes, and then . . . but actually less than that. It was twenty of eight and the nurse had told her to be there at eight which meant she had to take a taxi in only five or ten minutes. But she had decided eight-fifteen would be soon enough. She couldn't stand to sit more than fifteen minutes in that waiting room knowing that any minute the nurse might come out and call her—she would get there at eight-twenty, that would be enough time. Such was her state of nerves, waiting for the final hour to come. Little else had been on her mind for two days, this appointment, and now it was practically there and she couldn't believe it, it all seemed so unreal, as if it were happening to someone else, not her. However, it was her fate all right, not someone else's, and she had a few minutes, maybe fifteen or twenty minutes at the most, and that was all, then a taxi, and the doctor's office.

And there she was, sitting and having tea and toast in Bickford's cafeteria, calmly putting lemon in the tea and glancing around idly at the scene as if there were nothing wrong and she was going to meet a girl-friend or go to a movie. No one would have suspected, to look at her. In the last day, from nervousness and worry in her opinion, she had gotten a rash almost like chicken pox, felt feverish, and had a terrible headache, but that didn't show in her face and she looked normal enough. Anyone glancing at her would probably have thought she looked a little pale and tired, but not worried or especially bothered about anything. Actually, in those last minutes, her thoughts were racing around and around in terrible turmoil, as for the last time she went over the whole thing and once more thought through this decision she had made. As she ate the toast and drank the tea, outwardly calm, she thought about the whole decision once more, knowing it was her very last chance. For the last time, she convinced herself it was right. It *was* the right thing, that went through her mind over and over. It was the sensible solution to a dilemma that couldn't possibly be solved in any other way. How could she go off by herself, and even if she could, was it right to bring a child into the world under such conditions? Suppose her fears about dying like her mother *were* only a "complex," suppose she went away and had it without any trouble, what then? Could she keep it away from George, its father? Wouldn't things be really just the same? Suppose she went away as she had planned to do when she wrote her aunt, and had the baby all right, and then suppose he proved he wanted her and the baby too, what then? And on this, Sue was right—how could you "prove" such things anyhow? Don't you simply *know* such things, one way or the other? If he came after the baby was born and married her then, wouldn't it be almost the same as now, and worse than that, suppose he didn't, suppose it turned out that it *was* just his conscience bothering him now and he didn't want her or the baby really—how would *that* be? How could she bring a baby into the world to such a life? This is what she was really convinced of, that he might love her but didn't want to get married and stuck with a wife and a child, and inside would hate her and turn against her and the marriage would be utter misery, but as long as there was a chance of that, she'd never marry him in the first place, so the result would be that she would have the baby all by herself, and how could she take care of it and give it a home, and what kind of life would that baby have?

Look at her own experience, with no father and looked down on by people, even though she was a pretty girl and was liked by everyone. They all knew she had no father, such things are never a secret, and it affected everything they said or did. How could she stay in her own home town, when the boy who wanted to marry her (though she hardly as much as looked at him) was always apologizing to everyone in subtle ways about her background, pointing out how "nice" her aunt was, how nice *she* was herself, and so on, naturally assuming that a poor girl like her with such a past would be ecstatic with gratitude to marry *him*, from a nice family and everything. All the boys in that town would have acted exactly the same way and felt the same. And all of them waiting, including the old ladies, just waiting around to see when the bad heredity would come out, because everybody knows the apple don't fall far from the tree. Oh, yes! Everybody knows about that apple—as if human beings were fruit, or her mother was anything but unfortunate in the first place. But that was the way it was. No matter how well they thought of her, it was always there, and how could she herself even *dream* of bringing another child into the world under the same identical conditions? It would be completely unfair to the child. She had no right to have that baby, none at all. Of course such an operation was wrong, but George had been correct when he said that in some situations there are only two alternatives, and both are bad.

The real thing that was wrong was her ever getting into this situation in the first place, that was the sin, and the way she'd fooled herself was by not thinking, the way people always do. If she'd only stopped to wonder what she would do if this happened, maybe she would have known better. But her thoughts hadn't been on the consequences, she didn't even dream of the consequences, and so she had gotten into an impossible mess.

But so much for all that, once in the mess there was no use lamenting or thinking what else one could have done, the question now was how to get out of it. And it was all very well to think nobly of going away and having the baby, and being too good of soul to have any illegal operation, but was it fear to have the operation that made her write to her aunt, or real nobleness and the desire not to kill the baby? It was fear. She knew the baby was just a tiny thing hardly even the least bit alive and a million miles from being a real child, and what was the difference between stopping it from being born now and going to the Margaret Sanger institution, except that it had started to live? There was no point in being ridiculous. Besides, even if it was killing it, that was the correct thing to do, under the circumstances. It was a sin that she would simply have to take on her conscience and bear on her shoulders. She could have other children this way, but if she went off alone and miserably unhappy to some strange town where she didn't know anybody and all of them knowing at a glance what the story was, and she had that baby by herself in some strange hospital, she'd never survive it, and that was no complex, it was the truth, she'd die having that baby.

But to think like that made her wonder if she was getting the operation because she was afraid of the other—but oh no, she decided against that interpretation, it wasn't that she was afraid to go away, it was because she had no right to have the child, she'd already analyzed that again and again. She also wondered, maybe he loved her and she was making a mistake, but then she would answer in her mind—no, even if he does it would hang over them both and ruin their lives, he hadn't wanted to get married before. Back and forth, back and forth, thinking and thinking as time went by and only minutes remain, but the thoughts go faster and faster until everything is chaos and confusion. Such is the torment a person's mind can give them, when they're afraid to face the thing they are most frightened of in life.

All this and much more was on her mind that evening as she delayed those last few minutes. And besides that, now that the hour had come, she was terrified. The thought of that doctor frightened her so she could hardly sit in the chair and hold her cup of tea. She was so scared the cafeteria was a technicolor blur of light and color and sound, and now it was really late, these were indeed the very last minutes, or even seconds—the clock on the wall said three till eight, and when it got to eight she had to leave and take the cab. In three minutes—but it still seemed unreal, as if she had talked to that doctor a million years ago or just dreamed she talked to him—all the details she arranged, leaving the house on 58th Street, finding the other room, lying in bed at night unable to sleep, seeing the

270

doctor, all of it was like a dream—getting her money from the bank, being afraid of seeing George or one of them on the street, talking to that nurse, and the hours and hours at night in the new room by herself, then the fat doctor, arguing with her and she putting on a scene with him . . . none of it was real, it was all like a nightmare. Except that she wouldn't wake up from it, she was in it, the nightmare was life.

The truth is, she was in a state of such nervousness and tiredness that she couldn't even think clearly. Her forehead was hot as if she had high fever, yet the palms of her hands were wet with perspiration. She was very afraid. The reader might think she is a coward, but she *was* a coward, she had never had any courage and everything frightened her, she couldn't help it, she just had no toughness, and always wilted. The only thing she could do when faced with such things was cry like a child, it was too much for her, she just didn't have as much courage and nerve as other people. And what was about to happen was by far the most frightening thing that ever had happened to her, she didn't even dare think about it, much less remember the things Sue told her about how unbearable and gruesome the operation was. When she thought of that, terrified tears would come in her eyes and she would tremble, her hands would actually shake she was so afraid, and the thought would come in her mind that she couldn't go and couldn't do it.

At the same time, she was determined to do it and knew that she would. In another minute, she would go, she knew that. The way she had made up her mind was by deciding she would do it, even if she died or fainted or whatever else. Other girls had done it, and she could do it, too. She wasn't an utter coward, and even if she was, nevertheless she would do it, regardless of whether she was scared or not. How could she ever have a baby, if she was so afraid of something like this? Certainly this wasn't as bad as having a baby. There were many things in life worse than this, and she had to face it and go through it, that was all. God knows that after all that had happened, all the terrible scenes and misery and the endless

271

struggle to decide what was right, it would be pathetic now for her to weaken because of a few minutes of pain. She *had* to have courage, and that was all there was to it.

So she was thinking in those last minutes. Any reader who is a girl and has ever had the same experience, would know exactly what this was like. But the fact is, even those who are afraid have no other choice, because the alternative is worse. For all her letter to her aunt, she was terrified at the very idea of going away by herself like that, and even when she wrote it she had known she never could do that. Never. And besides, it was sensible and the right thing to have the operation, anyhow, just as she had analyzed it so many times. Of course it would take more courage to go off and have the baby, but that didn't mean it was *right* to do so. It would be exactly the worst thing she could do, for herself, for George, and for the baby too, and that was the truth. She *had* to have the operation, and therefore, she would.

Bobbie sighed and looked at the clock. It was seventeen minutes past eight. Her tea had gotten cold. She wet her lips and took her purse in her hand, glanced around the cafeteria, and stood up. There was no delaying another second. She left and got a taxi and gave the doctor's address, and got there at eight twenty-nine. On the sidewalk she looked at those brownstone steps and his name in brass, and she couldn't go up those steps. It was impossible. She wasn't afraid, she just couldn't move in that direction. But there was another minute left. She would walk up to the corner and then come back, and go up the steps and ring the bell. Tears came in her eyes as she walked toward the corner.

Chapter 35

PHIL SAID, "LISTEN, George, there comes a time when you reach a point of utter absurdity. That's the stage just before you really crack up, and blow your top. Now I'm warning you. Calm down. You're acting like a child. What the hell, be realistic. Both of us have tried to make you look at this business rationally and you refuse, but let me tell you something else—"

"I don't want you to tell me anything else," said George. "You don't know what the hell you're talking about. You don't know her, and you don't understand her, and everything you say about her is just as crazy as that goddamned analysis you made of her—that's what caused all this in the first place, that goddamnable analysis of yours."

"That's not fair, George," said Sue. "It wasn't just Phil, it was your whole attitude, and you know it. Don't make a scapegoat out of him."

"Right," said Phil. "And what I said wasn't so far wrong anyhow. I could have been basically correct, even though she'd already gone to a doctor and had had a test and thought she was pregnant. My analysis of her still stands. Everything I said to her was fundamentally correct; that's why she took it so hard. It hurt. I should have been easier on her and she was dead right to point out it was none of my business, but on the other hand I had the impression both of you wanted to talk about it. Are you listening to me?"

"No," said George. "I'm trying to think. I can't listen to you and think at the same time."

"Well, I've got something to say to you, and I want you to listen whether you want to hear it or not."

"Why don't you both go on and leave me alone and let me concentrate?" asked George. "Neither one of you understands Bobbie and all your jabbering does is confuse me. My God! She's probably off right now on the verge of suicide and you tell me to relax. Oh, God almighty why did I ever let her get out of this house? What was the matter with me? Was I insane? Where was my mind? Ohhhh, Lord."

"I'm going to shock you out of this right now," said Phil. "For Christ's sake, look at you. All this is is wounded vanity and childish insecurity. You're having a goddamned tantrum, George, just like a child. Why don't you lie down on the floor and kick your arms and legs? That's all this is, refusing to eat or shave or change your clothes; you're acting like a child. She's not going off committing suicide. That's ridiculous and you know it. First of all, she has no reason, and second, she's not the type. Now what the hell, George. You've known the girl for a couple of months, three months at the most, actually less than that. She's a nice little girl with a pretty smile, and a cute way about her—there's something very sweet about her, but good God, you're acting as if it's the first girl you ever knew. Get a grip on yourself. Bobbie's not the only girl in the world—you've got to be more independent about women than that. It never fails. Whenever a man gets sentimental and schmaltzy about a girl, she kicks him in the teeth. That's part of the answer to all this. She had some grounds for being angry at you, for browbeating her, but what the hell, she didn't play fair—she sat there like a clam and didn't say a word, when she should have told us she'd seen a doctor. How were we supposed to know? The way she presented the thing it was completely irrational. Were we supposed to divine the truth like mind-readers or something? I knew at the time you shouldn't have humbled yourself to her like that, even if it looked like you were in the wrong. She didn't play fair at all, and what you should have done was look her in the eye coldly and tell her so. You know as well as I do that the average girl doesn't

274

like a man to humble himself before her. They have contempt for a man who'll do that. The basic thing with women is that they want to respect a man, and if they don't, they'll always kick him in the teeth. Do you think a girl likes to hear a man slobber that he loves her and worships her and would die of ecstasy to touch the hem of her skirt or kiss one of her old gloves? She just thinks he's a jerk. It sounds reactionary to say so, but women like to be mastered. They like to feel that there's a man in charge. They lose interest completely when they sense that the man is weakening and becoming schmaltzy —sure they like romance, but not from the man, what they like is to feel the romance themselves. I'm telling you the straight facts and you know all this just as well as I do. One of the mistakes you made with Bobbie was humbling yourself. All that begging her to marry you. My God, George, you should never have done that. You should have just asked her, and if she said no, then to hell with it. What else could you do? She thought she was pregnant—but she wouldn't get an abortion and she wouldn't marry you. You offered to marry her, and we all helped in locating a doctor who'd do the abortion. She was being unreasonable. And when a woman is unreasonable, there's no use in trying to handle her by humbling yourself. If you take that, she loses all respect for you. Now if you think I'm wrong about all this, ask Sue. She'll tell you that I'm right. That's the way women *feel*, George. It's not only this society, it's part of their basic biological nature. They're *passive* by their very nature, it's a basic thing, and if a man fails to be *active*, they sense it immediately and it queers everything. I'm not saying women have no intelligence, all I'm saying is that they know in the deepest sense that it's no damn good, once a man refuses to take the lead, and starts crawling before them, the way you did with Bobbie."

"I didn't crawl before her," said George. "You're nuts. You haven't got bat sense."

"What he says does make a certain sense," said Sue. "I know it always bores me if a man treats me as if I'm on a pedestal."

"It has nothing to do with any of that," answered George.

"Everything you say is reasonable up to a point, but it has nothing to do with this case, because you're basing it on a false assumption."

"What false assumption?" said Phil.

They had argued throughout Wednesday and Thursday. At first, George had said that the truth was that she was going to North Carolina to her aunt and would have the baby there. He said she probably hadn't gone yet and probably was in some hotel under a false name, waiting to go through the motions of pretending to have another pregnancy test. She'd wait a couple of days, then send a card, and leave town. He was positive this was the answer and analyzed that she would be taking a train on Thursday afternoon. He had it all figured out. She was economical, therefore she wouldn't go by Pullman and she wouldn't take a plane, however she wouldn't go by bus because that was physically too tiring and took too long and she'd be taking care of herself on account of her delicate condition, therefore the answer was a streamlined coach train with reclining seats, and there was one of these that went through her home town, namely, "The Southerner," which departed from Pennsylvania Station on Thursday afternoon. That was the train she'd be on. He'd watch the gates when they were opened and catch her right there. And he watched the gates. Alone, because Phil and Sue refused to go along and help, it was such a foolish idea. In their opinion, she'd already gone, and even if she hadn't it was the worst thing he could do, to go there and try and bother her. He should let her go on down there.

This was what George said at first. He insisted that she was lying completely in her letter to Sue, and that she was still as pregnant as could be. That was where Sue and Phil disagreed with him. And their argument was very convincing. Phil said that it obviously had been a mistake about her being pregnant. That was no lie—why should she go to such lengths to lie about it? It would be crazy for her to deny it and completely against her own interests. The truth was that she had been under a nervous strain, was angry at George, and suddenly

276

when the pressure was released, all the tension burst forth and her suppressed anger at George came out and caused a temporary feeling of complete negativeness as far as he was concerned. He had been the cause of all her worry and trouble, and worse than that it hadn't even been any real trouble at all, it was just as ironic prank of fate, and that was the last straw. It infuriated her that she was suddenly left high and dry, with no dramatic problem, no awful situation that they were all worrying about, no more dilemma that made her the center of everyone's attention. All that steam suddenly being released was just too much, and on top of that, George had made the tactical error of humbling himself, so the natural, and even inevitable, result was that she'd simply gone numb as far as he was concerned. Of course she'd gone back to North Carolina, but she wouldn't stick around—the doctor could write her the result of the second test, and it was already obvious enough that the first one had been in error anyhow. She was nowhere near New York—why did she want her trunk sent at once to her aunt's? She was down there. And what would happen would be that she'd remain down there a week or two, perhaps three, then send a postcard or letter, probably to Sue. It would be a very casual communication. She would act as if nothing much had happened and there'd been no real unpleasantness. She'd say, "How's George?" And so forth. Then she'd come on back up to New York, when she'd cooled down, in just about a month's time, and she'd be the same old Bobbie, smiling and having a good time, her old self again. An emotional storm, that's what it was, caused by a sudden emotional "low" coming in contact with a "high," a region of cold striking an area of turmoil, tension, and psychological cumulus clouds. That was the whole explanation, obviously enough, and he was prepared to bet fifty dollars that it was substantially correct. It had to be. There simply was no other answer. She couldn't still be pregnant. She'd never write such a letter as that if she was, and merely think about it reasonably—if she still was pregnant and knew it, where could she go? Where, indeed? She couldn't go back to that old, Bible-breathing

277

harridan of an aunt. The aunt would burn her alive and the entire town would be buzzing and whispering about her. To assume that she'd go back to that town, if she was pregnant, was utterly unreasonable. It *was*. She'd *never* go back there, if she was pregnant. It would be the last place on earth she'd go. Simply look at her own personal history, didn't that make it obvious? She'd jump in the river before she'd go back to that town and be disgraced just like her mother and have the old aunt yammer at her and upbraid her for her wickedness, and all the old biddies calling and quoting scriptures and staring at her as if she was a monster—she'd rather be dead than face that, and never would return to that town in a million years, if she was pregnant. And if not there, then where else? Where else could she go, if not there? Off in the woods somewhere? Looking at it logically, one didn't have to analyze her letter to Sue or decide whether this phrase or that phrase rang true— the logical answer was that the letter was the truth, simply because no other answer was possible. And if there was any other answer, then let George suggest it.

Sue agreed. Her opinion was much the same as Phil's. But she looked at it a little differently. She said that in her opinion it was much simpler. She could understand it perfectly. She knew how Bobbie felt. The thing neither of them took into account in all their analysis of her, was the fact that first and foremost, she was an inexperienced and sensitive girl, with a romantic streak in her nature. They were both cynical about love and marriage and sex, but not her, she took it all seriously, and something that seemed casual to them, didn't seem that way to her. She could sit around and listen to all their talk, and not even pay any serious attention to it, her own idea of things was so different. It was clear just exactly what had really happened. She believed all the ideals about love and believed that George felt the same way she did—didn't he tell her all the time he loved her, in public and everywhere else? She naturally assumed he would marry her—of course he would, sooner or later, since he loved her, but then when the trouble came and George told her she was neurotic, her illusions were shattered.

What did it mean to her, the word neurotic? He was just calling her a name, as far as she was concerned, and she thought she'd been a fool to love a man who didn't love her. The whole thing was a clash between the realistic point of view, and the romantic point of view. And it'd been bound to happen sooner or later. This whole business had done nothing more than touch off an explosion that would have come anyhow. But it would all blow over. She knew—that last day or two—that George loved her, and practically admitted as much. She'd come back in a few weeks just like Phil said, and everything would be all right.

That was Sue's opinion.

"Here's the real answer," said George. "There's only one possible answer. She's going away to another city and have the baby. That's what she's going to do, and good for her. The letter to Sue is an utter lie, a deliberate lie. She's figured out what to say in order to make me believe it. If I didn't love her, I *would* believe it, that's how clever she is. If she was a romantic little silly girl, how could she begin to write such a letter as that, or for that matter do any of the things she's done? She's a very deep girl, that's what she is, all of us have had her wrong, the trouble with her is that she's just utterly irrational about her own feelings. Now look. Take that letter to Sue. That goddamned letter is calculated to give me an out, that's all. I don't say she's conscious of it that far—what she's trying to do in the letter as far as she knows herself is just to convince me she's out of it all and doesn't love me. Now let's analyze that. Why should she try and deceive me about it? What motive could she have? My God, we know enough to figure every bit of it to the last detail, even including exactly where she is. She knows what she's doing and don't think she doesn't. We've all underestimated her, including me. But the answer is there. She's planned it out so I can find the answer, if I understand her and put my mind really on it. I'm sure of that. There's an answer to every bit of this, she wouldn't just go away like this blindly, without knowing what she's doing. Now it's obvious enough that what she plans to do is go away and have that baby and let me go as I will, run around with other women, and all that, then after six months or so—notice that she mentions the time in her letter, very subtly—oh brother is she a deep one, this little nut—she thinks she has it all figured out—yes sir, after six or eight months, she thinks she'll get in touch with me in one way or another, without telling me anything about the baby, and she expects to be able to judge from my reaction how I feel. Her idea is that *then* if I'm still feeling the same way and want to marry her, knowing nothing about the baby, and even after she's gone away for half a year, and even after she's left behind that cold letter with Sue saying she doesn't love me—after all *that*, if I still feel the way I do now, then she'll believe me. A lot of what you say about her is true, but she is carrying out a fantastically fiendish test of *me*, that's what all this is. And the reason she's doing it is perfectly logical in her own eyes. It relates back to her insecurity as a child, and the sudden tragedy, to her, of being separated from this bootlegger and her mother's girl-friend. I can tell from the way she talks about it. A look comes in her eyes. What that meant to her was that love is a thing that can desert you, unless you are very careful. That's why it took me a month to ever get her in the bed, she wasn't taking any chances on being hurt, but then she did take a chance and when I acted queasy about her being pregnant, good God, all the alarums and sirens and everything else started ringing in her mind. That was my mistake, obviously, but there was no way on God's earth for me to have anticipated how she'd react, though of course everybody is insecure like this, more or less. But hell, it never occurred to me to marry her. Anyhow, that's the answer, and the question now is this: where is she? Where would she go? There must be some clue somewhere as to where she'd go. I'm sure that subconsciously she'd leave behind some sort of clue that would enable me to find her, if I try hard enough, so what could the clue be? There must be one. Did she ever mention any towns where she'd be likely to go have a baby?"

George had a "hunch" just after the conversation that morning. This was on Friday, after two days of almost constant argument. The hunch was that she was in New York, in a rooming house over on the east side in the mid-town area. He went out and walked there, looking for her on the streets and going up in houses that he could tell were rooming houses and asking janitresses and superintendents if a girl of such and such description had come there. He walked for miles and very probably covered the block she actually was on, but there was no vacancy sign on that house she was in and he didn't go in and ask about her. By the time he had walked all over that part of town, brooding and trying to find her, it was seven-thirty and he decided it was pointless to look for her aimlessly like this, in a city the size of New York. She could be anywhere. Merely because he had taken walks with her on the east side in mid-town was no indication that she'd go get a room there. She could have gone farther uptown, or to the west side on a street off Central Park, or for that matter down to the Village, any area in which there were rooming houses—in fact she would probably go somewhere strange, if she was in the city at all. He decided he had to go back to the room and look through her things once again and see if there might be some possibility of turning up a clue somewhere. When he decided this, he was on the corner of Lexington Avenue and 49th Street. The time was actually twenty-three minutes of eight, and at that time Bobbie was leaving the house she was staying at on 54th Street. He got on the bus and passed by the Bickford's where she was having toast and tea. It had been a pretty good hunch.

Sue finally found the letter from Bobbie's aunt, in the bottom of her trunk. They'd looked through the trunk before, but missed it, however now there it was, a long letter in spidery handwriting. George read it and sat for a long time and thought about it, and Sue and Phil also read it, and analyzed it and how it had affected Bobbie. Then George put his hands on his head and groaned.

"Good God," he said. "Do you know what I think she's doing? Christ almighty, she's gone and had an abortion, that's

281

what she's done and that's what all this is. Where's that letter to Sue? Let me see that letter—quick!"

"She wouldn't do that," said Sue.

"Not her," said Phil. "Don't you remember—"

"Shut up," said George. "Let me read this." He read the letter again, then looked up. "There's no question about it," he said. "This is the answer. She probably thought of going off and having the baby, but her aunt writes her this senile letter and it's all too much for her. She's gone and had an abortion and never intends to tell me a word about it. Her plan is to have it and stay away for a while—she meant for me to believe this letter she wrote Sue. At the end here, she leaves it open just a little bit, hinting that maybe later she'll see me—that's what she means by six months or a year. She thinks an abortion will clear things up, and she also figures there's no other answer. If she'd gone away and had the child, she'd still have to let me know about it. She couldn't go away and have the baby and not tell me, it'd be inhuman toward me and absolutely nuts, but she still felt that she couldn't marry me, so her solution is to have an abortion. But I'll tell you this—this is the end. She'll never marry me now and if she does she'll—it won't, it's no good . . . this is the end, I'll never get her now. But why didn't I think of this before? This was just what she'd do, what's the matter with me? The only hope is that she hasn't had it yet or that maybe she changed her mind. We'll have to—"

Sue said, "George, I think you're right. In fact, I think I know when she made up her mind. There was a change in her face the day before she left, and in fact, now I remember something, she asked me what that doctor's name was, on some pretext or other, you know that doctor Betty told us about? George, you're right. That's just what she's done."

"I'll call up that doctor and ask him," said George. "We can—"

"It's too late to call tonight," said Phil. "There wouldn't be anybody there. It's ten minutes after nine. Call him in the morning, but if I were you, I'd go down there."

"God almighty," said George. "If I'd only thought of this sooner, I could have gone and stood guard and watched and never let her go there. This is the end. It'll break her heart, she's not the type to have such a thing. God Almighty, what kind of world is this, anyhow?" George slumped back in the chair, his eyes shut, then he sat forward. "The only thing to do is go to that doctor's in the morning, and hope to hell she hasn't done it yet. But by now, she has. This is Friday, and she disappeared from here on Tuesday. Why in the name of God didn't I think of this before?"

So, George analyzed it correctly. She never had thought he would, but he did.

At nine twenty-five, the telephone rang and Sue picked it up. She said, "Hello?" And then, "Bobbie?! Where are you? Where're you calling from? Wha—"

"Give me that phone," said George. He took the phone and said, "Bobbie?"

"Hello," she said.

"Did you have an abortion?" he asked.

"A what?" she asked.

"You heard me. Did you have an abortion yet?"

"An abortion?"

"Don't you *dare* have an abortion, you little nut. Where are you calling from?"

"A drug store," she said.

"*What* drug store?"

"It's Whelan's drug store," she said.

"Where? Which Whelan's?"

"The one down on Eighth Street, at Sixth Avenue," she answered.

"You've driven me crazy," said George. "How did you get down there?"

"I walked down here," she said.

"Now listen here, Bobbie," said George. "I've had enough nonsense out of you. You've driven me out of my mind and taken a thousand years off my life. Now I want you to get in a taxi and come on up here immediately, do your understand?"

"Well," she said, "all right."

"And you're going to marry me in the morning, understand?"

"All right," she said.

"And no more of this goddamn crazy nonsense, is that clear?"

"Well," she said. "I just wanted a few days to think it over, so I took this room. And I thought it over. Did Sue show you that letter?"

"Yes, she did, and I didn't believe a word of it. What do you mean, writing a letter like that and running away like this? Are you trying to drive me in*sane*?"

"Well," she answered, "I was tired, you see I needed to get away by myself and think."

"Think. Huh. You get in a cab and come on up here immediately, and when you get here I'm going to give you a spanking."

"Well, all right," she said.

So much for the abortion. She knew she never would do it, the minute she looked at those steps.

He did give her a spanking, but not much, he was too relieved to see her. Later that night he said, "Tell me something, honey lamb. What made you call me up?"

"I just thought I would," she said.

And so they got married. But did they live happily ever after? That's another story and can't be told in this book, but there is indeed a little more, and therein lies the moral of the tale. Because that wasn't the end of Bobbie's troubles—it was only the beginning. The final twist to it all is yet to come. The rash she had was not from worry. George caught it from her, and was sick in Richmond, Virginia, with a fever of a hundred and three. He had German measles and that was what she'd had. Therefore, eight days after they were married, she went in the hospital and had an abortion. The measles, they said, would make the child be born feeble-minded. Three doctors signed the paper, saying so, to make the operation legal. But naturally she could have another baby, poor girl, to lose the baby after all that trouble—poor little angel—they'd have one soon, the minute she got all right, fate was so unkind to poor,

284

sweet little Bobbie. . . . But was fate unkind? It was only her reward for ever having thought of getting that operation in the first place, and serve her right, but too bad about the baby. It didn't take mysticism to see that.

And so, that's all there is to tell. If it seems to end slightly up in the air, the writer is sorry, but the truthful story of it all has been told, depressing and gloomy though much of it might be—however, maybe some day it will all work out. Troubles sometimes do, but now farewell.

Chapter 36

A Note to the Reader

DEAR READER,

Any court of law in a civilized land grants the accused the right to say what he will in his defense, before final sentence is pronounced, and on these grounds I have succeeded in persuading the composer of the foregoing lines, to allow me a brief word here, and I beg of the reader in turn his permission also, with the promise that I will make it brief, very brief.

God knows, the depraved wretch in this book called "George," could hardly say anything to convince even the most kindhearted soul that he shouldn't be shot, but that loathsome person is not *me*, dear reader. I would hang myself at once, if that were the case. Surely in all the wide sweep of literature, from the penny dreadful to the classic of yore, there is no more driveling idiot than this character. How anyone could manage to combine in this nature such a nauseating mixture of egotism and ill-temper is beyond my comprehension. And not only that, the character suffers from sheer stupidity, not to have recognized long before he did the whim of the gods, in confusing the heroine's emotions to such an extent that she would find him worth a second word. In fact, that is the first enigma of the book as it now stands—and I have not corrected it, tempted though I am—how such a girl, off the beaten trail in personality though she is, could find this toad interesting or worth while. The reader will agree that it would have been impossible, if my character were truly as depicted here. Actually, I am a likable cuss, who wishes no one any harm and finds much to admire in others, not an anti-social, noisy scoundrel as presented here.

But so much for all that, as the writer of this book was wont so often to say. I hope this brief comment will help bring it all into more accurate focus, but the reader will realize in any case that all women are eldritch, eerie, swamp-inhabiting creatures beyond the appeal of logic and reason. Against the deeper sex, blundering man has all the chances of the proverbial snowball in hell, when it comes to a psychological contest. The cave man who first made this observation forty thousand years ago was right. And his brother, who said, "No, and you can't understand them, either," he was right, too. Happy is the man who accepts these things, and doesn't worry about them, but only hopes that if he behaves himself, he can possibly keep his nose above water.

Now, in recent weeks, as angel lamb has gone her way with a project of her own, I have been engaged in the writing of a detective tale, consuming my life substance recklessly, exhausting what powers of imagination I have, in order to turn a penny, and gain at least some hollow semblance of financial security around here, before venturing into the horror of parenthood. My reasons for this were as altruistic as the reader can imagine, though I have no urges toward fatherhood and can eagerly suppress any that ever try to appear—in fact, having got out of it the last time as by a miracle, the whole lewd proposition jangled my nerves. Angel child tried to present it in slightly better terms—the only kindness she showed throughout—by suggesting that perhaps my hesitation had to do with fears on her account. However, it was just uncomplicated selfishness. The idea of having what little peace that remains in this world disrupted and shattered utterly by loud, demanding, diaper-covered brats was depressing to me, and still is, though one of these is well-nigh practically here at the time of this writing. She herself, however, seemed so extraordinarily gloomy and morbidly depressed, during the time when I was working at a dull job, wrestling against the final and fatal decision, and at the same time on the sly and unbeknownst to her, working on the aforementioned detective tale, that life around here wasn't fit for man or beast. The reader has no idea how difficult she was, and in the last extremity, one has to make concessions to an urge like that, as I decided —if she wants motherhood with such a fiendish and morbid intensity, then what the hell, why not? We'll all probably starve or be wiped out soon, but at least there'll be peace in the home in the meantime.

Thus it has been. It only remains for me to say, unfortunately, that 90 per cent of this strictly truthful account, given by the authoress, is not truthful at all, including even the identity of the authoress herself. In fact, the question no longer can be escaped, that is the second enigma of this work—who wrote it? Who indeed?

Surely, not Susan. She couldn't write any such lengthy work as this, since even a five-minute postcard tires her out.

And certainly not Phil; he writes only on Santayana.

Who, then? The obvious answer is angel child herself. She is the authoress in the cold-water flat, whatever the authoress says her name is. Considering the style of the work, and its heathenish anti-intellectual philosophy, she is obviously the author.

Yet one is bound to wonder, how could she ever stop talking long enough, to write all this? Could she ever write a work so grim and depressing, even though it has what must be regarded as a happy ending? Could she ever write in such a mean way, regardless of the circumstances, about yours truly, or for that matter, about anyone else? Not her. It would be beyond her.

Who did write it, then? By logical deduction, only one last possibility remains—I, myself. It certainly was one of us four, and I am the only one left. But this can be ruled out—I hardly would have spent over three hundred pages slandering myself, and exposing myself as a slobbering, insane ghoul. Instead, I would have pictured myself more accurately as the pleasant, intelligent, nice type that helps old ladies across the street. *This* character would have probably kicked them into the

288

gutter. Besides, the numerous artistic flaws in the work rule me out. Somebody else did it. It wasn't me. Maybe the cat wrote it.

Now, with that problem disposed of, I'll bid the reader adieu, with my congratulations on having seen Bobbie through all her troubles, and with a final, parting piece of advice. I would say just this: if the reader shares my own view and opposes domestic bliss and its horrors, then I eagerly wring his hand and advise him, stick to it, pal, and good luck; but if by any chance he should run into such a one as this one, and feel about her as I do, then I'd say, that's all, my friend, give up forever the idea of freedom and resign yourself to your fate. And above all else, don't hesitate, or there'll be all hell to pay. Strike quick! Marry her immediately! And if she wants a baby, then don't pussyfoot around, get in there and hit the ball.

On that word of advice, I beg sincerely to remain,

Your servant,
MR. X